HIGHER JUSTICE

Book One of the True Justice Series

D. E. Heil

Get an exclusive book related to the True Justice series!

One of the best things about writing is building a relationship with my readers. I love sending information to you: newsletters with details on new releases, special offers, and other bits of news relating to the True Justice series that my readers report finding very interesting.

If you sign up for the mailing list I'll send you a book related to the True Justice series entitled DELAYED JUSTICE. My books normally sell for $12.99, but this one can be yours for free.

Simply go to the back of this book to learn how to get your FREE copy.

TALKING HEADS

"What's the American public to do?" Chris Morrison, one of the hosts of the morning news program asked. "Begin carrying machine guns and hand grenades to the grocery store?"

"Of course not," Tom Littleton, his co-host, replied. "The President has to make sure Homeland Security is doing their job, but he's not."

"So you're going to blame it all on the President?"

The commentators of *Monday Morning Alive* were bantering back and forth to provide entertainment under the guise of news. Along with all their competitors, they had spent the last few weeks discussing the horrific events of recent months.

"If Homeland Security can't protect us, is it any wonder more and more people are roaming around with guns?" Tom asked.

"Do we really want people taking the responsibility for their own security? Someone will get hurt."

"Hundreds, maybe even thousands, of citizens were saved from injury or death but it's still not right," Tom replied.

"Congress is trying to pass common sense gun control laws to keep firearms out of the hands of terrorists, but the President is blocking their efforts," Chris said. "The Senate only needs 33 more votes to override his veto. He's hiding behind his interpretation of the Second Amendment."

"What good will more laws do?" Tom asked. "How many more innocents must die before Congress does something worthwhile?"

"So what do you suggest? Everyone begin carrying guns like the Wild West and have rivers of blood run in our streets? That's not the answer."

"Of course I'm not suggesting that everyone arm themselves. We still have police to protect the public," Tom replied hotly. "But on the other hand, we don't have a clue how many terrorists may already be on American soil."

"It's up to the government to stop these coordinated attacks," Chris said as he leaned forward to emphasize his point. "They're being carried out with military precision by people we think are bankers, doctors, or computer experts. Why don't we know who they are or what they're planning? Where's our intelligence community? Parents are afraid to send their kids to school."

"Some people are afraid to go to work because they wonder if they'll ever come home. That's hurting the economy."

"Worry about whether they'll come home? More folks are worrying about whether they'll have a home and family to return to."

"So what does Congress have to…"

"Wait!" Tom said as he put a finger to the microphone in his ear. "We have a breaking story!"

Chris dropped his finger from the microphone in his ear, and without uttering a word, he began to type furiously on the keyboard in front of him.

"It's being reported that there has been a shooting in a church in Nebraska during morning services," Tom reported as he continued to keep his finger to his ear and listened intently. "An unknown number of gunmen entered a small rural church, and without warning, began to shoot indiscriminately into the congregation gathered there. A large number of people have been injured but it's too early to report on any casualties."

"That can't be right!" Chris suddenly exclaimed with a look of utter astonishment on his face as he vigorously jabbed his finger toward his computer screen. A small drop of spittle flew from his mouth, and he shouted with great anguish cracking his voice, "It says right here that Nebraska doesn't allow guns in churches! Something has to be wrong! That can't be right!"

"Yeah," Tom said incredulously as he stared at the side of Chris' head. "There is definitely something wrong here…" His words trailed off without comment about his colleague's state of mind.

CHAPTER 1

POOR CHOICES

Amanda Freundin, a lifelong resident of Curtis Bay in the heavily industrialized area comprising the southern portion of Baltimore, giddily tottered home after a long night of partying with three of her girlfriends from school. As usual, she had partaken of the greatest portion of the Robert Mondavi Chablis the girls preferred. Her lime green flip-flops softly smacked the coarse-grained concrete as her ample bosom defied the chill winds by threatening to fall out of her low-cut V-neck sweater. A pink hooded fleece sweatshirt was loosely thrown over her shoulders more as a fashion statement to accompany her fashionably torn jeans than to offer warmth.

Like a small child on a warm summer day she meandered from one scraggly tuft of dying grass to another giving each a glancing kick then giggling hysterically at her own nonsensical antics. The fact the grass was growing in the numerous cracks scattered throughout the neglected concrete sidewalk instead of in a flower-studded meadow did not seem to faze her at all.

It had been easy for the slightly overweight fourteen-year old dishwater blonde to persuade Marty Donsbach, the forty-two year old maintenance man at the apartment complex where she lived with her alcoholic father, to buy wine for her. Marty was always willing to do little favors for the ninth grader. Because of her street-honed survival instincts she only spoke with him in the company of others.

She snaked aimlessly back and forth down the broken sidewalk in the desolate section of town she called home, totally oblivious to the danger lurking ahead.

John Dugan was six-foot two inches tall and 170 pounds of pure evil wrapped in a disarming personality. Greasy blonde hair hung in stringy clumps from beneath a black rayon watch cap perched rakishly on the side of his head. His stained, skin-tight denim jeans were bleached white on the front of the thighs and fashionably torn at the corners of the rear pockets. His chest muscles bulged seductively from beneath a well-fit white tee shirt that was partially concealed by an unbuttoned long-sleeved flannel shirt and the open front of a navy blue jacket.

He studied the desolate urban landscape before him as though he were surveying his personal empire. Like most career criminals, Dugan lived with the delusion he owned or somehow controlled the streets he prowled.

A swirling tornado of multicolored leaves blew down the deserted street signaling the beginning of winter. Seeing them, a shiver slithered down his back, causing him to dig his head deeper into the collar of his jacket.

"I need some, Man," Wayne Varecci, Dugan's toady cohort, spewed venomously as he leaned uncomfortably close to Dugan's right ear.

Varecci was of average height at five-foot ten inches tall. His protruding abdomen made him look squat and ill shaped with thick, short legs jutting from beneath a baby-blue hooded sweatshirt. His thick, short neck caused it to appear that his ears were growing out the top of his rounded shoulders.

Both men, barely out of their teens, had been hardened far beyond their years by growing up on the unforgiving streets of Baltimore's poorest neighborhoods.

"You always need some, you horny bastard," Dugan said through a tight-lipped sneer.

His mind flashed back to disgusting images of Varecci's past escapades, causing his stomach to churn with repugnance. Even the most liberal member of the American Psychological Association could not consider Varecci's sexual perversions remotely acceptable or non-violent.

Dugan glanced around the dirty, darkened alcove of the abandoned storefront the pair had sought protection in to partially deflect the biting late October wind. Faded, golden lettering was barely legible on the glass front of the door. It announced to the world that Yancy's Fine Tailoring was open six days a week. Dugan smiled silently to himself. Apparently, Yancy hadn't bothered putting a 'closed' sign in the window when he abandoned the business over twenty years ago.

"Here you go," Dugan said as Varecci's beady eyes followed his gaze toward the silent, seemingly abandoned rail yard.

"Amanda looks like she's got a good load on tonight."

Their eyes met as they silently acknowledged each other's intentions.

"I don't know about Amanda. She may have some incurable disease that'll make the Little Guy turn black and fall off," Varecci said playfully as his menacing grin glowed in the muted light reflecting off the dusty windows of Yancy's derelict shop. Dugan stared at him with disgust then remembered to smile. Varecci craved frequent verification that he was witty and Dugan was willing to play along to keep the dimwit happy.

"Beggars can't be choosers," Dugan hissed from between smirking lips. "Besides, she's the answer to your prayers. Or aren't you interested anymore?"

He noted the sudden snapping motion of Varecci's head and the hard, wicked glare in his eyes as he took offense. Dugan immediately and silently stifled his minion's rebellious attitude with a cold, hardened stare of his own. A slight shifting of his weight forward as though assuming a fighting stance, combined with a minute straightening of his carriage to accentuate his height advantage, established his unspoken dominance over Varecci.

"How do you want to handle this?" Varecci mumbled, accepting his place in the social hierarchy. A thin, crooked smile appeared on Dugan's lips signaling his acceptance of Varecci's surrender.

Varecci's hooded eyes furtively darted away to avoid Dugan's piercing stare then riveted on the chunky figure tottering steadily toward them.

"Follow me and you'll see," Dugan hissed menacingly.

Dugan and Varecci slunk nonchalantly onto the sidewalk in a fluid, unhurried motion. Years on the street had taught them to move swiftly but smoothly. Subconsciously they had learned the human eye and mind focus on sudden, unexpected movement. The more subtle their approach, the less wary their victims would become making it easier for the hard-edged young men to draw near their prey.

Amanda was startled when the two disheveled men seemingly appeared out of nowhere. The illuminated cones of dust-diffused light streaming directly downward from ancient streetlamps offered only limited visibility. Between the gauzy cones of illumination dancing shadows fooled the eye like a camouflaged optical illusion.

"Hey Amanda. What's a nice girl like you doing out on a night like this?"

Dugan kept his most disarming smile carefully fixed on his face. He knew his smile was one of his greatest assets. He also knew deep down that God had to be displeased when he used his gift as a weapon against his fellow human beings. Of course, he never gave a damn what God or anyone else thought of him so he was able to easily dispel any guilt he may have ever felt.

It took a second for Amanda's alcohol befuddled eyes to recognize Dugan's face. Her flashing smile instantly communicated the crush she had on him since they first met three weeks previously.

"Hey Dugan," Amanda bubbled.

"Varecci," She slurred as she disgustedly acknowledged Dugan's lackey without looking directly at him. Varecci's face darkened, highlighting his bloated, unshaven and pockmarked cheeks.

"Listen, you skanky little…"

Before Varecci could say more, Dugan interrupted by addressing Amanda with a twinge of false sincerity in his voice, "You've been out partying without me again Amanda. I'm hurt."

She knew he was only joking with her, but the doleful pouting of his fleshy lips was irresistible to the fourteen-year-old blonde.

"The night's still young Amanda. What do you think we can do?" Dugan slyly crooned as he flashed a smile.

Amanda's alcohol-limited attention was completely focused on Dugan. He wanted to keep the young girl's attention focused on him, which allowed Varecci to slip silently and unnoticed behind the unsuspecting teen. Dugan's heart began beating furiously because of the anticipated carnal pleasures permeating his mind.

"Amanda darling," he said while breathing heavily from between barely moving lips, concentrating on performing his best Marlon Brando impersonation. His eyes searched leeringly into hers as his hips moved forward with his hands following a split second later. He was proud of the moves he was making. They were working perfectly to charm the gullible youngster. She was totally absorbed by his presence. Her reaction confirmed his long-held belief that he should move to Hollywood and become an actor.

Amanda felt herself succumbing to Dugan's advances and began moving closer to him; all too willing to show him how much she wanted him. His hands began to gently fondle her golden hair. They could feel each other's breath on their faces.

"Now," Dugan said simply and calmly.

Instantly Varecci's huge hairy arms encircled and crushed Amanda's to her sides. She momentarily froze as her mind raced to make sense of what was happening to her.

"What the hell!" she yelped while jerking her head back in an attempt to crush her tormentor's nose flat against his ugly face. "Varecci, you BASTARD!"

The evil lurking in his soul was instantaneously revealed when Dugan's affable smile distorted into a contemptuous thin line.

He deftly flicked a snot-streaked blue and white kerchief from his back pocket and stifled the stream of profanity gushing from her cavernous mouth. The demonic look on his face was indelibly etched upon her mind as he cruelly jammed the rag past her teeth while her tongue vainly struggled to deny it access.

"Gag, you whore, it's all you deserve," Dugan muttered gleefully as terror grew in Amanda's tear-rimmed baby-blue eyes.

"Crank her arm up. I've got her head."

Casting a casual glance into the dark rail yard, Dugan's ominously calm voice directed Varecci like a puppet on invisible strings. "Drag her down to the creek."

An overwhelming sense of helplessness smothered her soul.

Damn! Not again! Amanda thought as she struggled with all her might to escape the horrors she knew awaited her.

CHAPTER 2

HOMEWARD COMMUTE VIA CURTIS BAY

"Yes Honey, I know. But these babies don't realize they're inconveniencing us by being born in middle of the night," Robert Fogler chuckled softly over the cell phone as he spoke with Irene, his lovely wife of 28 years.

Over their years together he had made a habit of calling her when he would be arriving home in the middle of the night to avoid startling her with the noises he made while pussyfooting into their house.

Robert may have felt much older than his 52 years, but he looked like an athletic 40 year old. His 6 foot 3 inch frame carried sinewy muscle with only a hint of paunch around his midsection. With close-cropped hair showing a slight smattering of gray and creamy ebony skin, the accomplished African-American could easily have been featured on the cover of GQ magazine.

"I am tired. I've been up for almost 36 hours and the last one was a difficult delivery," he uttered, barely above a whisper. Then he amusingly listened to the subdued complaint she murmured through the cloud of sleep that fogged her mind. He could almost recite it verbatim because it was the same grievance he had heard many times during their numerous years together.

"I am not too old for this," he protested. "Besides, what would I do if I gave up delivering babies?"

A gentle smile spread across his lips. He could tell by the silkiness in her voice that she was imagining him smiling in the darkness of the night. People could communicate without saying a word, knowing each other's thoughts, when they knew each other since age five as Robert and Irene had.

"You go back to sleep and I'll be home in 15 minutes," he said. "I'm going to hang up now because the old railroad bridge is coming up and the cell phone coverage is spotty down here."

"I love you too," he quietly replied to the muffled words of affection she had murmured. He kept his voice low and sultry, so not to rouse her from the half-asleep stupor she was obviously still in. His mind drifted toward his arrival home because there was little he enjoyed more than sneaking into bed to lay beside the roasty-toasty warmth of her body.

Just as he snapped the silver receiver of his cellular phone closed and reached to place it into the black plastic cup holder of the car's center console, a fleeting blur of motion caught his attention on the crumbling sidewalk running along the right side of the cheerless street.

His senses immediately went on high alert when a second rapidly disappearing swirl of motion caught his eye in the stygian depths of the rail yard and he fully realized what was unfolding before him.

His right foot eased the brake pedal toward the floor causing the heavy vehicle to slow to a crawl.

One was tall and thin with stringy blonde hair hanging from beneath a black watch cap. He was wearing a dark coat, he recited to himself. *The police will want positive identification.*

The other one was of average height with a big belly straining against his baby blue hooded sweatshirt.

His eyes scanned to the right, tunnel vision limiting his visual field. Then he saw it. A lime-green flip-flop was lying upside down in a scrubby patch of dead weeds at the edge of the sidewalk.

Robert began to gain confidence; secure in the knowledge he could recall so much of what he had seen. His brain raced to embed other details in his mind's eye as he simultaneously formulated a course of action.

The blond guy had the chubby girl's hair in both fists and was pulling her behind him. The fat toad-like one had the girl's left arm cranked up behind her back. His other hand held the belt loops of her blue jeans so he could drag her.

But where in the hell did they go? This damned rail yard goes on forever, he thought to himself as he struggled to remember the layout.

Suddenly he had an idea.

He hit the gas pedal of the powerful vehicle, immediately exhilarated by the surging momentum of the revving engine. With a deft flick of his wrist, he jerked the wheels to the curb where he had last seen the trio.

The right front tire of the shiny black Mercedes SUV jolted over the low curb and ground to a halt. Its halogen headlights threw a brilliant bluish glare deep into the black depths.

The coating of grime covering the street billowed into a swirling cloud of putrid red dust, which immediately overwhelmed the German-made automobile. The filthy haze ominously obscured his view between the railroad cars. As the sooty filth slowly settled to the ground, the unearthly yellow glow of the solitary streetlight lent a surreal air of unreality to the scene unfolding before his eyes.

Where the hell did they go?

His groping right hand flew to the cup holder where his phone was securely housed.

Like a man possessed by demons he flipped the phone open, held the emergency button for the requisite three seconds, then held the chilly plastic receiver to the side of his head. A pre-recorded message informed him the call could not be completed, making him wince.

He had driven into the dead zone and was now out of contact with the outside world.

Frantically, he held the illuminated screen at arm's length trying to decipher the glowing words without reading glasses. The dancing letters swirled in his blurred vision.

Damned my old eyes!

Squinting to force his sleep-deprived eyes to focus, he recoiled with horror when an absence of glowing bars confirmed he was out of touch with the rest of the world.

What the hell do I do now?

His options flashed through his mind. None of them were appealing.

A windy, rushing sound began resonating deeply in his head as time began speeding by like a runaway freight train. In the distance, a lonely train whistle sounded ominously in the night.

Damned! I'm going to jump into deep shit with both feet this time, the tall, ebony skinned man thought as his hands suddenly moistened with sweat. *I'm getting involved with something that's none of my business. But I have to.*

No I don't.

The hell I don't...

He tried to talk himself out of becoming personally involved, but he couldn't. He'd always possessed a conscience that wouldn't allow him to walk away from another human being in trouble. This wasn't the first time his conscience had gotten him into trouble; and it obviously wouldn't be the last.

He propelled himself from the Mercedes with wild abandon. Only when his feet hit the broken macadam of the street did he realize he was acting rashly.

The damned adrenaline is trying to get the best of you. Slow down, he thought as he struggled to remain calm.

He was not the type of person to panic in tricky situations but the taste of fear on the dry, cottony-textured surface of his tongue told him he was in trouble.

Just leave; it's the right thing to do. Call the cops; they can handle it better than you can.

All of the lessons he had learned as a physician and first-aid responder, as well as the instructions from the self-defense courses he'd taken on his own time and paid for himself, screamed from the recesses of his mind to get back in his vehicle; but he couldn't force himself to leave. His conscience wouldn't allow him to abandon anyone in trouble.

Activating the 9-1-1 emergency response system was the first action to take above all others when confronted by a crisis situation; or so they had taught him over and over again.

What they don't tell you in the safe, secure environment of the classroom is what the hell to do when you're alone and the damned cell phone won't work. How could there be such huge gaps of cell phone coverage in a city the size of Baltimore?

He fumed as he resisted the urge to fling the phone across the street and into the reflective waters of the Chesapeake Bay less than half a football field away.

In a fit of indecision and near panic, he leaped upward toward the driver's seat of the high-riding SUV. The non-slip pads glued to the top of the running board gave his foot a firm grip, allowing him to put all his strength into his skyward momentum. His body was split between gaining a better vantage point and returning to the safety of his vehicle in search of cell service. When the top of his head smashed into the unforgiving steel of the doorframe, his knees buckled and his hand went limp, allowing the cell phone to fall silently to the floor of the vehicle. An electrical convulsion of tingles rocketed throughout his entire body, reminding him of the sensation his sinuses experience when biting into a chocolate covered peppermint patty.

He didn't feel his body bounce off the seat or flop unceremoniously onto the gritty blacktop because the sudden, unexpected compression of his cervical spine momentarily snuffed out the electrical signals from his brain. The weighty darkness of unconsciousness fell upon him as willful thought and vision were swept away into a contented, satiny blackness.

It took a full five seconds for his mind to return to semi-consciousness.

The world around him appeared as a spinning collage of bursting colors interspersed with momentary explosions of dazzling brilliance followed by interminable gaps of dark nothingness. For a long time he dared not move. Finally, he struggled to right himself by pulling on the running board as his vision began clearing with agonizing slowness.

The fleeting memory of the blonde girl being dragged into the rail yard quickly displaced all other thoughts and caution from his mind. With his forehead resting gingerly on the running board, he suddenly felt the weight of the entire world on his shoulders.

He knew deep in his heart by the time the police got there the girl would be dead or wishing she were. The desire to help her jolted him back to near-consciousness.

With slow and deliberate movements, as though he were doing it for the first time, he pulled himself to his feet.

One agonizingly slow-motion movement after another lifted him out of the abyss of blackness that threatened to engulf him with each passing moment. Waves of nausea unceasingly racked his guts. His faltering mind was still groggy from the concussion he had inflicted upon himself.

Glancing around slowly, he realized the uninhabited and alien-appearing landscape surrounding him offered no assistance. The darkened fronts of the desolate, lonely bars lining the sooty, dingy street that polite society had long ago forgotten only added to his feeling of abandonment.

Industrial areas were almost always abandoned at this time of night. This forsaken hellhole was certainly no exception. Time seemed to hold him like an invisible vice as the fetid air of this God-forsaken part of the city crushed in around him.

You know you should go for help but there's just not enough time if you hope to have any chance of saving that child from only-God-knows-what.

His muddled mind began to reason with itself, trying to sway him from the crazy idea forming in the back of his head. He felt the heat begin to rise in his forehead as a cold, clammy sensation settled between his shoulder blades.

With a brilliant flash of intuition awakening him from his stupor, he realized that in a matter of minutes the three would be impossible to find in the millions of dark, silent hiding places scattered about the railroad yard. He knew he must act now if the girl was to have any chance of rescue.

You're on your own; so don't just sit there. Get moving.

He was now resolute and deliberate in thought and action. The fear and indecisiveness ruling his body just mere seconds before was replaced by resolve as he methodically began to prepare himself for battle.

Ignoring his matching alligator skin briefcase and wallet sitting on the passenger seat, he pulled his well-worn and weather-beaten bomber jacket from the front passenger seat where it had strategically hidden the pistol residing there.

After hurriedly shoving his arms into the pile-lined sleeves of the battle-originated garment, he noticed with an almost zen-like perception that the black leather jacket barely covered his broad shoulders. Rousing himself from his momentary lapse of concentration, he zipped the heavy brass zipper to his throat.

It's better to be wearing a dark colored jacket than glow in the dark with your white shirt exposed. Well Lord, when you led me to get training and carry a pistol for self-defense you sure knew what you were doing.

Leaning into the SUV just enough to reach between the driver's seat and middle console, he grabbed his Sig Sauer P220 from a kydex holster secured amidst the snug confines of the tawny leather seats. The weight of his upper body slumped onto the seat as it gave way to an unbearable fit of fatigue.

For driving comfort, he always removed the in-the-waistband holster he wore while working. A custom-crafted leather holster hand-made by the late Lou Alessi was tremendously comfortable standing but tended to gouge the hard steel of the pistol grip into his tender ribs while driving. To alleviate this uncomfortable problem he had purchased a specially rigged holster and installed it between the seats. A casually thrown coat or newspaper kept the pistol hidden as required by the laws governing his concealed carry permit.

Like most physicians, he did not like the inconvenience of carrying a pistol but the situations occurring in hospitals required him to be ready for anything. With an air of desperation he jerkily stepped away from his car.

The Sig he firmly clutched in his right hand was considered to be top-of-the-line in defensive pistols by law enforcement professionals. When your life is on the line, he had correctly reasoned, cost is of no consequence.

My instructor told me that if I needed to use a handgun for self-defensive it would probably be in semi-dark conditions. He was right!

He also said that the day might come when a reliable pistol may be the only friend I have with me. Unfortunately, he was right again.

Robert's Sig was chambered for the powerful .45 ACP round that had carried the U.S. armed forces through decades of fierce battles as the primary pistol cartridge of America's fighting men. Tonight, he was thankful for the destructive capabilities of the large caliber because he knew the likelihood of everything going smoothly was remote.

Flicking a tear of fear from the corner of his eye, he cleared his conscious mind, took a deep breath, and said a desperate prayer for guidance. A fleeting search for alternative answers flashed across his mind.

"Shit!" He muttered under his breath when he realized there were no alternatives. He was out of options and time.

Drawing a slow ragged breath into his suddenly oxygen-starved lungs, he shuffled on heavy, leaden feet into the swirling darkness of the seemingly abandoned yard. He held his only hope for success in the slippery palm of his sweat-soaked hand.

CHAPTER 3

BAD CHOICE

Moving cautiously while simultaneously analyzing every tiny sound reaching his attentive ears, Robert slinked furtively in the shadow of a gondola railcar carrying scrap steel. The smell of the rail yard was unique and puckered his nose. The matted dirt stank after having decades of heavy industry settle upon it. The gritty odor of gravel and the astringent aroma of diesel fuel mixed harmoniously with the musky, almost fish-like redolence of peeling paint and rust.

He hunkered beside the aged vehicle of burden to survey his surroundings. It took a few moments longer than he expected for his eyes to adjust to his shadowy surroundings. The almost total darkness found in the midst of the yard surprised him.

Only the faint twinkling of a smattering of stars was visible overhead. There was no appreciable illumination from the fading sliver of a moon. He found himself wishing the puny, orange-tinged glow of the filthy streetlights carried this far.

Just as he was beginning to be able to differentiate indistinct forms in the darkness, he caught a fleeting glimpse of stooped figures clumsily disappearing like limping Will-o-the-wisps between railroad cars.

That has to be them!

Most of the cars were open-topped with ancient barn-red paint flaking off their rusting steel skin. These brutes were designed to haul raw materials for industry, mainly bituminous coal or iron ore. However, the aged relics he hid behind were no longer up to the rigors of long hauls from distant coalfields. These octogenarians had long ago been relegated to short hauls toting waste metals. If they failed at that job, they were then carried to the smelting furnace by their surviving brethren and relegated to the mountain of soon-to-be-recycled scrap metal.

He cautiously approached the area he had last seen the trio, making sure to keep his form low to the ground while shuffling his feet just above the surface to avoid tripping.

Keep your ears open. They'll be of more use than your eyes.

A tiny scraping sound reached his ears, immediately riveting his attention to an area obliquely to his left where Amanda Freundin's feet and fingernail-studded hands flailed desperately in an attempt to escape Varecci's stench.

"Quit struggling or I'll let Varecci have you all to himself. And you don't want that, believe me," Dugan hissed into her ear, taking extra care to maintain a vise-like grip on a fistful of her hair so she couldn't smash his finely featured face. "He really likes it the more you struggle. It excites him."

Amanda went limp and Dugan thought his ruse had worked.

In a flash, she managed to free her left hand while spinning her body to the right and sunk her stiletto sharp fingernails into Varecci's face. His pustulous flesh separated in long, bloody welts from his right eye to the corner of his tainted mouth.

"You BITCH!" he roared like a wounded animal as his meaty fist smashed into her chest. Her breath whooshed out like compressed air being released from an overly inflated balloon.

Robert's head swung slowly and deliberately toward the trio as his ears pinpointed their exact location while the muzzle of his Sig tracked their movements.

He could only see specter-like forms in the murk, but he could clearly hear scuffling feet rolling diesel fuel-saturated stones on the railroad bed. His acute hearing was trying to verify there were only three of them. He hoped he had not missed seeing others when they vanished from the street.

"No yelling!" hissed Dugan.

"But…" Varecci whined as Dugan yanked a wad of Amanda's yellow hair toward the ground with a vicious sweep of his entire body. She gasped and whimpered pitifully as he smashed his knee into her back effectively pinning her to the ground.

"Quit your damned sniveling and pay attention! We're not going down to the creek. This is as good a spot as any."

Robert hurried in a shuffling gait, keeping his upper body as low as he could while trying to stay in the deepest, darkest shadows.

A rustling in the gravel brought his undivided attention to an area only twenty yards ahead of him. He stopped in his tracks.

Hell! They may be armed too! I didn't think of that!

He intelligently decided he was not able to confront two assailants under these circumstances regardless of how well he was armed.

I'm way the hell in over my head.

He spun around to make a stealthy retreat and accidentally glanced the Sig off the side of the railcar he was standing beside. The clang of metal against metal in the stillness of the night attracted more attention than a waiter dropping a tray full of wine glasses in a busy restaurant.

He instantly realized the folly of his actions.

Oh Shit!

"What the hell was that?" Dugan demanded, his ears striving to fix the location of the disturbance.

Varecci was too engrossed with beating Amanda to hear Dugan's words. He reveled at each wet, pounding blast his pummeling fist made when it contacted the delicate flesh of the hapless girl. The hollow sopping sounds held his rapt, though limited, attention.

Varecci's puny mind made it impossible to comprehend anything occurring outside the perverted pleasure he derived from the overwhelming aphrodisiac of dominating another human being. No minor disturbance would deter him from his planned rape and mutilation of their prey.

Seeing that Varecci didn't comprehend what was happening, Dugan grabbed his wrist. He could feel the piercing hatred of Varecci's searing glare searching quizzically for him in the darkness.

Robert sensed they had stopped and were listening to pinpoint his location in the shadows. He knew the moment of truth was at hand and moved forward toward the heaped mass of humanity with smooth, sure strides.

It was too dark for Dugan to fully comprehend the significance of the apparition sliding from the shadows beside the rail cars, but he knew it meant trouble. He reached for the Raven .25 ACP automatic pistol residing in his back pocket while simultaneously shifting his grasp from Varecci's wrist to the collar of his sweat-soaked sweatshirt.

Using his grip on Varecci's collar, Dugan jerked him around to face their opponent. He used the small silver-colored pistol clenched in his fist to point toward the dark form descending upon them. Robert was only thirty feet away and closing rapidly.

Varecci, seething with out-of-control anger over having his fun interrupted, swung a vicious punch to the back of Amanda's head, instantly stunning her into unconsciousness. As she collapsed into a rumpled heap Varecci rushed straight toward Robert in a blind rage.

A warning sounded in Robert's adrenaline-charged primeval mind allowing him to sidestep Varecci's attack a split second before he made contact. The move saved him from being bowled over by the much younger and stronger man but he was knocked off balance.

Holy hell! He just about had me! That was way too close. Create distance! Create distance!

Robert clawed madly at the side of the rail car with his left hand and almost spun wildly out of control in his haste to escape. The inky blackness of his surroundings removed any visual landmarks, which further disoriented him.

Varecci twirled in his tracks and promptly renewed his attack. Robert was forced to step backward, his hand sliding along the length of the car to avoid tripping.

As he stumbled backwards, the voice of his self-defensive shooting instructor echoed through his mind as though the words were being whispered into his ear:

When your assailant is attacking at bad breath distance, raise your gun up to chest level using both hands, making sure you keep it held close to your body so he can't grab it, square your body to the line of his attack and gently press the trigger.

The blinding muzzle flash of Robert's gun discharging in the near-total darkness temporarily blinded both of them and effectively disoriented Varecci because he did not feel the 230-grain Speer Gold Dot enter his belly just below the solar plexus. The bullet angled downward through his guts before exiting his turgid body just above his right kidney.

It was not an immediately fatal wound.

Robert's classroom training in self-defensive use of the handgun began to return to him in a flood of mental recollection:

Create distance between yourself and your attacker. Your superior skill from training will carry the fight to a successful conclusion. Regardless of whether he's armed or not, an attacker doesn't have to be skilled; he only has to be lucky. And the closer your assailant is, the luckier he becomes.

Varecci struggled to sort the bewildering bits of information flooding his limited mental faculties. Robert took full advantage of the lull in the action to put as much distance between himself and Varecci as he could before ducking between two fully loaded cars.

He began standing up to better assess the situation when Dugan fired his first shot.

The bullet ricocheted from one steel wall to the other in the confined space between the two rail cars where Robert had taken refuge. The slug barely missed his head twice during its zigzag flight.

Still blinded by his own muzzle flash, and now disoriented by the report of Dugan's gun, Robert frantically sought an escape route.

In his unsighted state, he turned and ran headlong into the rusted steel ladder attached solidly to the side of railroad car. During the day, workers checked the car's contents from these sturdy ladders. Tonight, this one caused Robert's second concussion of the evening.

At the instant his head collided with the ladder his legs sagged as a mushroom of exploding light erupted in his eyes. His left hand instinctively flew forward in a desperate attempt to arrest his fall. It found the bottom rung of the ladder and he clutched it frantically.

Realizing what he was grasping, Robert spontaneously formulated a plan as he one-handedly hoisted himself upright. Raising himself to his full height, he grabbed the highest rung he could reach. He pulled himself up until his foot was able to find purchase on the lowest rung.

Go quickly but silently if you hope to survive tonight. Hiding is your only chance!

Keeping the Sig firmly clasped in his right hand he used his right wrist to pull himself up to the next level.

If I can get above them maybe they'll lose track of me and that'll give me time to think.

Robert's hastily implemented plan failed before it began.

"There's the son-of-a-bitch!" Dugan screamed when he saw Robert's shadowy figure faintly sky-lighted against the starry background.

The instinct of any predatory animal in the wild is to pursue and kill any prey that is running away. The adrenaline-fueled predatory behavior of the younger man was triggered by the sight of Robert's fleeing figure and was further aided by the modern rendition of fangs; the .25 caliber Raven.

Dugan was impulsively driven to pursue Robert as pent up anger and bloodlust fogged his mind.

Firing the silver-colored pistol one-handedly, he rushed at Robert with savage abandon. In his homicidal haste he failed to notice that Varecci had begun climbing the ladder in pursuit of their prey. The electrifying exhilaration of the predator's pursuit engulfed Varecci in a shroud of invincibility common to young, testosterone-charged males.

Varecci was halfway up the ladder when Robert crested the crown of the railroad car. Scrambling to his feet on the ten-inch wide lip running completely around the top of the car Robert looked back down the ladder he had just stepped off of and was horrified to see Varecci reaching for his foot with one hand while clinging to the ladder with the other.

It was precisely at this inopportune moment that Dugan, in the midst of stepping down from a rail of the train track, triggered a 50-grain .25 ACP round. Dugan's bullet flew low; hitting the dull-minded Varecci in the hand he was using to hold himself to the ladder.

Varecci recoiled in shock and searing pain while staring dumbfounded at his wrist where the tiny slug ripped a path of destruction through brittle bones and stringy tendons.

Unthinking, he grasped his damaged wrist with his other hand to soothe the inferno erupting from its mangled joints. In the unreal slowing of time that occurs during times of severe mental stress, Varecci watched in horror as his bloated body peeled away from the ladder. His comic attempt to grasp the ladder with his uninjured hand was futile.

He tumbled clumsily out of control between the gondola cars and landed heavily with his rib cage straddling the steel rail of the tracks. A dull thud and sickening cracking sound occurred simultaneously followed immediately by an agonized, guttural scream. The three smashed ribs he suffered were not life threatening but the combination of this injury plus a blood-gushing bullet wound through his intestines rendered him incapable of standing.

Varecci was out of the fight.

One down, Robert thought as a smile of relief crossed his lips. His elation was short-lived. Dugan, using a two-handed hold on the tiny pistol, unleashed his final bullet at the shadowy figure tottering precariously on top of the car.

Robert felt the buzz of disturbed air from the bullet as it flew by his forehead.

Once again, his mind heard his instructor's voice whispering in his ear:

If your assailant is more than ten feet away you have to take careful aim and slowly press the trigger to make your shot count. Taking your time to precisely place one vital hit is infinitely better than wildly scattering bullets throughout the countryside.

Taking the advice of the voice reverberating through his mind Robert stood to his full height on the lip of the railcar and took careful aim using the outline of the gun instead of the night-obscured sights.

With a deliberate press of the crisp, three-pound trigger he sent a 230-grain .45 caliber Speer Gold Dot into Dugan's body, hitting a mere six inches to the left of his aiming point.

The bullet entered one inch above Dugan's right collarbone, angling downward to exit just below his right shoulder blade. The rapidly expanding bullet nicked the subclavian artery on its destructive path through his body. A wound to this vital artery, only half of a foot from Dugan's violently pumping heart, offered no opportunity to apply a tourniquet or otherwise staunch the pulsating gush of blood that immediately began soaking through the tightly woven fibers of his shirt.

The sudden disruption and severing of the nerves running from Dugan's neck into his right arm caused the silver gun to slip from his grasp. The lightweight zinc alloy pistol barely made a sound when it tumbled to the gravel-strewn ground.

Dugan knew instantly that he had been shot when the blinding muzzle flash and the almost-simultaneous thump of the heavy metal bullet smashing into his chest assaulted his senses. Adrenaline charged blood pressure forcefully expelled spurts of blood from the severed artery like a fireman's high-pressure hose; blood vital to carrying life-giving oxygen to nourish his now-starving brain. He did not know that his dying brain held only enough oxygen to operate for approximately 15 seconds before ceasing to function.

Dugan's sense of self-preservation had always served him well in surviving life on the streets. Without conscious thought his body pivoted 180 degrees and began pumping his legs as fast as his feet would move. Shards of gravel crunched noisily with every stride carrying him farther from the danger threatening his life.

Dugan never gave a second thought to his injured accomplice as he twisted his way through the maze of silent trains sitting idle. After detecting the sticky stream of warm blood snaking its way into to his shoes, his thoughts became fixated on the rapidly growing wet spot saturating his flannel shirt and jeans.

Robert focused all his attention on Dugan running between the trains and toward the run-down neighborhood beyond, but failed to notice the rapid, successive clamor of railroad cars jerking each other into motion.

Beginning with the train engine surging forward to supply forward momentum to move the train, each car began yanking its neighbor from a dead stop to a violent, lurching start, which then instantly slowed to a barely perceptible creep.

If he had understood the significance of the reverberating peal of heavy metal couplings smashing against each other, and it had sunk into his concussion-befuddled brain, he may have realized the train he was standing on was beginning to move.

Through a foggy bank of consciousness he slowly became aware of a slight tremor emanating upward from the steel skin of the railcar through the leather soles of his shoes. The trembling only occurred intermittently but grew stronger with each passing second. Thinking it may be Varecci renewing his attack, Robert focused his attention down the ladder as his fatigued eyes struggled to penetrate the murkiness under the gondola's belly.

With a sudden crash and jolt the open railroad car he was standing on lurched forward with a violent start, jerking itself from beneath his feet and sending him into an intractable free fall. His uncontrolled six-foot tumble into the car was not mitigated by any attempt to save himself.

The visual illusion caused by the car being partially full with heaps of discarded scrap steel added to his inability to discern where his body was in time and space. Clumped in uneven mounds, the soon-to-be-recycled waste created differing hues of mottled shadows scattered about the half-filled car. The distorted fluidity of the sky further confused his senses as he desperately tried to make sense of what was happening to him.

Robert landed upside down with a sickening crunch reverberating through the center of his chest when his upper back hit the corner of an ancient Maytag washing machine. Before his mind could register he had been injured, his head slammed onto the mangled tire rim from a 1964 Ford Fairlane, causing his third concussion of the evening.

His exquisitely crafted Sig P220 slipped unnoticed from his grasp and landed beside a mutilated lawnmower engine. The tool Robert had used to save his life and that of Amanda Freundin would be melted down as scrap metal when it reached the foundry.

Robert would never know he was knocked unconscious or that the hapless Varecci was sliced in half by the gargantuan silvery steel wheel belonging to the same railroad car he fell into. Ironically, both of the former adversaries had their lives irreversibly altered in the same irretrievable instant.

Amanda eventually awakened, beaten and bruised, having lain unconscious throughout the entire gunfight. After struggling to her feet she unsteadily staggered home to a warm bed with no recollection of Robert's involvement.

Two days later, railroad workers would find Dugan's and Varecci's grotesquely bloated bodies.

The police investigating their deaths would never uncover the truth linking the events leading up to their demise on that fateful night. Robert's disappearance and abandoned vehicle only added to the mystery.

CHAPTER 4

A RUDE AWAKENING

The train slowly meandered its way from the Baltimore railyards toward Virginia where the foundry and final destination for the scrap metal was located. In the outskirts of Washington, D.C., the train stopped to take on additional cars before continuing its journey. It was here that Robert Fogler, fourteen hours after he had fallen into the railroad car, awoke in agony.

Damned! My head feels like I've been out drinking for a week. I can hardly move I'm so stiff.

When he attempted to sit up a spasm of lightning-like pain shot from between his shoulder blades into his head. The pain was so great he did not notice or care that he was cutting his hands on sharp edges of scrap metal as he struggled to his feet.

Ow! Ow! My arm is numb and I can't move the damned thing!

Peering over the rusted lip of the gondola car he realized he did not know where he was. With Herculean effort, his stiff, uncooperative joints finally allowed him to laboriously crawl out of the car. His slashed hands dripped congealing drops of bright red blood onto his pants and the inside walls of the rusty metal hulk.

He did not know where he was going; only that he was in dire need of help. As he staggered across the railroad yard, a seemingly deserted neighborhood appeared on the far side of a chain link fence. The silvery diamond shapes of the woven metal fence separated the putrid brown of the railroad property from the mottled gray concrete sidewalks and grayish-black macadam street.

There must be someone there who'll help me, he thought groggily.

When he staggered closer to the fence his spirit plunged.

How the hell am I supposed to get over this thing?

Searching feverishly up and down the gray metallic fence, his eyes fell upon a ragged two-foot square hole cut in the fence many years previously by teenagers wanting to access a desolate place to drink beer.

After falling onto his hands and knees he flopped onto his belly and managed to crawl through the hole, miraculously avoiding most of the pointed wires jaggedly protruding from the edges. Only his scuffed leather jacket kept his belly from being severely cut by broken beer bottles scattered on the ground. His bare hands and knees did not fare as well.

Standing upright was almost an impossible task. He was hurting from his head to his toes. His hands began throbbing insufferably; shards of broken glass were now embedded alongside as well as in the cuts he received from the ragged edges of scrap metal in the railcar.

A blinding headache accompanied by tunnel vision began affecting his eyesight. He used his bloody hands to shade his hypersensitive eyes while squinting against the horrendously bright sunshine. The urge to vomit was overwhelming.

Robert was suffering external auditory exclusion with all sounds picked up by his ears appearing muffled while an almost intolerable din clanged inside his skull. His incredibly stiff upper back caused him to lurch in a rocking gait that would have made the Hunchback of Notre Dame appear nimble. Shuffling on unsteady legs he agonizingly staggered down the sidewalks of unfamiliar streets. His mind swirled in a tornado of befuddlement.

He looked for someone to help him but no one was to be found on the deserted streets. His injuries finally overcame him as the pain became too much to bear. Collapsing in the shade beside a foot-worn granite stoop leading up to the sun-bleached wooden front door of a crumbling red brick house, he closed his eyes for a moment to rest his pain-racked body; too weary to travel any farther. Unconsciousness mercifully enveloped him and cradled him in the boundless black depths of sleep.

CHAPTER 5

CHAUNCEY

When he awoke, it was cold and dark. There was a man talking to him and pushing his shoulder to awaken him. Robert could only stare dumbly at him and demand gruffly, "What the hell do you want?"

Slowly, the man's swirling facial features came into focus. It was the kind, gentle face of William Collonem, a thirty-two year old social worker at the Bethlehem Mission for Homeless Men. William's six foot five inch frame carried 320 pounds on it. The huge, intimidating size of his body often went unnoticed because of his constant, comforting smile.

"Can you hear me?" William asked patiently with a smile purposefully affixed upon his lips.

"Yes I can hear you. What the hell do you want?"

"I want you to get in the van so I can take you to the mission. It's going to be real cold out here tonight, cold enough to kill you. We have hot food, a warm bed, and biblical guidance waiting for you there. Are you OK?"

"I hurt real bad. I need a doctor."

"Let's get you in the van. We have a doctor who visits the mission on Tuesday afternoon, that's tomorrow. If you're in really bad shape we can take you to the emergency room. Did you get beat up?"

Getting no answer, William tried again, "Where are you all hurting?"

Robert still did not reply.

Seeing the man did not understand him, or could not respond, William helped him painstakingly gain his feet and led him to the van.

Must be drunk as a skunk to be this unsteady, William thought sadly.

"Have you been drinking?"

"I don't think so."

"You don't know?"

"I don't know. Who are you anyway?"

"I'm William. Are you diabetic? You're pretty unstable on your feet but I don't smell any alcohol on your breath."

"I don't know."

"What's your name?"

A quizzical look came over his face. "I don't know."

"You don't know your own name?"

"I can't remember. Please, I need help. I really hurt," he whined pathetically.

William was used to men occasionally showing up at the mission offering a false name to avoid being identified for past crimes. Having a man deny knowing his name was a much rarer occurrence.

"Come on; let me help you into the van."

He glanced toward the street and saw a white eleven- passenger van in desperate need of a car wash with "Bethlehem Mission" emblazoned on the side in large blue block-style lettering. A solitary cross of faded light blue paint adorned the passenger's door.

As William assisted him into the van, William's helper, an intern from Alexandria Community College named Scott Haldeman, asked him, "What's your name?" as he held a Ticonderoga #2 lead pencil poised over a piece of dog-eared lined yellow paper attached to a clipboard.

A dry mouth and cracked, thickened lips caused him to slur his reply, "I don't know."

"What's your name?" Scott asked with irritation and impatience in his voice.

I have to talk to him about the inflection and tone of his voice, William thought sadly. *Any affront to these guys can get the snot beat out of him in a skinny minute.*

"What's your name?" Scott repeated with increasing irritation in his voice.

Robert stared at him with a blank look on his face, "I don't know."

William sensed it was time to intervene.

"Just put down Chauncey, he looks like a Chauncey to me." The note of finality in his voice combined with a stern look as he glared down at the smaller man motivated Scott to take the hint without comment.

"Besides, we don't have another Chauncey at the mission so it'll help avoid confusing him with anyone else. Especially since he doesn't have a last name," William added consolingly.

Thus Robert Fogler became Chauncey.

Chauncey became a man without a past or legal name. Not named by his mother but by a large man named William from the Bethlehem Mission for Homeless Men. Chauncey had suffered total amnesia caused by a rapid succession of multiple head injuries and could not remember anything before being awakened by William.

"Grab a seat in the back of the van, Chauncey," William directed. "We still have a lot of men to pick up and it's better if they don't have to trip over you to get to an open seat."

As an afterthought William added in a mentoring, almost fatherly tone of voice, "Chauncey, you have to realize that the men who will share this van and the mission facilities with you are hardened by life. They're used to fighting for every scrap of food, clothing, and dignity they possess. They defend their territory, or even what they perceive as their territory, with sudden and devastating violence. Many of them are mentally unstable. Don't give them a reason to fight with you. Some of these guys will kill you before you know what happened."

Chauncey stared at William with no sign of comprehension on his face but finally gave a little nod of his anguished head. William's friendly smile broadened slightly before he turned away to continue his search for other derelict men to save.

Chauncey looked at the person he was to sit beside in the rear seat of the van, and was relieved to see a very docile older man whose face beamed above a warm, toothless smile.

Wanting to take William's warning to heart Chauncey decided to make friends with this seemingly harmless man. "Hello, my name is Chauncey," he said as he extended his tattered right hand. He fought back an obvious wince when a burning pain shot from his right shoulder blade to his fingers.

"I don't think you want me to shake your injured hand, man. It looks bad," the old man slurred indistinctly through puffing lips as he struggled to speak without the benefit of teeth. "My name is Wilbur. Do you have a last name?"

"No, I don't. Only Chauncey. And that's not my real name. William gave it to me when I couldn't remember my own."

"That's OK. I only use one name too and I don't want to explain why," Wilbur said. "I don't care about little things like being around people not having a name as long as I get me a good meal and a bed to sleep in."

"William said he'd feed us and give us a warm place to sleep. I need a doctor. I hurt bad."

"Yeah, that's too bad," Wilbur murmured absentmindedly, his attention consumed by the sight of another homeless man entering the side door of the van. The new arrival was well known to him.

"Be glad there are only two seats back here. This guy is pure trouble," Wilbur whispered as he gestured toward the man entering the van.

Chauncey, hugging his tormented right arm to his chest, glanced nervously at the man whose head had just poked into the van. Cautiously leaning closer to Wilbur, he asked, "Who's that?"

"That's Malik," Wilbur replied in a barely audible whisper.

Malik was a hulking, ill-mannered alcoholic smelling of filth, urine, and sweat. He glared with unblinking eyes at Chauncey and Wilbur before slumping onto the middle of the seat in front of them.

"Keep an eye on that one," Wilbur whispered to Chauncey. "He's a mean bastard."

Hearing him, Malik turned around to resume his menacing glare. Wilbur's fear was short-lived because Phillip, a man who had been sharing a steam grate with Malik, entered the van, stumbled, and landed heavily on the seat, jostling Malik in the process.

Chauncey watched in horror as Malik instantly launched into a vicious attack. He first hit Phillip in the middle of his chest then immediately threw a vicious right hook to his outstretched chin.

The blow to Phillip's chin glanced harmlessly off his whiskered jaw, doing no permanent physical damage. He quickly recovered and retaliated with a right cross to Malik's nose. The cartilage of Malik's nose snapped while his blood splattered across Chauncey and Wilbur's chests.

Chauncey sat transfixed as William Collonem launched himself into the van, savagely grabbed Phillip by the collar of his coat, and ejected him onto the sidewalk. When William's head reappeared at the van door it merely took a hand gesture to instruct Malik to follow him outside.

Only when Malik reached the van door did the realization hit him that he was about to be banned from the mission. He balked, shook his shaggy head slowly back and forth, then began backing up to return to his seat.

In a flash, William snatched a large handful of Malik's overcoat with his right hand and an equally sized handful of hair with his left. He easily pried the large man from the van and tossed him toward the steam grate as though he were nothing more than a plastic sack of garbage. Malik landed face first on the frigid sidewalk, bloodying the palms of both hands and ripping the knees out of his pants.

Chauncey stared in stunned amazement as William pointed his finger at the two prostrate forms lying on the ground and began spitting words at them with a venomous tone, "You bastards want to fight, go ahead. But you're not going to do it in my van. You can spend the night on that steam grate and I hope it keeps you warm enough to keep you alive. If not, then good riddance to both of you. If you do survive, I'll check back here tomorrow afternoon and see if you're ready to begin acting like human beings instead of animals!"

"He's different when he's mad," Wilbur observed in a quiet, awe tinged voice as he continued to stare at the spectacle unfolding before his eyes.

Turning on his heel, William spun his huge body agilely around, slammed the sliding door of the van closed, and unhurriedly took his place in the driver's seat. He motioned calmly with his index finger for Scott Haldeman to occupy the passenger seat. Scott obeyed immediately; reaching for his safety belt before his buttocks even hit the seat then swinging the vehicle's heavy door closed right away.

Malik, his broken nose bent at an awkward angle, blood running in an uninterrupted stream over his chin and pooling on the front of his dirt-stained nylon coat, sat beside an equally astounded Phillip on the cold, hard concrete in stunned silence, watching in dismay as the van pulled away.

Chauncey sat silently throughout the entire ride lost in his misery. Everyone, including Wilbur, paid him no attention.

CHAPTER 6

THE BETHLEHEM MISSION

To Chauncey, the ride in the van seemed to continue interminably and the seemingly endless number of stops plagued him mercilessly.

William, whom Chauncey quickly decided was not a very good driver, jerked the van to a sudden stop or bolted forward in a jackrabbit start at each stop, sending spasms of almost intolerable pain through his body. Even mandatory stops at red lights or stop signs resulted in agonizing convulsions of misery; each of which took Chauncey to the brink of unconsciousness.

In making their usual rounds William and Scott would quickly interview homeless people they found loitering on the streets or living under bridges. Most of the neglected souls they discovered were homeless waifs well known to them. The "usual customers" were often waiting for the van on street corners much like an employed commuter waits on a bus. The accepted custom of opening the van door, giving Scott their name as soon as it slid open, and entering in an orderly fashion went smoothly with those who knew the routine.

The homeless men who were not known to William had to be subjected to a short interview before being allowed into the van. Women were left on the street with instructions that the van for the women's shelter would be coming shortly.

He was amazed at how many homeless people refused the mission's offering of shelter. These hardy individuals, many of them suffering mental illness, chose to live in freedom on the streets. Scott gave them a brown bag lunch containing a ham and cheese sandwich on pasty white bread, an apple, and a non-descript chocolate candy bar with nuts. They had their choice of steaming black coffee or hot chocolate in a large Styrofoam cup topped with a shiny plastic lid.

Finally the van stopped and William turned in his seat. He then raised his voice to make sure everyone heard him, "We're here. File out of the van one at a time. There's no reason to push and shove. Nobody's going anywhere any faster than the whole group can move. You will all be processed together so help each other to speed up the procedures. Anyone who wants to fight or tries to smuggle alcohol or drugs into the mission will be immediately thrown back onto the street and into the cold."

He nimbly swung his bulk out of the van and took a position next to the side door. As the door slid open William continued his litany, "Go up the front steps and someone will assign you your job then direct you to the showers.

"After you're showered and dressed in clean clothes you can proceed to the dining hall. At precisely six o'clock the religious services will begin. The services will be officiated by the Reverend John Yates, the director here at the Bethlehem Mission. You will be courteous, pay attention to what is being said, and show proper respect, which means no talking during the service," he continued in a staccato voice.

"They always make you listen to the minister before they feed you. Just obey the rules and everything will be OK," Wilbur whispered into Chauncey's ear in a friendly, mentoring tone. Chauncey leaned away the best he could to avoid vomiting from the horrific, putrid odors wafting from Wilbur's toothless mouth.

The men began filing out of the van in a relatively orderly manner. Most of them were familiar with the workings of the mission having been there many times before. Chauncey had trouble getting out of the van. His open wounds and tormented joints had stiffened, increasing his misery.

William, seeing the problem Chauncey was experiencing, helped him step down from the van.

"It's a good thing tomorrow is Tuesday. The doctor will be in so I'll put you on the list to see him. I don't want you getting blood over everything so I'm going to excuse you from any assigned chores."

"Thank you," was all Chauncey could say from between pain-clenched teeth.

Chauncey's eyes followed the steps of the mission upward to the massive carved wooden front doors. The structure had once obviously been a government building. The twenty-three granite steps were foot-worn in the middle with the ends retaining their original squared-off edges. The stucco façade was painted white with six large columns holding up the portico's roof in the grandiose staging of hexastyle architecture.

Chauncey laboriously ascended the stairs. Each step increased his agony. The acidic odor of bleach and pine-scented disinfectant cleaner slammed into his nostrils as soon as he stepped into the cool, dimly lit lobby. Nausea overwhelmed him.

Slowly turning his body instead of his head to avoid worsening his headache, he surveyed his surroundings.

"Chauncey, you have to keep up with the group. Do the best you can. I'll meet you after you're showered. Make sure you work lots of soap into those wounds to get the dirt out, then I'll bind the cuts so you don't bleed all over your clean clothes," William said with concern in his otherwise deep, rough voice. He had obviously volunteered to be Chauncey's guardian angel while he was healing and unable to fend for himself.

He managed to shower but thoroughly cleansing himself was difficult considering the limited range of motion of his joints. While removing his clothes, he found cuts and abrasions over his entire body. He was shocked to find a ten-inch laceration running from the top of his left thigh to the knee. He gently worked the scant bubbles of the cheap, harsh brown soap he had been given into his wounds and obediently scrubbed lightly in all directions.

After the soap washed the grime away, stark light radiating from the bare bulbs illuminating the shower area caused shards of glass embedded in his palms and knees to sparkle like diamonds. He carefully plucked the fragments with his fingernails then tossed the shimmering slivers of variously colored glass into a dark green plastic trash can in the lavatory area adjacent to the showers.

After dressing in newly laundered but detergent-stiffened clothing Chauncey shuffled bewilderedly down the starkly lit hallway to the dining area.

He was glad the men moved down the hallway as a group. Being able to concentrate on the back of the man in front of him helped steady his faltering gait.

The dining hall had tables set end-to-end forming long lines from one side of the huge room to the other. Lines of chairs were neatly arranged on either side of the tables; six chairs per ten-foot table giving each man approximately three feet of table space. Such spacing had been closely analyzed by the mission director and was found to reduce the number of fights triggered by territorial instincts.

White lines painted on the floor assured the tables were in their correct place. This attention to detail guaranteed that six-foot aisles between tables were maintained. Guests bumping into each other or jostling another's chair as they carried their tray of food to a place at the table was a major precipitator of vicious, often-bloody fights.

A tall, thin, slightly balding man in his mid-thirties stood on a small riser at one end of the dining hall observing the men as they filed into the room. Trustees of the mission, usually bent and shuffling old men who were allowed to remain year-round as resident workers, offered guidance to seat the men systematically so they took the next available seat at the table.

Because of the orderly manner in which the men filed into the dining hall they were all seated within minutes waiting impatiently for the Reverend John Yates to begin his sermon and the food to follow. Tantalizing smells wafted from the kitchen causing the famished men to salivate.

Reverend Yates didn't hold anything back. He sermonized on every topic affecting the homeless men's lives. Some men paid token attention to his moralizing while others sat in bored silence. Most were staring at nothing in particular with a blank expression on their weathered faces.

And then there was Chauncey.

He found the words of John Yates absolutely fascinating. The concept of Heaven and Hell placed the four hours of the life he could remember into a workable framework. He now had a template to begin forming his future around.

Chauncey did not look upon the message as pontification but rather as personal counseling. The impact on him was so significant that when he sat with his food in front of him he could only pick at it because he was so deep in thought and introspection.

From the moment he first picked up his tray he had problems holding it. His hands had few areas not sliced or inflamed by cuts. He obviously had missed a number of glass splinters because touching those areas sent a nauseating bolt of pain shooting from his hand into his arm. He was relieved when he was finally able to send the tray down the conveyor belt to the dishwashing area without dropping it.

In the recreation area Chauncey gingerly set himself at the end of a light tan naugahyde couch smeared with smudges of filth embedded so deeply they could never be wiped away. A strategically placed lamp saturated the arm of the couch with a flood of light bright enough to read by.

The short-cropped commercial-grade carpet beneath his feet may have come from the factory with a mottling of dark-hued colors to cover up stains but the huge smattering of blotches contaminating the floor covering gave it an unintended camouflage appearance.

The instant Chauncey tentatively picked up a dog-eared magazine with his damaged fingers from the scarred end table abutting the couch, his eyes began devouring the words from the front page to the back. Feature articles, advertisements, and every sidebar were read word for word in a frenzied quest for knowledge. Neither the type of magazine nor the topic of the article mattered to him. He only wanted to absorb the thoughts and ideas conveyed in the writing.

Chauncey was so consumed by his passion that he did not notice the towering figure of William Collonem standing in the doorway with Reverend John Yates.

"Where did you pick him up?" the reverend asked in a low, conversational tone so the men didn't overhear him. In reality, it would have been nearly impossible to yell over the clamor of the television set or the ruckus rising from around the ping-pong table.

"Over by the old library on Mulberry," William replied as he continued his vigil of Chauncey.

"And he claims to not know his name or anything else?"

"That's the story I got."

"He sure gobbles up everything he can read. Has he paid any attention at all to the TV?"

"None. Few of these guys even touch those magazines unless it's to kill a fly that's bothering them."

Reverend Yates smiled knowingly.

"Maybe he's telling the truth, and that's why he wants to learn as much as he can. You don't think he's an extraterrestrial who needs to learn everything about us before launching an intergalactic invasion, do you?"

William chuckled softly.

"I don't know what to think about him. But I'm going to make sure Doc Reynolds sees him tomorrow. The poor guy is really hurting; and it's not just his hands."

"If you can, speak with the good doctor before he sees Chauncey. I would like to get his opinion of the man's mental condition. Keep an eye on him if you would, eh William?"

"You know I will," was all William was able to say before Reverend Yates disappeared down the hallway on the way to his office.

CHAPTER 7

DOCTOR REYNOLDS

"So what do you think, Doc?" William asked as soon as Chauncey had left the room.

"I'm not sure what to think about his mental condition if that's what you're asking. Physically, he's a mess. I removed the rest of the glass splinters from his hands and knees the best I could. There may still be some imbedded in there but it'll have to work its way out. I gave him some antibiotic ointment to apply to the wounds and he'll need to keep bandages over them for a few days until the skin begins to scab over. After that he should be OK as far as his cuts are concerned."

Doctor Reynolds looked directly into William's eyes.

"His musculo-skeletal complaints are something else all together. It looks like he took a pretty savage beating the best I can tell. He has bruises all over. Did you know he had a cut between his shoulder blades? That's not the type of wound a man can inflict upon himself. It wasn't very deep so I just put a few butterfly bandages on it instead of stitching it up. He told me he's grateful for the aspirins and extra blanket you gave him last night."

"Yeah, I saw him tossing and turning all curled up in a ball. I figured he was chilled through from lying on the sidewalk out there. I've seen it before," William replied.

"I'm sure you have. Did he tell you about the nightmares he had? He has crazy dreams about people shooting at him and babies in the hospital with tubes running in and out of them. The part about the numbers was pretty strange also."

"No, he didn't tell me about any of that. What was so strange about the numbers?"

"It almost sounded like phone numbers but it was all jumbled up. He seemed to get very agitated when he was telling me about the numbers. I guess it's like those dreams where you're trying to run away but can't."

"Could you make anything out of his dreams?"

"No, he couldn't remember specifics. You know how that goes. Is there anything that stands out about him in your estimation?"

"Well, he seems confused but that's not unusual for these guys. His mind seems to wander quite a bit also. Once again, not too unusual for our guests here at the mission."

"So you finally decided to use some of the psychology they taught you in college?" Doctor Reynolds asked chidingly referring to William's near-useless degree.

"Yeah, I guess so," William replied good-naturedly. "What do you think about those headaches he complains about?"

"They appear to be migraines; or at least a pretty severe tension headache. The headaches may be related to his neck and upper back pain. I know a pretty good chiropractor, Sarah Collins, who operates a clinic over in Northwest. She's a good friend and her husband's an orthopedist on staff at the hospital with me. She may be willing to take on a charity case if I ask her to. I'll give her a call."

"Thanks doc, I appreciate that."

"I know you do William. Sometimes it seems as though you've adopted these men to take the place of the family you lost."

As soon as he said it, he knew he shouldn't have. The sudden downward casting of William's eyes and the sagging of his shoulders verified he had said the wrong thing.

"I'm sorry William…"

"It's OK doc. Thanks for your help, I'll see you next Tuesday."

Not knowing what to say, Doctor Reynolds muttered, "Yeah, see you then," before turning and walking down the deserted hallway.

William spun around and yelled after him, "I'll keep Chauncey around here for a few days to let him heal up a little. Call me as soon as you can with that chiropractor's number, OK doc?

"Good idea. You'll be hearing from me," he replied without breaking stride.

CHAPTER 8

CHAUNCEY'S TALENTS

"Chauncey, I need you to stand here and check the boxes from this shipment as they come off the truck. We want to be sure we're getting everything we paid for. Can you do that?" William asked as he held out a dark brown clipboard and yellow #2 lead pencil.

"Yes I can," Chauncey replied with an eager-to-please tone in his voice.

"The mission usually has enough food donated to feed the men we take in nightly as guests," William explained. "But cleaning supplies and paper products have to be purchased from a supplier with monetary donations."

As instructed, Chauncey diligently checked off each box as it came off the large, white-sided delivery truck. Tyrone and Samuel, two of the mission's trustees, kept two hand trucks busy off-loading the delivery van; slowing only enough to allow Chauncey an opportunity to see what they were taking to the mission's storage room in the basement.

After the last of the boxes were off-loaded and stored in the basement of the mission, William returned and silently gestured with his hand for Chauncey to give him the checklist.

"Everything there, Chauncey?" he inquired cheerfully. William loved seeing the men work cooperatively. He knew it was good for them and offered them the best chance of becoming productive members of society.

"Yes, everything's there but the numbers don't add up," Chauncey said as winced from a jolt of pain that shot down his arm when he handed the clipboard to William.

William pretended not to notice him flinching.

"The boxes are all there but the numbers don't add up correctly? What doesn't add up? Aren't all the boxes there?"

"The numbers on this side of the paper," Chauncey explained, pointing to the right hand column where the charges for the items were listed.

"What doesn't add up?"

"We ordered three cases of toilet paper and we received three but they're charging the mission for four," Chauncey said as he pointed to the discrepancy with one of his undamaged fingers. "Everything else is OK."

"We'll get this straightened out with the cleaning supply office. The driver doesn't have a clue about this stuff. He only drives the truck," William confidently proclaimed while looking askance at Chauncy.

"Has this ever happened before?" Chauncy asked skeptically.

"I don't know. And I bet John doesn't know either. He's so absorbed with the day-to-day operations of the mission he usually doesn't have time to sort through paperwork with a fine-toothed comb."

William looked thoughtfully at the invoice in his hand, and then glanced at Chauncey with a sly look in his eye.

"Hey Tyrone! Can you handle it from here?" William asked the trustee who had just emerged from the basement.

"Sure, we only have to break down these boxes and put the stuff where it belongs," he answered matter-of-factly.

"Come on Chauncey, let's see if the good reverend has a minute to spare."

William knocked loudly on the wooden door to John Yates's office. It had obviously been covered with innumerable coats of variously shaded paint; each of which showed through assorted nicks and gouges on its battered exterior.

"Come in," John said in a calm, even voice that flowed like a comforting mist from behind the closed door.

"John, I have something for you to see if you have a minute," William boomed as he opened the door and sauntered into the room.

Chauncey followed William into the sparsely furnished office. At first glance, the office looked clean and well organized. Closer scrutiny revealed that it was only clean. Boxes holding piles of loose papers were neatly tucked beneath every table and desk in the office. Chauncey suspected that a door on the back wall of the office led into a closet holding more of the mission's neglected paperwork.

"John, would you please look at this invoice from the cleaning supply company?" William asked as he held the paper out to Reverend Yates. "Do you see anything not quite right about it?"

John took the invoice from William with a quizzed look in his eye; then he scanned it from top to bottom. "What's your concern? It looks pretty much like the one we get from them every week."

"Chauncey noticed that we were charged for four cases of toilet paper but we only received three. He asked whether this type of mistake happens often. I think it's a fair question and should be answered."

John's disgusted look told William he did not want to be bothered by trivial oversights. Without saying a word, he reached beneath the computer desk and pulled out a cardboard storage box filled to the brim with loose papers.

Searching through the jumbled mess, John finally found a yellow invoice matching the one he held in his hand.

"Let's look at last week's and see."

Holding them both at arm's length, one invoice in each hand, John squinted slightly to see the squirming numbers. Disgustedly, he laid one of the invoices down to pick up his gold-rimmed reading glasses lying upside down on his food-stained desk blotter. Taking a minute to scrutinize the invoices, he deliberately laid them down side-by-side on his desk.

Without a word, he once again rummaged through the overflowing cardboard storage box in search of another invoice. Triumphantly raising one from the bowels of the clutter he earnestly searched it for discrepancies.

"Well Chauncey, it looks like you've stumbled onto something here. Each week's supply order has one item we're being charged for but did not order nor receive. There definitely seems to be a pattern," John said with disappointment in his voice.

"Chauncey, I'll handle this but I have to know how long these shenanigans have been going on. Would you be willing to go through all these bills I haven't had time to? I should have made time but I didn't," he said as his voice trailed off while his shoulders slumped noticeably in resignation.

"Of course I'll help. I don't know what I'll find let alone what I'm looking for but I'll try," Chauncey said enthusiastically.

For a split second John's furrowed brow, which seemed to be a permanent fixture chiseled on his otherwise finely featured face, was overwhelmed by a smile of relief. Trying to keep up with the avalanche of paperwork and petty bureaucratic drudgery deluging his office was the bane of his existence. He had gone to Theology College and worked diligently for his degree in counseling to help people in need, and not to shuffle papers around his desk all day.

Forgetting his problematic workload for just a second, John's true calling shone forth as he remembered to inquire about Chauncey's well-being. "How are you feeling today, Chauncey?"

"I'm hurting terribly, but thank you for asking."

"Did Doctor Reynolds call with information about his chiropractor friend?"

"Yes, I have an appointment with a Doctor Sarah Collins tomorrow evening after her regular office hours; that's when she does her charity work. It's on the bus line, and William said he'd give me bus fare. He generously offered to pick me up in the mission van when I was done. He said he might be out all night checking on the people who refused to come inside."

"Yes, William is very generous with the mission's gasoline fund," John said with a joking tone to his voice as he threw a teasing glance at William.

"Well, that settles it," he continued with a tone of finality. "William, will you find a place for Chauncey to work undisturbed? And Chauncey, please concentrate on these cleaning supply bills first. I'd really like to know how far reaching this problem is so I can rectify it immediately. Please find out if there are any others."

With those words, Chauncey became the mission's bookkeeper.

CHAPTER 9

POROUS SOUTHERN BORDER

Muhammed Shah was unimpressed with the kaleidoscope of colors bursting from the Arizona desert as the breathtaking panorama swept past the windows of the Ford Econoline van. He was more concerned with the increasing dampness in the sweaty seat of his pants as his buttocks pressed into the sweltering plastic seat.

He was an unassuming man dressed in worn blue jeans and a slightly wrinkled short-sleeved dress shirt purposefully donned to blend in with the thousands of immigrants illegally crossing into the United States from Mexico every day. His natural walnut-hued skin allowed him to mingle unobtrusively with his fellow travelers. A day-old haircut and shave from a barbershop near the Mexico City airport offered a local touch of authenticity to his new identity as Jesus Jimenez, a citizen of Mexico. A tattered, sun-bleached green and yellow John Deere cap was pulled low over his eyes to complete his disguise.

I haven't been able to get the taste of this accursed land out of my mouth since arriving here, he thought disdainfully.

For what seemed like the ten thousandth time in the last three hours, he allowed his gaze to survey the other eleven passengers crammed in the van with him.

In three days we will arrive in Baltimore and I will be done with all but three of these chattering baboons, he thought, looking upon them with condescension while his deceptive, gracious smile never wavered.

Of course, I have to remain sociable until I have what I need to complete the mission Allah has ordained for me. It was only by His Grace that I was able to arrange a meeting with infidels who work at the Aberdeen Proving Grounds in Maryland - the location of the only remaining store of mustard gas from the American's World War I.

Without warning, the gringo driver jerked the steering wheel to the left to avoid colliding with a meandering armadillo; violently slamming the sun-wrinkled man seated beside him into Muhammed's shoulder. The man looked at him and shrugged his shoulders with his palms skyward in a submissive gesture of apology for the driver's actions.

The passengers relaxed when the van resumed its monotonous trek with the familiar hum of balding tires on scorched asphalt droning endlessly in their ears.

Thank you for allowing my border crossing at Nogales to proceed without incident, Mohammed prayed silently. *You are obviously allowing me to establish your rule over the people of the United States and to punish them for their shameful ways. It is by your will that the American politicians are too stupid to close their country's borders to the couriers of their destruction.*

Ignoring the rancid flatulence wafting throughout the van from one of his ill-mannered travel companions, Muhammed suddenly felt at ease. A satisfied grin spread across his craggy face as he settled back into the cramped seat to tolerate the rest of his journey in thoughtful silence.

The foolish infidels from the American's Department of Homeland Security don't even know I am the key to their destruction. I am the chosen one, the only person who knows the identity and location of all our followers who have been secretly living in Washington, D.C. for many years.

He looked out the dirt-streaked window impassively and smiled broadly.

It is I, Muhammed Shah, who has sole discretion on how to use these human resources to demolish the infrastructure of American society.

His furrowed brow relaxed and he began to snore gently as his head slowly settled upon his chest in sleep.

CHAPTER 10

ILLEGAL IMMIGRANTS AND MUSTARD GAS

"Commander, how did you meet these people?" Abdul-Haq asked Muhammed, trying to avoid having the doubt in his heart from being heard in his voice.

"It is none of your business," Muhammed said. "But I will tell you because I want you to be familiar with the operation we are about to embark upon."

"Thank you, Commander."

"Jose Padilla, Juan Martinez, and Jorge Diaz were in the group I was with when we came across the American border with Mexico," he said while staring intently at him. "They work on a construction crew that cleans and repairs air ducts in the buildings of the Aberdeen Proving Grounds."

"And why is that important to our mission?"

"Because, you fool," Muhammed replied haughtily. "The only remaining stores of mustard gas in the United States are stored in the Edgewood area of the Aberdeen Proving Ground in Maryland. It is being stored under heavy guard until a disposal plant can be built to neutralize what remains from America's World War I."

"That war was a long time ago."

"Yes it was, but the mustard gas is still potent and the Americans want to be rid of it," Muhammed replied. "Luckily, lawsuits from environmental groups have stopped the expected completion of the disposal facility which is good for us because we have an important use for the gas."

"And what is that?"

"It is none of your business," Muhammed said menacingly. "You will be informed of your duty and nothing else."

"I'm sorry sir," Abdul-Haq stuttered. "I---"

"Never mind," Muhammed said disgustedly. "Just be thankful the Americans are inept and stupid."

"I am, Commander," he said sheepishly.

"The environmental extremists have aided us for many years," Muhammed said with a tone of superiority in his voice, eager to flaunt his knowledge. "First these groups complained about the proximity of schools and communities to the proposed disposal plant so the government fitted the schools in the area with overpressurization devices to protect students and staff in the event of a catastrophic fire or explosion during incineration."

"That must have taken much money and a long time to complete."

"The Americans have too much money and they waste it," Muhammed said disgustedly. "The schools were protected and the local community was prepared for such an occurrence by undergoing training, planning sessions, installing additional emergency equipment, and other programs which were put in place to assure that no tragedy would occur during disposal of the gas. The news reports were very clear in explaining all the details."

"The fools," Abdul-Haq said heartily to ingratiate himself with his commander.

Without responding to Abdul-Haq's comments, Muhammed continued, "A disposal plant is the only way to neutralize the gas that would be acceptable to the American public but the environmental groups continued filing lawsuits to delay its construction."

"You are very knowledgeable."

"It was through the reporting of these lawsuits in the newspapers that I learned everything we need to know about where and how the mustard gas at Aberdeen is stored.

"And what role will these Mexicans play in your plan?" Abdul-Haq asked then immediately realized he had once again voiced a question he should not have. "I'm sorry sir---"

"Do not worry," Muhammed said. "Quite simply, they are our burglars."

"I am sorry, sir, but it sounded like you said they are our burglars."

"That's exactly what I said," Muhammed said as he puffed his chest out proudly. "I have promised each of them five thousand dollars to steal canisters of mustard gas from Aberdeen Proving Grounds for us."

CHAPTER 11

STEALING MUSTARD GAS

Muhammed, Abdul-Haq, Jamaal, and Hamza were standing idly in the empty interior of a dimly lit garage on a seedy side street in Dundalk, Maryland that Jamaal had rented under an assumed name. A solitary, bare bulb hung from a beam in the center of the vast, unused space illuminating the grease stained concrete floor with an eerie, anemic glow. The bare concrete block walls emitted a bone-chilling dampness even though it was late spring. Gasoline odor permeated from the pores of the decrepit concrete and made Muhammed nauseous.

Taking a deep breath in an attempt to calm his rebellious stomach, Muhammed strode to the center of the group.

"Now that we have gathered I want to explain what is to transpire tonight and why you will be doing the work Allah has ordained for you," Muhammed said commandingly.

"We have waited years for you to gather us together and reveal our destiny to us," Hamza said respectfully.

"Yes, it was important to keep each of your identities secret; even from each other," Muhammed responded. "It was necessary so you would not be able to identify your colleagues in case you were captured by the infidels and questioned. I alone have been entrusted with that information and am the key to open the secret of your years of hardship."

"Praise be to Allah that you have been sent to unite us to do his bidding," Abdul-Haq said. "Living with the infidels and their decadent ways has tested our faith many times."

"I am sure," Muhammed said as he raised his chin to signal his superior rank. "Now it is time to divulge the reason for us being here."

The three men attentively looked at him.

"The tools we need to accomplish our mission have been delivered," Muhammed said expansively. "We are here tonight to assure we are the only ones who are aware of that fact."

The three men stood silently and stared intently at Muhammed. He made them wait in silence for a few moments to underscore the privilege his superior rank afforded him.

"The plan involving the Mexicans was quite simple," Muhammed explained. "The only question was whether these infidels could fool the security people at Aberdeen."

"Commander, was it possible for these Mexicans to just walk out of the Aberdeen Proving Grounds with canisters of mustard gas? They are not very sophisticated or educated."

"Of course not you fool!" Muhammed sputtered angrily. "They work in an unsecured section of the same building where the mustard gas is kept. Unguarded air ducts connect the secured and unsecured areas of the building."

"And they can gain access to the secured area?"

"The plan was very simple," Muhammed continued without acknowledging the question. "They simply unscrewed the steel mesh grate blocking access between the heating systems of both areas."

"And do they know what they have stolen?" Abdul-Haq asked innocently.

"Do you think I am a fool?" Muhammed spat. "They only knew they were to take the cylinders that look like propane tanks painted with yellow and red stripes."

"Were they sure those are the cylinders containing the mustard gas?"

"The newspaper had a picture of the cylinders in the article about the environmental group's lawsuit to halt construction of the disposal facility."

"Surely the cylinders were big and heavy," Hamza said. "How did they get them past the guards?"

"It was simplicity itself," Muhammed replied. "They use crawlers, similar to those used by mechanics to work beneath automobiles, to haul tools and cleaning equipment through the air ducts. It was a simple task to load the mustard gas cylinders onto the crawlers and roll them past the steel mesh barrier."

"But weren't they seen removing the distinctively painted cylinders from the air ducts?"

"After reaching the area of the building they are authorized to be in, they spray painted the cylinders to match the other equipment used to clean the air ducts."

"Excuse me for being so inquisitive, Commander," Hamza asked sheepishly. "But didn't the scent of spray paint alert the guards or other people in the building?"

"It is a very good question Hamza and one that I too thought of. It is very good you are inquisitive; you will be a valuable asset," Muhammed replied with an obvious tone of approval in his voice as he looked disapprovingly at the other two men for not being as insightful.

"The workers used large fans to vent air from the ducts to the outside; they are normally used to stop fumes from chemicals used to kill mold and sanitize the ducts from sickening the building's occupants."

"It is a brilliant plan, Commander," Jamaal said in an attempt to ingratiate himself with his superior.

"Simplicity leads to brilliance," Muhammed agreed as he mentally congratulated himself for developing such a plan. "At the end of the day the workers simply hid the newly-painted cylinders beneath the rest of the equipment in their truck."

"Were they not stopped and searched as they left?"

"The canisters blended in with the other equipment they use every day in their labors."

"How many of the gas cylinders did they steal?"

"Ten in total but they only stole two per day otherwise they would have obviously been leaving at the end of the day with more equipment than they arrived with in the morning."

"Wouldn't the guards inspect the steel mesh grate and see that it had been removed?"

"After the workers replaced the grate, the duct surrounding it was painted. Painting is one of the contracted services for which they have been hired," Muhammed said smiling. "It looked the way it was supposed to appear after it had been cleaned, repaired and re-painted."

"And when are we to receive the mustard gas?"

"I already have it in my possession," Muhammed replied with a large smile on his face. "Each day they left the cylinders in the garage of a deserted house owned by our supporters. I picked up the cylinders after they left. They never saw anyone."

"So what are we going to do when we meet them here in half an hour?" Hamza asked innocently. "Pay them for their thefts?"

"No you fool," Muhammed said. "We are going to kill them."

"Won't someone miss them and ask questions about us?" Abdul-Haq asked with a trace of uncertainty in his eyes. "Surely they will have told someone about their theft, the money they expect to be paid, and about you."

"Yes, they may have told the people they live with. Their wives and children live with other illegal aliens in a rented house in Aberdeen," Muhammed said with a wicked grin. "I have already dispatched four men from another cell of true believers to kill everyone in that house then burn it to help hide the identities of the corpses. The authorities will suspect they are drug-related murders."

"And what would lead them to think the murders are drug related, Commander?"

"Because our men will leave a small amount of cocaine and heroin hidden in their vehicles parked in the driveway," Muhammed grinned, very proud of his clever plan.

"Will the authorities dig deeper for more information on the residents of the house?"

"No, they will have no identification in this country," Muhammed said. "They are illegal aliens living in the shadows of society. They have no documented job, do not pay taxes, and do not have their names on anything, not even an automobile. They do not exist."

"They will kill the children also?"

"They are infidels, Hamza," Muhammed said with deadly malice in his voice. "Are you unwilling to do what is necessary to complete our mission?"

"No sir," Hamza said with conviction. "It is Allah's will."

"Commander," Jamaal asked hesitantly. "Do you have plans for the mustard gas?"

"Yes Jamaal," Muhammed said quietly. "I have formulated a plan to use it on thousands of infidels at a Christian festival known as the Hallelujah Gathering. Of course, none of you will be participating in that operation. It is not what you were trained for."

"Praise be to Allah," the three men said in unison.

CHAPTER 12

SARAH COLLINS

The petite but athletically built thirty-four year old director of the District Spinal Care Clinic deftly flicked a wisp of her short-styled auburn hair from her eyes and forced a smile onto her face to energize her fatigued mind. After all, her day was winding down and she had a relaxing evening scheduled with her husband.

When she entered the room the tall, handsome, middle-aged African-American man lounging in one of the two chairs in the treatment room was casually studying the anatomical charts prominently displayed on the pink walls of the room.

"Well Chauncey, you've been under our care for four months now and it's time for a re-examination," she greeted her favorite patient as she bustled into the exam room.

After poising her pen over a clipboard, she began firing questions at him in rapid succession while writing furiously.

"How are your migraine headaches these days?"

"I haven't had one in about two months, thank God," Chauncey said with relief in his voice. "I didn't realize how much they hurt my ability to concentrate and work until they disappeared."

Sarah always marveled at how well this previously homeless man spoke. His diction was far above most of her other patients. As a matter of fact, he spoke more eloquently than most people she knew.

"I'm glad you can concentrate again," Sarah said with a smile, "especially since you're my bookkeeper now."

"I agree," Chauncey said as he returned her smile. "But you have to remember I was initially hired as a handyman so it wasn't as important to be headache-free for the first two months of my job."

"That may be true," she said. "But I'm always happy to see someone make progress and be relieved of horrendous symptoms like you had."

"And I'm very glad you were here to help me," Chauncey replied. "But I still feel funny about you treating me for free."

"Chauncey, all of my employees and their immediate families get chiropractic care for free as a benefit of the job," Sarah said. "And it's not all unselfish."

"What do you mean?"

"I mean that chiropractic is preventive health care," she replied evenly as she looked directly into his eyes. "It means my employees will not get sick as often and they'll be healthier while on the job and I like healthy, productive employees."

Chauncey smiled at his boss to return her broad grin. His admiration for Dr. Collins went beyond the normal employer/employee relationship because she had faith in him and gave him a chance when no one else would.

"Are there any areas of pain you're still having?"

"No, except for that stiffness between my shoulder blades," Chauncey continued. "I still wake up with a lot of stiffness in my upper back every morning but it loosens up in a half-hour or so."

"If you jump into a steaming, hot shower as soon as you get up, and let the warm water beat on that area, does it help you get moving faster?" she asked while continuing to write without looking up.

"Yes it does. And it stiffens up again just before bedtime."

"That's called the arthritic profile," she said. "You have some degeneration in that area, that's the type of wear-and-tear called osteo-arthritis, and you'll probably fight that battle for the rest of your life."

Chauncey nodded his understanding without saying a word, his face exhibiting no emotion at hearing the bad news.

"Just remember that seeing me for treatments will help to stop or at least slow down the degeneration as well as keep you moving with less stiffness and pain," she continued as a perky smile spread across the smooth, unblemished skin of her face. "I guess you'll have to work for me forever so we can keep you as healthy as possible."

Chauncey was amazed at how her entire face seemed to beam wholesomeness when she smiled.

"How about the shooting pains down your right arm?" she asked.

"They've been gone for about two months also," Chauncey replied. "Well, not totally gone. Occasionally it still flares up a little but an adjustment usually takes care of it. Will it ever go away totally?"

"Maybe, maybe not," she replied noncommittally. "Life in general, and gravity in particular, are constantly beating up on you. The areas still giving you trouble, especially if they recur on occasion, will probably plague you for the rest of your life. Once again, regular care will help keep it under control as much as possible. That's the best that can be hoped for," she explained in a calm, matter-of-fact voice.

"How's your new apartment working for you?" she asked to avoid having him dwell on bad news.

"It's great," he replied. "The mission was terrific in helping me get a place of my own. They fed and housed me until I could take care of my health problems- thanks to you- then helped me get this job. But I'm glad to be able to leave there. Having some privacy is really nice."

"Do you see William anymore? You two were pretty close."

"Oh yes! He comes over for lunch on Tuesdays and Thursdays," Chauncey replied, warming to the conversation. "He insists on bringing food, but it's not necessary."

"He's a very proud man," Sarah said. "He's just trying to be friendly without being a burden."

"Reverend Yates joins us when he can," Chauncey continued, thinking on what she said about William as he spoke. "I think they're both glad for an opportunity to escape from the pressures of the mission for a while."

"It's nice you have time to visit with your friends," she said.

"What's nice is having my apartment and this office only a few blocks away from each other so I can go home for lunch," Chauncey said. To change the subject he asked, "You have a big night tonight, don't you?"

"Yes, one of Josh's partners in their orthopedic practice is retiring and they're having a big party downtown," she replied. "The dinner is a dual celebration because they'll be officially welcoming Josh into the practice as a full partner. He signed all the papers and made everything legal and binding last week so now he has full partner benefits.

"And it's a personal celebration for Josh and I because the house we have been rehabilitating for the last two years is finally finished. I am so glad to have all the workers out of my house. Maybe now I can have some peace and quiet."

"You must be very proud of him."

"I am proud of him. As a matter of fact, he's waiting in the parking lot for me to finish so why don't we concentrate on getting you examined?" she asked, flashing a twinkling smile as she spoke.

Chauncey returned her smile, hoping that someday he would find a woman his own age as nice as Sarah.

Chapter 13

JOSHUA TOBIN, M.D.

Joshua Tobin, Sarah's loving husband, settled onto the plush leather seat of his BMW 550i. He knew she wouldn't leave her office until after the last patient had been treated.

I hope those are her last patients, Josh thoughtfully mused as he watched three well-dressed young men walk out of Sarah's office door before settling onto the tanned leather of his car seat to dream of a bright future.

It's been a long day and it's going to be a long night. Sarah can wake me when she's ready, he thought as he settled deeper into the comforting confines of the caressing leather and closed his eyes.

One of the men walking nearby, Tobias Masterson, was an eighteen year old patient of Sarah's who was recovering from an auto collision he had been involved in three weeks earlier. The other two men, Marias Phillips and Rolondo Hammon, were also eighteen years old and had grown up with Tobias.

The three men were almost inseparable growing up. They were cousins but looked so much alike they could easily be mistaken for brothers and often were. Each of them was almost six feet tall and weighed close to 200 pounds with closely cropped hair adorning the tops of their rounded heads. The various gold accoutrements each wore around their necks, pierced through their earlobes, or capping their front teeth were often the only distinguishing features to easily tell one from the other. Usually, if you saw one of the three, the other two were not far away.

The three cousins had a lot in common including long rap sheets for crimes ranging from simple theft to assault and battery. They almost always committed their crimes as a gang of three.

While growing up in their neighborhood, it was common knowledge that if someone started trouble with any one of the cousins they would assuredly have all three to contend with. The men were not overly well endowed with intelligence, but they were always willing to stand up for each other and that attribute alone was what had gotten them through scrapes with the law or other street thugs.

As they left Sarah's office that evening the three street-wise young men had only one thing on their minds.

A gorgeous, well-endowed girl had invited them to a graduation party in Chevy Chase. Her skin was as smooth and velvety as a rose petal and glowed like a piece of freshly unwrapped Godiva chocolate. The contrast of her luscious skin against the brilliant glow of a taut fitting white halter-top still haunted their daydreams.

"How the hell we supposed to get to this party?" Marias asked pensively. "Chevy Chase is way the hell on the other side of town."

"We need us a ride, Dawg," Rolondo pointed out before exiting the front door of Sarah's office. "He's right, Chevy Chase is way on the other side of the beltway and it ain't right for us to show up there on foot."

"That ain't right for sure, Home," Marias replied. "What if we meet the girl of our dreams? It ain't right to take a lady home on the Metro."

The three threw their heads back in unison as they laughed uproariously at Marias's sarcastic joke. In the back of their minds, however, they knew he was right.

"It ain't right, for sure," Rolondo intoned solemnly.

"We could have gone with Harold if Tobias didn't have to get his neck fixed," Marias suddenly added with irritation in his voice.

Tobias, angered by Marias's comments retorted, "Listen man, my neck hurts pretty bad. If it was you, you'd be cryin'. Besides, my lawyer said if I don't keep all my appointments, I won't get no money. You want that man? You want me to not get any money?"

"You been there every day you supposed to be, for sure," Marias said. "But you ain't ever been there on time. I heard that bitch at the front desk yellin' at you."

"She wasn't yellin' at me," Tobias replied jokingly. "She in love with me and want me bad, Man."

The three cousins burst into laughter once again.

"Besides, it don't matter none. My lawyer say I only have to be there, he didn't say when."

"If you had the damned money we'd have a ride, right?" Marias asked in a conciliatory tone.

"Yeah Dawg, we'd have a ride," Tobias replied in a manner accepting of Marias's peace offering.

Suddenly Tobias stopped in his tracks, his gaze focused across the parking lot on a shiny new metallic dark blue BMW 550i sedan. "There's our ride, Homes," he said as a broad smile broke across his lips revealing a mouth full of pearly white, evenly spaced teeth.

No spoken word was necessary. They had performed carjackings many times as a well-organized team and each knew the roles that had to be taken.

"I'm taking the passenger side because of my neck. It's the easiest and I don't want to be in pain at the party," Tobias announced with finality.

"So where do I go?" Rolondo asked hesitantly. "I don't want to pull open the driver's door. I always take the passenger side."

"Well, today you're taking the driver's door and you damned well better pull it plenty hard, I don't want Marias not being able to get him out of the friggin seat."

"Why doesn't Marias take the driver's door? He can handle it fine," Rolondo whined as he looked pleadingly at Marias.

"I always take the back. I like to pull them out and throw their sorry ass on the ground," Marias stated matter-of-factly. "And I'm good at it," he added with an obvious hint of pride in his voice as he puffed out his chest and shifted his weight to appear slightly taller.

"Just do what I tell you," Tobias said with venom in his voice. "Or don't you want to get to that party tonight?"

"Damned!" Rolondo muttered dejectedly. "Let's do it," he grumbled as he stepped in the direction of the 550i with a sauntering gait.

"Make sure there's nobody around. I don't want any witnesses screwin' things up," Tobias needlessly reminded his cohorts.

They knew he was a perfectionist and expected him to worry about details they considered unnecessary. He had shown signs of Obsessive-Compulsive Disorder since he was six years old and they surely didn't expect him to change now.

"It looks good and deserted," Marias crooned contentedly, more to console Tobias than to make a strategic observation.

"Look at that dumb-shit," Tobias said with a smile. "He just sleepin' like a baby. Not a care in the world."

Josh Tobin was totally unaware of what was going to happen to him in the next few seconds. In the end it did not matter; he was not a man of violence. All his life he had depended on others for his personal protection. He had always been able to live in the best neighborhoods with low crime rates and frequent police patrols. When the three hardened young men mentally checked off items during the victim selection process, they could have not done better than choosing a person like Josh Tobin. It was victims like Josh who made it easy for criminals to overcome them.

He was almost always oblivious to things happening in his immediate environment. Tonight was no different. He was only vaguely aware of Marias Phillips walking past his car. Only when Rolondo, following Marias by a few steps, yanked the driver's door open did it shock him from the murky depths of his nap.

"What the hell--" He began to sputter feebly, but was silenced at the sight of the deeply blued Smith and Wesson Model 19 .357 magnum revolver in Marias's tightly clenched fist. It's heavy, blunt faced barrel gave it a sinister appearance similar to the truncated snout of a venomous snake. The revolver, famed as the choice of lawmen for over two decades, had been in the possession of Tom McAdams, the sheriff of Prairie County, Illinois only three weeks previously.

No other possessions from Sheriff McAdams's burgled rural home had traveled to Washington, D.C.; however, the huge black market price fetched in areas where guns, especially handguns, were outlawed made it very profitable for the burglars to transport stolen firearms great distances.

Josh's vision could barely follow the blur of fluid motion as Marias's gnarly left hand grabbed a fist-full of his carefully coiffed blonde hair and jerked him out of the car headfirst.

"Give it up! Give it up!" Marias yelled in a commanding voice with his spittle-flecked mouth only inches from Josh's left ear.

Josh was so confused by the swift, savage attack that he did not understand what he was supposed to be giving up. The surprise attack had worked too well; the victim was completely disoriented and incapable of cooperating even though he was more than willing to do so.

As soon as Tobias saw Marias pull Josh from the car, he ripped opened the passenger door with his right hand and sprang into the passenger seat. Even before his buttocks hit the leather seat his eyes locked on the ignition switch. "I got the key! I got the key!" he chanted gleefully over and over again in a crazed fit of joy.

Marias was too engrossed in humiliating Josh to hear Tobias's gleeful gibberish.

Josh's buff tan calfskin wallet was jammed in the cup holder of the console between the two unblemished, leather bucket seats and it immediately caught Tobias's attention. Grabbing the wallet in his left hand, he began thumbing through it with his right, stuffing wrinkled, green cash and credit cards into the depths of his right front pants pocket. Tobias was too engrossed in pillaging his newly found treasure to pay attention to what was going on outside the car; he then tossed the empty wallet under the front seat.

"I got the money! Let's go!" Tobias yelled to his cohorts but Marias could not hear him because he was too engrossed with manhandling Josh.

"Give it up! Give it up Mutha Fucker!" Marias continued to bellow in a maniacal attempt to coerce Josh into handing over his wallet. His frenzied, shrieking voice rose in volume and shrillness with each repeated stanza.

Josh, in a surreal daze, was trying to comprehend what was happening to him. His mind reeled as he worked feverishly to grasp the reality of the situation and find a way out of it. In the protected cocoon of his sheltered life, he had incorrectly been taught that criminals were nothing more than fully-grown, misunderstood children who had not been treated correctly or fairly during the formative years of their childhood.

Marias was far from being a misunderstood child. Rather, he was a consummate life-long criminal who resorted to bursts of unrelenting violence to get his way.

Incorrectly assuming he could take control of the situation by acting like an understanding parent speaking to a misbehaving child Josh attempted to stand up and look Marias in the eyes.

"Don't look at me Mutha Fucka! What the matter wiff you!" Marias yelled insanely as a spritz of spittle flew from his mouth.

The situation escalated to lethal proportions. His lack of respect for Josh as a worthwhile human plummeted immensely while his disgust rose precipitously.

"Give me your money, Mutha Fucker!" Marias yelled.

They only want money.

Josh's befuddled mind was finally able to comprehend a portion of what was transpiring around him.

All I have to do is give them money and they'll leave me alone.

"What the matter wiff you Mutha Fucka?" Marias shrieked shrilly, his voice on the verge of being incomprehensible from rage as his clenched right fist, still clasping the blued steel Model 19, smashed into the fleshy tip of Josh's nose.

Josh slumped to his knees. If it had not been for Marias's unrelenting grasp of his hair he would have fallen to the ground in a crumpled heap.

Josh's mind wandered wildly as warm, sticky rivulets of blood coursed down his face. His ability to think rationally was diminishing rapidly and his once brilliant mind was now powerless to comprehend the scope of his swiftly deteriorating situation.

Still using his left hand full of Josh's hair, Marias tried unsuccessfully to lift him and force him backward toward the rear of the BMW, its dark blue metallic paint now splattered with variously sized droplets of Josh's blood.

"Get him between the car and those bushes," Rolondo excitedly instructed from his vantage point at the driver's door. "We don't want anyone seein' him like that and gettin' us in trouble."

"This fuck's too heavy."

"Lift him up, Dumbshit."

Marias savagely jerked Josh to a partial standing position making it easier to forcefully walk him backwards toward the brushy fencerow separating Sarah's parking lot from the pharmacy's lot next door.

Josh, his mind feeling like a piece of driftwood tossed mercilessly in an effervescent, storm-tossed sea, stumbled backward as he tried to regain his feet.

I can talk to these guys---I know I can, he thought desperately.

Pain induced nausea tore at the lining of his stomach and threatened to progress to vomiting with each passing second. Even with Marias lifting him by the hair of his head he was not able to stand vertically. His knees stubbornly refused to fully extend. A slight bend at his waist caused him to bear his weight precariously on the balls of his feet.

This time, when he began to speak, the blood dripping across his lips sprayed onto the front of Marias's pale pink silk shirt.

Marias went ballistic.

"What the fuck a'matter wiff you Mutha Fucker? What the fuck you do? What the fuck you DO? This my new shirt, you shit! I jus' got it today! What the fuck'm I gonna wear ta the party now?"

In his semi-conscious state, it appeared to Josh that Marias actually wanted an answer.

Suddenly a not-so-brilliant flash of intuition careened into Josh's befuddled mind.

If I buy this guy a new shirt, he'll leave me alone!

Marias released his grip on Josh, allowing him to fall heavily to his knees.

"I can buy you a new shirt -- and pants too, I have lots of money!" Josh said in a garbled voice as his head sagged toward his chest, suddenly feeling much too heavy to hold up.

Mustering the last of his strength he laboriously raised his eyes and looked at Marias with a sheepish, boyish grin spreading slowly across his puffy bloodied lips. With his neck craned back his head began bobbing side-to-side like an animated bobble-head doll as he tried to keep his assailant in focus through the watery mirage dancing before his eyes.

Smiling through blood-drenched teeth because he was sure he had hit upon a solution to his dilemma; he fought to focus his eyes on Marias. What he saw made him stop his friendly, disassociated chatter and stare in disbelief.

There stood Marias as if in a fencer's stance, pointing the Model 19 single-handedly at Josh's chest. For Josh, time seemed to slow to a near-standstill. He vividly saw the leisurely contraction of the muscles in Marias's trigger finger and the slow but steady blanching of the skin over his knuckles.

His mind snapped back to reality and he made a final, desperate move to save himself by throwing his body wildly to the right.

It was a valiant but futile effort on his part because all he accomplished was to redirect the 125-grain Federal hollow-point bullet to strike below his left clavicle instead of dead center in his chest. The bullet plowed through the second rib on the left side, shattering it into multiple sharp bony fragments that began ripping an ever-widening swath of devastation through his chest cavity. The gilding metal covering of the bullet peeled back from the soft lead core, increasing its destructive path.

The energy from the speeding projectile propelled the now-jagged edges of the disrupted metal and bone fragments through the rubbery, pulsating walls of his aorta. The tattered remains began fluttering like the tail of a kite in a high wind with each powerful beat of his heart. Life-sustaining oxygenated blood, now liberated from the guiding confines of the artery, began dumping into the depths of his thoracic cavity.

His blood pressure began plunging rapidly toward zero because the bright red blood now lay useless in a pool instead of being pumped to his brain to deliver its life-giving cargo of oxygen.

In a surreal bastardization of reality Josh did not feel the impact of the bullet.

A massive gushing sensation of warmth spread gently throughout his chest filling him with a sense of well-being and contentment. Quickly, a searing stab of pain between his shoulder blades replaced the rush of warm, pleasant comfort as his body acknowledged the disruption of major blood vessels. The flash of scorching pain instantly segued into a growing sense of serenity. With dissociated interest he realized he was falling forward.

Small gray stones covering the parking lot stood out vividly on the black background of the asphalt and fixed Josh's undivided attention. The visual clarity of the diminutive rocks increased with each millisecond as he focused his attention with laser-like intensity on each and every one of them. The pebbles began rushing toward him at warp speed.

He did not feel the slightest amount of pain when his nose crushed against the unyielding asphalt surface. The cartilage of his nose broke loose from its moorings and was forcefully driven into the recesses of his skull.

In agonizingly slow motion, he sensed his body settling onto the surface of the surprisingly cold, hard parking lot. In his mind's eye he imagined his body being absorbed by the unforgiving ground.

Toasty warmth spread throughout his body like butter melting on the nooks and crannies of a hot English muffin fresh from the toaster. He eagerly yielded to his growing desire to actively pursue the growing, unbelievably brilliant white light overwhelming his thoughts and mind.

The all-consuming warmth peacefully and silently lulled Josh Tobin into the eternal slumber of death.

The number of people a trained and skilled person such as Dr. Joshua Tobin could have helped over a long and productive life would never be known. A highly educated but deceased physician is no more an asset to society than any dead individual, regardless of education or their station in life.

"Let's get the fuck outta here!" Rolondo shrieked frantically as he swung his bulk onto the driver's seat of the BMW. Marias heaved himself into the back seat with a satisfied grin on his face.

"Did you see the look on that dissin' mutha fucker's face when I smoked him? It was great," he beamed.

"Great! What the matter wiff you? What the hell we do now?"

"We drive outta here real slow without makin' a fuss so we don't attract no attention," Marias said. "Then we get me a new shirt. This one's trashed."

CHAPTER 14

SARAH'S ORDEAL

"Damn this traffic! It's getting worse each week, I swear!" Ellen Murgen vented into her cellular phone.

"It's aggravating for sure," Stacey Johnson, Dr. Collins's receptionist sweetly crooned into the phone. "But don't you hurry and get into a wreck."

"I really appreciate it, Stacey," Ellen said.

"Dr. Collins is running a little late herself so if you're only fifteen minutes late it won't be a big deal," Stacey reassured her. "But if you're going to be later than that give us a call back and we'll just schedule you for next week. There's no use stressing you out any more today than you already are. OK?"

"I'm so glad to be able to work without pain and my entire life is back on track," Ellen continued without answering Stacey's question. "I know she's had a long, tiring day but it feels like I'm starting to go downhill. She's told me many times that if I catch problems early they're much easier to take care of."

Patients often wanted to maintain a conversation while they're in traffic to help the time go by more quickly and Ellen was obviously in a mood to chat. Stacey, however, was busy and anxious to finish her work so she could go home at a reasonable hour.

"We'll see you in fifteen minutes and get you taken care of," Stacey pleasantly replied, gently putting an end to Ellen's unnecessary chatter.

Stacey turned toward Chauncey's gray steel desk and said, "Chauncey, will you please find Dr. Collins and tell her that Ellen Murgen is going to be about fifteen minutes late because the traffic is bad?"

Chauncey lifted his gaze from the stack of tally sheets from which he was gleaning the daily statistics. Stacey noticed that his eyes were red and bloodshot, and he had to force a smile onto his face.

"I'm sure it will be fine with her," Chauncey said tiredly. "But just to be sure I'll tell her so she knows what to expect."

When Ellen wheeled out of traffic into the almost deserted parking lot of Dr. Collins's office, she scanned the lot for a convenient place to park. Even in the fading light of late afternoon it was easy to see there were plenty of parking spots in the middle of the lot affording an uncomplicated entry as well as effortless exit.

As soon as her car came to a full stop, she placed the gearshift into the "Park" position and climbed out of her car, being careful to place both feet on the ground before using her arms to push herself out of the driver's seat, straightening her skirt as she stood up. With an awkward heaving motion she swung the heavy car door closed, glanced briefly toward the brushy fencerow in front of her car, and simultaneously clicked the "Lock" button on the keyless remote. A mellow "beep" sounded and the brilliant halogen headlights automatically clicked on, which clearly illuminated a well-dressed man lying face down in a parking space 15 yards in front of her car.

Ellen Murgen was horrified to see the spreading pool of dark red blood flowing from him and slowly meander its way toward a storm drain.

Frantically casting her eyes left and right she made a mad dash for the lighted security of the office doors screaming hysterically as she ran.

Bursting through the front door in a terrified frenzy, she ran directly to the reception desk and blurted to Stacey, "There's a man- a dead man, I think- lying in the parking lot. He's bleeding- a lot! Oh My God!"

Her wild-eyed look spurred Stacey to immediately dial 9-1-1 with a manic outburst of energy. She did not need, nor did she want, to seek verification of what Ellen had seen.

"Chauncey, lock the front door please," Stacey instructed the perplexed bookkeeper as he stared in wide-eyed amazement, trying to comprehend what was happening.

Before he could move to lock the door, Sarah burst from the hallway leading back to the treatment rooms.

"What's wrong?" she asked as she and Dr. Joseph Holmes, her associate doctor, ran side-by-side from the back of the office. "What's going on?"

Sarah glanced at Ellen and saw she was too hysterical to offer an explanation.

"What's happening?" she asked, looking directly at Stacey.

"There's a dead man in the parking lot in a pool of blood," Stacey reiterated with all the information she had received from Ellen.

"Oh my God! Josh!" Sarah shrieked as she bolted for the door. She clawed at the door handle in a paroxysm of fumbling fingers and her face drained of all color. Her ashen complexion added to the anxiety felt by everyone in the room.

"Oh my God! Oh my God, NO!" she repeated over-and-over again, her voice becoming more hysterical and louder with each word.

Before rushing into the night, Sarah spun toward Dr. Holmes with a fierce look in her eyes and ordered, "Get examination gloves and as many clean towels as you can carry. Hurry!"

Dr. Holmes, assessing the situation in a flash, turned to Stacey and ordered, "You heard her. Get the gloves and towels and hurry! I'm going after her!"

Chauncey had already bolted out the front door in hot pursuit of the distraught Sarah by the time Dr. Holmes joined the exodus from the office.

Scanning the parking lot from the top step of her office, Sarah immediately identified the prostrate figure laying in the dazzling radiance of Ellen's headlights. Her eyes verified what her heart had known all along.

"Oh my God! Oh my God! No! No! NO!" was all she could repeat to an unhearing and uncaring parking lot.

She darted into the deepening shadows without hesitation. The billowing tails of her white laboratory coat lent silent testimony to the speed with which she propelled herself across the asphalt. Chauncey sprinted after her in a surprising burst of unexpected speed, which shocked the much younger Dr. Holmes.

"Sarah! Wait!" Chauncey called in a firm voice as he clutched her arms in a resolute, unyielding grasp. "You don't know if they're still in the parking lot. It may be dangerous. Let me go first."

He gently passed the sobbing, almost incoherent Sarah into the arms of Dr. Holmes where she slumped onto his chest. His encircling arms clutched her tightly to him to keep her rubbery legs from collapsing. Her feeble efforts to protest his grasp only further drained her ebbing energy, adding to her inability to capably support herself.

Chauncey cautiously made his way toward the fallen man, casting wary glances throughout the parking lot as he went. It was almost impossible to see into the lengthening shadows scattered throughout the lot.

I wish I had a flashlight and a club, he thought as he warily wended his way toward the prone form of Josh Tobin.

In a sudden fit of renewed vitality Sarah broke away from Dr. Holmes's supporting arms. Her headlong rush caused her to awkwardly bump into Chauncey and almost knocked him over as he warily made his way toward the prostrate, unmoving body of her husband.

"What the hell---" Chauncey exclaimed loudly as he stumbled out of her way and struggled to keep himself from falling.

Ignoring Chauncey's shocked exclamation she threw herself beside Josh's limp, apparently lifeless body before lifting his head gently onto her lap. His listless neck allowed his head to roll within her lap while his unseeing, slightly glazed eyes rolled back into his head.

An ambulance arrived with its red and white lights flashing as Sarah was rocking back and forth on her haunches, moaning an incomprehensible wail of grief while cradling Josh's head to her bosom. The ambulance pulled beside the throng of onlookers who had gathered around the fallen man.

The ambulance crew was accustomed to seeing a crowd of onlookers staring at and surrounding the sick or injured person. As usual, it irritated them because it made their job much more difficult.

"OK folks, move out of the way so we can work here," commanded Rosemary Scroggins, a petite woman with her jet black hair pulled back tightly into a bun and dressed in the dark blue uniform of an EMT as she pushed her way toward the victim.

"Come on folks, cooperate so we can get some help to these people," Harold Croft, Rosemary's partner added. Harold's six-foot five-inch frame carried two hundred and thirty pounds and the sheer presence of his towering body made most people take notice and follow his instructions. His shaven, bald head gleamed above those of most people and added greatly to his commanding demeanor.

The crowd parted just enough for them to see Sarah and the dead body of her husband. The gurney was moved as closely to the victim as possible then left sitting unused behind Sarah who continued her incessant rocking without acknowledging their presence.

"We're too late to do anything for this guy," Harold said as he leaned down and whispered into Rosemary's ear. "Let's just wait for the coroner and homicide unit."

"She's the one we have to take care of now," Harold continued whispering to Rosemary as he nodded toward Sarah. "Let's make sure she's stable then we'll play it by ear to see what we do from there."

After surveying the scene Rosemary silently nodded in agreement then moved toward Sarah.

"Honey," Rosemary spoke softly to Sarah as she kneeled beside her and placed her hands comfortingly on her shoulders. "Why don't you come over here and sit down so we can examine him. It will be better if you give us room to work."

"He's my husband and he's dead," a grief-stricken Sarah moaned to no one in particular.

"I know Honey, but you have to let us do our job," Rosemary gently urged Sarah.

"I should have been here with him. I could have helped him and he wouldn't be dead if I had been here," Sarah wailed pitifully.

Rosemary nodded to Harold to help by taking Sarah's arm as she tried to respectfully pry Josh's head from her grasp.

"That's it Honey, let go and we'll take good care of him," Rosemary's soothingly convincing voice prompted Sarah to cooperate. "You can't help us anymore except by going over to the ambulance and sitting down."

Sarah slowly opened her arms and relinquished Josh's head to the care of Rosemary then allowed Harold, who exhibited an unexpected gentleness in his touch, to help her to her feet.

After struggling to stand at her full height she shrugged away from his supporting arms.

"You'll take good care of him, I know you ...," Sarah never finished the sentence.

The sudden loss of blood pressure to her brain caused by blood rushing to her feet when she rapidly stood up combined with the emotional stress of seeing her husband's lifeless eyes staring into nothingness was too much for her to handle. Without another word

Sarah swooned backward, freefalling to the rear. She tumbled over the edge of the gurney and her feet flew skyward.

Rosemary and Harold both lunged in an attempt to break her fall.

Before either of the EMTs could reach her, the unprotected back of her skull smashed onto the hard, unforgiving pavement next to where her husband's blood ran into the storm drain. The cracking sound of her cranium hitting the ground sent shivers up the spine of every person within hearing distance.

Sarah Collins immediately became a victim in dire need of the EMT's life-saving medical attention.

"Oh shit!" Rosemary said as she rushed to Sarah's aid. "There's going to be hell to pay for this one."

"And a hell of a big pile of paperwork," her bureaucracy-savvy partner chimed in disgustedly.

CHAPTER 15

GOOD-BYE TO JOSH

Sarah was kept in a drug-induced coma in intensive care for four days to reduce swelling of her brain. After her vital signs stabilized, she was moved to a private room for ten days of recuperation and observation. Josh's brother Jeremy, known to his family as J.T., visited her hospital room daily regardless of whether she was conscious or not.

"I feel terrible that I wasn't able to be at Josh's funeral," Sarah sighed as she looked lovingly at her brother-in-law.

"You were unconscious in intensive care for four days for crying out loud," J.T. replied with empathy in his voice. "You were comatose until the day after Josh was buried."

And we're all damned glad we didn't have a double funeral, he thought while keeping a toothy smile plastered on his face.

"But I wish I could have at least visited his grave."

"You will when you're strong enough; I'll take you to the cemetery myself," J.T. said with conviction. "You've been in the hospital for a total of fourteen days. This is the first day you're really cognizant of what's happening around you. You have to regain some strength before you try anything too strenuous. Besides, there's nothing you can do there that you can't do here."

"Yes there is," she replied firmly, barely able to stifle a sob. "I can cry with him there."

"You'll have time," he reminded her. "It may seem like you have to rush things but you really don't."

"Without going to the funeral, it doesn't feel like he's really gone," she said, dabbing at her eyes with a tissue. "I can't seem to accept the fact I'm never going to see him again."

She sobbed gently while groaning deep in her chest.

"Now's the time to grieve," J.T. said gently. "If you don't grieve now it will just take you longer to get back to a normal routine."

"I don't want a normal life; I want my Josh," she said as she began sobbing heavily.

"I didn't say a normal life. That will come with time. For now let's settle for a normal routine. Grieving is a process that has to unfold in its own good time."

Sarah looked at her brother-in-law with a look of awe on her face.

He's just like a big brother to me; a smart, handsome, comforting big brother who is wise and always knows exactly what to say.

"You seem to have a good idea of how these things work."

"I've had too much experience in this type of thing considering my past employment and such," he added evasively as his mind wandered into the past.

"Do you regret working with the C.I.A.?" Sarah asked with trepidation, knowing it was a delicate subject and he was not supposed to ever talk about his association with that federal agency.

"Not at all," he said. "It actually led me into some very advantageous situations."

"Such as---" she prompted, suddenly interested.

"Well, we moved to Northern Virginia so I could commute into D.C.," he said. "I wanted a nice place to raise the kids and we certainly found it there."

J.T. continued conversing in a level, calm tone while looking intensely straight ahead as though he were viewing the last few years of his life on the institutional gray wall of Sarah's hospital room.

"Northern Virginia is definitely a nicer place to raise a family than D.C. will ever be.

"The crime rate there is certainly lower than it is in D.C.," he continued. "The Commonwealth of Virginia trusts its law-abiding citizens to carry concealed weapons and it's reflected in lower rates of murder and other violent crimes."

J.T. was sorry he brought up the crime rate in D.C. as soon as it was out of his mouth. Sarah's eyes lowered and her chest began heaving with deep, racking sobs of grief.

"There are a lot of good churches there also," he continued on quickly, trying to change the subject. "We attend a big Catholic church on Maple Street with a growing parish of young families. St. Boniface offers everything we need to get the kids started on a good moral and principled life."

"You're fired up about a Catholic church?"

"I'm not too fired up about the Catholic Church as a religious organization but you know how Stephanie is. She and the kids are deeply involved in church and school activities."

"Having a good church and school to be involved with really helps foster a feeling of belonging," Sarah said seriously. "It's what makes an area worth living in."

J.T. noticed that her sobbing had subsided and she was concentrating on their conversation.

"The kids are especially getting into the church," he said when he realized he was making headway in pulling her out of her doldrums. "They have a youth ministry group that organizes a Youth Retreat every summer."

"That sounds interesting," Sarah said, leaning forward with peaking interest.

"They go for an entire week to a place in West Virginia for a Christian get-together called the Hallelujah Gathering," he added. "Some of the parents use their week of vacation to volunteer as chaperones."

"They probably have a nice vacation," Sarah noted. "Especially if the kids are teenagers; they can be hard to keep happy on family vacations at that age."

"The kids really love it because they're on their own for a week; even though they're really not," J.T. explained. "The chaperones keep a close eye on them."

He saw that she was very interested in his litany about the kids and their Youth Ministry activities.

"What church do you attend?" he asked in a conversational tone hoping to draw her into the conversation.

"I don't really attend a church," Sarah replied. "At least I haven't for a while. I was raised Catholic like Stephanie but I fell away from it while I was in college."

Sarah took her turn to stare at the wall as though it were a movie screen playing the story of her planned but recently shattered life.

"Josh and I planned on moving to Northern Virginia to be closer to you and your family," she said as she looked directly at J.T., hoping he would understand they had wanted to establish stronger family ties.

"You talked about that when you visited last time," he said pleasantly. "You were looking at Loudon County if I remember correctly."

"Oh yeah," she said sheepishly. "We did talk about that. I forgot."

Then she looked at the folds of the sheets covering her svelte body under a thin sheet of starched cotton cloth, "We wanted the same things you have. A safe place to live and a family."

Sarah began to sob softly but continued, "We planned on having kids, you know. Three. He wanted three. He said it was a nice number."

"Stephanie and I are content with two," he said. "That was enough for her to handle since she was raising them mostly as a single parent because I wasn't home a lot of the time."

"Two weren't enough for Josh because they would barely replace us on this planet and four seemed like a number that a Catholic girl like me would want to have," Sarah continued, not giving him a chance to interrupt. "He liked to joke about my Catholic upbringing but he really didn't care."

"Josh didn't care about what religion anyone was," J.T. added hesitantly. "He never thought much about religion or God in one way or the other."

"I actually think he wanted our kids to be raised Catholic; he said it was a good training ground for the Protestants," Sarah said, hoping he would pick up on the wry humor in her statement.

She flashed a brilliantly white, even smile as she visualized a picture of Josh in her mind's eye. They both sat in silence; each lost in their personal thoughts.

A minute later Sarah looked at him and cautiously said, "I remember you holding my hand when I was going in and out of consciousness."

She watched J.T.'s eyebrows rise in astonishment at being caught caring about another woman who wasn't his wife. "I think you were really concerned about me."

"I was--- we all were--- are," he stammered.

"I never had a big brother that really cared about me, you know," Sarah said. "And whether you like it or not, you're now that big brother."

"Well, thank you for bestowing the title of Honorary Big Brother on me."

"Thanks for accepting," Sarah said as a girlish grin broke across her face. "It's easy nominating you for the position considering how close you and Josh were."

"What about Chauncey?" J.T. asked, hoping to deflect Sarah's attention from being focused on her dead husband. "He rode all the way to the hospital in the back of the ambulance with you, you know."

"I didn't know that."

"And he called me every day to ask how you were doing while you were in intensive care because they wouldn't let him in since he's not family. After they put you in this private room he came to visit every day, but only while I was here. He usually just sat quietly in that chair in the corner and watched you and the monitors hanging over your bed- never saying a word- and then he would use hand signals to let me know he was leaving. If he wanted to talk he'd motion for me to meet him in the hallway."

"I didn't know that either."

"Yeah," J.T. continued, happy to make Chauncey the center of the conversation. "The ambulance guy said he even hung the saline bag and other paraphernalia like he knew what he was doing. Are you sure he doesn't know more about his past than he's letting on?"

"No, I don't think so. He's pretty straightforward. There's really nothing shifty about him that I can tell."

"Well, keep an eye on him. He seems too good to be true."

"Aren't you just the most trusting soul?"

"Well, distrust of my fellow human beings has kept me alive on more than one occasion," he said distractedly as his eyes fell to the floor, staring at nothing.

"Have you heard anything about the guys who killed Josh?" Sarah asked, trying to pull him out of a dark reverie of his violent past.

"Yeah," J.T. said, snapping his thoughts from the past to the present. "The police grabbed them on the Beltway near Chevy Chase. They pulled them over in Josh's BMW for going 90 in a 65 zone."

"Can they prove they were the ones who killed Josh?" Sarah inquired, leaning forward with great interest.

UH-OH. This is the first time she's cognizant enough to bring up the topic of Josh's killers. Well, it had to happen sooner or later. I wish it were later---

J.T. became visibly uncomfortable and shifted nervously on his chair.

"Are you sure you're ready to talk about this?"

"Yes," she said firmly. "I eventually have to learn what happened and now is as good a time as any. Now, tell me what happened."

"When the cops stopped the car they saw one of the guys was nervous and became suspicious," he said as he again moved uneasily in his chair. J.T. was obviously ill at ease with the topic of Josh's killers and stopped talking until he could gather his courage.

"Are you sure you want to-"

"And---"Sarah said as she mimed with her hands for him to continue.

"And they found a .357 magnum revolver and a shirt with Josh's blood on it in the trunk. The revolver, shirt, and car all had blood on them. One of the guys even had blood on his hair."

Sarah sat with a stupefied look on her face. "They found the gun?" she asked in astonished disbelief.

"Yeah, ballistic testing confirmed it was the one used to kill Josh."

"There's no question? It was the gun?"

"Yeah, it was the gun," he said. He was stunned to realize she was fixated on the gun instead of the men who did the killing.

"How did they get the gun?"

"They bought it off a drug dealer in Northwest," J.T. said. "It had been stolen from a house in Illinois or Iowa; one of those Midwest states starting with an 'I' a few weeks ago."

"And that's legal?" she asked with ferocity in her voice and gaze.

"Of course it's not," he said, taken aback by Sarah's intense questioning. "They all had felony convictions on their records. They weren't allowed to possess, or even be near, a gun."

"They?" Sarah asked incredulously. It had just dawned on her that more than one person was responsible for the death of her husband.

"Yeah, there were three of them."

"What are their names? Who the hell are these animals?" she asked as her eyes took on a vicious, burning quality.

"Marias Phillips was the guy who actually shot Josh. They found his fingerprints on the revolver."

He was not anxious to continue so he allowed her plenty of time to digest the information.

"He was driving around without a shirt?" she asked innocently, trying to envision the sequence of events in her mind.

"No," he said evenly. "Apparently they stopped and robbed a clothing store so he could get a clean shirt."

"They what?" Sarah asked, astonished at their gall.

"The guy needed a new shirt because they were going to a party and he couldn't show up with blood on the one he was wearing," J.T. explained calmly as he watched her closely.

"And how did the police figure this out?"

"They found the price tags from the store in the trunk with the bloody shirt and gun along with some other clothes with the price tags still attached."

Sarah was assimilating this information when a flash of astonishment appeared on her face.

"Was anyone hurt in the store robbery?"

The look of dread on her face was agonizing to J.T. because he knew the private hell she was going through. She obviously had to confront the truth of what transpired regarding her husband's death but he was not sure she was strong enough.

"They pistol-whipped the clerk," he said factually after taking a deep breath. "And gave him a concussion and fractured skull."

"Will he be OK?"

"He's in this hospital somewhere," he said. "I don't know how he's doing, but at least he's alive."

"Yeah," she answered with a distracted tone in her voice. "At least he's alive. Who else was involved when Josh was killed?"

"Rolondo Hammons was the one who pulled Josh's door open to get him out of the car; his fingerprints were on the door handle and steering wheel," he answered in a guarded tone.

"Who was the third guy? What is his name?" Sarah asked in a commanding tone.

"His name is Tobias Masterson," J.T. said, waiting for the tid-bit of information to settle in her churning mind.

It hit like a nuclear bomb at ground zero.

"Tobias Masterson," she said repeating the name in a confused, uncomprehending tone, allowing the words to fall heavily off her tongue. "TOBIAS MASTERSON!" she shrieked in recognition and amazement.

She sat bolt upright in bed, the heavily starched sheets falling unnoticed to her waist.

"That bastard is a patient of mine- was a patient of mine- he---" she stammered as her face reddened and her mouth worked up and down, suddenly incapable of uttering another sound.

She broke down in a torrent of tears, which quickly drenched the front of her lime green nightgown allowing her bra to show through the thin saturated cloth. Her sobs came in gasping, raspy spasms sucked through her tightly constricted larynx.

"I was helping that son of a bitch and he killed my husband?" she asked with anguish in her voice and a look of incredulity on her face.

"He didn't kill him directly but since he was involved in a felony that resulted in the death of a person, he was charged with murder; the same as the guy who actually pulled the trigger."

He realized with a jolt that his directness in describing the murder of her husband might have been too much for her to handle this soon after her ordeal.

"Listen Sarah, I---" he stumbled in a halting, uncertain tone.

"NO! You listen! This is shit! A bunch of criminals who have no right to own a gun kill my husband in cold blood. For what? A car? I would have given them the damned car!" she screamed irrationally.

J.T. could only shake his head, unable to think of anything to say.

"What the hell! It's ludicrous. It's past ludicrous! What the hell am I supposed to do now?" she asked in a nearly incoherent, furious tone as she flicked her head back and forth in an agitated display of anguish.

J.T. didn't answer because he had no answer to offer. It was a legitimate question she had asked, and it had no answer that would make any sense to her or anyone else.

In a brisk move that startled J.T., she sat bolt upright on the rumpled mattress. "I'm going to see Nadine," she said with conviction. "She'll know what to do."

"Who the hell is Nadine?" he asked in a confused tone as his brow furrowed even deeper.

"Nadine Brand. My old college roommate," Sarah answered simply as though he should have known. "She was a school teacher for a few years but now she raises horses full-time."

"Why don't you find a young college roommate; those old ones get a little saggy after a while."

"What in the hell are you talking about?" Sarah asked, not believing what she was hearing.

"Young college roommates are much more exciting than those old ones," J.T. stated in his dry, quirky sense of humor.

"You're a pain in the ass, Mr. Tobin," she said laughingly with a look of disbelief on her face as she heaved a pillow at his head. He caught the pillow and laughed along with her.

"OK, OK. So where does this Nadine live? I'll take you there."

"She lives about two and a half hours west of here in the mountains of Virginia on a horse farm. I'll have to call her for exact directions."

"When do you want to go?" he asked.

"Tomorrow. As soon as they cut me loose from this place," she answered.

"But I'm going to L.A. tomorrow. I fly out first thing in the morning. I can't get out of it because it's business and all my meetings have been scheduled for weeks."

"I'll go by myself. I'll be OK."

"I know that but I'll feel better if you're traveling with someone."

"I'll take Chauncey."

"Chauncey? Can he drive? Does he even have a driver's license?" he asked in an unsure tone.

"If he can't drive then I will. Besides, who cares if he has a driver's license? They're giving driver's licenses to illegal aliens for crying out loud! At least he's a citizen."

"As far as anyone knows, at least," he added with a heavy tone of skepticism in his voice. "Who's going to watch your practice?"

"Joe Holmes is watching it."

"He's your associate, isn't he?"

"Yeah. I called him this morning and he's handling it just fine. When I got hurt he jumped right in, took control of everything, and now he's buying my practice," she said plainly.

"What?" he asked with shock in his voice.

"Do you really think I could go back to my practice? Seeing that parking lot where Josh died at least twice every day? I just can't do it," she said as rivulets of tears began coursing down her face.

"Yeah, I guess you're right," he acknowledged, not quite sure what to add to the conversation.

"I called him early this morning to get the ball rolling," she said between sobs. "I have him contacting a business brokerage firm to value the practice and he's talking to our bank to get financing."

"Can he get financing?"

"He should be able to. He's been with me for almost three years so he has his own practice established and knows how to run the business side," she said as she wiped the tears from her eyes with the corner of the bed sheet.

"That should be a selling point to the bank."

"It's golden," she said with her eyes looking levelly at his. "The staff are trained and dedicated. The patients are familiar with the doctors and facility so it's a viable and vibrant practice. That's what the bank looks at when they make a decision on whether they'll lend money to the buyer."

"I've never had to understand the business side of anything," J.T. confessed. "I collected my paycheck and paid our household expenses out of what money we had to work with."

"Well, the business side of life is interesting and a royal pain in the ass at the same time," she confessed. "With it being an active practice I can get more money for it. If I didn't have Joe already in place the practice would dwindle away to nothing in no time at all and be worthless."

J.T. was stupefied and didn't know what to say so he changed the subject.

"So you're off to see Nadine."

"I'm off to see Nadine. But only after I take a nap," she stated matter-of-factly.

CHAPTER 16

VIRGINIA-BRED ROCKY MOUNTAIN HORSES

Sarah's former college roommate, Nadine Brand, had been a loner since her husband left her for another man. She spent her days on the horse farm she received in the divorce settlement, raising and training Rocky Mountain horses.

When Sarah arrived at Nadine's farm, "The Shire," she found her busy in the barn finishing the morning tasks necessary to maintain a healthy herd.

"Why did you name this place The Shire?" Sarah asked after exchanging greetings.

Nadine's chuckling laugh bounced her slightly protruding, jelly-like belly.

"It's from the book *Lord of the Rings* by J.R.R. Tolkien," Nadine replied. "The main characters are Hobbits, little hairy human-like critters with a very formal social structure."

"So you named your farm after hairy little critters?" Sarah asked with a chuckle and smile.

"Kind of," Nadine replied as her belly continued to bob up and down with her laughing. "Hobbits have seven named meals during the day and take life with a smile and great attitude. The Shire is the village the main characters live in."

"That sounds like it's something worth emulating," Sarah said with a grin.

"Yes it is, in my estimation at least," Nadine said as she continued to laugh gently. "That's the way I want to live; plenty of meals and a great attitude."

"The Shire," Sarah repeated, mulling the name over in her mind.

"That name on the sign over the entrance of my lane reminds me of my lifestyle goals every day," Nadine said seriously. "We all need a little reminder of how life is supposed to be, you know."

She had a faraway, knowing look in her eye as she spoke. Suddenly she snapped back to the present and locked Sarah with a penetrating stare.

"That guy who drove you up here," Nadine said. "He didn't hang around very long and barely said anything at all while he was here. What's his story?"

"I'm not sure what his story is," Sarah replied plainly. "He works for me and the rest of his story is way too long to go into now. But he's turned out to be a really good friend when I needed support from the people around me."

"Well, now you have another really good friend to take care of you," Nadine said. "I'm honored to have you visit when the shit hit the fan."

Sarah wasn't ready to discuss her situation so early in their visit. She quickly changed the topic.

"So why did you decide to breed this type of horse?" she asked. "I thought everyone raised race horses."

Nadine gave another deep-seated belly laugh as she marveled at Sarah's naiveté of the world of horses. It seemed that Nadine took every opportunity she could to laugh.

"That's easy," Nadine replied after regaining her composure. "The Rocky Mountain Horse is really from the grass roots of this country. They're as American as Mom and apple pie."

"So it comes from Colorado, or what?" Sarah asked innocently.

Seeing she was serious and really didn't know anything about horses, let alone the Rocky Mountain breed in particular, the teacher in Nadine came to the forefront.

"No, their name has absolutely nothing to do with the Rocky Mountains out west. In the early 1800s, the breed originated in the hill country of Kentucky. The 'Rocky' name came from old-timers who claimed a single colt was brought to Eastern Kentucky from 'some place west of the Appalachians' around 1890," Nadine said, talking enthusiastically about her favorite subject, while a slightly crooked smile creased her sun-wrinkled face.

"So they're a working horse?"

"Originally, and because of the reality of the times, the surviving horses were the strongest and hardiest of the bunch. They led a hard life then, unlike these guys," Nadine said with a little chuckle as she pointed toward her herd.

She suddenly became very serious.

"The Rocky Mountain Horse is strong today because the people in the Kentucky hills could only afford a horse that survived without much care during the harsh winter weather. They either made it to maturity to reproduce or they didn't. The stronger genes survived in the herd."

"The survival of the fittest," Sarah said jokingly. "What a unique concept."

"The Rocky Mountain Horse has had a colorful history," Nadine continued conversationally. "Today the breed is a much sought after horse. Equestrians like them because they're gaited. That means they're easy to ride without a lot of up and down bumping and the horse has a good disposition."

"A good disposition?"

"Yeah," Nadine laughed. "Until you've had a horse get nasty with you and bite, kick, or otherwise beat you up you don't truly appreciate an even tempered horse."

"They are really pretty, that's for sure," Sarah stated in an attempt to show her approval of her friend's passionate love of her horses. "They have such pretty coats; the sunlight just shimmers and glitters off them."

"Yeah, they are pretty," Nadine agreed. "But they don't all have the same coloration that mine do."

"How's that?" Sarah asked.

"All of my horses have chocolate-brown bodies and flaxen colored manes and tails," Nadine continued. "That combination of colors is highly coveted; that's why I'm trying to breed it into my herd."

"So you want to breed the most popular coloration of horse so they're worth more?" Sarah asked, striving to better understand the situation.

Nadine exhibited a not-so-subtle air of pride in her voice and posture as she continued.

"These horses are the center of my life right now," she said. "I made a conscious effort to put all my physical and mental energy into them. I had to, it was either that or I knew I'd go crazy."

Knowing she was moving into dangerous territory with her comments, Nadine continued with caution, "Have you thought much about where your life may be heading?"

Knowing there was no use trying to avoid this conversation, Sarah replied directly to her question without missing a beat.

"I've already contacted a real estate agency about selling my house in Washington," she said, looking Nadine directly in the eyes. "They were really nice about everything and understood I wasn't able to handle much of the details so they arranged to have an auction company sell the furniture and such from the house."

Nadine noticed she had a look of longing in her eyes as she spoke.

"Did you ever go back to your house?" Nadine asked. "Since Josh was killed, I mean."

"I know what you mean," Sarah snapped as she continued looking directly into Nadine's eyes.

"No, I haven't," she admitted as her shoulders sagged noticeably. "I had Amy, a friend of mine from D.C., go in and take out all my personal belongings."

"It's good to have friends who are willing to help in times like these."

"Everything from my clothes to my toothbrush came out in cardboard boxes and brown paper grocery bags," Sarah said wistfully. "What I didn't bring with me is at a storage facility near my brother-in-law's place."

She looked away and stared into the baby blue sky, visualizing in her mind's eye what her house and furnishings had looked like.

"I just couldn't go back to that house again," Sarah said while continuing to look at the sky. "There are too many memories there."

"It's always a difficult time," Nadine said consolingly.

"I wanted to keep it in my memory as a happy place Josh and I shared," she said as she dabbed at a small tear that had formed in the corner of her eye. "I don't want to remember it as an empty shell of what was once my life."

"That was a good idea."

"After my personal stuff was out, I had J.T., my brother-in-law, go in and take all of Josh's stuff out," she said while wiping another tear from her eye. "His clothes were donated to The Salvation Army and his books and professional stuff were sent to his Alma Mater so students can make use of it."

"That was good thinking," Nadine said.

"I told J.T. not to give anything of Josh's to anyone we know. I don't want to see his favorite tee shirt on any of the relatives," she said with steel in her voice.

"That makes sense," Nadine confirmed, trying to assure her friend she had done the right thing.

"If I couldn't say good-bye to Josh at his funeral then I certainly wasn't going to subject myself to the emotional trauma of seeing remnants of the life we'd shared together scattered hither and yon," she declared. "I want to act like he was just a pleasant memory and move on with my life without delay."

She looked at Nadine, her eyes searching for emotional support from her old confidant.

"And you're on the right track," Nadine said seriously. "You seem to be making some very sound and reasonable choices without going overboard."

"That's why I escaped to your 'Home for Wayward Roommates'," Sarah said with relief and a smile, ready to drop the subject.

Nadine took the hint and commenced to steer the conversation away from Josh to Sarah's new chapter in her book of life.

"You came here right from the hospital. How are you feeling physically?" Nadine asked with concern in her voice.

"I'm OK. I really got hurt in that fall and I was in deep trouble for a while," she replied. "But I'm fine now. With that kind of injury there's always concern about permanent brain damage but that doesn't seem to have happened. Thank God. I have enough problems to deal with."

"If you spent that much time in the hospital, it must have been a pretty horrendous fall," Nadine said.

"I just can't get too physically active until all of the stuff inside has a chance to heal properly," Sarah replied, trying to put on an air of bravery she truly did not feel.

"Let's go sit in the shade so it doesn't tax you too much," Nadine said as she motioned for Sarah to follow her toward an umbrella-covered table and matching chairs. "We can talk more once we're more comfortable."

Sarah had arrived at The Shire just before lunchtime as Nadine was finishing her morning training session with the horses. Unknowingly, she and Chauncey had arrived at the most advantageous time because midday was used as a rest period for both Nadine and the animals.

The two former roommates visited for a few hours over raspberry iced tea and lunch-type finger foods. A large sugar maple tree in the front yard provided shade as well as a convenient place to hang bird feeders. The antics of ruby-throated hummingbirds kept them enthralled throughout the warm afternoon. Watching the miniscule birds flit about helped fill in the otherwise uncomfortable periods of silence that occurred in their conversation.

When it was time for the evening feeding of the horses, Nadine excused herself and went into the house to strap a floral-carved El Paso Saddlery holster onto her ample waist. It held a silvery stainless steel Smith and Wesson Model 60 revolver with five-inch barrel.

Taking a moment to organize her thoughts and gather her composure at the outside door leading to where Sarah sat peacefully under the sugar maple enjoying the peace and quiet of the farm, Nadine steeled herself for the scenario she knew was about to unfold.

Straightening herself to her full height, Nadine nonchalantly pushed the screen door open and strode purposefully toward Sarah.

"OK, we're ready to get these critters fed and put away for the night."

When Sarah saw the gun resting on Nadine's right hip she froze in place; her eyes glued on the Model 60. Nadine saw fear register on her face and immediately tried to console her.

"Sarah, it's OK."

"What's OK? That's a gun!"

"Sarah, you're looking at this gun like it's a snake that'll jump off my hip and bite you," she said as soothingly as she could. "You have to realize it isn't the gun that's evil. The men who killed Josh were evil. This gun and all of the others I use on this farm are used for good."

"What good can possibly come out of a gun?" Sarah shot back angrily, her eyes blazing with fury.

"Do you like to watch those horses run out there in the pasture?" Nadine asked levelly as she calmly waved her arm toward the pasture.

"Of course I do. We've been watching them all afternoon."

"Do you see that little guy running with his mother? The tiny pale chocolate colored guy with the blonde highlights?" Nadine asked innocently.

"Yeah, he's really an active little bugger. His poor mother must sleep well at night after keeping after him all day long. What does he have to do with you carrying a gun?"

"He has everything to do with me carrying a gun."

"How?"

"When we get them into their stalls, remind me to show you the long scars down his right flank and across his lower belly," Nadine said as she looked piercingly into her eyes. "Three coyotes tried to pull him down while two more kept his mother busy across the pasture."

"But they obviously didn't succeed," Sarah said evenly.

"They almost succeeded and would have if I didn't have my rifle handy. I had to kill two of them," Nadine said without a hint of regret in her voice. "The others ran for the hills where they probably killed a deer or went over the mountain and took a lamb from my neighbor's herd."

"You've killed things?" Sarah asked in horror.

"Sarah, God gives the good people of this earth the OK to kill the evil things," she continued as she reminded herself to keep her temper under control. "It's what keeps evil from overcoming good."

Before Sarah could reply, she continued.

"You can debate if coyotes are evil or just animals doing what they were put on this earth to do," Nadine said. "I've seen the results of when the neighbor's sheep were torn to pieces, having their guts eaten while they're still alive, and not actually dying until hours later when the sheepherder found them and put them out of their misery."

"That's horrible," Sarah gasped as her hand flew to cover her mouth.

"Yes it is," Nadine said as she looked levelly at her. "I will protect my animals and myself against any and all predators; whether they walk on two legs or four. Now I have to take care of my horses. You can join me if you want to or you can stay here."

With that, Nadine turned decisively and walked to the stables to begin her evening chores. Sarah was still in shock and taken aback by what Nadine had said.

Nadine would never know how long Sarah stood with her feet rooted solidly to the ground because she did not look back. Instead, she continued striding purposefully toward the barn.

Don't look back. Whatever you do, don't look back. She has to face this and you better not give her an out by starting a discussion because you'll only lose the argument then she'll never benefit from figuring out this whole shitty situation for herself.

Sarah felt she should be mad at Nadine for her attitude about guns and killing, regardless of how righteous she felt about it, but she wasn't. She knew deep down in her soul that Nadine was right.

Nadine unhooked the fence latch and let herself through before striding into the barn and out of sight while Sarah stood dumbfounded. She could only stare vacantly at the gaping door opening where her friend had disappeared. Her mind began working through a maze of confounding principles trying to sort out her conflicted emotions.

In the scheme of nature, Nadine's attitude made sense. Her words had appealed to Sarah's sense of righteousness and touched her natural instinct for self-preservation; and it all made perfect sense.

Sarah stumbled numbly after Nadine before leaning exhausted with her elbows resting on the wooden railing, being careful to avoid the steel wire strands of the electrified fence. She was feeling too confused and befuddled to follow her into the stables.

While Sarah watched the horses coming in for their evening inspection and feeding, her mind wandered in many different directions. It was as if she were not in her body, but rather observing the scenery surrounding her in a bizarre bastardization of reality.

She wondered about the frailty of life and the tenacity of humans to cling to it.

She looked at the setting sun and wondered how many millions of people would be watching that same sun teeter on the horizon before disappearing for the night. Out of nowhere, the thought popped unexpectedly into her mind that some of them would be watching it set because they had successfully defended themselves from evil people.

Before she realized it, searing tears began coursing down her cheeks. While she concentrated on the gush of tears dripping off her chin, sobs rooted deep in her core began racking her body with spasms of grief. She valiantly tried fighting against the urge to cry but soon succumbed to her emotions.

Damn him! Damn you Josh! Sarah thought through tearful sobs. *What the hell was the matter with you? Why didn't you defend yourself? Why didn't you learn to take care of yourself?*

What would have happened if I had been with you? We'd both be dead because neither one of us put any thought into being able to fend for ourselves.

"We had so damned much education between us. We're both doctors for Christ's sake! Why didn't we take time to learn how to defend our own lives? We gave other people lives worth living but were just too damned stupid to learn to take care of ourselves," she wailed at the top of her lungs without realizing she was verbalizing her thoughts.

"Now look at us!" she bellowed at the setting sun, not caring she was loudly cursing a man who had died weeks earlier.

"You're dead and I have no life at all!" she screamed in a rambling, cracking voice. "My life is being sold without me being there and I don't even have a place to call my own!"

"Damn you Joshua! Damn you! Damn you! DAMN YOU!"

Nadine heard the outburst and knew it was a necessary part of the healing process. She was actually ashamed to admit to herself that she felt a tiny bit of fear as she listened to the enormous amount of anguish and anger springing from the raving woman leaning on her fence.

Nadine was familiar with the mental healing process. She had gone through a similar soul cleansing when her husband left her. She knew it would continue until Sarah exhausted herself so she resigned herself to just talk calmly to her horses. They seemed to understand and went back to their feed buckets with only the occasional sheepish glance at her.

When Nadine finished with her nightly chores it was almost too dark to see the path back to the house.

Giving her horses a final pat on their long, silky necks she closed the last gate separating the pasture from the open yard. She slowly made her way to where Sarah clung desperately to the top rail of the wooden fence.

Even though she could not see her face in the gathering gloom, she knew she looked like Hell warmed over.

"Come on, I'll get you some soup and put you to bed," Nadine directed. "You'll feel better in the morning. You're not even taking a shower tonight. You need rest more than anything."

Sarah turned dazedly without replying and followed her back to the house, not saying a word or even attempting to walk beside her.

When they got back to the house they removed their dirty shoes outside the front door and went into the kitchen. Without saying a word Nadine removed a large plastic storage bowl of vegetable soup from the refrigerator, ladled a substantial amount into two mottled brown earthenware bowls, and heated them in the microwave.

"This is my mother's recipe and it's a closely-held family secret," Nadine said, probing with conversation to determine if Sarah was ready to open up.

Seeing she was not ready to talk, Nadine said, "Put two pieces of that whole grain bread into the toaster. When it pops up you can spread some of that organic butter I buy from my neighbor on it. It's heavenly; especially on a chilly night."

Sarah obeyed Nadine's instructions robotically and without comment.

When the soup was steaming Nadine set the bowls onto woven placemats to protect the finely finished surface of the ancient walnut table. "This table has been in my family for three generations. My great-grandfather made it with hand tools."

Sarah smiled feebly at her in acknowledgement but remained silent.

She picked up the ornately stamped stainless steel spoon set beside her bowl and was preparing to plunge it into her soup when she noticed Nadine had bowed her head. Hesitating slightly, she set the spoon back down and bowed her head slightly.

"Dear Lord," Nadine began, "thank you for the beautiful day and the ability to visit with dear friends. Thank you for keeping us safe and giving us health. Thank you for the food in front of us; please use it to nourish our bodies to do Your work, Amen."

"Amen," Sarah mimed uncertainly.

How long has it been since you've done something as simple as giving thanks for your life and food? Sarah wondered. *It's been quite a while,* she concluded.

The meal was eaten deliberately and in silence. Both women were tired from a long, emotional, and active day and were not eager to talk unnecessarily. When they were finished Nadine washed the dishes and Sarah dried then Nadine helped her carry her suitcase upstairs to the guestroom.

"The only bathroom is the one downstairs. Use this light to see in the middle of the night," she said as she pointed toward a yellow plastic flashlight setting upright on the dresser. "Those steps are pretty steep and it's totally dark out here in the country."

"If you need anything, don't be afraid to wake me up. I'm usually up a few times a night listening at the window to make sure everything's OK with the horses," she said as she turned and left the bedroom without any further comments.

Sarah's head barely hit the pillow when she fell into a deep sleep. Only when the sounds of rattling dishes and clanking of heavy pots roused her from slumber did she realize it was morning, or at least some version of it because it was still dark.

When she was finished dressing she held the flashlight firmly in her right hand and grasped the handrail determinedly in her left before descending the stairs one at a time. She was glad to get safely to the bottom without falling. A quick left turn took her into the bathroom.

After brushing her teeth and hair she deemed herself presentable and went to find Nadine.

When she got to the kitchen Nadine was nowhere to be seen. Glancing at the white enamel rimmed clock over the stove she saw the bold, black hands pointing to 5:15 a.m.

What an ungodly hour of the morning. Why don't country people sleep later? And where is Nadine?

Then she noticed a faint glow snaking from beneath the door to the Florida Room.

Why would anyone call it a Florida Room when the house is located in Virginia? she wondered.

Slowly and as quietly as possible, Sarah nudged open the stained wooden door leading to the Florida Room, the front entryway to the house. It had obviously started out as an open porch when the house was built over 100 years ago but was later enclosed. A bank of double pane insulated sliding glass windows lined its entire length from one end of the room to the other.

For times of cool weather, a solitary propane gas stove stood against the wall farthest from the door, ready to radiate warmth from its ceramic diffuser. In warmer weather, the windows slid up to reveal wire mesh screens. This allowed the cool air descending from the mountainside to supply a gentle cross-ventilating breeze. An eclectic collection of furniture modeled around an outdoors motif gave the room the panache of a Western-style hunting lodge.

Nadine was sitting sideways in an overstuffed chair enjoying her second cup of coffee as she peacefully observed her horses through the steam-rimmed windows. She had a woolen red blanket with white fringes thrown carelessly across her lap.

In the inky darkness of early morning, Sarah could see row after row of yellow tipped bluish flames hissing gently from the propane heater's diffuser, which offered the only source of light and heat in the room.

"Good Morning," Nadine said quietly as though she did not want to disturb the peacefulness of the new day. "You slept pretty well if all the snoring I heard coming from your room is any indication."

A wicked smile formed on her lips knowing that she was continuing a running joke she and Sarah had perpetuated since their college days as roommates.

"I don't snore! Never have and I never will!" she retorted as she mischievously returned Nadine's smile.

Nadine laughed heartily.

"The coffee's on the kitchen counter. It's decaf. If you need the real stuff we'll have to get some at the store today because I don't keep caffeinated beverages in the house."

"Decaf is fine. I get too worn out half-way through the day if I drink caffeine," Sarah replied as she covered her mouth with the back of her hand to stifle a yawn.

Nadine gave another chuckle as she watched her trying to wake up.

"Cups are to the right of the sink in the cabinet. Milk is in the fridge and sugar is on the table. Help yourself."

Sarah made her way to the sink and tugged at the burnished brass handle of the cupboard revealing a diverse array of multi-colored coffee mugs. She chose a white ceramic mug with a homey Christmas winter scene plastered on its side and poured a cup of steaming, thick black coffee. She added a dollop of cold, clear well water from the tap to weaken the obviously strong brew to make it palatable.

"Well, you still like coffee strong enough to take the enamel off your teeth, I see," Sarah said chidingly. "And you obviously prefer an eclectic assortment of coffee mugs. What happened to that nice set I gave you as a wedding gift?"

"My ex took them with him. I guess his boyfriend liked that style and decided they needed them more than I did."

A wan, mocking smile crossed Nadine's lips.

"Have you gotten over that mess or are you just putting on a good front?" Sarah asked cautiously.

"I've gotten over it. At least the best I ever will. When a woman chooses her mate she thinks it's for life. No one will ever be quite as important to her as the one she chose. It's not easy for a woman to lose her true love," she said philosophically.

A pall of icy silence smothered the room when the reality of what Nadine said hit them both in the same terrifying instant. They could not look at each other nor did they have anything to say for an uncomfortably long time.

Simultaneously but separately, and without a word being spoken, they decided to allow the painful pause to linger until it died by virtue of its own weight.

"Breakfast will be in about an hour," Nadine said, no longer able to stand the discomforting stillness. "If you need something right away you can make yourself some toast. There's whole grain bread left from dinner; otherwise, we'll have bacon and eggs in a bit. By the time we're finished with the breakfast dishes it'll be daylight; then it's off to tend to the animals. This is your last free meal. If you don't work around here you don't get fed."

Nadine flashed an impish smile, which Sarah returned enthusiastically.

"Some good honest work and sweat will be good for me," she stated emphatically to acknowledge Nadine's joke. "And I like to eat so I better work to your complete satisfaction."

After a few minutes of quiet contemplation and coffee sipping, Sarah asked tentatively, "Are coyotes dangerous to humans?"

Nadine shot Sarah a sideways, furtive glance, not quite sure where her line of questioning was going.

"They can be at times. Why do you ask?"

"When I think of coyotes I always envision good old Wiley Coyote. I never would've dreamed they could be as cruel as you say they are. Since you carry a gun, I started wondering if you actually feared them."

"It's not just the coyotes. I've had to shoot a rabid raccoon, and a fox that was killing my chickens. That revolver is a tool around here, the same as a shovel or rake. It has a specific job to do, otherwise it doesn't rate a place on the farm. You never know when you'll need it. But if you need it, you'll need it badly, and you better have it with you and not sitting in a drawer or in the truck. That's why I keep it strapped to my belt."

Nadine sat up straighter and continued on a topic she had put much personal introspection and thought into.

"As a matter of fact, the venison in the soup you ate last night for dinner was a doe that walked out of the woods while I was riding my horse in the back pasture last deer season."

"That was venison? Why didn't you tell me?"

"Why? Food is food. Besides, you didn't ask. You couldn't tell the difference between it and beef, because you ate it all, so you obviously liked it."

Sarah smiled, "Yeah, I did eat it all, didn't I?"

"You sure did and you had seconds also," Nadine said, once again seeing the smile on Sarah's face she remembered from the happy-go-lucky days of college.

They let the conversation drop for a minute but Sarah was obviously not satisfied with Nadine's answer. She asked in a serious tone, "So, do coyotes attack humans?"

"Yes they do. Recently there was a tragic incident where a small girl was killed in her front yard. There are about 30-35 coyote attacks on humans in California every year."

"That's terrible!" Sarah exclaimed as she raised the back of her hand to her open mouth in a subconscious gesture. The horrible picture of a child being torn apart by a pack of coyotes seared itself on her mind.

Seeing that Sarah was deeply and emotionally interested in the subject, Nadine continued after flicking a stray strand of gray-sprinkled jet-black hair out of her eyes. "The incidence of coyotes attacking humans is increasing rapidly, as a matter of fact."

"Why?"

"In a nutshell, coyotes are more frequently targeting humans as a food source. The experts seem to think they're getting bolder."

"Why are they getting bolder? What's it mean they're getting bolder? And how do you know this stuff?" Sarah asked with an interesting combination of aggression and disbelief in her voice.

"Look at it this way," Nadine said evenly. "If you're going to live in the city you better know the rules: don't cross the street against the traffic light, don't look like a goof-ball tourist in the Big City for the first time, etc. It's no different here in the country. You better know what you're up against and play by the rules or you're going to get hurt."

Before the last of her words were out of her mouth, Nadine saw a cloud of sorrow cross Sarah's face. Not wanting to allow her friend to fall victim to a deeper funk, she quickly forged onward with the conversation.

"If I remember correctly---" Nadine continued, strenuously searching her mind for a long-forgotten statistic. "There are four well documented steps coyotes go through in becoming acclimated to humans. At first, they're rarely, if ever, seen in the daylight. They're totally nocturnal because they're not sure about their human neighbors."

"That makes sense. Animals are shy and run from humans."

"Then they begin foraging for food during daylight hours," Nadine continued, ignoring Sarah's comment. "They're testing how much they can get away with. Since humans are most active during daylight hours, the yodel dogs get used to seeing humans while they hunt for food. Familiarity allows them to begin losing their fear of humans."

"Yodel dogs?" Sarah asked quizzically.

"It's a local name for coyotes because of the howling they make at night; it sounds like they're yodeling. Didn't you hear them about three o'clock this morning?"

"I didn't hear anything after my head hit the pillow. It must be this clean country air," she kidded with a girlish smile brightening her face.

"Oh right, I forgot. You couldn't hear anything over your snoring."

"You rat!"

"OK, back to coyotes attacking humans," Nadine said with a chuckle, returning to the subject they were rapidly drifting away from. "Coyotes are what are known as 'opportunistic feeders,' meaning they'll eat anything that'll fit into their mouth. It isn't long before coyotes become habituated to humans, and begin feeding on pets."

"Pets?"

"Yep, good ole Fido or Tabby becomes coyote food."

Sarah interrupted, "They can't eat many cats and dogs, can they? We'd hear about it all the time if they did."

Nadine laughed deep in her belly.

"Yes they can, there's a documented case where a coyote den was uncovered in the center of Erie, Pennsylvania and they found 51 dog collars. Cats usually don't wear collars so they have no idea how many fed that city-bred pack."

"So what about them attacking humans?" she asked as though she was being kept in the dark about this aspect of the coyote's eating habits.

"After the coyotes begin eating cats and dogs, they move up to killing them while they're being walked. Even getting so bold as to kill them while they're on their leash and the human owner is right there."

"No way!" Sarah said.

"I'm serious!" Nadine replied non-apologetically in a somber, earnest tone.

"It's at that point the coyote becomes more aggressive toward humans. It may be because they see humans as an impediment standing between them and their food. That's easy to understand considering most dog owners won't stand idly by while Fido is being eaten off the other end of the leash."

"Wow!" Sarah exclaimed after taking a few moments to absorb all she had heard.

After taking enough time to process all the information, she timidly asked, "So can you stop coyotes from attacking humans?"

"Yes," Nadine replied cautiously. "If you stop them from progressing up the ladder of aggressive behavior toward humans then they'll stay on the lower rungs of the food chain below people."

"At what point do you have to teach them the lesson?" Sarah asked hungrily as she leaned forward with anticipation.

"Well, it's better if you teach them the lesson as soon as possible. You probably won't see them when they're hunting nocturnally but if you harass them in the daylight by shooting or trapping them you'll force them to stay active only when they'll avoid human contact."

"And if you wait until they're eating your pets?" Sarah asked seriously.

"Then you've lost your opportunity to teach them the lesson. At that point they're way too familiar with humans and you'll have to fight them off when they're much too close for comfort. It's better to keep them in fear of you early in the game. Why?" she asked with a quizzical look on her face. "What are you getting at?"

"Because I want you to teach me to shoot," she replied cautiously, half expecting Nadine to refuse her request.

"Just so you can shoot coyotes?" Nadine asked with a slight, crooked smile beginning on her face as she set her empty coffee cup on the scarred oak end table.

"So I can teach predators that they better leave decent folks alone," she replied with a glint of steely resolve reflecting in her eyes.

CHAPTER 17

SARAH LEARNS TO SHOOT

"Wow! We sure finished quickly!"

"I think you put more energy into shoveling those stalls because you're motivated to get started shooting," Nadine chided her dear friend.

"There may be something to that," Sarah admitted as she gently hung a manure-encrusted shovel on a rubber-coated hook suspended from a ceiling beam in the barn. "But it really felt good to be doing some manual labor again. I didn't realize how sedentary my life had gotten."

After a light but filling lunch under the sugar maple tree, Nadine excused herself and reappeared from the house carrying a revolver nestled securely in a dark brown canvas handgun rug and a rifle housed in a jet-black leather case.

"I'll carry these if you'll carry the shooting bag," she said, handing a large dark blue nylon bag full of gear to Sarah.

Shrugging the rifle case over her left shoulder and turning on her heels Sarah said, "Let's go down behind the barn. There's a big dirt pile back there. It makes a good backstop to catch the bullets after we shoot them."

"Why do you need to catch the bullets?" Sarah asked jokingly, a tinge of stress tainting her voice. "Don't you think I'll hit the target?"

"Oh, I'm sure you'll be hitting the target soon enough but the bullet goes right through the cardboard and paper targets we'll be using. You have to catch them in something. Dirt is a real good bullet catcher."

Sarah picked up on the seriousness of Nadine's attitude so she remained silent.

The horses in the pasture watched them intently until they disappeared around the corner of the barn then lost interest and returned to munching flakes of compressed hay from the ground.

Nadine detoured into the rear door of the barn and reappeared with an old yellow, brown, and black striped horse blanket. She walked determinedly to an area where bare patches of earth showed between islands of well-matted grass and unceremoniously dropped the blanket on the ground. After kicking the blanket flat with the scuffed toe of her work boot, she gently removed a blued Ruger Single-Six .22 caliber handgun from its protective brown rug and placed it gingerly on the blanket.

"See this little gizmo here?" Nadine asked as she pointed at the revolver's right side.

"What's that?" Sarah asked.

"That's the loading gate," Nadine replied. "By flipping it open with your thumb, like this, it renders the revolver incapable of firing. That's the condition it will always be left in when we're not shooting it."

"That must be an old gun," Sarah observed. "It's all shiny along the edges."

"It's not that old. The shiny spots are where the bluing has worn off from it being carried in a holster," Nadine replied patiently. "This was one of my favorite woods bumming revolvers before I got the .357 Smith so it's ridden in a holster almost every day for a year or more."

"Woods bumming?"

"It's a term for when you're just bumming around the woods with no particular goal in mind; just taking a nice relaxing walk in the woods."

"Like hiking?"

"Just like hiking," Nadine replied. "Except that you carry a handgun for personal protection or to plink a little for the fun of it to sharpen your shooting eye."

"Plink?"

"Yes, plink," she said with a broad smile appearing on her face. "It's a term meaning to shoot at an old tin can or other target of opportunity."

"But all the safety rules of shooting still apply when you plink?"

"You bet they do. Even when you're plinking in the woods instead of on a formal shooting range, you still have to observe all the rules for safety's sake."

"Are we going to go plinking someday?"

"Someday," Nadine replied as she slid the rifle out of its black leather case. "Right now let's get you started correctly on the range we've set up here."

"What kind of gun is this?"

"This is a Marlin Model 39," Nadine replied patiently. "It's a .22 the same as the Ruger."

She then took the blue nylon shooting bag from Sarah, set it beside the firearms, and spun to face her. Nadine's graceful movements belied her bulky build.

"OK," Nadine began, "Now we're all business. Shooting is a serious activity and we'll treat it as such at all times. It only takes a split second of inattention for an unintended discharge to occur and you can never call that errant bullet back."

"Here are the rules of the shooting range," she continued without waiting for acknowledgement. Sarah stared at her attentively.

"Always have all gun barrels pointing downrange. There is no reason to have them pointing in any other direction. Our targets are down there and nowhere else," she said pointing toward the dirt piles.

"When we go down to the targets, the actions of all guns will be opened, and the guns left lying on this horse blanket," she said as she pointed toward the blanket on the ground.

Sarah's eyes began to widen as she listened intently to the instructions.

"That way we know that all guns have their actions open when anyone is downrange. If there is any breach of these rules we will immediately put the guns away and suspend shooting until we review the rules of the range."

Nadine's determined look left no doubt in Sarah's mind that she meant every word she said.

She continued unabated, "No one is to touch any gun, for any reason, while someone is downrange. If we have to fix something or adjust the sights there will be plenty of time after everyone is back behind the firing line."

"There are the four Rules of Gun Safety. They are never to be broken," she stated with a stern expression on her face.

"Number one," she said, "is to always keep the muzzle of your gun pointing in a safe direction. This is important because if you always have your gun pointed in a direction where it's safe for you to shoot; you'll never hurt or kill anything you don't want to."

"Number Two," she continued in an authoritative tone. "Always assume that every gun is loaded. If you treat every gun, even when you 'absolutely know' it's unloaded, as being loaded, you'll treat it with the respect it deserves. It's when you begin taking your gun for granted that unintended discharges happen. Please note I did not say 'accidental discharge.' There are no such things as accidents in gun handling, only stupid actions by the operators."

"What do you think number three is?" Nadine asked her pointedly.

Sarah was taken aback by the question and could only look at Nadine with a blank, puzzled stare. She hadn't planned on being tested before she was given the information.

"Keep your finger off the trigger until you're on target and ready to shoot," she said without waiting for Sarah to answer. "If your finger is not on the trigger it can't fire the gun. If the firearm discharges then something pulled the trigger. It's as simple as that."

"When you're on target and ready to fire, move the manual safety to the 'off' position," she said as she motioned with her finger without touching the rifle. "Always be careful to keep the muzzle of the barrel pointing down range toward the target backstop when you move the safety to the 'off' position as a safety precaution. Remember gun safety rule number one? This is one instance where it's applicable."

"That only leaves number four," Sarah said, anxious to complete the instructions and begin shooting.

"Keep your pants on, Missy," Nadine said evenly. "The safety rules are much more important than the actual shooting. A monkey can pull the trigger. It takes forethought and a conscientious effort to do so safely."

"Rule Four is to make sure of your target and what's beyond it. That's why we're shooting into a dirt pile. We know it'll stop the bullets."

Nadine flicked an errant strand of hair from her dark brown eyes.

Sarah began babbling on, asking one question after the other. Nadine tried to hide a smile she felt spreading across her face when she noticed the slight hint of nervousness in Sarah's voice.

Being a little nervous is good. It means she doesn't have a cavalier attitude going into this.

After getting their eye and ear protection in place, Nadine raised her voice so Sarah could hear over the sound-deadening earplugs and muffs.

"Now pick up that rifle and we'll get started."

"But I want to learn to shoot the pistol!" Sarah complained.

"And you will," Nadine replied calmly. "But first you have to learn the basics of sight picture, breath control, and trigger press. That's much easier to do with a rifle."

Sarah smiled at Nadine, realizing she was being a little too impatient. Nadine was gracious and seemed to expect it and accepted her eagerness.

Either Nadine was an exceptionally good schoolteacher and has tons of patience or she remembers what it was like when she first began to shoot. It's most likely a combination of both, Sarah thought.

When Nadine instructed her to do so, Sarah scrunched down behind the rifle, her heart beating wildly with excitement. As she was sighting down the barrel, Nadine gave more detailed instructions to her.

"Take a deep breath, let half of it out, hold it, and slowly press the trigger straight back."

Just as Nadine finished her instructions, she heard the signature report of a .22 long rifle cartridge being fired.

PpHTTTT.

The sound was muffled so well by the hearing protection Sarah wasn't sure if she fired the shot. Raising her head up to see the target she asked anxiously, "Did I hit it?"

"Look for yourself," Nadine replied as she handed Sarah a binocular.

It didn't take her long to find the hole in the lower right corner of the target.

"Yahoo!" Sarah hollered wildly, scaring Nadine with her blood-curdling yell.

After Nadine regained her composure, she returned Sarah's smile.

Thank you Lord. Giving her early success in learning to shoot helps keep her enthusiasm peaked.

If she can learn the difference between using something as simple as a gun for good or evil, then she may be able to make some sense of her situation.

"I want to shoot again," Sarah said simply as she snuggled onto the horse blanket and settled in behind the Marlin. Then she looked up at Nadine.

"If I do well with these guns, can I shoot some of the bigger ones tomorrow?" she asked.

"I have a plan on how you can progress all the way up to shooting my biggest guns proficiently," Nadine said patiently. "It may take us a few days to work our way up the power scale but we have time."

CHAPTER 18

ARI-1 COURSE

Each evening, after the animals had been cared for and dinner was in the oven, Sarah and Nadine would retire to the Florida Room with "Sundowners," the adult beverage of choice consumed after the day has ended and the guns are put away. Today, they were enjoying Kahlua and cream over ice.

"So what are we going to do tomorrow after we're done with the morning chores?" Sarah asked tiredly.

"Well, well, you seem to have a certain enthusiasm for this country life all of a sudden," Nadine said as she smiled at Sarah.

"Yeah, I guess I do. The last week has been great. I never realized I had spent my entire life living in cities and hadn't experienced true country living. Do you think I'll ever be able to go back?" she asked jokingly.

"No I don't," Nadine replied seriously.

"Really?"

"You may have enjoyed the lights and fast-paced nightlife of the city when you didn't know any better, but now you do," Nadine replied with a hint of devilishness in her voice.

"You are a wise old sage, Madam!" Sarah said cheekily.

They both rolled in their seats as they broke into uproarious, schoolgirl-like laughter. After calming down and taking a long draw on her drink, Sarah said with a dead serious tone to her voice, "I didn't think I would ever be able to laugh like that again."

"I knew you would. I just wasn't sure it would be this soon. Time truly is the greatest healer but sometimes it takes way too long to heal."

"Yeah," she said absently.

"So what do you want to do tomorrow?" Nadine inquired quickly to change the subject.

"I'd like to go to wherever they sell ammunition," Sarah said, then stopped for a moment to take a sip of her Kahlua and cream. "I want to replace your ammunition we've shot and I want to buy a bunch more so we can shoot it all up. Shooting relaxes me and I really enjoy it. I truly think it's therapeutic."

Nadine smiled knowingly.

"I know what you mean. When my ex left me all I had were my horses and my guns. It was the only thing I knew to be real and I could trust. So I rode and shot all day long for weeks on end. And lo and behold, somewhere along the line my life began to return."

"So you think I should shoot and ride horses for a few weeks?" Sarah asked with a hint of incredulity in her voice.

"Well, kind of," Nadine replied levelly as she glanced at the pasture from the comfort of the Florida Room. "What worked for me may not work for you. Not only are we two distinctly different people with disparate ways of working through our emotions, but your situation of losing your husband is vastly unlike my predicament. You may need a different set of circumstances to get yourself back on track."

"So what do you suggest, Oh Sage One?" Sarah asked with a broad smile on her face.

"Well, though I'm not a psychologist and I don't even play one on TV---," Nadine replied sarcastically. "I think that since shooting is a healing activity for you, you should take the ARI-1 course."

"What's that?" Sarah asked with great interest.

"It's the 101 course offered by the Armed Response Institute. ARI-1 is a 40-hour immersion course that teaches you how, when, and when not to use deadly force. It's a mainstay for lawyers and cops because it goes well beyond the stuff they teach in law schools and police academies about using lethal force."

Sarah looked at Nadine incredulously. "So! You think that since I've decided shooting is fun I need to learn to kill people?"

"Honey, you didn't want to learn to shoot to put little holes in paper," Nadine said in a level tone, trying to broach a delicate subject. "You want to learn to protect yourself from the coyotes and other predators in this world like the ones who killed Josh."

Nadine did not tread lightly enough.

Sarah glared menacingly at her, stood up defiantly, and slammed the yellow-fringed throw pillow she had been cradling on her lap onto the couch before stalking out of the room.

Nadine looked despairingly at the ice in her glass and let her go.

Well, maybe she wasn't ready for what you just dumped on her. What do you do now? Priority number one is to get dinner ready, she decided. *I'm starved.*

After checking on the progress of dinner, she decided the roast would be ready in twenty minutes.

I may as well make another Kahlua and cream then check my e-mail.

When the oven timer chimed the roast was cooked perfectly, the baked potatoes were soft, and there was no sign of Sarah.

I may as well dine alone. I'll set a place for her in case she cools down enough to eat. What the heck! I'm going to open that bottle of Foxhorn Cabernet I've been saving. It'll go great with the roast.

And I may as well catch up on reading this month's Today's Horse magazine. I guess I've gotten used to having Sarah here to talk with during dinner and have neglected my usual meal routine.

Just as she was beginning to clear away the dirty dishes Sarah appeared silently and stood at the doorway.

"Is there enough left for me?" she asked in a guarded but friendly manner. She forced a waxen smile upon her lips. Her eyes were red-rimmed and puffy, and her nose showed signs of redness from repeated wiping.

She's trying to make amends. That's a good omen.

"There's not only enough for you but it'll probably carry us over for lunch tomorrow," Nadine said as she smiled broadly in a gesture signaling her acceptance of Sarah's unspoken apology. "Sit down; it'll be easier for me to serve you since I know where everything is. Do you want wine with your dinner?"

"Yes, please," Sarah replied quietly.

Nadine sat with her as she ate, reading her magazine to avoid staring at every bite she placed it in her mouth. She began eating daintily, placing each forkful in her mouth with great care and chewing slowly, but progressed to a steady cadence as she hunched slightly forward over her rapidly emptying plate.

It's nice to see she's hungry. It's a good sign.

After she was sated, Sarah carefully placed her knife and fork side by side on the dirty plate, then slid it deliberately to the side of the table. Gently lifting her napkin from her lap she folded it with great care and placed it on the table then looked directly at Nadine.

When Nadine sensed Sarah's eyes locked on her she slowly looked up from her reading to meet her gaze.

"So tell me more about the ARI-1 course, Oh Sage One", she said with a smile on her face. "What do they do?"

"They teach people when, how, and when not to shoot in self-defense," Nadine replied. "And they teach you what to do and what not to do in the aftermath of a self-defensive shooting to deal effectively with the legal system."

"Who teaches it, some old, broken down Rambos?"

Sarah was immediately sorry for the sarcasm in her voice and was ready to apologize but Nadine continued without acknowledging her rudeness.

"No Rambos there, it's all either retired or active-duty police officers teaching the course," she replied in a matter-of-fact manner. She wasn't going to let Sarah control the tone of this conversation because it was too important for her emotional healing to treat the topic lightly.

"The Armed Response Institute is owned and operated by a wild, funny guy. Oh God, you wouldn't believe the number of jokes this guy knows!" she said while blushing and gently shaking her head back and forth.

"So they're a little off-color at times, I assume?" Sarah asked surreptitiously.

"That's an understatement, but they are funny," Nadine confessed.

"Any way, the owner is Sam Heydt. He's one of the cops who travel nationwide to train other cops. There're no Rambos there; just professionals."

"So there's a bunch of testosterone-fired cops teaching the course. What does a woman do in that type of environment besides make lunch?"

She was again embarrassed by her own sarcasm. "I'm sorry, I don't know why I'm being so mean. Maybe it's because I'm scared of what's happening to me and how my attitudes are changing so quickly."

"Don't worry about it. It's a legitimate question," Nadine replied then continued, "There're no testosterone-fired teachers in that bunch. Well, they obviously have the testosterone to be real men but they're more courteous and accommodating to their female students than a woman would be. They understand this type of training is basically out of character for women, at least until the women understand their role in protecting the weak among us."

"Sammie, that's the name he goes by, once told me he went to bat for female FBI agents in court because they couldn't pass their firearms proficiency test. Apparently, the more petite hands of the females needed a smaller grip on their handguns and they couldn't handle the large-gripped firearm the FBI was issuing to its agents."

"That's chivalrous of him, but did it do any good?"

"The FBI changed the equipment so it fit smaller hands and that allowed women to pass the shooting proficiency test," Nadine replied. "Now they're doing good work as career FBI agents. Of course, that situation didn't endear him to the FBI hierarchy but it doesn't seem to bother him. The bottom line is that he goes to bat for women."

"And you think this is what I need?" Sarah asked apprehensively.

"It's not me that thinks you need this. You brought yourself to that conclusion but didn't put it into those terms."

"Say what?" Sarah asked as a quizzical expression flashed across her face.

"It goes back to your Biology 101 lesson with coyotes. You even threw in a healthy dose of Psychology 101 from that Bachelor's degree you got back in undergrad," she replied.

"What are you talking about?"

"This isn't rocket science," Nadine said. "A coyote, the predator, will continue to kill and eat its prey as long as some outside force doesn't stop it. Human predators and coyotes act the same behavior-wise. They'll continue doing what they have always done until someone stops them."

"So the responsibility for violence lies with the predator that hasn't been stopped?"

"That's right. But it also depends on the prey. If the prey has the ability to stop the predator from preying upon them, then the predator will change their behaviors. One way or the other," Nadine said, clarifying her remarks.

"But aren't criminals just a product of a bad upbringing and it's not really their fault?" Sarah asked, knowing her deeply held concept of reality was being brought into question.

"It doesn't matter what their upbringing was like if you're the prey," Nadine said unemotionally. "You're still just a piece of dead meat to them."

"Yeah, but---"

"Yeah, but nothing," Nadine said with an edge of impatience in her voice. "Predators are not sensible and you can't reason with them. Don't think for a minute they're like us. They're a distinct breed and live by different rules. What you consider to be 'reasoning' or 'understanding' they perceive as weakness. Therefore, you deserve to be eaten."

"Are you sure that's the way they think?"

"It's the way the mind of any predator works," Nadine stated with finality. "And you know it."

"It seems so cruel---and cold."

"Predators do not reason with their food, they simply eat it. Like you just did at dinner," Nadine said. "A violent human attacker, the predator, can be expected to react in the same way as a coyote."

"But they're human. Not animals!" Sarah said with a twinge of hysteria creeping into her voice.

Nadine noticed that Sarah's hands were moving in anxious, twitching movements as she spoke.

"Violent attackers tend to be sociopathic, meaning they don't follow the same morals as the rest of society. That's why they're called 'career criminals.' It's the way they live their lives. Either way, you're still going to be eaten by the predator. It's not such a good deal for you, the victim," Nadine said plainly.

"So what do we have to do, put all the criminals in jail?" Sarah asked, her previous anxiety having subsided as Nadine began making sense.

"Or kill them," Nadine said matter-of-factly. "The threat of jail, death, or serious injury is enough to change the behavior of the smarter predators; at least if it's staring them in the face. It's the only way to keep them from preying on innocent people."

"Meaning what?" Sarah asked tentatively, still slightly shocked by Nadine's bluntness.

"Meaning that when a criminal is taken at gunpoint by a police officer or an armed citizen, the message is simple," she replied. "Stop your aggressive behavior immediately or be seriously injured and risk dying."

"So we have to shoot all the criminals?" Sarah asked incredulously.

"No, the majority of criminals understand their options are very limited at that point," she said. "They usually stop their aggressive actions immediately to avoid injury. That's why the vast majority of incidents where good people take criminals at gunpoint either end in surrender or, more likely, the bad guy running away. There are over two million such incidents in the United States each year."

"That's a lot," Sarah said. "If there's so many why don't we ever hear about them?"

"You never hear about them because it ends happily with the criminal running away," Nadine explained simply. "Since that's all the victim wanted in the first place, why get the police involved?"

"But you think you'd hear about some of these on the news."

"There's no news when a criminal runs away; only when they commit a crime and someone is injured or killed," Nadine said plainly.

"So all I have to know is how to point a gun at a bad guy and he'll run away?" Sarah asked innocently.

"Definitely not," Nadine said with a look of horror on her face. "You have to be willing and able to use lethal force, and you can only be confident enough to use lethal force if you know the law is on your side. That's why any citizen who makes the decision to carry a concealed firearm should take a course, like ARI-1, that teaches the legalities and tactics of self-defense."

"But if I live out here, which I just may do someday because I really like it in the country, I won't need a gun unless I go into the woods. There's really no crime out here, is there?"

"Honey, that's denial and you know it," Nadine said soothingly. "Just like the person who won't take a CPR course or buckle their seat belt because 'it won't happen to me' you're refusing to accept reality if you think you'll never need to defend yourself. Pretending that violent crime won't find you, regardless of where you live, is just sticking your head in the sand."

Nadine smiled softly with grandmotherly-like concern showing in her face.

"So you think a course is the way to go?" Sarah asked seriously.

"It's the only way to go," Nadine replied softly. "They teach you how to prevent bad things from happening and how to handle them when they can't be avoided."

"We're never done learning I guess," Sarah said submissively.

"You've paid for many years of college learning how to make a living," Nadine replied calmly. "This is the knowledge that may allow you live. Period."

Nadine saw a look of enlightenment cross Sarah's face.

"OK, what will I need?" she asked.

"You'll need a good quality handgun. It doesn't have to be new; there are plenty of gently used guns on the market," Nadine replied. "You'll also need five to six hundred rounds of full power ammunition. You'll be doing a lot of shooting over the week."

"The week!" Sarah exclaimed.

"Yep, it runs for five days just like a real job. There's a lot of information and it's all new to folks like you. You have to have time to absorb it and then put it into action. That's a big task and one that can't be accomplished in a short weekend."

"What else will I need?" Sarah replied with a tone of acceptance in her voice. "If I'm going to be serious about this I may as well do it right."

"You can visit their website and get a list of all of the stuff you'll need," Nadine said with a smile. "But to make it easier for you I already printed the material while you were upstairs."

"So you were pretty damned sure I'd do this," she said with a smile. "OK, let's see what you have!"

"Yeah, I was pretty sure you'd go," Nadine admitted. "We'll go shopping tomorrow afternoon to get you what you'll need. We deserve a break from farm work anyway."

CHAPTER 19

SHOPPING

The next morning after the farm chores were completed they headed to town. Nadine was determined to buy everything Sarah needed for the ARI-1 course before she changed her mind.

The shopping went quickly.

"That pretty well completes our list. How about some lunch?"

"That's the best idea you've had today," Sarah replied energetically. "Where do you want to go? I'm buying."

"Let's head on over to The Eatery. They have good food and I really get a kick out of how everyone seems to know everyone else in these small towns."

During lunch Sarah dominated the conversation with questions regarding the ARI-1 course, which Nadine answered patiently. After leaving the restaurant, Nadine said, "We better be getting back to the farm and start the evening chores if we want to finish before dark."

Within five minutes of leaving The Eatery and the town of Thompsonville, Sarah saw a 'For Sale' sign beside a long dirt lane perched atop a yellow wooden pole. Her head snapped to the right, striving to look at the property as they passed by. A fleeting glimpse of a small, well-kept white clapboard house surrounded by neatly kept outbuildings was all she needed to determine she wanted a closer view.

"Do we have time to go back and take a little better look at that house for sale?" Sarah asked, already knowing the answer to her question.

Nadine looked at her out of the corner of her eyes.

"So you're on a shopping spree and now even a house looks pretty good?" Nadine asked chidingly.

"No, I'm just open to all options right now. I'll need a place to live, or at least a place to run away to when the real world gets too stressful, and I really like this area. The people are friendly and it has a certain peacefulness about it," Sarah replied.

"You don't have to explain to me," Nadine said as she made a U-turn in front of a dilapidated red barn.

"I know," Sarah said as she blushed. "I guess I was just trying to convince myself that house shopping is OK. You know, that it's not too soon to begin rebuilding my life instead of just staying with you forever."

"Good idea," Nadine said, suddenly becoming very serious. "Are you sure you can find a way to make a living out here in the boonies?"

Before Sarah could answer, Nadine asked her second question, "Are you sure you'd be able to put up with the peace and quiet out here for the long haul? You're a city girl that's used to always having something to do from sun-up to well past sundown."

"Aren't we getting a little nosy?" Sarah joked.

"Cut it out," Nadine said as she smiled broadly and looked directly at Sarah. "You know what I mean. You'll have to be able to make enough money to pay the mortgage on this much property. The taxes alone on a piece of acreage this big are enough to curl your toes."

"Actually," Sarah said cautiously, "I should have a ton of money soon."

Nadine's eyebrows rose considerably but she was too polite to ask any more questions. She didn't have to because Sarah was in an expansive and talkative mood.

"My practice is in the process of being sold. Joe Holmes, my associate for many years, is buying it. We've already settled on a purchase price, the bank is willing to lend him the money, and lawyers are drawing up the papers," Sarah said as Nadine turned onto the dirt lane with the 'For Sale' sign beside it and came to a stop. "My house in D.C. is on the market and it should bring a fair amount of money. We moved into a neighborhood that was being 'gentrified' and rehabilitated the house from a wreck into a showplace."

"Rehabilitation takes a lot of work," Nadine said as she tried to steer the conversation away from the direction she knew it was headed. She failed miserably in changing the topic of the discussion.

"We only had three months to enjoy our showpiece residence before Josh was---."

Sarah's voice trailed off perceptibly. She then took a deep breath and steeled herself before continuing, "And Josh had a two million dollar life insurance policy bought by the group practice he was a partner in."

"That was nice of them," Nadine said innocently.

"It wasn't out of the goodness of their flinty little hearts," Sarah said bitterly. "Josh's partners are listed as the beneficiary on the policy and it's in their contract the money will be used to buy Josh's part of the practice from his widow."

Sarah looked out the side window of the car as tears welled up in her eyes.

"That's the first time I've referred to myself as a widow," she said tearfully.

"So what you're saying is you're filthy rich. At least for the moment," Nadine asked in an attempt to change the topic slightly and help pull Sarah out of her funk.

"Yep, that's what I'm saying," she said as a wan smile broke through her tears. "Assuming everything goes as it's supposed to. You know what it's like when a bunch of lawyers get their fingers into things that involve money."

"Oh yeah, unfortunately I do," Nadine said with a smile. "I've had my share of dealing with the law profession."

"Let's go down the lane a little ways and see what the house looks like. I really can't see much from here," Sarah said.

Nadine drove to the front of the house and gave a courtesy toot on her pickup truck's horn to alert the residents in the house that they had visitors.

It took less than two minutes for a small, grandmotherly woman with a floral print apron covering her below-the-knee length housedress to appear at the front door. She was wiping her hands on a white dishtowel with large yellow daisies printed on it and smiling from ear-to-ear.

She opened the door widely yet stood square in the middle of the doorway. The message was clear; if you're friendly then you're welcome. If you're not, you're in for a heap of trouble so you best mind your manners.

"What can I help you young ladies with?" she asked with a smile.

"Hello, I'm Nadine Brand and this is Sarah Collins," Nadine said. "I live down near Rapine and Sarah is up visiting for a few weeks. She isn't sure if she wants to move to the area but she saw your place and wanted to see it up closer."

Sarah quickly interjected, "Naturally, we'll call the real estate agent to set up a time to visit and get a good look at the property. I'm just not sure exactly what I'm looking for, or even if I'm in the market for a new house."

"Well, I'm a Sarah also. Sarah Schneider is my name but everyone knows me by my nickname, Minnie. Don't ask me where the name came from - it just kind of grew on me!" she beamed.

"You're right, the real estate agent is handling the actual showing of the house but if you want to sit for a few minutes, we can visit until my bread is finished baking."

"Thank you but we don't want to intrude."

"Nonsense, you aren't intruding," she said enthusiastically then pointed toward a small, squat white clapboard outbuilding. "Go get those folding chairs from over there by the springhouse and set them up here by the front door and I'll get us some sweet tea."

Without another word she turned on her heels and disappearing back into the dark confines of the house.

Nadine turned and went to fetch the folding aluminum chairs with Sarah close on her heels. Their eyes flitted observantly over the property as they walked.

"Minnie seems to be fairly old," Nadine observed. "She may have lived in this house all her life. If I'm right, she'll be able to give us a history of this property if we can get her talking."

"We don't have much time; don't forget about the animals," Sarah reminded her. "Besides, we just showed up unannounced. I should have just called the real estate agency."

"Don't worry about it," Nadine replied. "Minnie seems to be glad to have some company."

As Nadine was setting up the last of the chairs Minnie reappeared at the door with a tray holding three glass tumblers and a curved handle clear glass pitcher with daisies painted on the side. The pitcher was filled almost to overflowing with ice and murky brown tea.

"Fetch that little metal table off the patio there, Honey, if you would please," Minnie said as she smiled at Sarah.

Minnie patiently waited for Sarah to get the rickety table set up and as stable as it would ever be.

"Help me set this down, Honey," Minnie asked with a trace of straining in her voice.

Sarah took the slightly rusted metal serving tray with an ancient Coca-Cola advertisement printed on its face from Minnie and set it on the table then inconspicuously held it steady while Minnie served Nadine. She then poured a glass of iced tea for Sarah and handed it to her.

"Sit down there, Honey," Minnie said as she indicated an empty chair with a gnarled, arthritic finger. Finally, she poured and lifted her own glass of tea high in the air and made a toast.

"To your health," Minnie said.

"To your health," they said in unison as they held their glasses aloft.

A quaint smile spread between the three women.

After everyone had taken a deep swallow of their tea and the two visitors nodded their appreciation to their host, Minnie started the conversation.

"Now, what can I help y'all with," she asked in a matter-of-fact manner.

"Well, I'm not sure I'm really in the market for a house right now. Especially this far from where I'm currently living," Sarah said.

"Then why are you even looking for a house? And where are you living now?" Minnie asked boldly.

"Well, I'm living with Nadine right now, you see--" Before she realized it, Sarah had spewed out her entire life history to Minnie.

Sarah never thought she could ever tell anyone everything she revealed to Minnie in the next twenty minutes. Maybe it was because she looked like the perfect grandmother and Sarah needed grandmotherly advice at this very difficult time of her life.

"I'm sorry," she apologized. "I didn't mean to dominate the conversation."

"It's not a problem, Honey," Minnie replied.

"So why are you selling such a beautiful house?" Sarah stammered in an attempt to shift the conversation away from her.

"Well, I'm alone these days myself," she said dully. "My husband died of a massive coronary two years ago and I've been running this place by myself ever since. I'm eighty-two years old and while I do pretty well, I'm starting to slow down."

"You look much younger than your eighty-two years, Minnie," Nadine said.

"And you move like a much younger woman," Sarah opined. "As a chiropractor, I tend to notice things like that."

"You're both much too kind," Minnie replied as she blushed then continued with her story.

"My daughter Susan is sixty-two years old this year and has lived in Florida for the last twenty years," Minnie said. "She and her husband recently moved into a brand new senior citizen's housing development that's still in the process of being built."

"Some of the senior housing facilities I've seen recently are really beautiful," Sarah replied.

"She really loves it and says I can get an apartment in her complex," Minnie continued. "That way we can be neighbors and I don't have to maintain any buildings or cut grass."

"That sounds good to me," Nadine said. "How old do you have to be to get into a place like that?"

Minnie chuckled.

"It's a good deal for both of us because she worries about me, wants me close to keep an eye on me, and yet doesn't want me living with them."

She smiled palely as she looked ashamedly toward her guests.

"I hate to give up this place," she continued. "I was born here and I expected to die here like my husband did, but that's not likely to happen."

"Your husband died in this house?" Sarah asked with repulsion in her voice.

"No, he didn't die in this house, he died at the grocery store while picking up a few items," Minnie replied. "As a matter of fact, I don't think anyone ever died in this house."

"That's a relief, I'm a little uncomfortable about houses where people have passed on," Sarah admitted.

"There were a number of births, but no one ever died here," Minnie reflected, searching the recesses of her mind.

To change the subject, Sarah asked, "How much land do you have here?"

"We have one hundred acres or somewhere thereabouts," Minnie said. "There are fifty under cultivation and roughly thirty in woods, and twenty in overgrown pasture land."

"That's a nice ratio," Nadine offered as she looked at Sarah out of the corner of her eyes.

"Do you see that fence with the cattle standing behind it?" Minnie asked as she pointed with a shaky finger. "That's the property line with the Miller farm."

"They have some nice looking Black Angus cattle there," Nadine observed in a neighborly tone.

"And that fence over there?" Minnie asked, pointing in the opposite direction. "That's the property line with the Sabbatini farm."

"Both of the property lines go straight back to the woods and continue until they hit the National Forest property line," she continued, warming to the conversation. "The Forest Service marks their property real well with little metal tags on all of the trees along the property line."

"It's good to know some of my tax money is going toward something useful," Sarah said with a gentle smile creasing her lips.

"The federal government doesn't want anyone felling any of their trees," Minnie stated with finality.

Apparently, Sarah thought, *Minnie's dealings with the federal government in regards to the National Forest property line did not go smoothly over the years.*

"Have you had trouble with the Federal government over your property lines?" Sarah asked innocently.

"Nothing compared to the War of Northern Aggression," said Minnie with a fair bit of vehemence dripping from her voice. It was obvious that hard feelings ran deep and injustices were neither easily forgiven nor forgotten.

Nadine and Sarah looked at each other and muffled giggles beneath their hands.

"And you've taken care of all this property by yourself for the last two years?" Sarah asked to bring the subject back to the farm.

"Well, I haven't taken care of it all by myself. I've kind of overseen its maintenance," Minnie corrected her. "There's a nice man from down the road who farms the fifty tillable acres. Instead of getting a percentage of the profits as is the usual custom, he pays the taxes on the fifty acres and keeps my grass cut."

"That seems like a reasonable trade," Sarah said, marveling over the simplicity of the arrangement.

"Yes it is, as far as I'm concerned," Minnie said. "And he may be persuaded to continue the agreement if you bought the farm."

"Do you really think so?" Sarah asked with increasing interest.

"I think it's a profitable arrangement for him and it saves me quite a bit of aggravation," she assured her. "It doesn't seem as though you're really in any type of situation to run the place by yourself."

"After helping Nadine on her horse farm for a few days I know I don't have enough energy to take care of a place this size by myself," she admitted.

"And if I may be so bold, I don't think you're really cut out to run a farm as a business," Minnie stated as she thrust her jaw forward.

Sarah giggled politely.

"Minnie, you're so right. I would never consider running a farm as a business. This city girl just doesn't have the experience!"

Suddenly, she became very serious. "I don't really know what I want right now."

"That's a tough situation to be in," Minnie agreed with a barely perceptible nod of her head.

"I seem to need a totally different life than what I had a few short weeks ago," Sarah admitted. "I had my life all planned out and now that's all been shattered. I'm left with nothing, or so it would seem."

"I've been there and done that," Nadine added as her mind wandered back into her own past. Sarah shot her a quick sideways glance and continued with her story.

"One thing I do know; if I were to buy a place like this, even if I only used it during the weekends, I would keep it as a viable, working farm."

"That's what it was meant to be and should be kept as one," Minnie agreed.

"The history is too deep here and it's a good place to raise a family," Sarah agreed. "I could never allow a fine farm like this to fall into disrepair."

"For a city girl, you seem to have a firm grasp on what a good piece of land deserves and what it can offer the right person," Minnie said with a warm smile directed at Sarah.

"That's why I would keep it a viable operation," she declared. "Even if it cost me more money than I made out of it." Sarah surprised herself with such a strong statement and was even more astonished that she meant every word of it.

"How would you keep it as a working enterprise if you aren't here all the time?"

"I'd find someone to farm the land like you've done," she replied, looking Minnie directly in the eyes. "I don't see any livestock in the pasture so I'd renovate it to support either horses or cattle. I'm partial to cattle for some reason."

"Probably because you're tired of shoveling out the stalls at my place," Nadine said chidingly.

"That may have something to do with it," Sarah joked back and they all laughed uproariously.

"There are farmers who would watch your livestock while you weren't here," Minnie said. "The local growers are usually looking for additional income and most of them are honest, hard workers."

"Is there any tax advantages to keeping the property as a farm?" Sarah asked, her business acumen peaking.

"The agricultural designation definitely reduces taxes," Minnie replied. "I'm impressed by your grasp of the importance of watching overhead expenses for an agricultural operation."

"I've run my own business for a number of years," she reminded her.

"And you think you can keep tabs on the business aspects, keep the place in reasonable shape, and still have time to relax here?" Minnie asked with a heavy dose of skepticism in her voice.

"It depends on what you call relaxation," Sarah replied as she smiled. "Farms and lounging around don't seem to go hand-in-hand."

The women again broke out in laughter. Nadine was laughing hard enough for her bulbous belly to bounce deliriously.

"I know what you're getting at, Minnie," Sarah said, suddenly very serious. "But you have to know me. I can't sit still for more than ten minutes. I need to keep moving."

"A farm will keep you moving, that's for sure," Minnie replied.

"Relaxation to me would be to have a day that starts at five o'clock, involves manual labor all day long, and ends at half-past dark," Sarah said. "No mind boggling paperwork, no major decisions regarding another person's life, not having to put up with ten staff members bitching because four of them are going through PMS at the same time. Now that's relaxation!"

Minnie looked at her incredulously then burst into uproarious laughter.

"Your daily grind must be a real hum-dinger!" she bubbled. "After all that, shoveling horse shit must be relaxing!"

Nadine and Sarah sat stunned for a split second then began laughing until their sides hurt.

"Minnie!" Sarah said still laughing. "To hear such a prim, proper lady like yourself put my situation into such succinct terms is hilarious!"

After visiting with Minnie for another hour, Sarah and Nadine reminded each other they had to get back to care for the horses.

As they were driving down the lane from Minnie's farm, the delicious scent of freshly baked bread wafted throughout the pick-up from the warm loaf sitting between them on the seat.

"Minnie was elated when you said you'd call the real estate agency and set an appointment to see the rest of the property," Nadine said. "I think she can see a lot of herself in you when she was your age."

"You mean beautiful and worldly?"

"No, I mean full of piss and vinegar."

They both laughed boisterously until they couldn't speak. The rest of the drive to The Shire was made in silence.

She's really thinking deeply, Nadine thought. *I don't know what she has going around in her mind but I'm certainly not going to interrupt. She needs a lot of quiet time, I think. Besides, there's nothing I can add that would be helpful right now anyway.*

Sarah continued to be strangely quiet and contemplative during the evening chores. Her mood continued throughout the evening as she ate dinner with a minimum of small talk.

After clearing and washing the dinner dishes, Sarah said, "I'm going to bed. I didn't realize how exhausting this has been. Maybe it's just the fresh country air, what do you think?"

"I think it's the two huge slices of Minnie's homemade bread with apple butter you wolfed down at dinner and not the fresh country air making you sleepy," Nadine said jokingly.

"Maybe that's it!" she replied with a chuckle. "Good night."

When she reached the kitchen door, she stopped and spun to face Nadine and fixed her with an intense gaze.

"Tomorrow after we do the morning chores, can we shoot the guns we haven't shot yet?" she asked.

"Of course we can," Nadine replied. "But it's supposed to get pretty hot tomorrow afternoon so we better get the shooting done early to stay out of the heat."

"Will it be too hot up on the mountain to take a hike after we're done shooting?"

"No, as a matter of fact, it's usually cooler up there," Nadine offered as a questioning look crossed her face. "Do you want to take a little walk up there?"

"If you don't mind. I would actually like a few hours to myself and see if I like the woods," she stated succinctly.

"It's a fine idea. Just remind me to give you my compass," Nadine said in an encouraging tone. "As long as you don't go over the crest of the mountain you can take a northern compass reading and it will always bring you out to the road because it runs east and west."

"Thanks," Sarah said as a gleeful smile spread across her face.

Now what's that all about? Nadine thought as she watched Sarah walk away.

CHAPTER 20

SARAH'S REVELATION

In the morning, Sarah entered the Florida room in the dark and had the coffee ready long before Nadine made her appearance.

"Well, well, it looks like you're getting the hang of this country living," she said as she settled into her easy chair.

"It really feels great to get an early start on the day!" Sarah beamed.

What's up with her that she's so upbeat and vibrant at this hour of the morning?

"So what are your plans for today?" Nadine asked tentatively.

"We're going to take care of the animals as quickly as we can then we'll shoot the rest of your guns, have lunch, and then I'll take a walk up the mountain so you can have a few moments of peace," Sarah said brightly. "You need some personal time."

"Bullshit! I don't need any personal time and you know it!" Nadine joked.

"OK, I need some personal time," Sarah admitted. "Do you think I'll need a gun while I'm up on the mountain?"

"You can carry a gun with you if you want to, you're certainly proficient," Nadine replied. "Take your pick."

"What about the legality of carrying a gun, even if it's in the woods?" she asked with concern in her voice.

"Virginia allows 'open carry' so long as it's in a holster and in clear view," Nadine replied. "Besides, when you're on my property you're legal."

"What else will I need?" Sarah asked, realizing the seriousness of being in the woods alone.

"Usually, there isn't anyone up on the mountain at this time of year so you should take your cell phone."

"Can I get reception out here?"

"You may not get a signal until you're near the top," Nadine informed her. "But it's better to have it than not."

"Is there any drinking water on the mountain, like a stream or anything?"

"You'll have to carry water," Nadine said seriously. "Never trust untreated water. Most of the surface water has parasites in it these days."

"What do you want for dinner?" Sarah asked unexpectedly.

"We haven't even had breakfast yet and you want to start dinner?"

Sarah laughed.

"I wasn't thinking of starting dinner," she said, showing a full set of even, brilliantly white teeth in a broad smile. "I was thinking of buying you dinner. There has to be a decent restaurant that has a wine list around here someplace."

"D'amato's is over in Spinale. It's only about twenty minutes from here and they have a really good lasagna special on Wednesday nights."

"Italian it is!" Sarah gushed enthusiastically. "Can we finish with the horses and still have enough time to get over there before they close?"

"Yes, we'll probably have time to get showered after doing the evening chores and get over there with plenty of time to spare."

"Let's plan on it then."

"Are you sure you'll have enough energy left after climbing the mountain?" Nadine asked seriously.

"For a dinner with wine served on white linen tablecloths, I'll find the energy," Sarah said with finality.

"It sounds like a plan!" Nadine replied cheerfully.

The morning chores went quickly. By 9:00 a.m. Sarah and Nadine were behind the barn situating their shooting gear at the firing line. The ritual of setting up the gear and range had become an organized, efficient task for the two women.

"What would you like to shoot?" Nadine asked as she began unpacking various pistols, revolvers, and rifles.

"I want to pick up where we left off the other day," Sarah said without hesitation. "I want to learn to shoot the larger pistols we haven't shot yet."

"Pistols it is then," Nadine said with a smile.

It pleased her to see Sarah so enthusiastic about shooting. She had worried that she and Sarah would no longer have much in common since they had gone their separate ways after college but the shooting sports gave them common ground on which to renew and build their relationship.

"Let's start with this Glock nine-millimeter," Nadine said as she picked up a black, plastic-looking pistol.

"What are those funny sights on that pistol?" Sarah asked with a questioning expression on her face.

"Those are XS Sight System's 24/7 Big Dot front sight and express rear sight," Nadine offered.

"They're a lot different than the other sights I've used so far."

"These sights are for fast shooting in emergency self-defensive situations," Nadine patiently explained. "These were developed in Africa for hunting dangerous game."

"In Africa?"

"Yes, in Africa. If an elephant or rhinoceros is bearing down on you with the intent of stomping your miserable human carcass into the ground, you have to be able to shoot fast and accurately at very close range."

"Cool!" Sarah exclaimed.

"They called them 'express sights' and on dangerous big game rifles they used a big, round front bead made of elephant or warthog ivory to pick up the reduced light in the thick, brushy areas where that type of game is hunted."

"Why elephant ivory?" Sarah asked.

"Actually, they preferred warthog ivory because it didn't turn yellow with age like elephant ivory."

"So why don't they use warthog ivory since it has a proven track record?" Sarah quizzed Nadine.

"Modern technology allows the use of tritium, a low-level radioactive material, to put a glowing light into the sights."

"Why's that important?" Sarah asked.

"It's important because most violent encounters, or attacks, occur in low-light situations if not in total darkness," Nadine replied. "The glowing sights allow you to place the front sight on your assailant and get your shot off as soon as possible. Remember, this type of shooting is only in life threatening situations so it's a last ditch effort and you better be on target."

Sarah sighted downrange with an unloaded gun to try the sights. "They're real easy to see and line up," she said.

"Speed and accuracy are everything when you're faced with a violent encounter," Nadine explained.

"I like these a lot," Sarah opined.

"And the glowing sights are very helpful for finding your pistol in the dark," Nadine pointed out. "It's much better than fumbling blindly around your nightstand drawer in the middle of the night."

The shooting session went smoothly until Nadine observed, "It must be close to noon. The sun is straight overhead and my belly is growling."

"I'll make lunch," Sarah said enthusiastically, "if you'll get me a compass and any other stuff I'll need for my foray into the wilds of Virginia."

"It's a deal," Nadine said as she laughed deeply at Sarah's mocking reference to the mountain behind the farm.

As soon as lunch was finished and the dishes washed, Sarah took her leave.

"I'll be back by five o'clock to help with the evening chores," she called over her shoulder as she turned toward the mountain.

"I'm going to take a nap while you're gone," Nadine called after her. "You wear me out."

Sarah laughed and gave a carefree wave with her hand above her head before strolling out of sight with long, confident strides.

"I hope she knows what the hell she's doing," Nadine said to herself before shuffling into the cool innards of the house for her afternoon respite.

Nadine awoke after a thirty-minute nap then sat under the sugar maple tree in her front yard with a tall, frosty glass of ice water within easy reach.

Maybe I shouldn't have let her go hiking alone. She doesn't have any experience in the woods. She shouldn't have any trouble from wildlife but there's always the chance she'll fall or twist an ankle.

The searing heat of the afternoon sun was losing its fierceness and began mellowing as the day slid toward evening. Nadine's worrying made her antsy and she made more trips to the restroom than necessary to burn off her nervous energy.

I should have warned her about the methamphetamine laboratories that occasionally spring up in the wilderness areas around here. The owners aren't afraid to shoot someone to protect their investment.

Fifteen minutes before her deadline, Sarah appeared at the edge of the pasture. Nadine exhaled a huge sigh of relief when she spied her walking with purposeful strides across the meadow.

"Hello, Lady of the Mountain!" Nadine greeted her as she struggled to fight her way out of the chaise lounge she was reclining in.

"Hello, Flatlander!" Sarah quickly quipped. "I've made some decisions and some plans."

"Well, well, and what may they be?" Nadine asked as she handed her a frosty, sweating glass of freshly made iced tea.

Sarah paused to remove the lemon wedge from the rim of the crystal clear glass before guzzling most of the murky tea in a cascade of gulps.

After wiping tiny droplets from her upper lip with the back of her hand, Sarah began excitedly, "I've decided that I'm definitely interested in Minnie's place. I called the real estate agent from up on the mountain. By the way, you're right; I had to be almost at the very top before I could get any cell phone reception."

"Anyway," she continued without letting Nadine get a word in edgewise, "she agreed to show me the property tomorrow and called Minnie to make sure it's OK."

Before Nadine could reply Sarah continued, "I asked the real estate agent if she knew any foresters and she gave me the phone number of her cousin. I hired him to make an appraisal of the timber on those thirty acres. If the property line is as well marked as Minnie says it is, it should be easy to get an accurate appraisal."

Nadine's mouth dropped open. "My, my, aren't you just the little business woman---."

Sarah blushed and started where she left off without skipping a beat, "I also had the real estate agent recommend a colleague from a competing agency. I called and hired him to get some background information on the value of similar properties that have sold in the last few years."

"You're going to steal that land from a nice, little old lady! Shame on you!" Nadine gasped with a display of fake surprise on her face.

"I'm doing no such thing, you witch! And you know it! That farm has been on the market for almost a year. Apparently its way overpriced and I want to be able to make a realistic offer for it. If I have a few figures to show Minnie where it's overpriced she may get to Florida while she can still enjoy it!'"

"So you don't think that Minnie's just some robber baron waiting for a star-struck Yankee to come along and overpay for her idyllic plantation?" Nadine chided her friend.

"No I do not," Sarah said seriously. "She truly is a nice lady. I tend to think that either her daughter, or the real estate agent, or both for that matter, want to get a lot more for the place than it's worth."

"You may be right," Nadine agreed. "It wouldn't be the first time grown children put their interests above those of their dear, old mother."

"That's the way I have it figured," Sarah said defiantly. "It would be much easier for her if poor, old Minnie passed away before she had to put up with her living in the same development."

"And you're going to set Minnie straight so she can retire to Florida and aggravate her daughter until she takes her final breath. Is that it?"

"Something like that," Sarah replied flatly. "Is there any more of this iced tea? It's the best tasting I've had in a coon's age. How do you like that hillbilly lingo, eh? I've been practicing."

After getting her refill of iced tea, Sarah sat in the shade with Nadine under the sugar maple then continued detailing her plans. "Now for the best part; I really had to think this one out since you brought it up the other day."

"What did I bring up?" Nadine asked in confusion, totally baffled by what she may have said to put Sarah into such a whirlwind of activity.

"You asked me the million dollar question," she explained. "I hadn't considered if I could stand to live out here in the country full time."

"And the million dollar answer is?"

"The answer is 'no'," Sarah answered pointedly. "I couldn't stand all this peace and quiet."

"What?"

"I'd go crazy in a few weeks but you already knew that because you know me," Sarah replied evenly. "But on the other hand, I can't ever see myself living the fast-paced, heavy-on-the-nightlife lifestyle I used to; so I had to find a compromise."

"You're not one for compromise either," Nadine added accusingly as her eyebrows rose in a ruffled frown.

"No, I'm not, but that doesn't mean I can't meld the best of both worlds and make it work," she said, speaking quickly as though afraid of losing her train of thought. "A colleague has been looking for a doctor to take over control of his satellite practice in Northern Virginia. I have my Virginia license because Josh and I had been planning to move there one day to raise a family."

"You mentioned that," Nadine said, not wanting to dwell on the subject.

Sarah fell silent for a few seconds to regain her composure before forging onward.

"I called him and asked if the position is still open and if he wanted me to take over that clinic," she said with so much excitement she was on the verge of babbling. "He was ecstatic because he knows I can run a profitable operation."

"And he just happened to have this position open?" Nadine asked skeptically.

"He's going to open it," Sarah replied plainly. "He hasn't been able to get a decent associate to make that place work in the five years he's owned it. He always hires screw-ups who don't understand what it takes to make a practice profitable."

"So he's going to fire the guy he has working for him now?"

"He was thinking of firing him anyway. Don't worry about it."

Sarah took a minute to regain her composure once again, still breathing rapidly as she contemplated the lifestyle changes she was considering.

"I insisted that I only work Monday through Thursday," she said, having organized her thoughts and was once again warming to the topic. "That gives me three-day weekends to spend at the farm."

"What about the other three days of the week?" Nadine asked. "Can a practice run profitably with it being closed three days out of seven?"

"I'll hire another associate as soon as I get the practice up and running," Sarah said. "It's important to have a doctor covering the entire week."

"And how long do you estimate it'll take you to get the practice up and running to your satisfaction?" Nadine asked incredulously.

"That'll take me about two months, I figure," she said as she turned the plan over in her mind.

"So you're going to work in Northern Virginia?" Nadine asked in astonishment.

"And spend my weekends out here on the farm," she said as her breath continued to come in excited gasps. "I already have my brother-in-law Jeremy, I call him J.T., looking for an apartment for me."

"Now let me get this straight," Nadine said slowly as she tried to digest all that Sarah had just explained to her. "You're going like a possessed woman and I just want to make sure all the pieces fit. You're going to work in Northern Virginia and then spend your weekends out here?"

"Yep! An apartment in the suburbs, very busy and congested suburbs, I might add. Then I'll have a farm out in the country for long weekends. No grass to mow or maintenance to perform at the apartment but all kinds of chores to do on the farm."

"And if Minnie won't sell you the farm at a price you'll accept?"

"Then I'll find another farm. She doesn't have the only one that's for sale, I'm sure."

"And you think you'll be able to keep up with all the demands of a farm only working it during the weekends?" Nadine asked in a voice heavy with disbelief.

"Exactly," Sarah said. "Remember what Minnie said about the guy she has farming the cultivated land? He also cuts her grass and that's the biggest job needing to be done on a weekly basis with the entire property."

"Honey, there's a lot more to running a farm than harvesting crops and mowing the grass," Nadine said in a condescending tone.

"Every other job can either be hired out to a professional if it's too big for me or I'll be able to work on it over a number of weekends," she continued on undeterred.

"Oh, by the way, I also called the County Extension Service and I have them helping me determine if the farmer is taking advantage of Minnie's generosity."

"You are something else!" Nadine said as her eyes flew wide open.

"I may be able to get someone else to farm the fifty acres with a deal more profitable for me, maybe pay the taxes on the entire property instead of just covering half the taxes, and still have enough left over to pay someone to cut the grass," she explained.

Nadine could only stare wide-eyed. "You certainly are a business person if I ever met one!"

"It's only thinking things through and discovering all the possibilities that may occur then picking the most likely to succeed," Sarah stated flatly.

"Oh, and another thing. When I talked to J.T., he told me I could establish residency in Virginia within 183 days then I can apply for my concealed carry permit."

"So what are you going to do between now and then?"

"I'm going to take three weeks' vacation before I start work at the clinic," Sarah beamed triumphantly. "Until then I'm going to ARI-1. I called while I was up on the mountain and gave them a credit card number to hold my reservation so now I'm all set for the course."

"You've been busy today," Nadine said with a smile.

"If you don't mind, I'd like to keep your place as my base of operations until I'm able to get everything settled," Sarah said with a questioning tone in her voice as she scrunched her face up in a cute, girlish expression.

"Of course, you're welcome to stay whenever and as long as you want to, you know that," Nadine replied sincerely. "Besides, I have to see how this is all going to play out."

"Will you come with me to look at Minnie's property?" Sarah asked as she changed subjects without taking a breath. "Two sets of eyes are better than one and you know what to look for in the outbuildings."

"I wouldn't miss it for the world!" Nadine said enthusiastically. "I love helping you spend your money."

They laughed giddily, smiled at each other, then allowed their conversation to lag into silence as each concentrated on their iced tea and allowed their minds to drift.

CHAPTER 21

SARAH'S LIFE MENDS

"It was nice of you to come along to the hardware store to help me find the fixtures I need for those leaky faucets at the house," Sarah said to Nadine as they drove down a lonely two-lane country road. The daisies and tiger lilies lining the roadway were in full bloom and gave a picturesque quality to the unraveling scenery.

"I'm happy to have time to catch up with you," Nadine said. "You've been way too busy trying to get your apartment and farmhouse together at the same time."

"And rejuvenate a practice. It was in shambles," Sarah added tiredly. "Taking on that flagging business was more than I'd bargained for. It took the better part of the winter before I was able to hire an associate to work the weekends and that put me behind getting settled at the farm."

"How about the farm?" Nadine asked. "Was that more work than you had bargained for also?"

"No, it actually came together pretty well and within expectations. I'm thinking of remodeling the entire house once I get settled in a little better. I just want to keep it functional for now."

"Were there many things that needed attention?"

"No, Minnie took pretty good care of the house but there are definitely some repairs she put off doing."

"And your apartment's working well for you?"

"It's great," she said, brightening noticeably as she warmed to the discussion. "It's a nice area with lots of stores. I can get just about anything I need within a fifteen minute drive."

"How do you handle making the switch from the routine you have here at the farm and when you're living in the city?"

"I get up at five o'clock or so to run a mile around my apartment complex then shower and begin my day feeling invigorated," she said. "Then I dash off to church or to the office depending on the day."

"Church?" Nadine asked incredulously.

"Believe it or not, I actually go to church two mornings each week," she replied. "I joined St. Boniface, the church J.T. and Stephanie go to, and began attending morning service."

"You? In Church?

"Yes," Sarah replied huffily. "Me in church. Is that such a terribly hard thing to believe?"

"It's certainly not something I would have expected from you in the past."

"Well, it's me now," she said with a smile. "I even join women from the church on Thursdays for breakfast at the Double J Diner before dashing off to the office."

"Interesting. If you want to, you can come to dinner at my place tonight and fill me in on the details," Nadine said with a disarming grin. "It's not as hopping as a visit with your church buddies but the food is plentiful."

"I'll bring the wine," Sarah replied. "And I have a loaf of nice crusty French bread from a little bakery around the corner from my apartment."

"That sounds like it'll go well with the chili I have slow-cooking in the crockpot," Nadine said cheerfully. "And if you want to go to the Baptist church down in Rapine with me this Sunday, it would give you a chance to meet some of the people from around here. It's time you began expanding your sphere of friends in this area."

"You? Going to church?"

"We all change as we go through life, don't we?" she said as she flashed a knowing smile.

They just crested a hill when Sarah saw a Golden Retriever puppy run from the side of the road at the bottom of the grade and begin trotting in circles while wagging his tail furiously and barking energetically at their vehicle.

"Watch out!" Sarah screamed as her right hand flew to brace herself against the dashboard of the pick-up truck.

Nadine slammed on the brakes hard enough to throw their bodies against the seat belts. The heavy vehicle glided gently to a mildly jolting stop. The last Sarah saw of the prancing floppy-eared canine was of him disappearing below her line of sight in front of the truck.

"Oh my God! You hit him!" she screamed as she battled clumsily to free herself from the restraining shoulder harness. Her fumbling fingers finally found the door handle as she awkwardly hurled herself out of the truck.

Before she could fight her way past the swinging door and front fender she was met headlong by the trouncing form of an out-of-control-with-delight puppy whose roly-poly body shook with each bounding leap.

She was so elated to see he was unharmed, she stooped and almost scooped him into her arms but froze when she saw how filthy his matted coat was.

"He's a mess!" she said with disgust.

"Is he OK?" Nadine asked when she ran panting from her side of the truck.

"He's fine," Sarah said simply. "But look how muddy and knotted his hair is!"

"And he stinks!" Nadine said as she shielded her nose with the back of her left hand. "Does he have a collar?"

"No, at least I can't see one," Sarah said, unwilling to search through the smelly mass of hair surrounding the puppy's mane.

"That doesn't surprise me," Nadine said evenly. "Most farm dogs don't."

"How do we find who he belongs to?" Sarah asked as she squirmed to avoid having the odoriferous beast's prancing paws soil her fashionable jeans.

"There's a farmhouse down the road about a quarter mile," Nadine said as her searching eyes spied a building on the horizon. "It looks like that's the most likely candidate. Let's load this little guy into the back of the pick-up."

"How are we going to do that?" Sarah asked skeptically. "I mean, without getting all smelly and muddy."

"There is no other way," Nadine said succinctly. "We can't leave him here in middle of the road to get run over by the next vehicle that comes along."

"That's not an option," Sarah replied in agreement. "Let's get smelly and muddy."

Sarah enticed the puppy to follow her toward the back of the truck while Nadine lowered the tailgate with a resounding metallic thud.

"He's obviously well fed with all that fat on him," Nadine said as she stood watching the frolicking dog. "I wonder if he was dumped out here because he's too active."

"Forget about him being fat," Sarah said with an exasperated tone in her voice. "Which end do you want?"

"I'll take the back," Nadine said. "The front seems to be preoccupied with jumping on you."

"Good choice," Sarah said as she reached down to grasp the overactive canine while trying to keep her face away from his flailing front paws and lashing tongue.

"He's going to jump out of there," Nadine said critically after dumping him on the tailgate. "We better tie him to the load tie-downs on the sides of the truck if we expect to get him to the farmhouse."

"Another good idea," Sarah replied as she reached for a coil of jute rope riding in the bed of the pick-up. "I better ride back here with him so he'll stay calm. Please try to avoid as many bumps as you can."

"Put those tarps over here for him to lie on," Nadine instructed as she pointed to the other side of the pick-up's bed. "You'll want to squat on your feet to help absorb the bumps you're so worried about."

Sarah's bouncing ride in the ribbed steel bed of the pick-up was much wilder than she thought it would be. The stiff springs of a pick-up truck like the Ford F-150 were designed for carrying heavy loads and transmitted shock waves from every pothole in the crater-rutted dirt lane directly to her legs.

This is lunacy but he's calmed down just knowing I'm here. The poor little guy is just lonely. He must have been frantic being alone out there.

"I see someone down by the barn. I'm heading down there," Nadine yelled out the driver's side window of the truck hoping Sarah could hear over the whipping wind.

When she hit the brakes Sarah lost her balance and flew into the rear window of the truck. Before they slid to a complete stop on the dusty lane, a man with a creased, weather-beaten face dressed in light tan Carhartt coveralls appeared at the door of the unpainted barn wiping his hands on a grease-smudged red rag. He needed a shave and did not look happy at seeing the unexpected visitors.

"Hello!" Nadine greeted him without stepping out of her truck.

"Hello," the man answered in a grizzled voice. "What can I help you with?"

"We found this puppy roaming around on the hardtop road and wanted to find his owner before he gets run over."

Sarah remained silent while the puppy tried to climb into her lap and share his stench with her. The man kept flicking his eyes toward her but did not address her.

"He's not our dog," he replied as his ogling eyes flitted over her again.

"Do you have any idea who may be missing a dog from around here?"

"Nope," he replied noncommittally. "And I don't want him around here."

"There's a problem with this dog?"

"With any stray dog," the man replied as he stuffed the greasy rag into his back pocket. "He was probably dropped off by someone from the city. They think some 'kindly old farmer' will take their rejects in," he said with a heavy dose of sarcasm in his voice. "But feed costs a lot of money we don't have so I don't want him around here."

"If you don't know who owns him, I'm not sure what to do with him then."

"I don't want him," the man said again. "Just keep him away from here so he's not chasing my steers. That'll kill my livestock and I can't afford to lose any."

"We'll figure something out. Thanks for your help."

"What do we do now?" Sarah asked as she hung over the side of the pick-up to address Nadine without having to raise her voice.

"We go to the hardware store and see if any solutions to this problem show up."

"Well, I'm riding with you," Sarah said as she began dismounting the pick-up. "I can't handle riding back here. He'll be just fine."

The rest of the trip was uneventful but the puppy began straining wildly at the rope tether and yipping loudly when Nadine and Sarah disappeared into the double glass fronted doors of the hardware store.

Sarah continued checking on the puppy every few minutes while they were in the hardware store. Each time the pup saw her he would begin his gyrating antics anew.

By the time we get out of here she'll have added an additional twenty minutes to our shopping trip just from checking on that puppy so many times, Nadine thought.

The clerk who assisted them seemed to have an uncanny ability to identify the various rusty bits and pieces of plumbing they brought and replaced them with shiny new parts from huge bins scattered throughout the store.

"Will you ladies need any tools or adhesives to finish these jobs?" he asked politely.

"No, I think we have everything we need to get things back together," Nadine said as she flashed him a warm smile.

"I'll just ring up your items then," he said as he walked behind the ancient wooden checkout counter situated to the right side of the front door. A state-of-the-art computerized cash register perched prominently at the farthest end seemed oddly out of place in the old country-style store.

While Nadine was placing their purchases behind the seat of the pick-up, she noticed Sarah was greeting the puppy with as much enthusiasm as he welcomed her.

"Well, that's rather telling," she crooned with a sly look in her eye.

"What do you mean?" Sarah asked.

"You know exactly what I mean," Nadine replied. "He's your dog and now you have to figure out what to do with him."

"Rex is not my dog," she retorted snippily.

"Rex?" Nadine replied. "You gave him a name and still deny that you've just adopted a stray hound?"

"He's not a hound," Sarah said testily. "At least I don't think Golden Retrievers are considered to be hounds."

Sarah broke down laughing and looked at Nadine with pleading eyes.

"OK, so we've adopted a dog."

"So what are you planning to do with this non-hound retriever named 'Rex?'" Nadine asked. "And what is this 'we' stuff?"

"I figure I'll be responsible for his feed bill, veterinary costs, and all other expenses," Sarah said thoughtfully. "He'll live with me when I'm at my farm on the weekends and he can live with you when I return to work in the suburbs, if that sounds OK to you."

"I think that will be OK," Nadine said thoughtfully as she weighed the ramifications of what she was agreeing to. "As long as he doesn't chase my horses or chickens. If he does, he loses his happy part-time home."

"It should work out well because he'll have the run of two different farms with a changing cast of owners taking care of him."

"Well," Nadine said in resignation. "Let's head over to the feed store for all the stuff you'll need to care for him."

"Yeah," Sarah consented. "We'll need a lot of brushes and dog shampoo. I think we'll have to use scissors to cut most of that matted hair off him."

"We'll probably get enough hair off him to knit a Chihuahua," Nadine joked.

"A big, fat Chihuahua," Sarah added with a chuckle.

In the next six months, Rex grew into ninety pounds of energetic, brilliantly glistening Golden Retriever. Daily grooming with Nadine's horse brushes contributed greatly to his radiant coat. He remained trim even though he had an astronomical daily caloric intake of puppy chow because his self-appointed job of protecting the farms from intruders of all types kept him busy twenty-four hours a day.

CHAPTER 22

COYOTES WILL BE COYOTES

Sarah and Nadine were just settling down after stacking hay and tending to the horses at The Shire. They had hurried with the chores to save time at the end of the day to shoot pistols on Nadine's range behind the barn.

"We only managed to fit in a half-hour of shooting, but it was a welcome break at the end of such a busy day," Sarah said. "I was glad to get a chance to sight in my new gun."

"That's why a lot of folks like to end their day with a little bit of target practice," Nadine replied. "It's relaxing and a whole bunch healthier for you than watching TV."

"How's dinner coming?" Sarah asked. "I'm starting to get hungry."

"The hot Italian sausage has to cook in the spaghetti sauce for at least another forty-five minutes," Nadine said. "Why don't you mix up a few sundowners and we'll sit under the maple tree."

"That's the best idea you've had all day," she replied. "The weather tonight should be just about perfect to sit outside though we may need some light jackets later."

After mixing their drinks they settled into Adirondack chairs facing westward to watch the sun as it dipped toward the horizon. The first few minutes were spent in silence as they absorbed the peace and quiet of the evening.

"You did pretty well out there on the range today," Nadine said after a few minutes had gone by. "Your shooting has really improved."

"Chauncey and I set up a range at the edge of the woods on the back of my farm," Sarah explained. "We shoot .22s at least once a week."

"I didn't think Chauncey was allowed to handle a gun," Nadine stated.

"He can't buy or own a gun because he doesn't have positive identification to prove he's not a felon," Sarah explained. "On the other hand, since there's no proof he is a felon there isn't any prohibition against him handling firearms."

"That makes sense," Nadine said in agreement. "How do you pay him if he doesn't have a last name or social security card?"

"There are millions of illegal aliens working and getting paid in this country every day," she replied without further explanation.

A moment of silence enveloped them as they searched for a topic that would not be of such a sensitive nature. Suddenly, without warning, Rex lunged from beside Sarah's chair where he had been lying peacefully and ran hell-bent for the woods on the far side of the pasture.

"What the hell's up with him?" Nadine asked. Then she heard them.

"Coyotes!" she yelled, starting forward.

"Oh no!" Sarah cried. "He's going after the coyotes. They'll kill him if they get hold of him!"

"Grab a gun and let's go get him," Nadine bellowed with a twinge of fear evident in her voice.

Sarah bolted for the range bag she left on the side of Nadine's porch. It only took her a few seconds to locate the Para Ordnance Companion she had been breaking in with target ammunition.

"It's lucky I sighted this thing in with the Cor-Bon Pow'RBall ammo I plan on carrying for self-defense," Sarah yelled over her shoulder as Nadine raced inside to retrieve her .222 Remington rifle.

"You go - I'll catch up," Nadine yelled without looking back as she ran into the recesses of the house.

Sarah thumbed six of the fat .45 ACP cartridges into a magazine and shoved it into the butt of the pistol, racked the slide, and flipped the safety upward into the 'on' position with her right thumb. She dumped a handful of the stubby cartridges and an empty magazine into the left rear pocket of her jeans in case she needed them.

Racing across the yard, she contemplated turning the electric fence off but decided against it.

It'll take too long. I better just slither under the wire.

Jamming the Companion into the rear waistband of her jeans, she slid onto her belly and hurriedly inched her way under the fence. Three of the horses stood nearby and watched her with bored amusement.

Stay low! If you touch that wire with your back it'll light you up.

With only the lower half of her body left to pull beneath the electrified fence, she placed her left hand into a warm, steamy pile of fresh horse manure. In an unthinking, reflexive action she pulled her hand up at the same time she raised her body to get away from the offending material.

SNAP!

The electric jolt hit the side of her lower back with a mind-numbing detonation of pain that dazzled her nervous system like a jangled mass of quivering spaghetti. It took her a few seconds lying flat on her belly in the fragrant meadow to regain her composure.

Crawl like a soldier on your belly using your elbows to move forward. Move slowly. Keep your butt low. Don't let the pistol touch the wire or it'll fry your ass.

Just after Sarah cleared the fence and stood shakily on the other side, looking vacantly at the smeared manure covering the front of her shirt and jeans, she heard the snarling and yipping of coyotes interspersed with Rex's barking. It only took a few seconds for Rex's growls of bravado to turn to yelps of pain and terror.

Oh shit! They're killing him!

Fear caused Sarah's heart to beat faster. Her legs began pumping up and down as she haltingly sprang into a run.

Calm down and run faster. Don't let excitement make your heart beat faster and use your oxygen more quickly. You run a mile every day, you can make it! Lengthen your stride!

I'll never get there in time!

Run faster! Must run faster!

The edge of the woods loomed forbiddingly in Sarah's path like an impenetrable wall of black vegetation.

Damned it's dark in there!

Her flying feet took her past the slightly brighter border of the pasture and into the shadowy realm of the forest.

At least it'll be easy to find them with the racket they're making. Unless they kill Rex then it'll be quiet and I'll never find him.

Sarah's legs pumped with renewed vigor as she dodged between trees and vaulted over fallen logs. Vines tore at her arms, face, and neck as though they were alive.

There they are! Oh shit! There're six of them!

It only took a split second to realize that every time Rex tried to flee or attack one of the coyotes the others lunged in to rip at his unprotected belly and hindquarters.

Oh no! He's covered with blood!

Trying to ignore the gore staining Rex's golden coat, she slid to a stop behind a locust tree, her breath coming in wheezing gasps as watery snot ran from her nose onto her upper lip. Her mouth and throat were dry as crunchy leaves.

Rest the side of your hand on the tree to steady your aim or you'll miss for sure. You're breathing much too heavily for accurate off hand shooting. Don't rest your gun on the tree, just your hand.

No sooner had she steadied herself than two of the frenzied coyotes immediately launched into a full throttle charge directly at her. Their brilliantly white canine teeth hung like opposing daggers and seemed to glow in the deepening shadows of the forest.

Don't fixate on them, get your pistol up and ready!

The thoughts had barely formed in her mind before the Companion came up to eye level seemingly on its own volition. Sarah subconsciously allowed her training to take over. Her actions were governed by the lessons she ingrained into her muscles and nervous system with redundant drills.

Taking aim on the smaller of the two coyotes, a reddish-brown female with a white-flecked face, Sarah unleashed a .45 caliber pill of devastation.

BAM!

The model 1911 variant pistol bucked in her hands as a 165-grain Pow'Rball bullet left the muzzle at 1,225 feet per second and slammed into the female's right shoulder between her neck and shoulder blade. The bullet ranged lengthwise through her body burrowing a path of destruction as the Pow'Rball expanded to .68 caliber before coming to rest against her diaphragm.

The result was instantaneous.

She fell onto her nose with her hind legs pumping wildly but uselessly at the carpet of fallen leaves littering the forest floor in a nervous reaction caused by instantaneously meeting death.

The second coyote, a large grayish-black coated male, continued his attack, coming in fast and low to the ground. Using the tree for cover, Sarah smoothly aligned the front sight with the crown of his onrushing head.

Concentrate on the front sight. Press the trigger smoothly to the rear. Don't jerk it.

The .45 automatic bucked in her hand but Sarah's practiced response had the big bore pistol back on target in a millisecond.

Don't think about where your first shot hit, just shoot again. Front sight- BAM!- front sight- BAM!- front sight- BAM!- front sight- BAM!

The evenly spaced roar of the gun's muzzle blast reverberated throughout the wooded hillside. At the sound of her fifth shot the large male ceased to be a threat. The slugs had expanded and dumped all their energy into the yodel dog's vitals. Not a single organ in his thoracic cavity was untouched by the barrage of deadly missiles catapulting through him.

Holy shit! Both coyotes fell within 5 yards of me!

Don't let your mind wander," she admonished herself. *Look for more threats. There were six of them and you only stopped two.*

Her well-learned precautions were commendable but unnecessary. The four remaining coyotes had disappeared like will-o-the-wisps into the gathering murkiness of the rapidly approaching dark.

Sarah allowed herself a quick glance at her pistol and the gravity of her situation fell upon her like a ton of bricks.

Holy shit! It's at slide lock!

The gun's empty! Reload now! Reload!

Her left hand flew to the butt of the pistol to catch the magazine as she hit the release button with her right thumb.

You don't have any loaded magazines! You have to recharge the magazine!

Shove the gun into your waistband to free up both your hands so you can reload.

After using her right hand to jam the Companion into her waistband, her left handed off the empty magazine to her right, then flew to the rear pocket of her jeans to retrieve the loose cartridges she dumped there in her fervor to run to Rex's aid.

Keep looking around while you load the magazine. Don't let your guard down.

Put three cartridges into the magazine from the gun then slam it home so you at least have a loaded pistol then load the other one from your pocket until it's full.

Keep your eyes scanning for the threat to return. Don't bet your life on the coyotes continuing to run away. They could come back just as quickly as they disappeared.

Even with her mental admonitions to remain alert in a 360-degree circle around herself, she realized she had been concentrating on watching Rex limp aimlessly in circles when a sudden rustling of brush behind her caused her heart to jump.

Shit!

She snatched the Companion from her waistband and slammed the half filled magazine into its butt, briskly racked the slide with the strength and speed only possible when danger has the nervous system on high alert, and pivoted from her waist in a continuous blur of motion.

"It's me," Nadine gasped as she laboriously puffed each breath through pursed lips. She was preoccupied with pushing her way through the heavy underbrush, her hands and the knees of her jeans caked with horse manure.

"What's going on?" she asked as she slumped heavily against a poplar tree beside Sarah. "What's happening? What are you shooting at?"

"The coyotes ran away but Rex is injured," Sarah wailed as hot tears began streaming down her sweaty, brush-scratched face. "And I'm beginning to shake like a leaf."

When he heard the voices of his masters Rex ceased his aimless meandering and hobbled up to the two women with an obvious limp hindering his movements.

"Oh my God!" Sarah wailed. "His muzzle is ripped and half his ear is torn off!"

"Oh shit!" Nadine exclaimed as she bolted upright. "Look at his side!"

"Oh no!" Sarah bawled from deep within her throat. "His intestines are falling out!"

She flew to Rex's side while stuffing the .45 into the waistband of her jeans just to the right of midline in the small of her back where it wouldn't be in her way. The coyotes had slashed a foot long gash in Rex's left side.

"OK, we'll need some bandages," Sarah said as she stood up and tore her flannel shirt open, buttons flying in all directions. "We can use this to tie around his middle to hold his intestines in and keep them as clean as possible."

"Oh my God!" Nadine wailed as she unthinkingly threw her manure-encrusted fist to her mouth. "This is horrible!"

"Shut up and give me your shirt," Sarah ordered.

Nadine, realizing in a flash that she was panicking in a situation demanding a cool head, immediately followed Sarah's example and ripped her shirt from her back as the buttons pinged off the crispy leaves on the forest floor.

"What else do you need?" she asked.

"I need you to run back to the house, grab a cell phone to call the veterinarian and get your truck. Meet us at the woods edge out in the pasture," she said. "I'll have to walk Rex out of here because he's too heavy for us to carry."

Nadine turned and ran back to the pasture as fast as she could move, the Remington rifle bouncing wildly against her back as it flailed about on its sling.

"Don't worry, Rex," Sarah crooned to him in soothing tones. "I'll get you out of here."

His loving and trusting eyes met hers and she had to turn away to avoid breaking down in tears.

"Stand still now," she said calmly. "And let me tie these shirts around your middle."

He cooperated by standing placidly while Sarah tied the shirts tightly around his middle. He whimpered pitifully when she tightened the second shirt around his midsection.

"I know boy," she said quietly. "It hurts but we'll get you taken care of."

"OK boy," she said soothingly. "Now let's walk out of these woods and get to the pasture while there's still enough light to get a better look at you."

By the time they got to the pasture it was almost pitch dark under the canopy of trees in the woods.

Thank God we got to the pasture when we did. If it took any longer we'd be stumbling around the woods in the dark. This is not the time to get lost.

The coyotes began howling from half way up the mountain. A shiver slithered down Sarah's back as Rex began whimpering pathetically and moved closer to her.

"Rex, lay down," she said, pointing to a grassy spot beside where she had flopped on the ground just outside the edge of the woods. "I'll finish loading my magazines and make sure we have enough firepower to keep those bastards at bay."

Keep talking to him in subdued tones; it'll keep him calm. Hell, it'll keep you calm.

Suddenly the headlights of Nadine's pick-up truck flashed across the pasture and began bouncing wildly toward them. Sarah stood up and began flailing her arms high over her head. The radiant glow of her white bra bouncing frantically in the glowing illumination of the headlights allowed Nadine to feverishly guide the pick-up truck directly to them.

"Put this on," she called as she threw a shirt toward Sarah. "Then help me spread this horse blanket on the ground and we'll use it as a litter to lift him into the bed of the truck."

It was a difficult maneuver for the two women to lift ninety pounds of dead weight into the bed of the pick-up but the Golden Retriever tolerated the handling with only a single, muted moan when his bulk thumped onto the hard steel flooring.

"OK, let's tie him to the sidewall of the bed to keep him from panicking and jumping out then we'll be on our way," Nadine said. "The vet is expecting us."

"Let me spread this other blanket over him to keep the wind off," Sarah said. "He shouldn't be stressed any more than necessary in his weakened condition."

As they leaped onto the front seat of the truck Sarah said, "Drive safely, there's no need to speed on these winding country roads."

"Yeah, running into a slow moving tractor won't do us any good," Nadine said in agreement.

The journey to the veterinarian's office was uneventful other than Sarah frequently turning around to watch Rex through the sliding rear window of the pick-up's cab.

Bursting into the reception area of the veterinarian's office, Sarah almost ran headlong into a stately woman bustling out to greet them.

The veterinarian, Maggie Sjostrom, was a tall, willowy twenty-six year-old woman of Norwegian extraction with her long blonde hair pulled tightly into a bun on back of her head. The combination of blonde hair and white lab coat caused her pasty complexion to wash out in the flickering glow of the fluorescent bulbs in the reception room.

The young veterinarian was not the least bit alarmed to see two women, one with the butt of a .45 automatic peeking out of the waistband of her jeans, arrive in disarray at her office with an injured Golden Retriever.

"Let me guess," Sarah said in the manner of a greeting. "You're the junior member of the practice so you get the privilege of covering evenings over the weekend."

"Is it that evident?" Maggie asked with a flashing smile.

"I've been there and done that," Sarah replied.

"I graduated last year but I'm perfectly capable of handling all manner of animal emergencies," Maggie assured her.

"I have no doubt you are," Sarah replied with confidence in her voice. "The best I can tell, he has a gash on his left abdomen with protruding intestines and lacerations on his muzzle and left ear."

"OK, I'll check him out after we get him up on the exam table," she said as she looked past Sarah and out into the parking lot. She saw Nadine lowering the truck's tailgate and offering solace to a sick looking but friendly Golden Retriever.

Rex slowly raised his massive head and licked Nadine's hand.

"I'll get a transport board. It'll be easier for us to use than the blankets you have him lying on."

Sarah and Nadine heaved the transport board with Rex securely strapped to it onto the stainless steel examination table. The penetrating light from the bank of halogen bulbs suspended above the table allowed Dr.Sjostrom to determine his wounds were serious but not life threatening.

"This will go much faster and easier if you help me," she said looking into the eyes of the women to see their reaction. "Do you think you can do that?"

"I'm a Doctor of Chiropractic and have been through all the courses for this type of work but it's been years since I've worked with any of the gooey parts," Sarah said evenly.

"And I always help Mitch when he comes to work on my horses so I'm used to the 'gooey' work as my esteemed friend here refers to it," Nadine replied with a smile, her attitude relaxing in the presence of Maggie's confident demeanor.

"Good," Maggie said with enthusiasm. "Let's get started."

"I'll need to use a general anesthesia to knock him out otherwise he won't let us work on him; particularly when we get around that muzzle area," Maggie said while looking at Sarah. "And he may bite us, any of us, when we try shaving around his mouth and nose.

"What are your names?"

"I'm Sarah Collins and this is Nadine Brand," she responded while slightly nodding her head toward Nadine.

Maggie strung a vinyl bag of clear solution from a stainless steel stand, positioned the stand at the head of the table then inserted a small needle into a vein in Rex's right front leg. She then carefully measured a minute amount of clear fluid into a syringe and injected it into the plastic tube.

"He'll begin to relax in about three seconds," she said. "Then we can shave the hair from around the wounds, clean them up with antiseptic, and sew them up."

Before she was finished explaining the sequence of events Rex closed his eyes and began breathing deeply.

She moved down to the belly area and shook her head.

"What a mess," she said. "But it's not as bad as it looks."

"Meaning what exactly?" Sarah snapped with a little more edge in her voice than she would have liked.

"Meaning," Maggie continued, nonplussed, "That there's only one small hole in the intestines. That's not bad at all considering how long and ragged this tear in his belly skin is."

"That's good then," Nadine said in an attempt to appease Sarah's fear.

"It will take about ten minutes to shave his belly, another ten to suture the intestine and cleanse the area, then another ten to close him up," Maggie said evenly.

"Let's get to it then," Sarah said with resignation sounding heavily in her voice.

Twenty-five minutes later Maggie snipped the last thread from Rex's belly.

"Now let's have a look at his muzzle and ears," she said simply before moving toward his head. "In another fifteen minutes we'll be done and have an almost-like-new dog resting comfortably."

"Let's finish up," Sarah said flatly.

"Sarah, can you please hold this oxygen mask near his mouth and nose?" Maggie inquired pleasantly. "Just keep it about an inch from his nose so I have room to work."

"I'll follow your lead," Sarah said with conviction. "Just tell me what to do."

Maggie examined Rex's muzzle and nose more closely.

"I'll have this cleaned up in a few minutes," she said.

With sure, smooth movements Maggie proceeded to shave the hair from the damaged areas, disinfect the wounds, and then sutured them with deft hands.

"Now we have to move him to a temperature controlled kennel to recover. Call about three o'clock tomorrow afternoon to check on him and he'll be ready to go home the day after if all goes well."

"Thank you, Maggie," Sarah said before breaking down in a torrent of tears with great sobs violently shaking her shoulders.

"Nadine," Maggie said as she ignored Sarah's meltdown. "Help me move him into the kennel then take Sarah home and let her get some rest."

CHAPTER 23

ANOTHER SHOPPING SPREE

"I don't know about you," Nadine said as she wheeled her F-150 off the hardtop road and onto the dirt lane leading into The Shire. "But this has been one harrowing day and I'm too pumped up to go to sleep right away."

"I could use a hamburger cooked over a campfire," Sarah said. "And a couple glasses of red wine as an appetizer would be nice."

"I have some smoked hot-pepper cheese and crackers to go with the wine while we wait for the fire to burn down to embers," Nadine replied with a laugh. "I don't need you drunk as a skunk before the fire's ready for cooking. I'll turn off the slow cooker and we'll have the spaghetti tomorrow. Besides, sauce is always better if it sits overnight."

"I'll call Chauncey at my place and let him know what happened," Sarah said with fatigue evident in her voice. "He worries about me if I'm out too late."

"You two are something else."

"And what's that supposed to mean?"

"I mean that the two of you are like two spinster sisters fretting over each other," Nadine said evenly. "And don't you try to deny it. You two are almost inseparable."

"Well, we do look out for each other," Sarah admitted. "But that may be changing. He has a girlfriend over in Sharpsville."

"Oh really!" Nadine exclaimed. "And how long has this been going on?"

"Oh, he's been seeing her socially at the Baptist church there for a while," Sarah said. "Her name's Annie. I don't know her last name."

"Well good for him," Nadine replied enthusiastically.

Two hours later they were vacantly staring into the embers of a dying fire with full bellies and the remnants of a bottle of Merlot sloshing in the bottom of their glasses.

Sarah shifted in her chair and had to use her right hand to move her holster around the plastic arm of the folding aluminum chair to get more comfortable. The Kydex holster held the relatively new Para-Ordnance Companion .45 she used on the two coyotes that rushed at her in the forest. It was stoked full with fresh ammunition.

Nadine carried her Glock 19 that was none the worse for wear-and-tear since Sarah borrowed it to complete the ARI-1 course.

It was a great comfort to both of them knowing they had a means of protecting themselves and their animals immediately at hand especially considering the events that had unfolded earlier in the evening.

Sarah was eyeing Nadine's AR-15 leaning against the woodpile, its chamber empty but its thirty round magazine full and ready to load a .223 cartridge with the flick of a wrist.

"So what do you think?" Nadine asked with no particular topic in mind. The silence was irritating her and she wanted to begin a conversation.

"What do I think about what?" Sarah asked with a bit of irritation in her voice for having her quiet reverie interrupted.

"Oh, I don't know. Coyotes, country living, life in general. The usual stuff," Nadine finished, not sure if she really wanted to chat now that she knew Sarah was agitated.

"I think these predators; whether they're coyotes or otherwise, are beginning to really get on my nerves," Sarah stated emphatically.

"Well, you have to learn to live with them one way or another," Nadine replied.

"No, I have a right to be here. They're going to have to learn to live with me and I'm going to set the rules."

"And how do you propose to do that, Oh Master of the Universe?" Nadine asked with a chuckle.

"I'm planning on instilling the fear of Man back into those animals. At least the fear of Woman, as the case may be," Sarah said with a steely smile crossing her lips. "What's the name of that black rifle sitting over there?"

"The AR-15?" Nadine asked, trying to figure out what Sarah was talking about.

"It's a Bush something," she continued, racking her fatigued brain for more information to describe the rifle.

"Yeah, it's my Bushmaster. At least Bushmaster is the brand name. The type of rifle is called the AR-15, the semi-automatic civilian version of the M-16 the military has used for the last 30 years," Nadine filled in as she wondered where Sarah was going with this conversation. "Why are you interested in the AR-15?"

"I'm interested in it, Oh Nosy One," Sarah said, mimicking her. "Because I think I want one."

Before Nadine could question her further, Sarah verbalized a question of her own. "Where do you learn all this stuff you know about guns?"

"I read a lot."

"No--- seriously."

"I am serious," Nadine replied. "I subscribe to Women and Guns magazine, I'm a member of the National Rifle Association so I get the American Rifleman magazine, and I'm a member of the Second Amendment Foundation and get their Gun Week bi-weekly newspaper as a perk of my membership. Why do you ask?"

"I want to know more than I do about guns and shooting," Sarah explained simply. "I know it's fun because we shoot for recreation and a serious responsibility because of my ARI course but---" she hesitated while her mind searched for the correct words, "I want to know which guns are best for different situations."

"That's easy enough," Nadine said simply. "All it takes is some study. Why do you bring this up now? Because of what happened to Rex?"

"Because after all the shooting was done, and the coyotes had run away, I got scared," Sarah said with her voice rising as her emotions took control of her. "Those coyotes actually came for me! A human being! They're not supposed to try and eat me! I'm at the top of the food chain for crying out loud!"

Sarah was visibly shaking again.

"You're only at the top of the food chain if you have bigger teeth than the other predators," Nadine said in a soothing voice in an attempt to calm her down.

Sarah took a moment to gather her thoughts and relaxed her jangled nerves by taking a deep, cleansing breath.

"That's what I'm talking about," she said in a much calmer voice. "I wasn't so sure if I did have the biggest teeth in the woods; at least for a few terrifying moments out there. Why do I keep shaking like this?" she asked as she held up her trembling hands.

"It's a delayed reaction to the adrenaline leaving your system after a frightening situation," Nadine said calmly. "Every time you think about the event your body experiences the same reaction it did during the crisis."

"Luckily, I had my .45 with me," she continued in an even tone without acknowledging that she heard Nadine's explanation.

"But even with it I felt the coyotes could have taken me if they all attacked at once. I ran my pistol dry just killing two coyotes. What if the others would have attacked instead of running away?" she asked with a quivering voice.

"You're not just traumatized about Rex getting attacked," Nadine realized in a flash. "You had to face the reality of being attacked and you were alone."

Sarah could only drop her head and stare at her hands with a dumbfounded look on her face. A solitary tear dropped onto the front of her jacket.

"You and your .45 did a great job, just like you trained for, and that's why you practice frequently. You never know when the stuff will hit the fan," Nadine said soothingly as she tried to assure her everything was OK.

"The .45 did work well in that situation, at least against the two that attacked me," Sarah said analytically. "But I'm not sure I could have placed all my shots quite so accurately if the whole pack had attacked."

"Your training would have pulled you through," Nadine said half-heartedly.

"After running the situation over in my head a few times I've decided I need something with more firepower than what my pistol offers," she continued. "I want greater magazine capacity than a concealed carry type of pistol offers."

"I can't argue with you wanting another gun," Nadine said. "Exactly what do you expect from an AR-15?"

"I want to be able to shoot any coyote that shows its face on my property or anywhere near it," Sarah replied with conviction. "I may even want to start hunting them to keep their numbers down so they don't get bold enough to attack me or my animals."

"Well, it's a good type of gun for predator hunting," Nadine said as she scrunched her face in thought. "There're a lot of folks that use it for coyotes with excellent results."

"And I assume it's good for human predators considering the military has used it for over thirty years," Sarah surmised.

"Yes it is," Nadine confirmed. "A number of police agencies use it successfully and have gotten almost 100% one-shot stops with it when using hollow point ammunition. That's the same type ammunition you'd use for coyotes."

"What's 100% one-shot stop mean? And where did you learn all of this again?" Sarah asked, showing genuine interest.

"I told you," Nadine said. "I read gun and shooting magazines. I'll even buy you a subscription to a few if you promise to read them."

"Thanks, I'll read them. I promise," she said with a chuckle. "Now, what's this 100% one-shot-stop stuff all about?"

"It simply means that cartridge, when using hollow point bullets, usually takes only one shot to make the aggressor cease their hostile actions."

"So you only have to shoot the bad guy once?" quizzed Sarah.

"Usually," Nadine said. "But remember, in your ARI class they taught you the idea is to stop the aggressor from being hostile."

Nadine took a deep breath and continued with the lesson reminder.

"The objective is not to kill the aggressor even though they may pass away from their wounds," she said. "You only want them to stop being violent and trying to hurt you or a loved one. That's why you should keep shooting until they stop their hostile actions."

"Keep shooting until the threat ceases to be a threat," Sarah confirmed.

"Exactly," Nadine replied. "This particular cartridge and ammunition combination, when fired from a rifle, usually takes only one properly placed round to stop their aggressive action."

Sarah was listening intently, so Nadine continued.

"For example, take your coyotes this afternoon. If they had stopped attacking Rex and ran away you wouldn't have had to shoot them," Nadine explained. "Instead of leaving they started attacking you, which required you to use deadly force against them. Only then did they stop attacking."

Nadine was sure her explanation was sufficient and would satisfy Sarah's curiosity for a while. She was wrong.

"That's what I'm getting at," Sarah said.

"What are you getting at?"

"When those coyotes attacked me, Rex was useless," Sarah replied. "He couldn't even help himself anymore."

"He had his guts hanging out for crying out loud!" Nadine whined loudly in defense of Rex's honor.

"That's my point," Sarah continued unabashedly. "I was on my own and wasn't sure I was armed well enough to handle that many coyotes."

Sarah looked at Nadine and saw the confused look on her face so she continued.

"Don't you see?" she pleaded. "We're usually alone most of our lives. Especially you and I. We're women, and we're on our own with almost no chance of help arriving to get our Skittles out of the fire if anything terrible happens."

"Go ahead," Nadine said as Sarah's message began sinking into her fatigued mind. "I'm following you now."

"So what would happen if human predators like rapists and murderers for two examples, decided they want to treat us like prey? Are we really armed well enough with just a handgun? Or do we need a rifle handy also? Especially out here on the farm where the shooting distance may be more than a few feet. I'd rather take on a predator across the yard than at bad breath distance."

Sarah looked at Nadine with unwavering resolve in her eyes.

"I've thought of that many times," Nadine assured Sarah in subdued tones. "That's why I keep various firearms scattered around my farm. A good gun strikes me as being the best form of feminine protection a woman can have in certain situations."

"I've seen at least two down at the barn," Sarah admitted as she smiled at Nadine's joke.

"I haven't had an experience like yours, and I hope I never do, but I've tried to learn from other people's situations so I don't get into the same trouble they did," Nadine said plainly. "Re-inventing the wheel is not my idea of fun especially when my life or that of my loved ones are on the line."

Sarah smiled at the tolerance and patience Nadine showed her on what seemed like a daily basis.

She'll always be a teacher. When she left the teaching profession years ago, she certainly didn't quit being a teacher.

"So what do we do now?" Sarah asked.

"We go shopping," Nadine said matter-of-factly. You won't be happy until you get yourself an AR-15."

"So, where do we go to buy one?" Sarah asked innocently. "I'm not familiar where many gun stores are around here or what's all involved in buying a gun like this."

"The Conestoga Trading Post has the best selection of ARs that I know of in this area. It's as good of a place to start as any," Nadine said as she mulled the list of local gun dealers around in her mind. "And all you'll need is a government issued form of identification so they can do a background check and enough money to pay for it."

"Oh! I have that in my purse if they'll take a personal check," Sarah replied happily as her eyebrows rose in surprise.

"They open at ten o'clock in the morning. I'll pick you up about nine."

"I just wish they weren't so ugly," Sarah said dejectedly. "Basic black has never been one of my favorite colors."

"Then you're in luck," Nadine said with a laugh. "Now you can get them in every color from aqua to desert camo."

"Cool!"

The next morning when Nadine wheeled into the front yard of Sarah's farm, Chauncey was coming out of the barn, his hands filled with wrenches of various sizes.

"Hello Chauncey!" she greeted him.

"Hello Nadine," he said cordially. "It's nice to see you again."

"Is Sarah around?"

"She's in the house waiting for you," he said. "She'll be out in a minute. She's been chomping at the bit to get moving this morning."

"She's on a mission."

Just then Sarah came out of the house with her purse slung over her shoulder and a spring in her step.

"See you ladies later," Chauncey said as he waved with a wrench-filled fist and smiled at Nadine. "I gave her a list of things I need from the hardware store. Please don't let her forget to pick them up."

"Don't worry," Nadine assured him. "I have a hardware list myself so I'll make sure we get there."

Sarah strode directly to the passenger's door of Nadine's truck, placed her hand on the handle, then turned and said excitedly, "Let's go!"

CHAPTER 24

CHAUNCEY GOES TO
THE HALLELUJAH GATHERING

Chauncey threw his duffel bag into the back seat of Sarah's Chevy 1500 Crew Cab. It was Thursday and he had just commuted on the Metro to Northern Virginia from his apartment in Washington, D.C. to work at Sarah's suburban office.

"Sarah, would it be a major inconvenience if I took off from Wednesday to Sunday the first week of next month?" he asked. "J.T. asked me to help chaperone his church's youth ministry camping trip to the Hallelujah Gathering. Dr. Holmes has already given me Monday and Tuesday off."

"So you're finally taking my advice and vacationing for a few days to recharge your batteries, eh?" Sarah asked emphatically. "You can catch up on everything when you get back. I've told you that before."

"I know you've told me to take some time for myself," he replied. "But I enjoy my jobs so much, and with the long weekends up on the farm it's like I'm always on vacation. Seriously!"

"I'm really glad to see you and J.T. getting along so well," she said. "I think it does both of you some good to have someone to chum around with."

"Well, as you know, I've been visiting his church during the latter part of the week when I'm out this way and help him a little with the kids at youth ministry. The priest even knows my name," he said. "But then I attend the Baptist church near the farm on Sunday. It gives me variety in my spiritual life."

"Not to mention that Annie attends the Baptist church," she said with a smile.

"Well, that may have a little to do with the variety part," he said as he averted his eyes sheepishly toward the ground and tried to stifle a grin.

"So tell me about this Hallelujah Gathering."

"It's a weeklong Christian event up in West Virginia," he replied. "The farm where it's held has camping facilities and everything."

"That sounds interesting," she lied. "I'm sure J.T.'s kids will enjoy it."

"They went last year and couldn't wait to get back this year," he said.

"You won't be sleeping on the ground, will you?" she asked when the chiropractic angle of the trip sunk into her mind. "You might wake up with your back in a major snit."

"No, I won't have to sleep on the ground," Chauncey laughed. "Most of the chaperones wouldn't tolerate that very well. The youth ministry group has camp cots for us. The kids will be on air mattresses with sleeping bags on the ground."

"Well, have a good time," she said with a chuckle. "Just don't get lost in the wilds of West Virginia."

"It should be an experience," he replied without knowing how true his prophecy would be.

CHAPTER 25

THE HALLELUJAH GATHERING

"So what have you gotten me into, J.T.?" Chauncey asked as the church van loaded with camping gear pulled off the interstate onto a two-lane state road.

"You got yourself into it," J.T. replied with a chuckle. "I just asked you if you'd be willing to help chaperone the youth ministry group at the Hallelujah Gathering."

"Well, you've been here before, what can I expect?"

"The Hallelujah Gathering is an annual event that's held on the five hundred acre farm owned by Peter Giovanni," J.T. replied. "It's a mixture of Christian rock concerts, lectures, and good old-time revival meetings for all denominations. It's geared toward teenagers but the adults get a lot out of it."

"Is the campground right on the farm?"

"Peter has set aside two hundred of his acres for the actual events like revival meetings and concert stages," J.T. explained. "And he keeps about a hundred acres for a campground and concessions."

"They don't use the entire farm?"

"No, the rest of the property is the actual working farm and it's off limits to the Hallelujah Gathering participants," he replied. "It's a rule that's strictly enforced to ensure no one is hurt by animals or machinery."

"That makes sense," Chauncey said. "Do we have reservations at the campground or do we just take what's available when we get there?"

"Actually, we aren't staying on the farm."

"We're not?"

"We're staying on the Hager farm across the road from Peter Giovanni's place."

"Why?"

"It's very crowded in the campground Peter has set aside and that makes it miserable in this sticky, humid weather," J.T. replied. "We'll use the concessions at the Gathering but it's much nicer camping at the Hager's. They also have fewer campers so it's easier to keep track of the kids. That's important."

"Peter's campground is full?" Chauncey asked. "How many people will be attending this event?"

"The first weekend is the busiest with about seven thousand attendees," he replied. "But it'll fall off to half that for the rest of the week."

"It's going to be a mess with that many people jammed into such a small space."

"I told you it would be interesting," J.T. said as he laughed to himself.

CHAPTER 26

RADICAL ISLAMISTS AT THE GATHERING

"You have taken good pictures, Omar," Muhammed Shah, the commander of six terrorist cells secretly living in the United States, said approvingly to his newly-acquainted soldier. "They will give us the information we need to carry out our mission."

"Thank you Commander," Omar said with humility in his voice if not in his heart. "It is very informative to combine the knowledge gleaned from the satellite pictures taken off the Internet with the ones Samir and I took from the ground."

"How did you get such good pictures and detailed information on the property where the Hallelujah Gathering will be held?"

"It was simple, Commander," Omar said as he puffed out his chest proudly. "Samir would drive down the valley in a van with darkened windows and I would be in the back with a camera taking pictures out the partially opened window."

"And these aerial photos?"

"I took those from the top of the mountain overlooking the farm where the Hallelujah Gathering will be held," he explained. "They have been preparing for the event for months so it was easy to see where the various buildings, tents, concert stages, and campgrounds will be located."

"It was not difficult to get to this vantage point?"

"No sir, the road winds across the top of the mountain," he explained. "There are many places to pull to the side and take pictures without being seen."

"You have done well, Omar," he said. "Allah will be happy with your work."

Omar smiled broadly at the praise his commander was bestowing upon him.

"And you have mapped the prevailing winds?"

"Yes Commander," he replied enthusiastically, sure he was due more praise. "We dispensed puffs of talcum powder from a plastic bottle to monitor the winds all along the dirt road bordering the property where the Hallelujah Gathering will be held."

"According to the arrows you drew on this map, the winds blow from the dirt road directly across the grounds where the infidels will be performing their barbaric worship ceremonies?"

"Yes, Commander," he replied proudly. "The winds always blew the same way every time we tested them."

"Allah is smiling upon us," Muhammed said. "We will kill and injure many thousands of the Christian infidels. It is especially important since most of them are of warrior age."

"Commander, is it too early for you to tell us the plan?" Samir asked respectfully.

"It is time to give you the details," Muhammed said. "Three dark colored vans will be stolen to transport cylinders of mustard gas. The vans will move from the head of the valley under the cover of darkness down the dirt road you reconnoitered. The van I will be driving will have four mustard gas canisters and the others will carry three. Each vehicle will stop at a designated landmark and begin placing cylinders approximately every thirty meters as you move down the road."

"Will thirty meters be close enough to cover the entire grounds with the gas?"

"Yes, the eddying winds will swirl the gas around so it is spread far and wide."

"Won't the gas just rise up into the sky and be rendered useless?"

"No, Samir, the gas is heavier than air and will hug the ground as it is carried along. That is the way it was designed for use in the American's World War I."

"And what landmarks will be designated to begin dropping the cylinders, Commander?"

"The first van in line will be driven by Jaafar with Basel in back handling the gas cylinders," Muhammed informed them.

Pointing to a spot on the map with a gnarly forefinger, Muhammed continued, "He will stop here at the dead tree with the bark peeled off. You can see it on this picture right here. Basel will then jump from the van and place the first cylinder upright at the base of the tree. Remember to keep the tanks upright so the gas is released upward to get maximum dispersal."

"Will we be opening the cylinders to release the mustard gas immediately after setting them on the ground?" Basel asked seriously.

"Yes," Muhammed replied. "I want the gas to begin drifting across the fields as soon as possible in case there are problems."

"And what will I be doing, Commander?" Omar asked.

"You, Omar, will be in back of the second van with Samir driving," Muhammed replied as he motioned in Samir's direction. "He will stop here at this small machine shed to place your first cylinder then set the other two every thirty meters."

"That leaves you and me, Commander," Waseem said.

"I will be driving the third van with you in the back," Muhammed said. "We will stop here to place the first cylinder at the edge of the campground where the tents begin. Then we will place them every thirty meters. The mustard gas should cover the entire Hallelujah Gathering. I am particularly interested in the gas reaching the campground and concert areas."

"And the gas will be carried across the Hallelujah Gathering grounds by the wind," Omar said in astonishment.

"The plan is simplicity itself," Samir said with equal astonishment. "And when will this take place, Commander?"

"Satuday evening at ten o'clock," Muhammed said definitively. "Over 7,000 infidels will be gathered at the Christian rock music concert or moving about the grounds. It is the main attraction of the weeklong event. The gas should totally cover the entire Gathering at a time when the attendees are tired and most vulnerable. That fact alone will add many more casualties to the count."

"How did you learn about the specifics of what transpires at The Gathering?" Samir asked inquisitively.

"I looked it up on the Hallelujah Gathering website. The fools put information that is very important to our success on the Internet," Muhammed said with a laugh rumbling deeply in his belly. "They advertise their weaknesses!"

Muhammed continued, "They begin their day with a sunrise worship service and stay busy all day long. This leads to inattention and makes it more difficult for the infidels to think or react while under stress of an attack."

"That is excellent."

"Yes, Omar," Muhammed said expansively. "Such knowledge will allow us to add hundreds more casualties to the tally because of their inability to act swiftly in an emergency."

"Praise be to Allah."

CHAPTER 27

EVENING AT THE HALLELUJAH GATHERING

The day had been grueling.

J.T. and Chauncey were hot, sticky, and exhausted from being up since 4:30 a.m. to monitor the activities of the teens from the St. Boniface Youth Ministry group all day.

"So how did we get campsite duty?" Chauncey asked to avoid having to stand up from his folding aluminum chair and begin working again.

"The other counselors wanted to hear the rock band tonight," J.T. replied wearily. "After getting up at 4:30 for the sunrise service then sweating like a Missouri mule all day long, I was happy to have a little quiet time and just do camp chores without having to keep tabs on all the kids."

"And all that mud! I'm so sick and tired of wiping it off my shoes I could scream," Chauncey said emphatically. "Thanks for including me on the camp prep team."

"Not a problem," J.T. replied with a smile. "We really didn't have a choice. Everyone else was dead set on seeing the concert."

"From what I understand, the band is the most popular Christian rock group in the world," Chauncey said. "Apparently a lot of people attending The Gathering are here just to hear them."

"Yeah, Peter says there are an additional 1,500 people here today just to hear the concert," J.T. replied. "Thankfully they're not camping overnight or we'd be crowded right out of this meadow."

"At least there's a nice breeze coming down off the mountain now," Chauncey said as he lifted his face toward the surrounding ridge to allow the chilled draft sliding from the highlands to cool his feverish face. "Jason said we could expect a cool wind to pick up in the evening."

"It always blows down off the mountain in the evening because when the sun goes down the air cools," J.T. replied.

"And cold air falls while hot air rises," Chauncey said, finishing his sentence.

"That's why the evening winds are almost always moving from west to east in this valley," he said picking up where Chauncey left off. "The cool air slides down off the eastern face of that mountain before continuing across the road toward Peter's farm."

"So we get first dibs on the cool air," Chauncey said with a satisfied grin augmenting the peaceful look on his face. "We better get moving if we expect to have this campsite set up when the kids get back."

"Yeah, they'll be hungry so we better make sure we have a fire going for hot dogs," J.T. said.

"Should we divide and conquer or do you think we'll get things done faster if we work together?"

"We may as well work together," J.T. replied. "We'll probably be more efficient and if we get done before the kids return we'll just relax and wait for the onslaught of teenage energy."

"That would be good," Chauncey said. "I don't know how late I'll be staying up tonight; we old guys need our sleep."

"Most of the kids will fall asleep shortly after eating," J.T. replied. "Once their bellies are full, they should sleep like a bunch of logs."

J.T. reluctantly heaved his aching body out of the captain's chair then said, "We should get ice to fill the coolers because when the concert lets out, the concession area will be flooded with wet, muddy, smelly, hopped-up-on-soda kids."

"That's a great idea, especially when you put it in those terms," Chauncey said as he propelled himself from his chair. "Oh brother! Am I stiff!"

"Well, keep moving so you don't freeze in place Tin Man," J.T. joked. "Apparently age and grace do not necessarily go well together."

"You wait, youngster," Chauncey chided him back. "You'll have your turn to be this old."

"In that case, I'll race you to the concession stands," J.T. said with a chuckle.

"You calm down and we'll just mosey on over there," Chauncey replied while he returned J.T.'s laugh. "We have to conserve our energy to carry all that ice back here. You'll learn things like that with a little more experience."

"Yeah, right," J.T. said with a chuckle. "Hey! Let me show you something experience has taught me. Come on, let's go."

"Do we need a flashlight?" Chauncey asked as he looked up the hill. "We've sat here so long it's gotten pretty dark."

"I have my SureFire light in case we need it but that moon is half-full and should give us plenty of light to see our way through the meadow."

The two men walked stiffly up the slight rise leading from Hager's meadow to the Gathering campground. When they reached the top of the rise J.T. stopped, raised his arms so they were held out straight from his body, and began twirling in a circle.

"Uh! Oh! Now he's lost it," Chauncey said jokingly as he laughed lightly.

"I haven't lost it," J.T. said as he slowed his twirling then stopped and looked directly at Chauncey. "Can't you feel it?"

"Feel what?"

"See this little rise in the road between the Hager and Giovanni farms?" he asked. "It directs that wind you were talking about upward and makes it seem cooler than the slightly lower areas surrounding this little knoll."

"Now that you mention it, it does seem a little cooler, or is it just my imagination now that you've put the idea in my mind?"

"It's not your mind playing tricks on you," J.T. replied. "I always like to stand here for a few minutes and let the nice cool breeze wash the stench of the day away."

"It is a nice, peaceful place to take a rest," Chauncey said agreeably.

"Usually there's no traffic on this road after the activities start but here comes a convoy," J.T. observed as he stood looking up the otherwise deserted road.

"There are only three vehicles," Chauncey noted as his gaze followed J.T.'s stare. "Does that constitute a convoy?"

"I guess not," J.T. replied. "But we'll stay here enjoying the breeze until they pass then we'll go get the ice. I really hate having my quiet time disturbed."

"Life's rough all over."

"So I hear."

Both men watched in silence as the vans got closer.

"I thought they were traveling together," Chauncey said conversationally. "But that one pulled over and stopped by the edge of the campground. Maybe they're visiting someone."

J.T. remained silent and continued watching the vans intently.

"There's someone getting out of it," J.T. said. "Maybe you're right and they're just visiting."

"Maybe... but see- he's watching the other vans."

"Yeah," J.T. said softly.

"Now the second van is stopping beside that old shed," Chauncey said quizzically. "And the guy from the first van is unloading a canister and setting it up on the side of the road."

"If they're delivering propane tanks to the concession area you'd think they'd pull right up to the stand to avoid a lot of heavy lifting.

They sure as hell wouldn't be leaving them in a deserted field," J.T. said suspiciously. "What the hell's going on here?"

"I don't know but now there's a guy getting out of the van by the shed."

"And the van now at the front has pulled all the way down to that old, dead tree," J.T. noted. "Peter said he was going to cut that tree down this year but he obviously didn't get around to it."

"I'm sure there are a lot more important things that need to be done on a farm than chopping down dead trees."

"I'm sure there are."

"Now someone has gotten out of each of the vans," Chauncey said observantly. "They all seem to be unloading cylinders and leaving them standing upright on the side of the road."

"There's something strange here," J.T. said as internal warning bells began clanging alarmingly in his mind.

"There's definitely something strange here but I can't put my finger on it," Chauncey said as he took a curious step forward. "They look strange."

"Holy shit! They're wearing gas masks," J.T. whispered in an urgent voice. "And the guy by the tree just ran away from that canister like he expects it to blow up."

"What is it? What are they doing?"

"Chauncey! It's an attack! That's some type of gas!" J.T. cried breathlessly through hushed tones as he stooped down and began pawing at his left pant leg. His groping right hand surrounded the polymer grip of a Glock 26 then gave it a jerk to free it from the DeSantis ankle holster that had kept it concealed all day long.

Thank you Lord for letting Virginia and West Virginia have concealed carry reciprocity otherwise I wouldn't have been armed. Thank you for allowing me to tolerate the sweat and discomfort of having this ankle holster on my leg all day.

This was not the first silent prayer that had flitted across J.T.'s mind today and it certainly wouldn't be the last.

"Go to the Hager farmhouse and tell Jason to call 911. Our cell phones don't have reception way up here in the mountains," J.T. instructed Chauncey in muffled tones as he kept an eye on the vans with laser-like intensity. "Tell them to expect casualties so they can put all the region's hospitals on alert to handle a potentially large number of patients. The types of injuries are unknown at this time. Go!"

Chauncey took off running, taking care to lift his knees high like a broken-field running back to keep from tripping over the uneven ground.

J.T.'s mind reeled with scenarios trying to formulate the best plan of action to most effectively handle this threat.

Shit! You're on your own again. Calm down. You've been alone on a lot of assignments and you came through just fine. Focus on your mission. Take the closest ones first then move on to the others in a systematic manner.

J.T. moved forward in a shuffling crouch with his knees bent to keep his profile closer to the shadows of the dirt road's uneven surface. He held the Glock low and pointed toward the ground, its Tenifer surface slick under his glistening, sweaty hands. Ten rounds of Cor-Bon 115-grain hollow-point bullets were ready to be launched at 1,350 feet-per-second to perform the work they were designed for.

I better work myself up this side of the road until I'm directly across from the van then take them out as efficiently as possible. What is that gas? It's thick and yellow. Maybe its chlorine, that's a common gas they may have gotten hold of. No, chlorine's not dense enough and it'd dissipate too quickly in this wind. This stuff is hugging the ground.

It took him less than ten seconds to cover the uneven ground to the van parked beside the dead locust tree.

Whatever it is they're afraid of it. They're really backpedaling away from the canisters as soon as they open them. It must be really nasty stuff.

J.T. lifted his feet just enough to avoid rolling the stones littering the surface of the road to avoid making noise that may alert the men in the van to his presence. He was able to get close enough to see the driver and suddenly a plan popped into his mind with crystal clarity.

He's looking over his shoulder watching the other guy unload the canisters. He can't see me. I can probably work my way around to the back and get the drop on that guy then I'll deal with the driver.

I hope to hell there are only two of them in there!

Shuffling sideways and being careful to never cross his feet by sliding his forward foot sideways then slipping his back foot up next to it before repeating the sequence, J.T. inched his way around the back of the van. Just as he was about to begin moving around the bumper with his Glock at the ready, Basel leapt into the back of the van and Jaafar drifted forward.

What the hell!

A fleeting glance over his shoulder assured J.T. that the occupants of the other vans had not seen him.

The bastards are too busy doing their dirty work to notice me but that won't last long.

When the van stopped, Basel sprang out then twisted to snatch the second gas cylinder from its moorings in the back of the van as J.T. fired two rapidly triggered rounds from only eight yards' distance into the side of his chest just below the armpit.

BAM! BAM!

The first round smashed the fifth rib on its way to ripping through both lungs and tearing the aorta at the top of the heart to shreds. The second whizzed through the spongy space between the fifth and sixth ribs to tear a walnut-sized hole through both lungs three inches from the destruction wreaked by its mate.

Basel fell to the ground, rolled onto his right side, and then flexed into a quivering fetal position. J.T. did not waste time admiring his handiwork but instead took two steps forward. His Glock was held in an unwavering two-handed grip as he smoothly swung the black pistol to his left and settled the front post sight onto the juncture of Jaafar's neck and chest. The flat, pug nose of the black gun spitting a volcano-like flame was the last earthly sight Jaafar's mind registered.

J.T. fired only one round into the hollow of his neck where his breastbone gave way to the soft, fleshy waddles of his throat. The hollow point bullet soared through the delicate dermis and met just enough resistance as it punched through the tough, cartilage rings of the trachea to begin expanding. Its nose mushroomed from .355 to .401 inches by the time it perforated the rear of the trachea and collided with the soft tissues covering the front of the cervical vertebrae. The continually expanding .423-inch chunk of lead and gilding metal pulverized the body of the sixth cervical vertebra and shattered into smithereens. The meteoric shower of sharp, needle-like bony shards and broken metal masticated the spinal cord into a mass of useless, gooey pulp.

Before he could trigger a second round, Jaafar caved in upon himself and collapsed across the console of the van as his flexor muscles went into spasm; twisting his hands and feet into useless claws. It would be minutes before the lack of oxygen from his now unresponsive lungs rendered his brain void of electrical activity.

No time to waste. I have to turn off those gas canisters.

Not bothering to waste time checking whether Jaafar was still a threat, J.T. spun on his heels and bolted toward the only gas cylinder Basel was able to open before his demise.

Making certain he stayed upwind and out of reach of the escaping gas, he jammed the muzzle of the Glock into his waistband to free the use of both hands. Grasping the gray, perforated metal valve he twisted mightily.

A frosty, deadly fog continued spewing into the moist, humid air. The rapid release of escaping gas, contained for decades under tremendous pressure, froze the valve and frostbit his hands as soon as he touched it. Ignoring the skin being torn from his fingers by the frigid metal, he doggedly completed his task. It took four complete revolutions of the valve to stem the flow of gas from the cylinder.

Tossing the sealed cylinder to the ground, he snatched the Glock from his waistband.

OW! Damned! My hands really hurt! Ignore it. You have more work to do. Your kid's lives depend on what you do in the next few minutes.

CHAPTER 28

CHAUNCEY ALERTS JASON

Chauncey was puffing like an old steam locomotive by the time he reached Jason Hager's front porch. The rickety planking hadn't seen a coat of new paint in three decades and the flaking patch that remained was of an indeterminate color. Long longitudinal cracks had formed in the planks but were now filled with compacted mud.

Wrapping his left hand around the grimy white column supporting the roof, Chauncey swung his rocketing body toward the front door. He was surprised to see that the dirty, mustard-yellow wooden door boasted a surprisingly ornate and clean leaded, beveled glass window. A single, bare bulb hung from the peeling paint-flecked ceiling of the hallway making it easy for him to see into the house.

BANG! BANG! BANG!

Chauncey's closed fist pounded against the frame of the door surrounding the sparkling glass window. He only waited a few short seconds before beginning his incessant pounding again.

Jason Hager vaulted into view at the far end of the hallway from what Chauncey guessed to be the kitchen. He was obviously agitated by the pounding on his front door. His long, forceful strides caused his heavily cleated boots to smack noisily off the polished wood floor of the hallway.

"What the hell do you want?" he yelled into Chauncey's face as he burst through the ill-fitting door. "Don't you know enough not to pound on people's doors? You'll break the damned thing then I'll charge you for it! And what the hell can be so important at this hour of the night?"

Chauncey had a difficult time getting his words formed because of the dryness of his throat from running across the meadow. Jason's furious outburst only added to the problem.

"There's an attack against the Gathering, a gas attack, and they're trying to kill the kids," he finally managed to force out of his mouth. "J.T. has gone after them and sent me to tell you to call 911."

"What the hell---"

"Call 911 damn it!" Chauncey screamed at him.

He saw Jason was perplexed by his claim and would need verification before acting.

"There! Up there on the road," he yelled as he pointed impatiently back the way he had come. "They're opening gas cylinders and the wind is carrying it across the fields toward the crowds at the Gathering."

Chauncey did not get the chance for further explanation before two shots rang out from the direction he was pointing followed by a third less than two seconds later.

"Call 911. Please!"

Jason Hager was not very bright but once he understood the gravity of any situation, he always acted swiftly and decisively.

"Mary Anne! Call 911 and get the sheriff up here. Now!" he bellowed over his shoulder to his wife in the kitchen.

"You have to tell them to alert the hospitals," Chauncey said as he forcefully sucked in another breath. "They have to know to expect a lot of injured people so they can prepare."

"Mary Anne! Tell them to call the hospitals. There may be a lot of hurting people showing up there soon," Jason bellowed toward the kitchen. "And we may need a lot of ambulances; I'm going up there to see what the hell's going on."

"Did she hear you?" Chauncey asked with a tinge of horror in his voice.

"Mary Anne! Did you hear me?"

"Yes I heard you, you pain in the ass," a rough, tired female voice answered from the kitchen. "I'm dialing the phone now."

"Come on," Jason said to Chauncey as he snatched a twelve-gauge side-by-side shotgun with the bluing worn off its receiver from behind the front door. He expertly slung its cracked walnut stock under his right armpit and pushed the opening lever with his beefy thumb. "We're going to see what the hell's going on!"

Before shuffling out the door, he grabbed a dog-eared cardboard box of shotgun shells off the shelf of the coat rack hanging from the wall and began shoving them into the open tops of the button-down pockets of his sleeveless flannel shirt.

CHAPTER 29

J.T. MOVES ON

"What is that?" Omar asked Samir as he leaned into the side door of the van after placing his second cylinder upright on the ground.

"There is a man shooting into Jaafar and Basel's van," Samir said as he pointed directly down the road in front of him.

"Then we must hurry," Omar said as he whirled and grabbed the third cylinder before he jumped from the van. "This is the last cylinder we have. I haven't had time to open the second one yet. I will open them both after I place this one in its spot."

"Don't bother putting it up the road; just place it here," Samir yelled but it was too late. Omar had already begun running up the road with the canister hugged securely to his chest with his knees bending precipitously under the tremendous weight.

He had a spot visually marked as the location where Muhammed wanted the cylinder to be placed. Grunting loudly, he slammed the bottom of the heavy cylinder to the ground but it landed on a hummock of grass and fell silently onto its side. Bending from his waist to lift the hefty canister he suddenly felt a sharp, stabbing pain in his lower back like a red-hot knife being driven into him just above his right buttock.

It had been two years since he'd last suffered from lower back pain but he knew immediately the searing pain was from a herniated disc. He grabbed desperately at his low back but stayed bent forward because he was unable to stand straight. Severe, unrelenting pain froze him in his tracks rendering him unable to move.

His misery was short-lived.

Before he could do anything more than raise his head to face the threat he knew to be bearing down on him, he heard the shot that signaled the end of his agony.

The nine-millimeter Cor-Bon round was loosed from a distance of ten yards by a specter of death zooming out of the stygian darkness of the night. The impact of the bullet whacking into his upper chest at slightly less than 1,350 feet-per-second knocked him to his knees.

The brilliant, blinding muzzle flash temporarily blinded J.T. but he was able to make out the figure of Omar kneeling on the ground beside the fallen gas cylinder.

J.T.'s second shot, fired in rapid succession after the first, smashed the glass goggle of the gas mask covering Omar's left eye; his body began to crash to the ground in a crumpled heap as his legs buckled uselessly beneath him.

Before the crash of the first shot striking Omar finished echoing across the valley, Samir threw the van into drive and smashed the accelerator to the floorboards. By the time the second bullet pulverized Omar's brain, Samir was accelerating the 2,000-pound instrument of death directly at J.T. in his desperate attempt to escape.

J.T. spun toward the sound of the racing engine and snapped off a round sending it uselessly through the windshield on the passenger's side, shredding the headrest of the seat Omar had occupied less than four minutes previously.

With the headlights blinding him, he threw himself wildly to the side of the road as Samir's van missed him by mere inches. He landed face down on the stony shoulder, scraping the palm of his frostbitten left hand into the sharp-edged gravel. His right hand resolutely gripped the Glock even as jagged stones tore strips of skin from his knuckles.

He did not wait to evaluate his situation before rolling into the grass on the side of the road. Only when he was sure he was safely out of danger as the van whizzed by did he attempt to stand up. Taking a second to orient himself and reevaluate his situation, he astutely determined he should turn off the solitary gas cylinder spewing gas in huge, billowing plumes.

Remembering the freezing metal of the first gas cylinder, he tore his shirt off and used it to protect his hands from the ice-covered valve. As he worked, he kept an eye on the third van. Just as he gave the valve a final twist, he saw the van begin careening wildly toward him with a plume of nearly invisible dust flying from its rear tires.

Dropping his wet, chilled shirt between his feet, he once again snatched the Glock from his waistband and took aim at the lurching vehicle.

Just as he was pressing the trigger, Muhammed swerved perilously to the left, throwing up a shower of stones and dust. The evasive maneuver caused the bullet to crash into the passenger's side window. Before the exploding glass finished falling from its frame, a second slug entered the passenger's door. A third poked a dimpled hole in the sliding door and buzzed between the two men seated in the van.

J.T. did not waste time watching the taillights of the fishtailing van disappear into the night. Instead, he twirled to face where they had left cylinders in the field. He grimaced when he saw four plumes of dirty, yellow gas gushing across the grass. The leading edge of the plume had almost reached the tent city of the campground.

He began sprinting toward the spurting canisters but reversed direction to snatch his shirt from the ground.

I'll need this if I want to get all those turned off before my hands give out.

As he stooped to pick up his shirt he took one last look to survey his surroundings and rethink his next move.

It's always so silent after a gunfight...

BOOM! BOOM!

The sound of two distant shotgun blasts reached his ears just as he finalized his plans.

I better get those valves shut off, then try to find a way around that cloud of gas to warn the people at the concert. I don't know who's shooting down there but I hope it's the good guys.

He was barely able to finish shutting the valve on the last cylinder. His badly blistered palms gushed an increasing torrent of slick, red blood making it difficult to grasp the slippery metal.

CHAPTER 30

JASON HAGER STEPS FORWARD

"See there," Chauncey said with gasping breaths as he and Jason Hager stopped at the edge of the dirt road. "See the yellow gas moving across the field?"

"What is that?"

"I don't know," Chauncey admitted. "J.T. thought it was some type of poison because they're wearing gas masks."

"Here comes one of the bastards," Jason said excitedly as he pointed at the headlights lurching wildly toward them.

"Did you see that? He tried to run someone over but they jumped out of the way or else they got hit and was knocked down, I'm not sure which."

"That must have been J.T.," Chauncey said worriedly. "I hope he's OK."

"Well, let's stop that bastard and find out what's going on," Jason said as he stepped onto the road and began flailing his right arm above his head in a futile attempt to flag down the van. His grizzled left fist grasped the shotgun as it hung by his side.

Samir did not care that he had failed to run over the American who killed Omar. If he had wanted to, he could have swerved and ended his meddling ways but he was not interested in killing a single man. His goal was to escape.

*Allah will be pleased with what you have been able to accomplish
and will forgive you for escaping to fight another day.*

Samir steered the van to the left side of the road where Jason Hager
stood waving his hand back and forth as he strode nearer and nearer to
the center of the road.

Fool! You will die!

With an uncharacteristic flash of intuition, Jason realized the van
was not going to stop. He began running toward the side of the road as
fast as his stubby legs would take him.

"You're not going to run me down you son-of-a-bitch!" he
growled as he spun around to face the van and raised the shotgun to
his shoulder. He concentrated on a spot in the center of the windshield
where he guessed the driver's face would be. The shot was similar to
picking a single bobwhite quail out of a flushing covey.

With the flat face of the dark blue van rocketing out of the
darkness and bearing down on him, its chromed grill glittering dully in
the reflected moonlight, Jason Hager calmly slapped the forward
trigger of his shotgun.

BOOM!

The shatterproof glass of the windshield remained largely intact
but developed a twelve-inch circle of spider webbing in the center of
its glittering surface. In the center of the spider web was a small,
three-inch hole completely devoid of glass.

Sensing he was in danger, he took four hurried steps farther from
the road. Carefully gauging where it would pass by, he stopped, faced
the oncoming vehicle, then slipped his finger to the rear trigger of the
antique side-by-side and fired the second barrel into the side window
as it sped by. A shower of debris caught Samir in the side of his head
and neck.

Both shotgun blasts were not as effective as Jason would have
liked because the soft lead pellets deformed on impact. When the
flattened metal penetrated the van's glass, it lost most of its
momentum but retained enough force to shower Samir with a blinding

wash of lead shot and glass particles. He was stunned and disoriented when he swerved across the yard, barely missing Jason Hager.

"Damned! He's gonna run into my tractor!" Jason yelled in an anguished voice.

Samir's van missed the once shiny green and yellow John Deere by mere inches and imbedded itself into the cushioning boughs of an ancient blue spruce on the other side of the worn tractor.

Breaking the shotgun's action open, Jason fished two fresh shells from his shirt pocket and plunked them solidly into the chambers before snapping the action shut with an angry flick of his wrist.

In a fit of rage, he rushed to the driver's door and ripped it open as he muttered, "You son-of-a-bitch! I'm gonna smash your ass up and down this mountain---"

"Jason! Calm down and be careful," Chauncey yelled as he ran to his side. "He may be armed."

"He ain't shit!" Jason rebuked him loudly. "Get your ass out of there you miserable son-of-a-bitch piece-of-shit!" he screamed in a nearly incoherent screech as his rage fed upon itself, fueling his escalating anger with every passing second.

He grabbed Samir by the front of his blood-covered shirt and yanked him out of the van with his left hand while keeping his finger on the trigger of the shotgun with his right. Samir pitched head first from the driver's seat and spun uncontrollably to the ground. With a heavy thud, his limp body belly-flopped on the scraggly grass of Hager's front yard.

Pointing his dilapidated shotgun at the middle of Samir's back Jason said venomously through clenched teeth, "Don't you dare move before the sheriff gets here or I'll blow a hole through you so big a groundhog kin get lost in it."

Chauncey cautiously walked up to Jason and stopped beside him. They both stood dumbfounded and stared at Samir's unmoving form then slowly looked at each other.

In a flash, Muhammed's van sped by with Waseem's shattered body lying motionless on the floorboards. As the escaping van hastened by, Chauncey and Muhammed locked eyes for a split second, each one etching the other's features onto their mind indelibly before it disappeared into a cloud of dust.

CHAPTER 31

DELIVERING THE WARNING

The dirty, yellow gas continued to slowly roll over the uneven ground, wrapping itself around tents and working its deadly way toward the Grand Stand where the concert was being held. It was still concentrated enough to be visible to the naked eye but was becoming thinner and more difficult to see as it slowly meandered across the fields.

Damned! The gas is between the concert and me!

I have to warn the people in the campground and at the concert. But how am I going to do it without breathing the gas myself?

The shots he fired had alerted everyone and many were looking in his direction trying to see what the commotion was all about.

Oh no! There are a lot of campers staggering around gagging.

Checking the direction of the wind, he bolted toward the south side of the campground while keeping the specter of gas in sight.

It's so quiet. The band has stopped playing!

They probably heard the gunshots and stopped the concert. Good!

When he got as close to the campers and the Grand Stand as he could without inhaling the gas himself, he began yelling, "Hey! Hey! Run! There's poisonous gas coming your way! Run! You have to get out of there to save yourself! Run!

Oh Lord! They don't realize which way to run! They're just milling around! Oh no! They're freezing in place because they're confused. Oh Lord! Give me guidance...

In an unexpected flash of inspiration, J.T. realized that if he fired his last two rounds it would get their attention centered on him so he could convey his message via voice commands and hand signals.

It only took a split second to snatch the Glock from his waistband but it took three precious seconds for his damaged hands to prepare to fire it.

Oh man, this is going to hurt

Ignoring the searing pain shooting up his arms like lightning bolts, he took a firm grasp on the pistol and fired two evenly spaced shots into the soft earth at his feet. Looking toward the campground and Grand Stand he saw everyone looking directly at him.

Now's my chance!

Raising his hands high over his head and waving them back and forth he hollered as loud as he could, "Run to that side or that side to avoid the poisonous gas!" His hand and arm signals pointed right and left to correspond with his voice commands.

At first everyone just stood motionless and stared in wide-eyed confusion.

It's a natural reaction for people to just freeze when they're unsure what's happening. I have to be more specific with my instructions.

"Don't run with the wind. Run to the sides this way and that way," he bellowed at the top of his voice. Again, he used hand signals to give visual clarity to his verbal instructions.

Keep it up! You have no other options. Keep it up.

He continued to scream his warnings over and over again. He never felt so inadequate and hopeless in his entire life.

Don't let despair overcome you. You have to fight to the end. You have no choice.

Slowly, some of the campers closest to him began to understand when they saw others coughing and wheezing as the gas overtook them. And like a huge herd of wildebeest they ponderously began turning and moving toward gas-free areas, guiding others before them as they went.

They're helping each other! Of course! It's who they are. Since they were small children these people have been taught that serving others is what God wants them to do.

That's quite a bit different from what the bastards who did this are taught.

"Yes! Hurry! Keep moving in that direction or that direction!" he continued yelling as he feverishly directed them with hand and arm signals.

"Yell warnings to the others so they'll understand what they have to do to save themselves! Tell them about the poisonous gas coming toward them!"

And they did.

Like a droning buzz resonating from an angry beehive, the warnings spread throughout the crowd rising to a crescendo as more and more people began understanding the gravity of their situation and spread the word. Motivated chatter rippled through the horde in an uncontrollable flood.

The unintelligible babble was being transformed into motion as the message spread.

It's working!

Then he heard it.

A booming voice over the speakers at the Grand Stand announced, "We have gotten word that poisonous gas is being carried by the wind and is moving this way. To avoid breathing the gas you are being instructed to move quickly at a ninety-degree angle to the wind. You must move that way or that way as quickly as possible. Leave your blankets and coolers so you can help others. Hurry!"

The guy on the stage is using his hands and arms to signal to the crowd which way to run so there won't be any confusion. Just like I was doing! Thank you, God!

Yes! The band has a better view of what's going on from the stage. He can see and hear me from up there while the crowd down below can't. He heard me and used hand signals like I did!

By this time, the deadly gas had dissipated enough to become almost invisible and was rapidly swallowed by the darkness of night.

I've done all I can do here. I better get back to our campsite and set up a command center for our church's group. That's where they'll return.

If they don't come back then at least I'll know whom to look for, he thought as a great sorrow fell upon him.

He began staggering as he made his way back across the field. The strobe effect from the flashing red, white, and blue lights of emergency vehicles racing up the road added to his disorientation.

I guess Chauncey made it to Jason's and raised the alarm. Now I have to flag down the police and explain what happened before going back to our campsite.

A unique combination of fatigue and vertigo knocked him to his knees before he could take another step.

CHAPTER 32

ONE WEEK AFTER THE GAS ATTACK

"How are your hands?" Chauncey asked after he and J.T. sat down in the Tobin's living room.

"They're healing pretty well," he replied as he held up his hands. "These bandages can come off in another week or so."

"You look like you have mummy hands. Are your hands so bad that you need that many bandages?"

"It's more to keep the burn salve off anything I touch than it is to protect the wounds at this point. That nasty stuff gets onto everything and you can't get it off."

"Your hands must have been badly burned."

"The doc said my hands were only frostbitten by the cold of the metal valve and I didn't really come in contact with the mustard gas at all. So it's not really a chemical burn but the damage is the same as if it were burned."

"They figured out it was mustard gas pretty fast."

"Yeah, when that many people were injured they analyzed it as soon as possible so they'd know how to treat their injuries," J.T. replied. "I spoke to the doctor quite a bit about it and he filled me in on a lot of things I didn't know. Then I contacted some old friends and got some additional information that's not available to the public."

"Tell me about it, at least as much as you can."

"Well, mustard gas is an odorless gas that was used extensively in World War I," he explained. "The investigation showed this was left over from that war and was stored at the Aberdeen Proving Grounds in Maryland. That's where these canisters were stolen from."

"Did they figure out how it was stolen?"

"That's not public knowledge, sorry."

"That's OK," Chauncey said with a knowing smile. "What else can you tell me?"

"Mustard gas is very powerful and only a very small amount is horrendously injurious to the human body but the symptoms may not show up for twelve hours."

"That's why the people who came in contact with it didn't die right away."

"That's right," J.T. said. "The stuff stays active for several weeks. Peter Giovanni has been instructed not to allow humans or livestock onto those fields for at least six months. Further testing will show when it's no longer active."

"Will he be able to survive financially without being able to use those fields?"

"He said he can manage to keep the farm by getting on the road as a truck driver for six months," J.T. replied. "He had to sell the cattle he was planning on putting back onto those pastures because he doesn't have enough feed for them on the unaffected acreage."

"Did you find out what mustard gas does to create so much damage?"

"The doctor said it causes the skin to blister but only after four to twenty-four hours after exposure. That's why they suspected my hands were suffering from frostbite instead of contact with the gas. The damage occurred immediately," he said as he held his bandaged hands up.

"How many have died so far?"

"So far we've lost eighteen," he said, his voice catching as a tear escaped from the corner of his eye. "And the doc thinks the fatality rate may go as high as sixty or more."

"So we'll know how many casualties we suffered in about two months."

"No," J.T. said simply. "Anyone that had more than fifty percent of their body exposed may die over the next few years. Then there's the carcinogenic aspect that may take years to develop into cancer."

"I'm just glad none of the kids from our group were injured," Chauncey said. "It was our good luck they were all on the side of the crowd farthest away from where the gas was released."

"It certainly gave them extra time to get out of there before the gas drifted in," J.T. said with a slight quiver in his voice. "And for that I am eternally grateful."

Chauncey could only stare at the floor. He was at a loss for words.

Regardless of the valiant efforts of J.T., Chauncey, Jason Hager, and all of the police, EMTs, and hospital personnel involved in the Hallelujah Gathering incident, a total of 57 people died and another 453 suffered lung and skin injuries over the next two months.

How many victims will still be added to the list can only be guessed.

CHAPTER 33

THANKSGIVING PLANS

"What are you doing about Thanksgiving?" Nadine asked Sarah as they entered the lower pasture at The Shire after an early morning horseback ride in the crisp chill of October. "Do you want to spend it with me?"

"Thanks for the invitation but I've already accepted an invite from my brother-in-law to join his family for Thanksgiving," Sarah replied. "They told me to bring Chauncey. I think they're under the incorrect assumption we're having an affair."

"Oh really!" Nadine gasped.

"Speaking of Chauncey," Nadine said. "Have you been making any headway into finding out anything about his identity or past, you know, especially since that terrible situation that developed in West Virginia at the Hallelujah Gathering and all?"

"No I haven't," Sarah admitted. "The hypnotist was only able to ascertain that he could remember jumbled sequences of numbers but it's not clear whether they're telephone numbers, a social security number, or a combination to a safe. Hypnosis was worth a try but wasn't very helpful."

"Are you sure Chauncey was really under hypnosis and not just faking it?"

"No, he was under," Sarah replied tiredly. "Dr. Hambra has a good reputation and he believes Chauncey was definitely under. He said it's a sign of superior I.Q."

"What about fingerprints?"

"We've run into a catch-22 situation with fingerprints," Sarah said with exasperation weighing heavily in her voice. "The police won't run his prints to see if he's in the NICS system which would at least give us his real name."

"Why not?"

"Because he hasn't committed a crime."

"Well, have him apply for something, anything that requires a background check," Nadine said. "Then they'll run his fingerprints."

"There's where the catch-22 comes into play," Sarah replied. "Most applications, like applying for a concealed carry permit for instance, require you to provide truthful information under threat of jail. They always require your signature at the bottom of the form to make it a legally binding document and providing false information is a felony."

"So he can't get his fingerprints unless he commits a crime," Nadine said as she organized the situation in her mind. "But if he makes up a false name to get his background and fingerprints checked then he'd be charged with a felony."

"Exactly."

"But at least he'd know who he is," she said. "Even though he'd be in prison for committing a felony."

"It's not funny Nadine," Sarah said with irritation still evident in her voice. "I have an attorney checking into it to see if we can find a way around the catch-22."

"Life's a bitch and then you die," Nadine replied. "It seems that attorneys have to be consulted about every damned thing these days."

"Even when you die the government and attorneys still get a piece of your estate. Just like a pack of vultures cleaning up your remains."

"Why are you worrying about who Chauncey is? Are there problems?"

"No," Sarah said as she rolled her eyes in exasperation. "But his lack of identity is beginning to get me wondering what I'm involved in and it's burdensome for him."

"What do you mean?

"I mean that total amnesia from a head injury, assuming it was a severe beating he suffered, is extremely rare."

"What about emotional amnesia?" Nadine asked. "The beating may have come afterward and has no bearing as a cause for his condition."

"Once again, it's a very rare occurrence."

"So your question is?"

"Does Chauncey really suffer from this super rare situation," Sarah said as she chewed on her lip as she searched for the correct words. "Or am I being duped into helping an impostor move anonymously into another life?"

"Chauncey's not a mass murderer, at least he doesn't seem like one, if that's what you're getting at."

"What does a mass murderer act like?" Sarah asked in an agitated tone. "Ted Bundy was supposedly the nicest guy until he threw unsuspecting girls into his Volkswagen, bound them hand and foot with duct tape, then killed them."

"I see what you mean," Nadine said as she began gnawing thoughtfully on her lip just as Sarah had done.

"That's why I'm footing the bill for an attorney to help me find out who Chauncey really is. It will give both of us some peace of mind knowing who he is."

"Are you starting to get second thoughts about Chauncey? Is there anything I should know about?"

"No, not at all," Sarah said with firm conviction. "It's just that it's very difficult to live in our society without an identity. I don't want him living in the shadows like an illegal all his life if he doesn't have to."

"And that's the only problem with Chauncey?"

"That's the only problem I know of," Sarah replied.

"Which you have basically turned over to the attorney," Nadine concluded. "So the only thing you have to deal with immediately is how to convince your family you're not having an affair with Chauncey."

"That and how to find time to bake pies for Thanksgiving dinner," Sarah said with a look of mild trepidation remaining on her face.

CHAPTER 34

MUHAMMED'S REVENGE

The three men sat in the sparsely furnished but immaculately clean kitchen with two of them on one side of the yellow floral Formica-topped kitchen table. The third sat across from them in a haughty, detached manner, silently pecking at the keyboard of a laptop computer. None seemed to notice or care that the chairs were of a non-matching olive green.

"You have called for us, Commander?" Haady asked.

"Yes Haady," Muhammed replied as he looked up from his computer screen. "I have need of your and Bishr's skills."

"What do you want us to do, Commander?" Bishr asked submissively.

"You two have been very helpful in the past," Muhammed replied. "You disposed of the van with the bullet holes and blood in it and you found a fellow true believer to oversee Waseem's burial and keep the cause of his death secret."

"You asked that both those tasks be handled discretely and efficiently," Haady said. "It honors me to have you say you are pleased with the completion of our assignments."

"I am pleased, as is Allah, I am sure," Muhammed replied with aloofness in his voice. "That is why I have asked you to help with these tasks."

"What are those tasks, Commander?"

"These men who interfered with our blessed work at the Hallelujah Gathering; this Jeremy Tobin and his friend, Chauncey," Muhammed said haltingly as he chose his words carefully. "They must be punished for their meddling."

"Their meddling must be avenged," Bishr and Haady said in unison.

Muhammed looked at both of them from below hooded eyelids until they became uncomfortable under his unwavering gaze.

"It is your task to find out about these men," Muhammed said slowly as he laid a short stack of newspaper articles on the table in front of them. "The newspapers and television say that Jeremy Tobin lives in Northern Virginia. I want you to find his house and gather information about him and his family."

"And the other one?"

"And him also," Muhammed replied with deliberation. "His name is Chauncey and he gives two addresses. One is in Washington, D.C. and the other is a farm near a town called Thompsonville."

"Does he have a last name, Commander?"

"None of the news articles mentions a last name for him."

"And how are we to gather information on these two men?"

"You are to wait until the cover of darkness and take the trash they put on the street curb for disposal," Muhammed said. "There is much to be learned from what these Americans discard."

"Are there other ways besides taking their garbage that you would have us do to gather information on them?"

"Start with their trash," Muhammed said. "Only if it does not give us the information we need will you resort to riskier methods such as stealing their computers."

"We will report back to you regularly, Commander."

"I expect you will," Muhammed said menacingly.

CHAPTER 35

VALUABLE TRASH

"It was very easy to look in the telephone book on the Internet and find Jeremy Tobin's home address," Haady said to Bishr as they slid onto the torn front seats of a dirty brown Toyota Corolla.

"And it was even easier getting directions to his house," Bishr responded as he jammed the key into the ignition switch. "Now all we have to do is drive by the house every evening until they place their trash out for pick-up."

"Will we take it as soon as we see it?"

"No, you fool," Bishr replied. "We must wait until the middle of the night when the chance of us being discovered is very small. Even then we will try to replace the plastic bags with similar bags so they are not missed. Jeremy Tobin cannot know we are interested in information about him and his family."

Two days passed before the men saw what they had been looking for.

"Good!" Bishr said as he slowed the Toyota to more closely inspect the trashcans. "They are using Glad Trash Bags with the red pull strings."

"That is a good thing?" Haady asked quizzically.

"Yes," Bishr replied gleefully. "It is one of the brands of bags I bought and have in the trunk. All we have to do is crumple old newspapers to fill the bags and make them appear full to replace the bags we take away."

"I counted three bags that were visible and two trash cans," Haady said. "Assuming there are two full bags in each of the cans that makes a total of seven bags we will need."

"Then we will fill nine bags in case they put out more trash before we return."

"Will all those bags fit into this small car?"

"No, that is why I have borrowed a van with a side door from Abdul-Qaadir, a man I work with," Bishr said slyly. "I told him I need it to move my girlfriend to a new apartment."

"What is your plan?"

"I will drive the van with the newspaper-stuffed trash bags stacked just behind our seats," Bishr said enthusiastically. "You will very quietly get out of the van, open the side door, and begin loading Jeremy Tobin's trash into the back portion of the van then I will hand you the bags we stuffed to replace the ones you took."

"It will be like an assembly line in a factory," Haady said with amazement in his voice.

"And very efficient so we can quickly be gone with that which we seek," Bishr said with a satisfied grin on his face.

THANKSGIVING DINNER

"Watch those pies, Chauncey," Sarah called out as he tried to balance a third pie on his outstretched arms. "I've been up half the night baking and I don't want them splattered all over the driveway."

"Don't worry about me," Chauncey replied. "And don't forget the wine."

"I'm not forgetting anything," she shot back.

"You two sound like an old married couple for crying out loud," Stephanie Tobin called from the front porch where she stood holding the door open for them.

"I'm not good at very many things," Chauncey said jokingly. "But I'm real good at complaining and bickering."

"I can see that," she replied with an air of joviality. "It's nice to see you again Chauncey."

"And it's nice to see you too, Stephanie," he said as he sidled his way past her and into the house. "Do you want these in the kitchen?"

"Yes, if you would please. You can put those pies on the counter there," Stephanie directed as she pointed him in the right direction. "And Sarah, you can put the wine over on the microwave hutch if you can find any space."

After helping her guests unburden themselves of their contributions to the Thanksgiving Day feast Stephanie said, "Let's go into the living room. There's someone I'd like you to meet."

Stephanie led the way to the sunken living room, descended the two steps with the grace of a ballet dancer, and turned to face them after planting her feet directly between a tall, lanky man and a much shorter, more compact man with a handlebar mustache.

"You know J.T.," she said as she took the arm of her tall, lanky husband. Then with a flourish of her left hand she said, "And this is John Myers, J.T.'s friend. John, this is my sister-in-law Sarah and her friend Chauncey."

"Hello Sarah, it's a pleasure to finally meet you," John said with a slight bow as he extended his hand toward her. "And it's an equally pleasant honor to make your acquaintance, Chauncey. J.T. has told me quite a bit about you. He says you're a good man to have around in an emergency."

"J.T. is much too kind," Chauncey said uncertainly, not quite sure how to proceed with this new acquaintance.

"And I've heard about you also, Sarah," John continued. "I understand you have an excellent reputation as a chiropractor and recently acquired a farm up in the mountains. What is it you named your farm? It's a unique name but I can't remember what it is."

"I call it Predator's Bane," Sarah replied, also a little unsure how to react to him. "And it's a pleasure to meet you, John."

"How did you arrive at that name?" he asked inquisitively as a puzzled look crossed his face. His eyes bore into Sarah as he awaited an answer.

"It's a long story," Sarah replied as she averted her eyes away from his.

"If we have time later," he said with a smile popping out from beneath his thick, brushy mustache. "Maybe you'll indulge me and fill me in on the details."

John looked at Stephanie with an ingratiating smile and Sarah took the opportunity to appraise his physical bearing with her professional eye.

He only looks short and chubby but that's all muscle under his khaki shirt and he has huge gnarly hands like a steelworker. They must take a lot of daily abuse.

He stands with such ease as though he fears nothing. I'll bet this is J.T.'s old boss from the CIA he talks about. At least now I know his name.

"Make yourselves at home," Stephanie said. "I'm going to put a few finishing touches on dinner then I'll call when it's ready."

"I'll help," Sarah offered.

"No thanks, I've got it. It's only one or two small things," Stephanie replied cheerfully. "You better stay here and keep an eye on these three."

"OK," Sarah said as she shared a smile with the three men before turning to John.

"I'm afraid J.T. hasn't had time to fill us in on you as well as he has obviously done about us," Sarah said coyly with a polite smile. "What is it you do?"

"I'm a businessman dealing in the Middle East," he replied quickly. "I dabble in any number of adventures but always in that area of the world. They're the ones with money these days, you know."

"So I've heard," Chauncey said. "I've been studying the Middle East a little since that region of the world is in the news so often."

"Yes, it's an intriguing area," John added. "What in particular interests you about the Middle East?"

"Nothing in particular," Chauncey replied. "The fact that it's in the news so often, as I've mentioned, keeps my interest piqued."

"And what have you learned about the Middle East that continues to pique your interest?" John asked innocently as his mustache twitched back and forth.

"I've learned there are many mysteries and few concrete truths to be learned other than geography."

"And how is that?"

"Take the culture for instance," Chauncey said. "As far as I can figure out, it's not a homogenous culture even within each country."

"That's true to a certain extent I imagine," John confirmed with a small nod of his head. "And what else have you discovered?"

"The main thread that binds the Middle East together is their religion," Chauncey replied. "And curiously, it's also the thing that seems to cause the most strife among different factions."

"Very true," John confirmed once again. "Historically, the jihadists have been fighting and following in the footsteps of their warrior Prophet since the seventh century."

"And that attitude continues on today?" Chauncey asked inquisitively.

"Absolutely," John said as he warmed to one of his favorite subjects. "The radical Islamic movement is dedicated to converting the entire world to Islam at the point of a sword."

"Go on," Chauncey said simply, making an effort to maintain a low, calm voice while listening intently.

"To comprehend the situation you have to know and understand the teachings under which the radicals are operating," John said unemotionally.

"And those teachings are?" Chauncey asked quizzically.

"For example let's look at Osama Bin Laden. He didn't refer to his organization as al Qaeda," he went on in a learned manner. "Rather, he called it, 'World Islamic Front for Jihad Against Jews and Crusaders.'"

"That's a mouthful," Chauncey said. "But why do they single out Jews and the so-called Crusaders?"

"It is a mouthful," John agreed. "But in Middle Eastern terminology, Jews and Christians - Christians are the crusaders - are described as 'the vilest of creatures' because they reject Islam. At least according to Qur'an 98:6."

"You seem to have committed certain pertinent information to memory."

"Yes I have," he said. "When the command found in Qur'an 47:4 is to 'smite the necks' of 'unbelievers' you'd better start paying attention especially if you're one of the unbelievers because the radical Islamists may take it upon themselves to behead you and feel quite righteous about it."

"Surely that's a misinterpretation of the Qur'an."

"Not really," he replied. "These affirmations are rampant within the Qur'an but since it's written in classical Arabic, and must be read and recited during prayer in that language only, most Muslims really don't understand what principles they're pledging allegiance to."

"So if all Jews and 'Crusaders' as they're referred to are considered to be unbelievers, why don't the Muslims just start killing us all by cutting off our heads?" Chauncey asked unbelievingly.

"If they followed the last passage to be revealed to Muhammad, that's sura nine, they most assuredly would," John explained calmly. "Sura nine states that Muslims should wage war against the People of the Book- that's the Jews and Christians who follow the teachings found in the Bible or 'Book'- until they either convert to Islam or are subdued as second-class citizens called dhimmis."

"And that's why you say Muslims want to convert the world to Islam at the point of a sword?"

"That's why."

"And is this attitude what's behind the unrest in the Middle East?" Chauncey asked seriously.

"It's a large part of it."

"Then why don't we hear more about these teachings?" Chauncey asked with a hint of desperation in his voice. "Are we being lied to?"

"That's a distinct possibility," John said gravely. "Religious deception, as long as it's practiced on unbelievers, is taught by the Qur'an."

"What do you mean?" Sarah asked sharply.

"I mean that Qur'an 3:28 tells Muslims to not make friends with unbelievers except to guard themselves against them," John said as he stared directly at Sarah to emphasize his point. "Islamic spokesmen may be downplaying or even denying aspects of their religion that unbelievers, that's folks like you and Chauncey, may find unpalatable, disgusting, or repulsive."

"Oh my God!" she said when the reality of John's words had sunk in. "They do that all the time! I remember thinking how much the Muslim representatives lie when they give interviews on the news. They don't even seem ashamed when they're caught in an obvious untruth."

"So you've noticed that, have you?"

He remained silent for a moment, leaving a pregnant pause to allow his words to settle like a veil of truth upon everyone's mind before attempting to make his next statement. Before he could continue Sarah interrupted in an agitated manner.

"So the Muslims consider those of us who are unbelievers to be second-class citizens unworthy of respect or the truth, and Muslim women are not much better off than us unbelievers?"

"That pretty well sums it up," he said simply. "One cleric puts unbelievers into the same category as urine, feces, dogs, pigs, and dead bodies. Nice company to find yourself lumped in with, eh?"

"John, be realistic, you can always find some crackpot in any group who makes stupid statements," Chauncey said defensively.

"But this isn't some crackpot," he said calmly as he looked directly into Chauncey's eyes. "This list of unclean things is from the Iraqi Shi'ite leader Grand Ayatollah Sayyid Ali Husayni Sistani, a man considered by many in the West as a reformer and moderate thinker."

"Oh brother!" Sarah said. "What do the radicals think about us if this guy lumps us in with pigs and shit?"

A stunned silence fell over the room followed by an avalanche of laughter that left Chauncey and Sarah gasping for breath.

"OK, so why hasn't the huge number of Muslims around the world risen up and wiped us infidels off the face of the earth?" Sarah asked when she was finally able to breathe without laughing.

"Like I said," John replied. "The vast majority of Muslims only have a glancing knowledge of what Islam really teaches."

"That's why you differentiate by speaking of the radical Islamists."

"That's right," he said. "There are groups around the world who believe it's their responsibility to wage war against non-Muslims and impose Islamic law upon all the lands. Those are the guys we have to be concerned about."

"But you've been saying that the passages the radical Islamists are basing their perverted, distorted vision of their religion on are actually in the Qur'an," Sarah said as she sifted through the information in her mind. "Which means that it really isn't perverted or distorted; it's the way Islam is."

"If you don't believe me maybe you'll believe Omar Ahmad, the board chairman of the Council on American-Islamic Relations who said that Islam is in America to become the dominant religion and the Qur'an should be the highest authority in America. He finished by saying that Islam should be the only accepted religion on earth."

"Isn't that the group that likes to call themselves CAIR so it sounds like the well-known humanitarian group?"

"That's them."

"It sure sounds like world domination to me," Chauncey said in agreement as he nodded his head solemnly.

"Surely the media would be all over this if it were true," Sarah said with fear beginning to creep into her eyes. "They wouldn't stand by and see us conquered from within."

"Don't hold your breath on that one," Chauncey said as he interrupted. "Even the FBI can't seem to admit that this threat exists within our borders."

"What do you mean?" she asked.

"I'm referring to an explosion that occurred in Texas City, Texas," Chauncey replied as he warmed to the topic. "The FBI immediately ruled out terrorism even though they didn't visit the site to investigate until eight days after the explosions occurred."

"But it was terrorism," John said quietly. "Wasn't it?"

"So it would seem," Chauncey replied. "From what I can remember from the magazine article, it was discovered there were five different explosions at the refinery. That's definitely suspicious since a group calling itself Qaeda al-Jihad claimed responsibility."

"That's a situation where Americans have invited millions of Muslims to live amongst them, assuming they could live as equals," John said. "Unfortunately we're now finding that Islam must struggle to make itself supreme to all other religions and political systems."

"That's scary," Sarah said with a tremor in her voice.

"And that's only one instance of Muslim involvement in violence within the United States that may be religion-motivated," John said. "You can keep your head firmly buried in the sand, Sarah, or you can begin preparing for when they come for you and your loved ones."

A cloud of fury immediately exploded on Sarah's face at the same instant Stephanie bounded into the living room with a flourish.

"OK y'all, it's time for dinner," she announced. "The girls are putting the finishing touches on the table so it's time for everyone to wash their hands."

"That's one of the sweetest sounds in the world," Chauncey mused.

"The call to dinner," John said in finishing Chauncey's sentence with a chuckle. "J.T. and I'll catch up to you two in a minute if that's alright with you."

"Any time I get first dibs on the bathroom it's alright with me," Sarah said as she headed toward the door while still obviously deep in thought.

"Chauncey, there's a bathroom down the hall and Sarah can use the one upstairs in our bedroom," J.T. said as he verbally guided his guests to the restrooms.

After everyone except John left the room, J.T. said quietly, "That was quite a lesson for those two."

"Yes it was," John replied seriously. "Every word I uttered was the truth. And you better take some major precautions for you and your family. You've had one run-in with these bastards, your name was in the media for days for Chrissake after that Hallelujah Gathering affair, and the jihadists don't forgive or forget."

"I've taken some precautions," J.T. said as he carefully picked his words. "Sarah brought a Bushmaster with her; it even has a CompM4 sight, and she made me borrow it indefinitely. Though I may be too embarrassed to take it to the range and practice with it."

"And why is that?"

"Sarah had a hot pink paint applied to it. It looks like something Barbie would own."

"You don't have a rifle?" John asked as he stifled a chuckle.

"I didn't have a need for one until recently," he said evenly. "Stephanie and I both carry pistols and that seemed to be sufficient until the Hallelujah Gathering."

His voice trailed off as he fell into deep thought.

"J.T.!" Stephanie called from the kitchen. "Would you and John please come to the table so we can say Grace?"

"Uh-oh!" John said boyishly. "We'd better hurry or we'll be in deep trouble with the boss!"

"You got that right," J.T. said, his face beaming with a large smile.

CHAPTER 37

AFTER DINNER CONVERSATION

"J.T., will you please clean the meat from the bones so I can boil them down in the stock pot?" Stephanie asked politely. "I want turkey broth for soup this week."

"Yes dear," he intoned in a slavish, downtrodden voice meant to poke fun at his lovely wife.

"Chauncey and I'll begin washing the dishes," Sarah volunteered. "If that's OK with you, Chauncey."

"It's fine with me if I can still move. Thank you all for such a wonderful dinner."

"I'll second that," John added sleepily. "And I'll begin wiping down the table and counters."

"Y'all don't have to work," Stephanie said. "You're guests."

"And you're a very gracious host," John replied. "But many hands make light work."

"Mom, are you sure you don't want us to help clean up?" Mary asked solemnly. "We still have five minutes before Maria's mom picks us up for the movie."

"You'd better get going so you're not late," Stephanie replied as she snuck a quick glance at the kitchen clock.

"Besides," John added in a teasing manner. "How are we supposed to eat your share of the pies if you're still here?"

"You better not eat my pie, Uncle John," Joan cried with glee at being teased by her favorite visitor before running upstairs to brush her teeth.

"The girls really enjoy spending time with all of you," Stephanie said.

"And we enjoy them," Chauncey replied.

The clean-up went quickly.

"Why doesn't everyone go into the living room and I'll bring the coffee in as soon as it's finished brewing," Stephanie said as she began removing heavy ceramic coffee mugs from the cupboard and arranged them on a silver serving tray.

"Coffee sure sounds like a good idea," John said with a satisfied sigh as he turned to follow the others into the living room.

Stephanie had just finished serving coffee to her guests and taken a seat when Sarah sat back with a weary look on her face.

"All that turkey is making you sleepy, I see," Stephanie said as she smiled at Sarah.

"Maybe a little. I just realized this is the second Thanksgiving since Josh's murder," Sarah replied. "But thanks to y'all I'm not having as bad of a time with it as I thought I would."

A pall fell over the room.

"But I don't want to dwell on that," she said with a breezy air of enthusiasm as she physically roused herself out of her funk by sitting up straighter. "Today is a day to give thanks for the gifts we've been granted over the last year. There's a lot for me to be thankful for and you're a large part of it."

A beaming smile spread across Stephanie's face showing she was gladdened by Sarah's recovery.

"John, you've really piqued my interest," Sarah said as she spun in his direction so quickly that it startled him as he sat entranced in his feast-induced stupor. "What impact will a Muslim jihad have on us directly?"

"It can affect you in many ways," he began. "To fully appreciate the impact jihad may have on you and your country, you have to understand their mindset."

J.T. cringed noticeably at the turn this conversation was taking and looked sheepishly at his wife.

"You see," John said as he warmed to the subject. "Jihad does not recognize universal human rights; therefore, they're very brutal in their ways. It's because they view infidels as inferior to Muslims."

"That's understandable," Chauncey said. "Considering they lump infidel unbelievers in with pigs and excrement."

"Exactly," John replied. "You have to understand their point of view is vastly different from those of us raised in a culture of Judeo-Christian values."

"How do their values differ from ours?" Chauncey asked innocently.

"War is despised and hated while peace is praised in the Judeo-Christian cultures," John explained cordially. "But under jihadist ideology, it is war that is praised and the killing of infidels is held in high esteem."

"So the traditional sentiments we feel about war are not valid when the outlook of the jihadist is taken into consideration."

"You're so very correct, Chauncey," John replied. "Jihad warriors do not accept the tenets of the Geneva Convention or the conventional rules of war. All that matters to them is the death of infidels by any means."

"That's scary," Sarah added intuitively. "Coyotes play by the same lack of rules. No emotion or feelings- only the death of their prey counts to them."

"That's a good analogy," John said with a nod of satisfaction. "But at least with coyotes you know they're predators designed by nature to kill. With jihadists, the media has repeated misinformation over and over again about Islam being a religion of peace. So people are confused and aren't prepared to defend themselves like they would against a known threat."

"For crying out loud!" Sarah interjected as she sat upright in her seat. "President Bush called Islam a religion of peace within a few days of 9-11."

"And the result of this disinformation," John continued, "is that citizens have their concept of reality clouded and any chance of developing a clear, honest understanding of who their enemies are and why they're coming to kill them is lost."

Sarah stared intently at the floor as though seeing a movie reveal itself in the woven golden threads of the carpet.

"Are you still with us Sarah?" John asked in a kidding manner. "Maybe the turkey is finally getting to you and you need a nap, eh?"

"No," she said with a smile. "It just settled in is all."

"What settled in?" Stephanie asked with concern.

"The fact that jihadists are just like coyotes," she said evenly. "We're told they're cute and cuddly but in reality they'll rip your throat out just for the fun of it."

Silence descended upon the occupants of the room like a fog bank as the truth of Sarah's words sunk into their psyches.

"If the jihadists try to kill us," Sarah asked with a slight hitch in her voice. "How do you think they'll attack?"

"WorldNet Daily reported that captured al-Qaeda leaders and documents revealed a plan for an 'American Hiroshima,'" John said, making sure J.T. knew it was information that had been released to the general public. "Their plan is to use nuclear devices in major U.S. cities simultaneously. New York, Boston, Washington, Las Vegas, Chicago, Los Angeles and others would be hit at the same time if the reports are to be believed."

"They can't do that!" Sarah cried with anguish in her voice. "They don't have the missiles to hit that many cities at the same time!"

"They don't need missiles," John said deliberately to allow his next statement to sink in. "Al-Qaeda has obtained over 40 nuclear devices.

Suitcase nukes, artillery shells, missile warheads, and nuclear mines from the former Soviet Union. Then there's always the possibility of them making their own bombs from fissile material they purchase on the black market."

"But they can't smuggle those into the United States!" Sarah wailed. "We have Customs stopping---"

"Oh God!" she wailed, interrupting herself. "They can't even keep bales of pot out of the country!"

"There may already be nuclear bombs here," Chauncey said solemnly. "I remember reading about it. Retired Spetznaz agents, the former Soviet Special Forces, are helping al-Qaeda find nuclear weapons they hid in the United States during the Cold War. I remember that article."

"Bin Laden's goal is to kill four million Americans with the 'American Hiroshima' attack," John said with resignation in his voice. "And he wants two million of those to be children in order to 'avenge the Arab and Muslim world'; whatever that means."

"How would they hope to get so many nukes into the U.S.?" Sarah asked while Stephanie remained strangely silent. "That's a lot of nukes."

"It's surmised they used the MS-13 street gang and other organized crime groups to smuggle them over the southern border of the United States."

"What?"

"You heard me," John said evenly. "The entire furor you hear about illegal immigrants coming across the border with Mexico is not about Mexicans seeking honest work. It's about our sworn enemies coming into our county to kill us where we live."

John allowed his last statement to lie upon the air like a cold, wet blanket.

"You didn't know that Islam is making major gains in converting the native populations of Mexico and Latin America, did you?" John asked snappily. "And our Pentagon has confirmed that Latin

American smuggling rings are attempting to sneak al-Qaeda operatives over the southern border of the United States?

"All Central and South American countries have become springboards for smuggling extremists into the United States. The most common route involves Middle Easterners wending their way to Brazil where a false identity is assumed before entering Mexico.

"U.S. officials have long known about the growing Muslim influence in what has become known as the Muslim Triangle: Brazil, Argentina, and Paraguay. Even Islamic "charities" moved their bases of operations to Central and South America since international pressure coerced them into cutting their traditional ties with terrorists and other allied Islamic organizations such as al-Qaida. It was released in the news but no one paid it any attention."

"That's scary," Chauncey said as he began searching his memory for information related to the news John had just dropped upon them. "Now I remember!"

Everyone looked at him with open mouths and wonderment in their expressions.

"You have your memory back?" Sarah squealed with glee.

"No! No! I don't remember everything!" he said as he chuckled at their misunderstanding. "I remember reading that the FBI director, I can't remember his name, informed congress that al-Qaeda supporters had crossed into the U.S. after adopting Hispanic names while in Brazil and Mexico."

"I seem to remember reading something like that myself," John confirmed with a nodding of his head. "And I was surprised to read that tens of millions of Muslims of Arab descent are living in Latin America."

"But they're not all al-Qaeda or terrorists," Sarah said.

"You may be right," Chauncey replied. "But there may already be terrorists here who crossed over that porous border and our government doesn't seem interested in doing anything to stop them."

"And on that high note of setting our minds at ease," Stephanie said airily as she stood up. "Does anyone want a refill of coffee or some pie?"

CHAPTER 38

DRIVING HOME TO THE FARM

"That was a nice visit," Chauncey said as he and Sarah pulled out of the Tobin's driveway, a cache of leftovers securely stashed in the trunk of Sarah's new Mercedes C-300 Luxury Sedan.

They gave an enthusiastic good-bye wave toward the Tobins standing on their front porch as Sarah turned the 4-spoke steering wheel.

"It certainly was," Sarah agreed emphatically. "It's always nice to get together with family; especially on Thanksgiving."

Out of the corner of her eye she saw Chauncey's head drift slowly to his chest and his eyes drop dejectedly downward.

"I'm sorry, Chauncey," Sarah said sympathetically. "I didn't think about your circumstances before I said that."

"That's OK," Chauncey replied with a twinge of regret in his voice and a faint smile dimly cast upon his lips. "You and the Tobins treat me like family, and y'all seem like family to me."

"Thank you," she said. "You don't know how happy it makes me to hear you say that."

"So, are you planning on going to the Christmas Youth Ministry mass at St. Boniface?" he asked, trying to change the subject.

"I don't think Joan and Mary will let us miss it," she said with a smile, allowing herself a quick glance away from the road toward Chauncey. "They're both part of the ceremony."

"You're probably right," he said with a chuckle.

"And they expect you to be there too," she said. "Did you see how their faces lit up when you said you'd come?"

"Yeah, it's great to see such fine young people being involved in their church," he said. "This bunch of kids has really come together since the Hallelujah Gathering tragedy."

"It's great seeing adults volunteering their time to guide the kids in their ministry with the church," she replied. "A lot of adults wouldn't want to be bothered with someone else's kids, especially during the teenage years."

"I think it's nice how the young people provide everything from the music to the entertainment for the mass," he said. "If I'm not mistaken, Joan is even doing sign language while the youth choir sings *Silent Night*."

"No, it's Mary who's signing. Joan is a candle lighter," she corrected him.

"I think you're wrong," he said standing his ground.

"Well, we're either going to argue about it or put our money where our mouths are," she said with a teasing lilt to her voice.

"Are you so sure of your memory that you're willing to bet the maximum bet allowed by law?" he asked.

"There is no bet allowed by law," she said with a laugh. "So you're willing to bet an entire five bucks on your memory?"

"That's not funny, Sarah," he said returning her laugh with a hearty chuckle. "And yes, I'm willing to bet five bucks because I know it's an easy win; and I always like winning money from you!"

"Oh, is that so? Well, let me tell you---"

And so it went for the rest of the ride to the farm.

CHAPTER 39

UNWELCOME VISITORS

"Are you OK?" Chauncey inquired after a long period of silence. "If you're too tired I can help drive."

"I'm fine, just thinking a little and enjoying the silence," Sarah replied hoping he would take the hint. "Besides, you don't have a driver's license."

"The chances of getting pulled over out here are remote to say the least," he said with a tiny bit of irritation evident in his fatigued voice.

They were almost to Predator's Bane when Chauncey sat straight up in his seat and said, "Your lane is coming up soon."

Sarah ignored him.

"Do you have all the electricity hooked up in the old machine shed the way you want it?" Sarah asked inquisitively. "Is it ready for the inside to be finished?"

"I prefer to refer to it as my cottage now that it's been converted into living quarters," Chauncey replied playfully. "I don't want people getting the impression I live in a shed."

"You know what I mean."

"Yes I do," Chauncey said. "I even have that old computer hooked up so I can do work from either office, even when I'm here at the farm. Maybe someday I can telecommute and work from here and not have to go back to the city."

"That way you can be closer to Annie all week long. Right?"

"Well, yeah," Chauncey replied with a slight blush reddening his face. "That and I can be here to keep an eye on the place. Besides, Nadine needs some help doing the heavier work at her place during the week."

"How can you telecommute from way out here?" Sarah asked as she carefully steered her vehicle from the paved road onto the gravel of her farm's lane.

"I can use an internet service that allows me to access the computers at both offices," Chauncey said.

"How much does the service cost?" Sarah asked seriously.

"Don't worry, it's less than thirty dollars per month," he replied solemnly. "That's less than it costs me to commute to and from both offices on the Metro every month. I keep an eye on the office overhead just as much as you do."

"I know you do," she said feeling a bit guilty for doubting his decision. "And I appreciate that."

Chauncey's eyes abruptly riveted on the farmhouse, his searching gaze scanning rapidly for the anomaly that caught his attention.

"Stop!"

"What's wrong?" Sarah asked as she applied the brakes and brought the Mercedes to a sliding halt as a billowing cloud of grayish dust overwhelmed it, momentarily obliterating their view of the buildings.

"I thought I saw lights on in the upstairs bedroom," he said breathlessly. "Now I can't be sure with all this dust."

"I never leave those lights on," she said with a hint of fear creeping into her voice. "The kitchen and living room lights are on timers."

"Pull up a little so we can see the house better, that tree is in our way," Chauncey instructed as the dust began to settle. "Try and stay over toward the fence so it helps block the headlights."

"OK," Sarah replied as she began moving the Mercedes forward at a snail's pace. "I can definitely see the upstairs bedroom light is on from here."

"Oh shit!" Chauncey swore in an uncharacteristic utterance of profanity. "It just went out. Back out of here. Don't get excited. Just be careful you don't run off the lane because the grass may be soggy from the rain we got yesterday."

Sarah did not reply but began backing the Mercedes toward the road. When she reached the macadam road she stopped to look for traffic. Seeing no headlights she backed onto it.

"What do we do now?"

"We call the state police," he said unemotionally.

"Shit!" she said as she took her turn muttering a profanity. "The cell phones don't pick up any signals until we almost get to Thompsonville."

"Well, let's get moving then," Chauncey replied solemnly. "Hurry but watch for deer crossing the road. We don't need an accident on top of everything else."

CHAPTER 40

BREAK-IN

Tom Mahoney, a thirty-five year old with fair skin and even features quickly swung his long legs out of his police cruiser and rose to his full six feet in a matter of seconds. His lithe form carried a compact 170 pounds and was topped by a smattering of closely cropped light brown hair. He was a thirteen-year veteran of the Virginia State Police having applied to the organization before finishing his stint with the United States Marine Corps.

His eyes rapidly perused the scene with a single glance as his mind processed all the visual information his gaze could glean.

He took a brief moment to smooth the front of his uniform and glanced rapidly from top to bottom to make sure he was presentable to maintain the honor and dignity of his job.

He angled toward the two occupants of the metallic gray Mercedes. His eight-hour shift was to have ended an hour and a half ago but a recent outbreak of the flu demanded mandatory overtime from the officers not yet affected by the virus.

A light misting rain had begun to fall adding to his dreary mood.

"Ma'am, it's OK to return to your home now," the tall, lean officer said as he approached Sarah and Chauncey as they walked across the convenience store parking lot to meet him. "I'm Officer Mahoney and I'll escort you back. Follow me please."

"Was there a break-in?" she asked with a barely perceptible tremor in her voice.

The lightly falling rain made the grayish-black macadam surface of the parking lot appear slippery but it was just an optical illusion. Tom Mahoney turned slowly to face them and said, "There does seem to have been a break-in but the perpetrators are gone."

"Was anything stolen?" she asked shakily as the earthworm-like smell of newly moistened soil reached her nostrils. She absent-mindedly tried straightening her now ruffled hair as it blew in the gusting wind.

"We don't know," the officer said evenly. "That's why I need you to follow me back to your house so you can tell us if anything is missing." His unchanging expression did not add any further clues as to what the situation was at the farm.

Without another word, Officer Mahoney turned and walked back to his cruiser.

"It looks like we better hurry," Chauncey said as he took Sarah by her arm. Normally she would have been offended at his motherly attitude but tonight she felt violated and agreeably followed his lead.

The familiar landmarks flew by as the State Police cruiser motored down the wet, deserted two-lane road well above the posted speed limit. Only a smattering of Holstein cows watched their journey back the exact way they had sped only forty-five minutes earlier.

In a short period of time they arrived back at the farm, and when she turned into the lane, Sarah's stomach lurched at the scene that met her eyes. Eerie, flashing lights glinting from the light bars of three police cars shimmered off the white painted outbuildings and gave the familiar landscape a surreal appearance.

"Please don't touch anything until the fingerprint team has completed their work," Officer Mahoney said unemotionally when he met Sarah at her car door. "If you can just walk through the house and tell me if anything is missing it will help us."

"Oh! They smashed the front door!" she said as her shaking fist flew to her mouth. Previously stifled tears threatened to begin coursing down her cheeks. She started to run toward the door as though she were somehow able to rescue the shattered remnants.

"Yes Ma'am," he said as he trailed behind her with long, even strides. "There's a clear print of a tennis shoe on the door near the lock. It appears they just kicked it in."

"God knows how strong that door was," she said as she surveyed the devastated door lying cock-eyed off its hinges. "It was pretty old."

"It wasn't very strong," he observed. "Before I leave, I'll give you a brochure on what to look for when you buy a new one. A more secure door may deter them in the future."

"Do you think they'll come back?" she asked with fear in her eyes.

"It's been known to happen," he said solemnly. "Where's the man who was with you?"

"He went to his cabin," she said as she pointed toward Chauncey's vanishing form in the strobe-pulsing blue lights. "He's been rehabbing the old machine shed into living quarters."

Sarah slowly surveyed the entire house room by room with Officer Mahoney following her closely. She was careful to not touch anything that may hold fingerprints from the perpetrators.

"Sorry, I can't see anything that's missing other than my laptop," she said after walking through the entire house. "My desk was rifled through, and papers are scattered all over the floor, but it looks like everything is there."

"Are you sure?"

"The best I can tell," she replied. "I don't have a list of all the bills and other paperwork I was working on."

"That's strange," the officer said with a troubled look on his face. "Even the gun safe didn't show signs of attempted forced entry, and there're other items worth more than the laptop computer that haven't been stolen, but your papers have been disturbed."

"Maybe they didn't have time to steal anything else before we showed up."

"Maybe," he said absently with his mind trying to sort out the situation. "But I doubt it. Burglars usually stack the items they want beside the door or window they used to enter the building so they can easily carry it all out when they leave. There's a Bose stereo and flat screen television in the living room on the first floor that are untouched yet they took your laptop from upstairs."

"Was anything stolen?" Chauncey asked Sarah as he walked up.

"Only my laptop and they searched through my desk," she replied with a shiver. "Anything stolen from your cottage?"

"Just that old computer I told you about," he replied.

Tom Mahoney's eyes narrowed noticeably.

"They were after information," he said evenly. "What data did you have that was valuable enough to commit a felony?"

"I don't know," she replied with a look of puzzlement on her face.

"Neither do I," Chauncey added. "We don't have anything to hide and the information we have wouldn't be worth anything to anyone. It's only bills for the farm and chiropractic offices."

"Yeah," Tom Mahoney said as he looked at the two with suspicion.

CHAPTER 41

MUHAMMED'S CHRISTMAS PLAN

A single table lamp with a stained yellow shade sat precariously on a rickety card table, giving off an anemic glow in the corner of the dimly lit room. It was enough illumination for the six men seated in middle of the floor to conduct their nefarious business.

Muhammed Shah was the only man who knew the identity of all the jihadists under his command. They had been implanted into American society and waited for his arrival to gather them together and lead them to glory.

"Bishr and Haady have done well," Muhammed said expansively. "They have been able to supply us with information that will give us success in accomplishing our next mission. The infidels who interfered with our operation at the Hallelujah Gathering will pay for their impudence."

"They have found valuable information that makes our next undertaking possible," Muhammed continued. "Obviously Allah is guiding us."

"With your leadership and Allah's blessing we will succeed in any endeavor, Commander," Bishr said.

Not to be outdone, Haady asked, "Commander, what was of such value in the trash the Americans discarded that will be helpful to us?"

"A very good question, Haady," Muhammed said as Bishr flashed an angry glance in Haady's direction. "The discarded papers contained a permission slip for Jeremy Tobin's daughters to attend the Children's Mass at the St. Boniface Roman Catholic Church."

"And what does that mean, Commander?"

"It means that there will be a large number of infidels gathering at one place," he informed them. "And the man whom we seek to annihilate will be there with his family."

"But Commander, if I may be so bold in asking, doesn't the fact that the permission slip was discarded mean they will not be attending?"

"Very good, Zayd," Muhammad said proudly. "But there is information you do not have that shows this permission slip was likely discarded by mistake."

Zayd was obviously of Middle Eastern extract with very dark walnut hued skin peeking out from beneath a shockingly black head of hair and a full beard. At six-foot two and 170 pounds he often towered over any crowd he was standing in. He had entered the United States on a student visa ten years previously and had stayed after the visa expired. He worked as an auto mechanic in a service center owned by one of the group's supporters.

"And what is that information, Commander?" Zayd asked respectfully.

"There was a weekly bulletin from St. Boniface's Church that had a large red circle around the Children's Mass," Muhammed replied. "And the bulletin went so far as to give the number of people expected to attend the celebration.

"We also have an e-mail he printed out then discarded that discusses family members who will be attending. And more importantly, the e-mail is from the man named Chauncey whom we also seek."

Tortured thoughts of retribution and his hatred for Jeremy Tobin and Chauncey twisted Muhammed's mind. The vengeance he would wreak upon them had occupied his thoughts every day and night since his defeat at the Hallelujah Gathering.

"We will annihilate the meddlers at the same instant we unleash Allah's wrath upon the infidels," he shrieked hysterically as flecks of spittle flew from the edges of his mouth. "The Americans will see the devastation resulting from their ill-chosen ways on their television sets and hear about it on their radios. They will understand that a greater power is not happy with them and their decadent ways."

"Praise be to Allah," the men said in unison.

"What is your plan, Commander?" Najeeb asked after quiet fell once again upon the men.

"I want you and Haady to go to the St. Boniface Church during their worship times and reconnoiter," Muhammed replied immediately. "You will determine the physical layout of the church, note where the worshippers congregate at different times, determine if there are any armed security people present, and see if there are any areas of the structure that may present problems for our attack."

"Why have you chosen Najeeb and Haady, Commander?" Mahdy asked. "What tasks will Bishr, Zayd, and I perform?"

"It is not your place to question my decisions, Mahdy!" Muhammed screamed as his face reddened with rage. "It is because they look more like the lily white Europeans who make up the majority of worshippers at the St. Boniface Church."

Mahdy was obviously not able to blend into a crowd comprised mainly of people hailing from European backgrounds. At five-foot ten inches tall and two hundred pounds he looked much like every other earth-toned Egyptian in Cairo. Even in the three-piece suits he wore in his profession as an economics professor, he was identifiable as a Middle Easterner.

"You have been to the church, Commander?"

"Yes I have been there," Muhammed said irritably. "I cannot wait for you. It is my responsibility to complete this task and I will do so whether you are ready or not!"

A silence fell over the room as the men looked toward the floor in shame.

"Najeeb and Haady are both fair skinned and clean shaven," Muhammed continued. "They have been in this cursed country for most of their lives so speak without accents. They will not only blend in with the worshippers, but will be welcomed as one of their own."

Najeeb and Haady looked discretely at each other to confirm this was true, and it was. Each was as Muhammed described them.

Najeeb was tall at six-foot two inches and had a shock of jet-black hair closely trimmed to his head. His elongated face was highlighted by an oversized nose that gave him a comic, open look, an impression that was further enhanced by his ever-present smile showing narrow but even teeth.

Haady was almost a total opposite of Najeeb. He looked short at five-foot four inches tall and dumpy with a rounded head and belly to match. His fleshy lips and puffy cheeks hid a mouth full of crooked, discolored teeth. While he rarely smiled, his overall appearance led anyone meeting him to regard him as being a harmless, jolly fellow. There was nothing about either man that would raise suspicions about them. Neither would stand out in a crowd, especially an assembly in a church where people rarely noticed or acknowledged other attendees.

"Commander, if you have been to the church, why is it important for Najeeb and Haady to get the same information you must already have?"

"Because, you fool," Muhammed said maliciously. "I want their input without me influencing their observations. The more independent each observance is, the more opportunities we will have of formulating an effective plan of attack."

"While you are there," Muhammed continued as he thought of other angles to his plan. "Make sure you obtain a copy of the weekly bulletin and read all the messages on the various bulletin boards scattered throughout the building. All information is important to us regardless of how inconsequential it may seem."

"What type of information should we specifically be looking for, Commander?" Najeeb asked respectfully.

"The bulletin I took when I visited the St. Boniface Church revealed when the worship times are to be held, which services are most crowded, which aisles are to be kept open for emergencies, and where the children will be seated during the special Children's Mass being held for their Christmas celebration.

"The infidels do not realize how their unguarded gibberish reveals information that makes our tasks more profitable," Muhammed boasted as he warmed to the topic. "They even mention that the Fire Marshall has warned them to keep the crowds below 1,500 people and not to allow more than 300 to stand along the side walls of the church.

"It is very convenient that they will herd the children into a small area where we can kill many of them in one fell swoop," Muhammed said. "This is the seed of the next generation. Their deaths will impact the future of this decadent land and break the morale of the survivors."

"Have you formulated a plan yet, Commander?"

"Yes, I have."

"We are willing to follow you and lay down our lives for Allah. He will reward us for our sacrifice in satisfying his will."

"That is correct, Zayd," Muhammed said. "Allah will reward his true believers but I do not want you to sacrifice yourself unless it is absolutely necessary. There are other tasks needing your skills before you can collect your reward. My plan will allow us all to live more days and continue doing Allah's work."

"Is it too soon to tell us of your plan, Commander?"

"I will tell you my intentions because I want Najeeb and Haady to understand what I have planned when they attend the St. Boniface Church," Muhammed said. "It may help them to understand what may be important during their reconnoitering visit."

Muhammed began speaking in an expansive voice, "A plan must be kept simple to be successful. If it is complicated there are more things that can go wrong. This project is so elementary that it should be foolproof."

"Prior to Christmas Eve on December 24 when the Children's Mass will be held at St. Boniface's Church, we will procure three vans with sliding side doors. The vans must be stolen so they are untraceable and should be work vans that do not have windows on the sides," Muhammed lectured to an audience whose attention he held with every word. "Two will be parked at a Park-and-Ride located three miles from the church. We will ride in the third to launch our attack."

"Commander, if I may interrupt," Bishr said. "Won't we be observed by others at the Park-and-Ride lot?"

"No, you fool!" Muhammed roared, incensed for being interrupted. "The Park-and-Ride lots are located along major thoroughfares so commuters can share rides. Their purpose is to save gasoline and reduce traffic congestion into the major cities. Do you suspect there will be many commuters in the lots on Christmas Eve? A major holiday when few people work?"

Undeterred, Muhammed continued, "The Park-and-Ride lots are perfect for filling our needs. There will be few people, if anyone, there at that time of night."

He stopped to glare menacingly at Bishr then continued.

"Even if anyone is there, the lots are where strangers are not uncommon so new faces are not noticed nor remembered. It is also common for commuters to be leaving one vehicle and get into others," he said with an air of finality. "It is where we will return to make our getaway after our work at the church is done."

"By abandoning the van we use at the church it will throw the authorities off our trail for a short time. When we transfer to the other two vans to make our escape, we will dispose of our firearms by discretely throwing them in the pine trees surrounding the Park-and-Ride."

"Commander, will separating the group into two vans be enough of a deception to confuse the authorities?" Mahdy asked respectfully.

"No it will not, Mahdy," Muhammed explained patiently. "That is why each van will proceed to various small towns in the immediate area surrounding the interstate highways. There, you will each find a discharge man at their privately owned vehicles which have been parked there earlier in the day. The driver of both vans will abandon them when they arrive at their own automobile."

"So we will have men driving their own vehicles in six different directions to various locations within a few short minutes of leaving the church. Since we will have disposed of our rifles the authorities cannot easily connect us to the church raid," Zayd said admiringly. "It is a good plan, Commander."

"Thank you, Zayd," Muhammed replied before scowling perilously at the other men for not acknowledging what he considered a brilliant plan. "If anyone is stopped by the authorities he can claim to be driving to a friend's home in a distant city for the Christmas holiday; a visit each of you should arrange as soon as possible."

"You have planned well, Commander," Haady said in an attempt to redeem himself in his leader's eyes. "Can you tell us about how we will kill the infidels?"

"Yes, Haady," Muhammed said. "The plan is simplicity itself. Now pay close attention."

"I will be attending the Children's Mass on Christmas Eve seated on the right side of the church near the door leading to the outside exit. It is upon my command, given over a disposable cellular telephone that will only be used for this project, that the attack will begin," Muhammed continued. "Just so there is no confusion, when I refer to the right or left side of the church, I am referring to the view from the rear of the building. This is the direction you will be attacking from so it is the perspective which offers the most clarity to avoid misunderstanding."

"Thank be to Allah that you have the gift of planning with great detail," Haady stated emphatically.

"Praise Allah," Muhammed said in an obligatory manner before continuing. "I have discovered that these Catholics are very obedient and rigid in their rituals. Any disruption is disdained and will not elicit an immediate reaction from those attending the service."

"And you were able to discover this just by observing them?" Zayd asked seriously.

"Yes, Zayd," Muhammed replied patiently. "On the one occasion I was there, an old lady fell unconscious. Unlike other settings where Americans will rush without thinking to help the fallen person, these Catholics stood in place without moving and just stared at the old lady's body lying on the floor. Apparently, their training forbids them from immediately leaving their places during a mass even when a fellow worshipper is obviously in need of their assistance. They will not act but will only observe any disturbance as long as it is not immediately apparent they are personally in any danger."

"And we will use this defect in their training against them?" Najeeb asked, not wanting to be outdone by his fellow jihadists.

"Yes," Muhammed replied. "It is the key to my plan. Now let me continue.

"I will wait until the priest begins preparing for the Communion time of the service before giving the signal to attack; it seems to be the time when they are most reluctant to act outside of their worship rituals. The aisles will not yet be filled with worshippers waiting for their turn to get their piece of bread.

"During that time they all seemed to be waiting quietly in their seats. The communion ritual started in earnest approximately forty-five minutes after the mass began. That is when they leave their seats and stand in the aisles.

"This may be different during the Christmas worship, I do not know, just wait for my signal and be ready to go at any moment. We must attack before they jam the aisles and make it impossible for you to maneuver. We only have a small window of time in which to act. Do not allow yourselves to be lulled into complacency while waiting."

"How will we assure that we are close enough to act immediately when we receive your signal, Commander?"

"The weekly bulletin speaks of automobiles parking on the grassy areas because it is such a crowded gathering," Muhammed said with a glowing sense of satisfaction in his voice. "That is why the bulletin is such an important source of intelligence for us. You will park among the hordes then sit quietly in the back of the van to wait for my signal."

"That is why it is important that the vans do not have windows in the rear area," Mahdy mused.

"Very perceptive, Mahdy," Muhammed said approvingly.

"What will we do when we get your signal?" Haady asked, his physical appearance mistakenly giving the accomplished computer programmer the appearance of suffering from low intelligence. The people he worked with at the Union Bank knew he was a very bright and educated man but even they often looked into his black, beady eyes poking out from beneath brushy jet-black eyebrows and spoke to him as if he were brain damaged.

Muhammed laid out three poster-sized photographs showing the front entrance of the church. "I had these photos enlarged at Wal-Mart when I bought the disposable cellular telephones," he said. "These Americans offer anything for mere money even if it will lead to their own destruction."

"Upon my signal you five men will drive the van up to the front of the church," he said as he pointed to heavy wood framed glass-fronted doors situated under a large portico built to protect church-goers exiting their vehicles during inclement weather. "In this next photo you can see the driveway leading up to the front entrance."

"Najeeb, you will be driving the van so one of your duties will be to get a close-up view of this entranceway. It is a foyer approximately twelve meters wide and three meters deep," Muhammed said. "I want the driver to be intimately familiar with the building by actually seeing it in person. Haady, you also will pay attention to these details, especially the escape route, just in case something happens to Najeeb - you will be our back-up driver."

Haady nodded his large, round head in acknowledgement then asked, "Commander, is it possible to see through the foyer into the lobby?"

"Yes," Muhammed said patiently. "The glass fronts of the doors are full-length top to bottom and almost the entire width of the door except for the wood frame. There are eight doors side by side so you can see into the lobby very well. Now let me continue."

"This third picture is from across the street and shows a larger view of the entire building," Muhammed pointed out. "While Najeeb and Haady are in the church, they will discretely use their cell phones to take many pictures of the interior so the rest of you will know how the facility is laid out."

"And after we all arrive at the front doors of the church?" Bishr asked anxiously, concerned about Haady's observation of the glass doors.

"Then you will exit the side door of the van, with Najeeb staying in the vehicle," Muhammed said as he gestured toward the four men. "Each will have an AK-47 that has been smuggled into this country from our friends in Pakistan hidden under a long coat. Each of you will carry a backpack on your back."

Picking up a blank piece of white photocopier paper Muhammed drew a crude map of the inside of the church.

"Najeeb will park the van here," he said as he pointed with a dirty fingernail in need of a trimming. "The four of you will proceed through these doors into the lobby."

"Bishr, you will veer to the left to go down this long hallway," he said as he continued tracing with his filthy finger on the map. "It leads to an entrance near the front of the church where the altar is located.

You will place your backpack half-way between this door and the altar."

"Haady, you will proceed straight through the lobby and enter this door then walk with long strides up the aisle that's situated slightly to the left of center," Muhammed said as he took a quick glance at Haady's face to make sure he was comprehending the instructions. "You want to walk rapidly but smoothly. Do not run. Such movements will not raise an alarm with the worship participants. Then you will place your backpack about halfway down the aisle."

"Mahdy, you will go down this aisle that is slightly right of center of the church's main hall and do exactly as I have already instructed Haady."

"Zayd, you will veer to the far right and go down this long hallway mirroring the one Bishr is going down on the left side," Muhammed said expansively. "You will place your backpack halfway between the door you enter and the altar. We are targeting the churchgoers, not the priest. We want to maximize the injuries and death among the worshippers, especially the children."

"Commander, how do you know that the children will be sitting toward the front near the altar?"

"The weekly bulletin given out by the St. Boniface Church instructs the parents of the younger children to sit in the front of the main hall so it will be easy for the children to find them when they are finished performing their songs at the altar," Muhammed replied. "I told you the bulletin was a treasure trove of information."

"And where will you be sitting, Commander?" Haady asked in his slow, wandering voice while his pig-like eyes bored intensely into Muhammed's.

"I will be here," he said as he pointed to a spot near where he had showed Zayd to place his backpack. "I will leave just before you arrive, pass Zayd in the hallway on my way to the van, and there I will wait for you to finish your work."

"How much time do you think we will need to place our backpacks?" Bishr asked seriously.

"I estimate fifteens seconds from the time you enter the doors until you place your backpacks."

"And what is in the backpacks, Commander?"

"High explosives with small pieces of metal to wound and maim," Muhammed answered unemotionally. "You each will activate the timers on your explosives at the same instant just before exiting the van. The timers will be set for one hundred forty-five seconds. That will give you sixty seconds to place the backpacks then return to the rear of the church, and thirty more seconds to shoot three magazines from your AK-47 into the seated crowd. Each magazine holds thirty cartridges so many infidels will be killed or wounded. The AK-47s are fully automatic like the ones you trained with in Afghanistan and Somalia."

"Commander," Mahdy asked politely. "Will we have an opportunity to shoot these rifles before we use them at the church?"

"There is no need," Muhammed replied in a snobbish tone. "They have been tested for reliable functioning before they were shipped and I have been assured they are 'mechanically perfect' for a mission such as this. Besides, at the close range you will be deploying them, sights will not be necessary. Killing unarmed infidels is not difficult."

"Why should we shoot the infidels if they will be killed by the explosions?" Bishr asked impatiently while fidgeting.

"You are too stupid and impudent for your own good, Bishr!" Muhammed growled angrily. "If you were paying attention you would have noticed that all the backpacks are toward the front of the church; that is by design. By shooting from the back of the church you will not only be killing infidels in that area of the building but you will also terrify those sitting in the front. When they panic they will begin running from their seats toward the backpacks when the explosives detonate."

"And there will be a greater number of casualties because they will be closer to the explosives," Zayd said admiringly.

"As well as having dispersed the infidels," Muhammed added. "If they are tightly packed into the pews, that is what they call the rows of seats they sit on, the flying metal from the explosion will be absorbed by the bodies closest to it. By spreading the infidels out, the explosion will have greater destructive effect against more people."

"Are there any other ways to increase the destructive effects of the explosion?" Mahdy asked.

"Yes, there is, and it has already been discussed," Muhammed said impatiently. "By having the bombs coordinated to explode at the same time the combined effect from the concussion will amplify the destructive effects."

"Who is this bomb maker?" Bishr asked suddenly. "And where is he located? Can we be sure he is competent in his craft?"

"Why do you ask, Bishr?" Muhammed asked suspiciously as his internal warning alarms began sounding in his mind.

"I ask because this is a wonderful plan and I want to be sure the bomb maker constructs explosives that will wreak massive amounts of destruction upon the infidels," Bishr answered meekly, knowing he had overstepped his bounds.

"I will take you to the bomb maker so you can observe his work firsthand, Bishr," Muhammed answered slyly. "It is time that you meet more of the people in the organization."

"Thank you, Commander," Bishr answered gleefully as his spirits soared for having his talents recognized.

"So the terrified infidels will be exterminated by the explosions after we have left the building?" Mahdy asked quizzically.

"Yes, we will maximize the destruction by spraying the infidels with automatic weapons fire directed from side-to-side," Muhammed instructed them as he mimed with his hands as though he held an AK-47 in front of him. "Kill as many as you can by shooting into the crowd. Do not pick out single targets unless they resist and threaten you. If that occurs then you must deal with them individually. Then immediately return your attention to again shooting into the crowd in the way I have described."

"Commander, how will we know when our time is up and the explosions occur?"

"Each of you will carry a common digital kitchen timer which you will coordinate and set for one hundred twenty-five seconds. That will give you twenty seconds to return to the van before the explosives detonate," Muhammed explained patiently as if he were speaking to a child. "When the kitchen timer sounds you must leave immediately even if you have not expended all your ammunition."

"Won't survivors be able to identify us?"

"No, you fool," Muhammed snapped. "Everyone except me will be wearing a face mask as the infidel children do when sled riding. I will not be associated with the attack because I will be observing the worship service from the crowd."

"What will I be doing while the others are performing their tasks?" Najeeb asked.

"You will be guarding the van: it is our only means of escape," Muhammed replied. "Then you will cover the others as they leave the main worshipping area of the church. If any of the infidels interfere with them, you are to intervene. Each man will carry four thirty-round magazines when they enter the church. Shoot three into the crowd and save the fourth to fight your way out if necessary."

"When the shooting starts, won't the infidels just want to escape?" Najeeb asked.

"There will always be the possibility that some of the infidels standing in the back of the church or in the lobby will attempt to stop you even though they only have bare hands against your rifles," Muhammed replied. "Do not forget the attempt to stop our brothers from destroying the U.S. Capitol Building on 9-11. All perished in the fields of Pennsylvania, but the people in the Capitol Building were spared. The American fighting spirit is not to be underestimated, Najeeb."

"Will there be infidels standing in the rear of the church instead of sitting in the, what did you call them? Pews?" Mahdy asked respectfully.

"The weekly bulletin from the St. Boniface Church spoke of this phenomenon," Muhammed replied sagely. "It told of the Fire Marshall warning the church elders to keep the aisles clear and restrict the number of worshippers standing toward the rear of the main hall and in the lobby. That is how I know you should have unrestricted access up the aisles but returning to the van may bring problems."

"How large is this lobby in the rear of the church?" Mahdy asked with concern in his voice.

"It is large," Muhammed replied. "I estimate it is forty feet from the front doors where the van will be parked under the portico to the doors leading into the main worship hall and sixty feet wide. It will hold a large number of people. There are many infidels who worship at St. Boniface's church and the Children's Mass is a special event so many of their out-of-town relatives will be attending."

"Commander, what if the authorities intervene before we escape or interfere before the attack can begin?" Zayd asked.

"They will not," Muhammed replied simply. "I have another group of men, men you will probably never meet, placing stolen cars packed with explosives at three other churches. The worshipping services at those churches are starting at 8:00 p.m. That is one hour after the Children's Mass begins at St. Boniface's. The timers on the car bombs will be set to detonate at 7:40 p.m. precisely when most of the worshippers will be arriving at those churches. That is approximately five minutes before the attack will begin at St. Boniface's."

"The authorities will be too busy with those incidents to be concerned about St. Boniface's," Zayd said admiringly.

"Yes, Zayd, but you have to understand the large impact this will have on the infidels because it is more than just a diversion,"

Muhammed replied as he smiled smugly. "The media will report this as four churches being attacked simultaneously with hundreds killed or injured."

"And the simultaneous attacks will shake the faith of the non-believers, forcing them to convert to Islam," Zayd said admiringly. "It is a brilliant plan, Commander. Allah has blessed you."

"Yes he has, Zayd," Muhammed said. "Yes he has. Praise be to Allah."

"Praise be to Allah," they chanted in unison.

CHAPTER 42

THE BOMB MAKER

Muhammed Shah's flint black eyes flashed incessantly across the table filled with chemistry equipment. The thirty-four year old native of Saudi Arabia had trained ten years for this event and he did not want to risk failure when he was so close to achieving his objective.

"Be careful," Muhammad reiterated unnecessarily to Idries Iqbal, the master bomb-maker of the terrorist cell he commanded. "We don't want to have to explain to our Almighty Allah how we blew ourselves up without killing any infidels."

"What is it?" Bishr asked inquisitively.

"It is hexamethylene triperoxide diamine. HMTD is easier for you to remember, I'm sure." Idries said with contempt and disdain clearly evident in his voice as he spoke to Bishr.

"Do you have enough of the explosives to meet our needs?" Muhammad asked, trying to assuage his curiosity and fears.

"Do not be so nervous," Idries consoled. "There are one and a half times more explosives than we need. I made sure to add extra."

"Do you think we will need extra?" Bishr asked and was greeted by a steely stare from Idries.

"I want the destruction of the building to be extensive," Idries explained calmly as he fiddled with the glass beakers containing clear liquid being gently heated over the bluish-orange flame of a Bunsen burner. "The American television news crews will fly over the remains of the church taking pictures and video from a helicopter. I want them to have a strong visual image of utter destruction to show the people watching at home."

"That is true," Muhammad said with a faraway look in his eyes and wonder in his voice. "The infidels will not be touched by the death of hundreds of children and their parents if they are strangers, but one picture of a destroyed building will remain in their minds."

"The pictures of the destroyed Murrah Federal Building in Oklahoma City and the piles of rubble from the World Trade Center still haunt the Americans."

"How will these bombs be constructed?" Bishr asked innocently.

"Each of the men running into the church will carry a 100 pound backpack filled with HMTD and many shiny, steel ball bearings," Muhammed replied. "The HMTD will be stuffed into a section of small-diameter metal stove-pipe that has small holes drilled into it to hold the ball bearings in place. This will then be slid into a larger diameter pipe that also has ball bearings imbedded in it. More HMTD will be placed between the two ball bearing laden stove-pipe sections in a shaped charge configuration to maximize the outward thrust of the explosive's blast."

"Will it be placed into the backpacks like that?" Bishr asked.

"Of course not," Idries replied. "If the device is not held upright, the ball bearings will fly into the ceiling and floor instead of into infidels."

"How will you keep the device in the proper position?" Bishr asked while feeling important for having input into the details of the plan.

"The entire assembly with the pipes and ball bearings will be secured to a plywood base that has been cut to perfectly fit the bottom of the backpacks," Idries replied unemotionally. "This will assure that when the backpack is set on the floor it will remain upright which is very important to guarantee that the maximum amount of damage will be inflicted upon detonation of the bombs."

"Is that all that is needed to direct the flying ball bearings into the crowd of Christmas Eve worshippers?" Bishr asked expansively as he puffed out his chest, realizing he was being given information the others were not. He was quite proud of the elevated level of trust he had ascended to.

"No," Idries answered dryly. "A steel plate on the top and bottom of the assembly with a threaded steel rod running between them and secured with a washer and nut will securely hold it together. Such a sturdy apparatus is necessary to direct the ball bearings laterally instead of allowing the blast to dissipate skyward."

Bishr tried to slide his chair back from the scarred kitchen table the three men were huddled around, but the chair legs became entangled in the thick, shiny plastic drop cloth spread over the floor.

"Why do you have plastic on the floor?" he asked.

"It is because the chemicals in the explosives can bleach the color out of anything it touches and this is a rented apartment," Idries answered with irritation in his voice. "And to catch other messes I do not want on my floor."

Bishr smiled and settled back into his chair when Muhammed walked behind him and placed his left hand on his shoulder in a fatherly gesture.

"Do not be aggravated, Idries," Muhammed said. "Bishr is the inquisitive one of my group."

The smile that spread on Bishr's face when he heard his Commander brag about him was like a child's after hearing his father boasting of his good grades. This elated emotional state lulled Bishr into a false sense of security and complacency that allowed Muhammed to slip a ten-inch butcher knife under his chin and slice his throat from ear to ear.

Blood poured freely from the severed ends of the carotid arteries on both sides of his neck while his last breath spewed a spray of thick, red blood across the length of the kitchen table. His lungs instantly began shrinking in size as the pressure difference between them and the surrounding atmospheric pressure equalized.

Muhammed pushed the panicked man firmly into the chair with his left hand then used his right to plunge the butcher knife into Bashir's chest in order to pierce his aorta where it exited the top of his heart. The additional wound served to speed the loss of blood while offering Muhammed a handhold to control his victim's thrashing body.

Idries leaned toward the dying man and looked directly into his terrified eyes and asked, "Which of the accursed American intelligence agencies do you work for Bishr? Who has paid you to ask all these questions? Why did you want to know who I am and where I live?"

Not expecting to get an answer from a man whose throat had been cut, Idries continued harassing him in his last moments on earth, "To answer your question before you die, this plastic drop cloth was placed here to catch your blood and wrap you in to make it easier to dispose of your cursed body."

When Bishr ceased thrashing, Muhammed allowed his body to drop gently to the floor.

"Idries, you will take care of this?"

"Yes, Commander," he said simply.

"You will take Bishr's place carrying the backpack of explosives down the left side of the church on Christmas Eve."

"Yes, Commander," Idries replied. "I am honored."

"Are the car bombs ready?"

"Yes, commander," he replied respectfully. "My men are prepared to perform the tasks Allah has ordained for them. Creating the three diversions at the other churches was very intuitive of you."

"Thank you, Idries."

CHAPTER 43

CHRISTMAS EVE AT ST. BONIFACE

Sarah usually scheduled patients until three o'clock on Christmas Eve and New Year's Eve to assure they have the care they need to help them through the holiday. Two emergency cases had called for appointments shortly after two o'clock, causing her whole afternoon to be delayed. She was late getting out of the office because she never turned down a person in need.

"Why do people wait until the last minute before coming for treatment?" Chauncey asked as he placed gifts for the Tobins into the trunk of her Mercedes C-300 Sedan.

"Oh, it's because they're busy shopping, or baking cookies, or decorating, or any of the hundreds of things people do to prepare for the holidays," she said noncommittally. "Everything but their health is on their minds until the last minute, then it's a crisis because they realize they can't enjoy the holiday when they're in screaming agony."

"It's rude and inconsiderate to ruin your holiday because of their lack of foresight," he said irritably. "They both had pain for weeks but suddenly this afternoon it became a top priority. Why didn't they get it taken care of weeks ago?"

"I've learned to expect it and not get upset by discourteous behavior," she said whimsically. "Don't let their lack of consideration ruin your holiday."

"I won't," he replied as he mentally admonished himself to calm down. "I called J.T. and told him we'd be late. They're going ahead to the church because it begins filling up at five-thirty for the 7 o'clock mass."

"The Children's Mass is really big," she said. "The entire family from Grandma and Grandpa all the way out to aunts and uncles want to see the kids do their thing. It's more of a circus than a serious religious service."

"And that's probably OK with God," he replied seriously. "I'm sure He's happy when the children have fun going to His House for worship. Religious services don't always have to be solemn and boring."

"Are you saying that going to the Baptist church with Annie is livelier than attending the stodgy, formal masses at the Catholic church?"

"Something like that," he said with a huge smile breaking over his face and a glimmer of vivaciousness twinkling in his eyes.

It was only a twenty-five minute drive from Sarah's office to St. Boniface's Roman Catholic Church but traffic was light and the trip went smoothly. The parking lot at St. Boniface's was a different story.

"Look at those idiots!" she said heatedly. "They're parking on the grass and in the little spaces with the yellow lines painted on them!"

"Calm down, there's no reason getting all worked up over other people's inconsiderateness," he said teasingly. "Isn't that what you told me just a little while ago?"

"Yeah, well--" she sputtered. "Damned! Who do these people think they are? Seeing their grandkids can't be that important! Get out of my way you moron!"

"Calm down, calm down," he said with a chuckle. "Let's get away from here a few blocks and see if we can find parking on the street."

It took Sarah over five minutes of impatient waiting to work her way out of the church's parking lot.

"I'll be glad when you have a license and can drive," she said as they sped down a side street. "Then we'll see how patient you are with these imbeciles."

"If I ever get a driver's license you'll see the quintessential example of coolness under pressure," he said chidingly. "If you look in the dictionary under 'cool' you'll see my picture."

Sarah laughed until she had to wipe tears from her eyes.

"OK, OK, you win. I'll calm down. Assuming I don't run over a few of these halfwits first!"

"How about parking in that supermarket lot?"

"That will work. They're closing soon so they probably won't mind."

"It's only a few blocks to walk," he said. "We'll be able to get there on time if you can walk that far in those heels."

"I'll manage," she replied determinedly. "Just as long as there're any seats left by the time we get there."

The walk to St. Boniface's went quickly. Upon entering the church, Chauncey was shocked to see how many children were in attendance.

"This is a real zoo!" he gasped. "There are kids everywhere! Where are those kids' parents?" he asked incredulously as he pointed wide-eyed at a pair of boys wildly having a jumping contest.

"A real children's zoo you might say, eh?" she said with a kidding tone in her voice.

"Very funny," he said as he guided her by her elbow toward the main hall. "Let's go over here to the right and see if we can find any seats."

"Some of those little kids may have never seen a crowd this large. It's really exciting for them," she said. "Try not to step on any kids."

"What do you think?" she asked with exasperation in her voice as she tried to see around the main hall of the church.

Chauncey, being much taller than Sarah, saw there were ushers cruising up and down the aisles seating people in available seats.

"Let's go over this way," Chauncey said, indicating they should go farther to the right side of the church. "This is the side J.T. usually sits on."

"Lead the way," she said.

The teenage usher was standing halfway up the aisle. When he made eye contact with Chauncey, his inquisitive eyes asked "How many?" without a word having to be said.

Chauncey held up two fingers and the usher took three steps forward and motioned for the people sitting in the pew to move toward the middle. The grumpy glances from the people in the pew clearly conveyed they were not happy with having to slide closer to their neighbor.

"There are some seats," he said as he again took her arm. "Let's go."

"You sit on the aisle so you have room for your long legs," Sarah said considerately.

After settling themselves and offering a smile of gratitude to the disgruntled people in the pew Sarah asked, "Do you see them anywhere?"

"No, I can't see them," he replied after standing and looking around.

"Stay standing," she instructed him. "They'll see you if you don't find them first."

"There they are way over there," Chauncey said as he waved his right hand high above his head.

"I'm going over to say hello. Save my seat," she said as she prepared to slide past him and into the crowd once again. He stepped into the aisle and let her pass.

"Leave your coat here to save your place," he said helpfully. "I'll stay here."

In the lobby of the church, Sarah saw children beginning to take their places for the beginning of mass. This left a multitude of grandparents, aunts, uncles, and cousins scrambling to find the best seats or places to stand beside the walls to get a good view of the children.

"Why did you sit all the way over here? Don't you always sit on the other side?" she asked in way of a greeting. She hugged them tightly as though she hadn't seen them for years.

"This side will give us a better view of the children as they perform," Stephanie explained.

"Why are you wearing that raincoat?" Sarah asked J.T. "Are you cold?"

"No, I'm comfortable, thank you."

"I must admit, J.T., that light tan raincoat makes quite the fashion statement but you'll roast in here with all these people giving off body heat," she said chidingly. "At least open it up before you pass out from the heat if you're not going to take it off."

"I'm fine, thanks," he replied.

They enjoyed small talk but the specter of the Hallelujah Gathering debacle still hung heavily over the parishioners of St. Boniface's.

"It's a little scary that this is the first Christmas since the Hallelujah Gathering massacre," Stephanie remarked.

"Did they ever find out why they attacked the Gathering?"

"The terrorist Jason Hagen captured said it was because they took offense at the Pope's comments about the views held by a twelfth century cleric regarding the Islamic faith," Stephanie replied with trepidation in her voice. "It was the words of a guy who died centuries ago for crying out loud! But it was enough for those crazies to attack a bunch of churches around the world and the Hallelujah Gathering. I wonder if they're still mad at us."

"It's a concern," Sarah replied. "That's why I'm a little better prepared than usual. And I'm sure a number of others are also."

Confessing to anyone, even Stephanie, that I'm armed is something I never do, something the trainers at ARI warned us not to do, but I had to say something to help assuage her fears.

Stephanie smiled as her eyes made an unconscious sweep of Sarah's body.

She says she's armed but I can't see where she would hide it. How does she conceal something as big as a pistol on that slim figure she has?

Maybe I should have worn my pistol but it's such a burden. Besides, this is a church.

"I'd better get back to Chauncey before he gives away my seat. I'll see you at your house tomorrow," Sarah said then turned and began wading back through the crowd.

"Thanks for saving my seat," she said breathlessly as she popped out of the crowd at Chauncey's side. "I think this show is about to begin."

The beginning of the Children's Mass was signaled by the sounds of the organ reverberating around the cavernous hall. A massive jumble of bodies began scattering in every direction as everyone scrambled to take his or her seat.

Children of differing age groups performed each presentation and the time passed quickly. Before long the presiding priest began preparing for the communion offering and Muhammed made a discrete cellular telephone call from the last pew on the right side of the church.

I shouldn't have drunk that decaf coffee on the way over here. This mass has gone on way too long. I can't wait.

"I'll be back in a few minutes," she whispered into Chauncey's ear as she made her way out of the pew.

Look at how all these people are crammed in here. If there was a fire they'd never all get out safely. The Fire Marshall must be having a bird

The bathrooms are on the other side of the lobby. I hope there's not a long line because of all these people overloading the facilities.

When she pushed her way through the glass front doors leading from the main hall of the church into the spacious lobby, she was aghast at how many children and parents were moving about. Barely audible over the din was a broadcast of the events from the mass so people in the spacious lobby could follow the proceedings.

J.T. told me this building won an architectural award for its innovative design when it was built ten or so years ago. It does have some nice features.

As she looked beyond the swarms of people, she took greater notice of the unique architectural aspects of the building itself.

Those large ceiling-to-floor windows forming the outside walls of the lobby give a commanding view of the front yard and really make it pleasant to sit out here on sunny days. I never realized how peaceful I am when I sit out here in the mornings before attending mass. I'm glad I started attending services here those few mornings during the week.

She began to wend her way through the throng of bodies.

A lot of these people probably couldn't fit into the main hall of the church. I wonder how far over the maximum allowed capacity we are tonight?

When she was halfway through the lobby she had to make a decision.

The large three-by-six foot carved natural Pennsylvania stone baptismal fountain sat ten feet away from the wall. Its round-bottomed basin sat grandly on a laid stone foundation four feet tall. The entire structure formed a narrow alleyway between it and the wall.

Thirty feet of open space lay between the fountain and the front doors. Both the area in front of and behind the fountain was jammed with a seething, multitude of smiling, chattering people of all ages.

J.T. says that baptismal fountain is a full sixteen inches deep and was designed to perform full-body infant immersion baptisms if the parents opt for that type of ceremony.

I better go toward the outside doors to avoid the congestion behind the baptismal fountain. I'll never get through that mess.

She excused herself over and over again as she crossed the lobby, dodging left then right as she sidestepped around individuals and groups. She was forced closer and closer toward the glass-fronted doors leading to the portico. When she was standing ten feet from the doors, she detoured around a group of children dressed as shepherds and happened to glance through the foyer toward the portico outside and saw a very strange sight.

What is a van doing discharging passengers now? The mass is almost over.

I hope these kids get out of my way. I'm really getting desperate.

She was pushing past a group standing in her way when she noticed a pair of men wearing long trench coats and black facemasks jump out of the van's side door.

The gravity of the situation hit her like a slap in the face.

In a flash, a ball of fear and dread settled in the pit of her stomach and her legs buckled slightly when the shock of reality struck her.

"What the hell's going on here?" she heard herself say without conscious thought.

Then the dumpily built Haady jumped from the van and allowed his trench coat to fall open revealing an AK-47 swinging wildly on a black nylon sling.

Oh my God! she thought as her right hand dove into the confining bowels of her Coronado Leather Classic concealment handbag.

The Velcro closures sealing the hidden compartment holding her holstered pistol parted with a loud ripping sound. Her groping hand gripped the polymer stock of the Glock in an adrenaline-vitalized fist and yanked it from its moorings.

I hope this isn't just a bunch of kids playing an elaborate prank, she thought as time seemed to slow precipitously.

In a spasm of fear and surprise, she began backpedaling away from the glass-front doors as the heart-stopping scenario began playing out in front of her eyes. Just as she brought the Glock up to eye level, her back slammed into a harried mother chatting amicably with a woman in a coyote fur coat. The collision jostled them all.

"What the hell are you doing?" the woman growled angrily as she spun around to give Sarah a piece of her mind.

Sarah did not hear her. Her attention was glued on the armed man rocketing directly toward her.

Haady had already passed the first set of glass-front doors with Mahdy directly behind him by the time she recovered from the rear-ender. Just as his sweat drenched hand grasped the brass handle of the inner door Sarah placed the XS System's 24/7 Big Dot front sight on his upper chest and pressed the Glock's safe-action trigger.

BAM!

The woman Sarah had collided with screamed, grabbed her golden-haired daughter, and blindly fled as the panicking hordes surged forward in mass confusion, desperately trying to escape the violence erupting behind them.

The look of shocked horror and surprise on Haady's face as the glass in front of his eyes disintegrated into a shower of glittering shards was clearly etched into Sarah's mind. Because of his adrenaline-charged nervous system, he did not feel the 115-grain CorBon DPX bullet smash into his chest at 1,250 feet-per-second then release its 399 foot pounds of energy into his lungs and heart.

The solid copper DPX, laboriously heat-treated for toughness with a deep cavity in the front end peeling back in six razor-edged petals, retained 100% of its weight as it bore a straight path of destruction along the entire length of its travel.

Suddenly Sarah was acutely aware she was suffering from tunnel vision and auditory exclusion. Her instructors at ARI had warned her about the reduction of sight and hearing when involved in a gunfight, which is understandable when someone is trying to kill you. She ignored both phenomena and concentrated on the threat staring her in the face.

Create distance between you and the threat. Distance is your friend.

Shuffle your feet backward. Never cross them to avoid tripping.

Concentrate on the front sight.

Press the trigger. Don't jerk it.

BAM!

Shuffle backward. Front sight. Press trigger.

BAM!

Shuffle backward---

Training and repetition had engrained the lessons into her subconscious actions.

Move! Move! Move! Keep moving. Don't give them a stationary target!

Deadly slugs slammed into Haady's upper chest with sickening regularity. The terrorized crowd assumed Sarah was the perpetrator and parted like the Red Sea under command of Moses's staff clearing a path between her and the baptismal fountain. Their only concern was to save themselves and their children.

She continued to step backward toward the fountain because it offered the only cover within the immediate area capable of stopping incoming bullets. At the same instant her buttocks met the chilling, wet torrent of water flowing over the side of the cold, stone fountain, Haady tried to take a step over the lower portion of the wood doorframe.

His oxygen-starved, befuddled brain would not allow him to pick his foot up high enough to clear the frame. When his toe caught, the 100-pound mass of explosive material on his back plunged his body forward. His mind registered the six-inch by six-inch Georgia Red Clay tiles of the lobby's floor just before his forehead made contact.

He did not hear the abysmally loud cracking noise that accompanied the shattering of his cranium.

Sarah did not waste time staring at Haady's crumpling body.

Her eyes scanned for other threats while her feet felt blindly around the raised stone rim surrounding the fountain. Before she could maneuver to the backside of the fountain, Mahdy and Idries bolted through the doors on either side of Haady's limp body. They hurtled toward the main hall of the church, their eyes locked on the doors they must breach to deliver their payload of death.

Before the crash of the first gunshot faded away, Muhammed pushed himself to his feet from the kneeling position he had assumed to imitate the other worshippers and launched himself from the end of the pew where he had strategically situated himself.

What is wrong?

What has gone wrong with my perfect plan?

A legally armed citizen had not been calculated into Muhammed's scheme.

A spasm of fear clawed at his guts as he propelled himself through the side door to the small hallway leading toward the lobby. Ninety feet away, in the same lobby Muhammed was running toward, Sarah was battling a similar spasm of fear gnawing at her.

Now! You have to shoot now! If those two get too far into the lobby you're toast because they'll outmaneuver you. Keep them contained as best you can.

Mahdy was running to his right while Idries maneuvered to his left. Their respective positions would indeed allow them to outflank Sarah if they were allowed to continue unimpeded in their headlong rush. Both terrorists had begun clawing at their trench coats in a struggle to free the AK-47s hidden beneath.

This is not supposed to be happening! Mahdy's terrorized mind screamed. Swinging the Big Dot sight on her Glock toward him, Sarah loosed a round.

BAM!

A miss! Damn it! Slow down and concentrate. Speed only slows you down. Concentrate!

Settling the front Big Dot sight into the 'V' cradle of the rear, Sarah carefully caressed the trigger. Six pounds of pressure on her finger tripped the safe-action trigger mechanism sending a 115-grain pill into Mahdy's humerus.

SNAP!

The unbelievably loud noise when the bullet blasted the bone of his upper left arm into innumerable shards startled him even before the pain began searing into his brain. The hardened warrior had experienced pain many times in his young life, and it was not unfamiliar to him, but the flaming agony he now experienced sent his fevered mind to the brink of consciousness.

The fact that his arm now moved where it had never moved before, in an area four inches below his shoulder, overwhelmed his increasingly confused thoughts.

After demolishing the arm bone, the DPX disintegrated the lateral aspect of his sixth rib before lodging in his lung when its momentum was finally spent. He tried unsuccessfully to ignore his useless arm swinging lazily at his side then began staggering like a drunk.

Ignore him. He'll wait. Deal with the one to your right.

Before Sarah's body could respond to her mind's commands, Idries managed to rip open the restraining buttons on his trench coat and was frantically tearing at the interfering cloth to bring his AK-47 into play. Sarah planted the Big Dot squarely on the center of his upper chest.

WHOCK! WHOCK! WHOCK! WHOCK! WHOCK!

A swarm of 123-grain, full-metal jacketed bullets began slamming into the polished wood covering the concrete block wall behind her. Najeeb the driver was assuring that the men with backpacks were not hindered by anyone while at the church.

He was positioned in the center of the van's side doorway with his AK-47 held tightly to his shoulder. His right eye sighted down the barrel as he had been taught to do in the training camp situated in the relative safety of the Somalia desert.

But one fact had escaped him and his comrades. Their rifles were not sighted in for them and were not shooting to point of aim.

Najeeb's rounds were impacting a full three feet high at twenty-five yards. Such carelessness did not matter when the goal was to mow down unarmed victims at point blank range with automatic rifle fire, but became crucial in a firefight against an armed and capable opponent.

Shifting her attention from Idries, who was still struggling with his overcoat, to Najeeb, she established a flash sight picture on the silhouette in the van and loosed a double-tapped flurry of bullets.

BAM! BAM!

Through a shimmering starburst of shattering glass she saw him flinch but not fall. Sarah would have shot Najeeb again because he was still standing, and was therefore still a threat, but a specter of movement caught her attention as Zayd made his move. In a blur of motion, Zayd erupted from the far right glass door between the foyer and the portico.

He had flattened himself against the wall when Sarah began shooting, and now that he had sorted out the situation unfolding before his eyes, he was ready to act. His headlong sprint for the main hall of the church was hindered by the staggering bulk of Mahdy who continued wandering aimlessly in tight circles holding his drooping arm with his uninjured right hand, his AK-47 and mission forgotten.

Seeing him dashing by out of the corner of her eye, Sarah swung her nine-millimeter ahead of the running man and loosed a single round.

BAM!

She instantly knew it hit low because a puff of shredded cloth and bloody tissue burst from the side of Zayd's hip just above the joint. He fell face first onto the unforgiving surface of the tile floor sprawling helter-skelter beside the prancing feet of Mahdy. The weighty mass of the backpack and its contents pinned him to the floor, crushing the breath from his lungs.

Before Zayd had stopped bouncing from his impact with the unyielding floor, Sarah shifted her sights slightly upward and centered them on Mahdy's upper chest, sending a pellet of destruction into the boiler room of his body. It tore into the area where his lungs joined the bronchial tubes shredding the once vital tissue into useless flaps of gelatinous goop.

Mahdy stopped his nonsensical movements and stared dumbfounded at her before his eyes rolled back into his head. He fell onto his haunches and sat for a second on his ankles then tottered gracefully to his right before sprawling ungraciously across the cold floor, the pain in his broken arm forgotten.

PPTTING! PPTTING! PPTTING!

The splattering of bullets on the rounded underside of the baptismal fountain's stony side did not register at first. It was only after Sarah saw the deflected rounds smashing into the floor tiles and tossing up a cloud of debris did it register that she was under attack from behind.

Pieces of broken terra cotta became injurious secondary projectiles springing from the traumatized floor.

Just as Najeeb's shots had been high, Idrie's rounds were striking low. Sarah ducked behind the craggy basin and stooped low. She didn't want to expose herself by moving from behind the protective bulk of the stone, but she had to in order to see what Idries was up to.

Staying as low to the ground as she could, she peeked around the side of the basin with the Glock thrust forward on straightened arms, her elbows locked in place to stabilize the wavering pistol. What she saw made her blood run cold.

There stood Idries, half hidden behind a massive laminated wood structural support, aiming his AK-47 directly at her. Her trigger finger tightened instinctively at the same instant Idries squeezed off a long burst from the thirty-round magazine of his rifle. The thunderous roar of full automatic fire blasting from Idries's barrel drowned out the crashing sound of her solitary pistol shot.

The flurry of rifle bullets chewed a huge chunk of stone from the lip of the basin. Chunks of granite the size of tennis balls flew from the mangled rock with terrific force. One exceptionally large piece of the jagged ore flew like a well-thrown baseball and smashed into Sarah's left temple.

She crumpled to the ground in an untidy heap not knowing what hit her. Her left hand flew to her head in a natural reaction to touch the injured area and came away drenched with bright, red blood.

Get up!

You can't lie there and let them run up on you.

Get up and fight! Fight for your life!

Now!

With almost supernatural strength she caught the edge of the fountain's stone base and heaved herself to a seated position then tugged until her feet were beneath her. She raised her eyes cautiously above the jagged edge of the destroyed fountain as water cascaded down its side growing into a puddle on the tile floor. What she saw made her breath catch in her throat.

Oh shit! He's coming for me! He's only two car lengths away!

Idries was slinking toward her and was taking great care to carefully place each step. His AK-47 was held at the ready with the pistol grip of the butt end held close to his armpit. Sarah saw the whitening of his left hand as it forcefully grasped the fore end of the sinister looking rifle as though he were afraid it would escape if given the chance. With a sense of relief flooding over her, she also noticed the rapidly spreading splotch of bright red blood flowing freely from an incredibly small hole in his upper chest.

The nine-millimeter DPX had found its mark. On its deadly path through Idries's body, it had shredded the left atrium, pulmonary artery, and ascending aorta at the top of his heart. Before she could command her fear-frozen legs to flee, Idries pitched forward never to move again.

Jerking herself to her full height she again raised her hand to her bleeding temple.

Where's my gun? What happened?

In her semi-conscious state she could not locate the Glock lying only three feet behind her. She had also forgotten that her assailants might not all be incapable of carrying on the fight.

Zayd shrugged off his unbelievably heavy backpack and forced himself to ignore the pain screaming at him from his masticated butt muscles and the pulverized hole in his pelvis as he struggled to right himself. In an effort only known to desperate men, he compelled himself to sit on his injured hip before pulling himself up to kneel on his right knee.

He did not believe what his eyes were showing him.

It was a woman who did this!

There stood his opponent: an unworthy, disrespecting infidel woman with her back toward him. The left side of her baby blue sweater was quickly becoming saturated with blood from a wound to the side of her head.

With extremely deliberate movements, Zayd raised his AK-47 to eye level and sighted on her upper back between the shoulder blades. Wavering vision shimmering like a mirage in front of his eyes made him unsteady. Timing the swaying of his body he tugged heartily on the gritty trigger of the AK.

BRRRP! BRRRP! BRRRP!

The fully automatic fire spewing from Zayd's rifle ripped into Sarah's delicate body, scattering chunks of bloody debris from her left shoulder.

She crumpled to the ground so quickly her upper body bounced from the waist up when her buttocks hit the floor. Almost immediately, she toppled backward with her legs curled beneath her. The back of her unprotected head cracked off the rock-solid ground.

Ever so slowly her twisted legs relaxed and straightened, allowing her to lie flat on her back. Holy water splattered over her from the shattered remains of the fountain.

His swaying body and pain racked brain resulted in his shots flying far wide of the middle of Sarah's back. Only one of Zayd's bullets found a mark, totally destroying the integrity of her shoulder joint; its once solid bony components now lying shattered in miniscule shards.

She lay semi-conscious, not quite sure what had happened. She did not attempt moving her useless left shoulder.

Zayd fought his way to an unsteady standing position.

"You infidel bitch! You killed my comrades and tried to kill me!"

He took one faltering step after the other while holding the AK-47 at port arms across his chest.

"You deserve to die in the worst way, but I do not have time to cut off your head," he said maliciously. "I have your fellow infidels to deal with before I die."

He staggered drunkenly toward her, his undivided attention glued to the area behind the fountain where she fell.

When he rounded the corner of the sprawling pool with the fountain in its midst he saw Sarah lying on her back, her left arm uselessly flung to the side at an odd angle. She was pawing at the front of her navy blue, pleated, mid-calf length skirt. The creamy smooth skin of her bare thighs was exposed as she pulled the skirt ever higher toward her waist.

"Infidel bitch. You cannot save yourself by offering me sexual pleasure in order to spare your life," he said cruelly. "Even with your decadent garter belt you will not be able to tempt me enough to spare your---"

The hateful words Zayd uttered were the last he ever spoke.

Time seemed to stand still when he realized the garter belt had a holster attached to it and the Smith and Wesson Centennial .38 Special revolver it once held was now in Sarah's clenched right fist and swinging deliberately toward his face.

The luminous red dot from the Crimson Trace Laser settled a half-inch above Zayd's voice box as he spoke his last words.

BAM!

The Centennial's one and seven-eighths inch barrel propelled the Winchester 158-grain lead semi-wadcutter bullet to hit exactly where the red dot lay superimposed on his throat.

When the soft lead projectile entered Zayd's throat, it soared easily through the cartilage rings of his trachea then punched effortlessly through the fleshy, flaccid esophagus. It began expanding with the lead mushrooming on the front portion of the bullet, which slowed its forward momentum but certainly did not stop it. Continuing its deadly trek through his neck, the slug angled steeply skyward to smash into the forward, lower edge of the first cervical vertebra where it pulverized the anterior arch on its way to destroying the dens of the second cervical vertebra before severing his spinal cord at the brainstem.

Zayd died instantly. His body unceremoniously crashed to the ground as Sarah's right hand fell limp, allowing the Centennial to clatter noisily to the floor. Her mind slipped effortlessly into the comforting silkiness of unconsciousness.

CHAPTER 44

MUHAMMED'S REWARD

The entire firefight in the lobby of St. Boniface's had taken less than twenty-four seconds.

Muhammed burst into the lobby from the side hallway just as Zayd's body crumpled to the ground in a disorderly heap. He cast his eyes around the devastation of his terrorist cell with a veil of dread falling over him like a death shroud. The emotional stress was so overwhelming he almost fell unconscious.

Regaining his composure, he swore to carry out the operation on his own.

The infidels will be afraid to run toward the sound of gunfire. They will be huddled in fear asking their impotent God for mercy that will not arrive. It is I, Muhammed Shah, who will avenge the deaths of my men.

He ran wildly to where Zayd lay unmoving and yanked the AK-47 from his dead hands. Bolting to where Zayd's discarded backpack lay, Muhammed shimmied into the straps and hefted the pack onto his own back with a mighty grunt issuing from his pursed lips.

Turning on his heels he sprinted spryly toward the main hall of the church.

CHAPTER 45

CHAUNCEY THE HERO

Before the first gunshot finished echoing throughout the main hall of the church, Chauncey was on his feet.

Sarah just left and that's the direction she headed, he thought as panic gripped his guts.

He sprinted toward the rear doors of the main hall and had almost reached them when a crush of panicked people poured through the doorway and overwhelmed him, sweeping him back the way he had come. Even Chauncey's strong desire to aid his beloved friend could not overcome the fear driving the hordes of people streaming side-by-side through the narrow entryway.

Screaming children, hysterical mothers with tears streaming down their terror etched faces, and wide-eyed men flooded into the main hall as a frenzied mob.

This is lunacy!

Oh my God! More gunshots! What's going on?

Chauncey began clawing his way into the crowd, forcing his way upstream like a lovesick salmon in the springtime. He powered himself past one or two hurtling bodies only to be pressed backward three steps by the unrelenting onslaught of wild-eyed people driven past their mortal capacity for calm, deliberate and orderly action.

In an attempt to gain an advantage over the blitzing crowd, he sidestepped the smothering throng to place himself beside the pews hoping he could use the wooden seats to pull himself forward.

Valuable time is being wasted. How can I get past these people? She needs me!

Chauncey looked to the other side of the church in a vain attempt to find J.T. but the pandemonium between them prevented him from locating his friend.

Just as it looked as though the crowd was beginning to thin and may give him a chance to get through, a small girl tripped and fell flat on her belly six feet in front of him. He couldn't ignore the child's plight regardless of how pressing his desire to rush to Sarah's side.

"Hey! Stop! There's a kid on the floor here!" he screamed at the top of his voice as he rushed toward her. He used his elbows to bowl people out of the way in his mad dash to save her.

"Get back! Stop!" he shrieked as he savagely elbowed a fat woman to the side, preventing her from stepping on the hapless youngster. She bounced off him and continued fleeing toward the front of the church without breaking stride.

Chauncey's actions prompted an older man in a black three-piece suit with a red and gray striped silk tie to step out of his pew, scoop the child up, and shove her into the pew to his wife before being swept away by the surging crowd.

Throwing caution and gentlemanly decorum to the wind, Chauncey began plowing his way through the multitude of people rushing toward him. Those he could not shoulder aside he flung violently out of his way.

Where are all these people coming from?

He used his height to look around and determined that the hundreds of people who had crammed themselves into the rear of the church, the choir loft, and along the sides of the rows of pews were joining the mass exodus toward the perceived safety at the front of the church like a frenzied herd of migrating lemmings.

Churchgoers in the pews began streaming into the aisles to join the mob fleeing the conflagration occurring in the lobby.

The pews are emptying out!

They're empty enough that I can jump from one seat to the next until I get to the back of the church!

Stepping into the nearest pew, Chauncey vaulted onto the seat and began jumping from pew to pew by slinging one of his long legs over the back of the bench and firmly planting his foot on the seat of the next.

The crowds began to dissipate. The rear of the main hall of the church near the doors was almost devoid of people. Since he was making good time, Chauncey continued jumping from pew seat to pew seat.

When he finally reached the end, he jumped to the ground and began sprinting across the twelve foot space separating the last pew from the door. He was so intent on reaching Sarah that he ran headlong into the door when Muhammed smashed it open from the lobby side.

Chauncey was stunned and his nose bloodied in the collision but he remained upright.

The men stood face-to-face staring at each other for a bizarre moment. Time seemed to stand still and the pandemonium surrounding them was temporarily forgotten.

Stunned and gazing dimly through watery eyes, Chauncey did not immediately recognize the swarthy man with a backpack slung over his shoulder and an AK-47 held at port arms. But Muhammed immediately recognized him. The features of Chauncey's face would forever be seared on his warped mind.

This is one of the men from the Hallelujah Gathering, Muhammed thought.

He was standing over Samir as he lay on the ground after making him crash his van. This is one of the infidels we are seeking to wreak vengeance upon!

A split second later, terror gripped Chauncey's heart when in a flash of recollection he remembered where he had seen this man.

Before Chauncey could react, Muhammed swung the AK-47's steel butt plate into the side of Chauncey's face, just below the left cheekbone. He crashed to the ground, his mind momentarily blank.

When his sight began to clear he was appalled to see the glaring Muhammed standing menacingly over him in an obvious posture of dominance. The sinister eye of the rifle's muzzle was staring directly at the center of his forehead. A wicked grin spread across Muhammed's face as he scowled down at Chauncey.

So this is how it's going to end.

Dear Lord, I have sinned. Please forgive my transgressions and take me into your Home---

A very strange sight interrupted Chauncey's final prayer.

The man whose name Chauncey did not know suddenly had a bewildered look appear on his face at the same instant a starburst of brilliant red mist spewed from a tiny hole in the center of his chest.

A .22 caliber 55-grain hollow point bullet from Black Hills Ammunition Company traveling at 3,300 feet-per-second had just blown a grapefruit-sized crater in the Muhammed's left lung.

What the hell?

Then Chauncey heard the answer as if it came out of a muffling fog. The crash of a rifle being fired from the other side of the church rumbled through the cavernous hall.

The report of the shot was accompanied by the instantaneous appearance of a second spurting rouge starburst erupting adjacent to the first on Muhammed's chest. Before the splatter from the second bullet's impact dissipated, Muhammed crumpled beneath the crushing weight of the explosive-filled backpack. He landed heavily beside Chauncey's outstretched body.

Chauncey slowly rose to his feet. His head swam in a kaleidoscope of swirling images. He laboriously tried to recalibrate his senses and regain his balance.

Looking around the church as if he were seeing it for the first time, he saw a ridiculous sight. J.T. was standing on the seat of a pew with Sarah's hot pink Bushmaster AR-15 held to his shoulder, the CompM4 sight in line with his eye, and pointing in his direction.

As soon as J.T. saw Chauncey he began waving his right hand wildly above his head while using his left to keep the Bushmaster in a ready position against his shoulder. His long tan raincoat hung open revealing the black nylon sling that had held the rifle with its collapsible stock folded to its shortest length.

"Chauncey! Get that backpack out of here! It's probably a bomb!"

Chauncey looked numbly around the floor in front of him and finally located the pack still strapped to Muhammed's dead body.

"Get it out of here!" J.T. continued to yell. "I'll get Sarah!"

As if in a parallel world, Chauncey stooped and began sliding Muhammed's flaccid arms out of the straps of the backpack.

Holy Hell! This thing is heavy!

Slinging the right strap over his shoulder, Chauncey heaved himself to his feet then staggered toward the door leading out the back of the church into the lobby.

It had been one minute and ten seconds since the terrorists had set the timers on their bombs and exited the van.

CHAPTER 46

GRAND FINALE

"Stephanie!" J.T. yelled above the din of mass confusion that had gripped everyone in the church. "You and the girls run up front and lay behind that small brick wall beside the altar. Run as fast as you can then stay put and stay still. Play dead!"

Knowing he would be delayed in reaching Sarah if he tried to run toward the back of the church via the aisles, he began leaping from pew seat to pew seat like Chauncey had.

If Chauncey hadn't stood up on the pew I would have never seen him in trouble. It's good for him he's so tall.

Thank God Sarah insisted I keep her rifle when she brought it for me to borrow at Thanksgiving.

He managed to vault over each seat with ease, and arrived at the rear door of the church in less than ten seconds.

I hope Sarah's all right and this isn't just a body recovery exercise. That had to be her shooting because I saw her leave the main hall of the church just before the shooting started. There were definitely at least two different guns being fired.

He cautiously approached the glass-fronted door and saw Idries lying face down and motionless in a pool of blood. Sliding smoothly to his left in order to place himself behind the protective shield of a brick wall, he began 'slicing the pie' with the AR-15 held to his shoulder and ready to bring into action with the flick of his trigger finger.

He continued to 'slice" the room into visual pieces until the prostrate form of Haady came into view. His feet were still suspended above the floor by the wood doorframe.

Holy shit! They all have identical backpacks!

What the hell happened here?

He had seen as much of the lobby as he could from inside the main hall of the church so he cautiously pushed the door open with his left foot making sure he shuffled to never allow his feet to cross and trip him. His eyes continually scanned back and forth as he warily trundled forward.

Only after moving ten feet into the lobby was he able to see Sarah's feet sticking out from behind the baptismal fountain.

Oh no! Oh God NO!

With his goal in sight, he hastened his advance until he had the entire lobby under visual observation. Only then did he allow himself to rush to Sarah's side.

Crouching beside her he laid his fingers along her neck to feel for her carotid pulse.

There it is! At least she's alive.

He glanced around to make sure of his surroundings and saw the backpack on Mahdy's body.

I better not waste any more time.

If those backpacks are bombs they're probably on timers or a remote detonator. Either way they may blow at any moment.

At that instant, kitchen timers on the bodies of Haady, Mahdy, Zayd, and Idries began chirping in unison.

Holy shit! Time's up! I've got to get her out of here.

He allowed the Bushmaster to slide under his tan raincoat where it dangled idly on its nylon sling. With both hands free he scooped Sarah into his arms.

I better take her to the church office. It's sheltered and has telephones to call 9-1-1.

He ran across the lobby with her dangling limply in his arms. He was ready to duck into the long hallway leading to the office when Chauncey burst back into the building from outside.

"Chauncey! This way! Come on!" he yelled as he bolted past him. "Did you get rid of that backpack?"

"Yeah, I dumped it off the side of the handicapped ramp into the Blessed Virgin's grotto," he yelled back, matching J.T.'s pace. "I figure if it is a bomb that brick wall will deflect the blast away from the building."

"Good!" J.T. said breathlessly as they reached the end of the hallway and burst into the priest's office.

"Get under that desk, curl up and cover your head!" he screamed loudly as he gently laid Sarah under a desk on the opposite side of the room. He had no sooner covered her body with his own than all the bombs detonated simultaneously.

The results were spectacular.

CHAUNCEY MEETS HIS WIFE

J.T. and Chauncey rode in silence from Washington, D.C. to Baltimore. Neither had much to say because they were lost in their own thoughts and the uncertainty of events that had enveloped them.

"I hate these parking garages," J.T. said as he spun around beside Sarah's Mercedes C-300 Luxury Sedan and shinnied sideways between it and the powder gray Buick LeSabre parked beside it.

"I guess they're a necessary evil in a city as crowded as Baltimore," Chauncey opined as he slid sideways on the passenger side of the car. "At least Sarah was nice enough to loan us her car. It's not as wide as your van."

"You're still always looking for the one bright angle aren't you?"

"It'll make your life go a little smoother if you try it," Chauncey replied chuckling.

They walked very slowly through the parking garage, not willing to rush into an unknown stage of Chauncey's life.

"How did you reserve the Baltimore Courthouse to meet your wife in?" J.T. asked.

"I didn't reserve it," Chauncey replied. "Apparently I knew some important people, at least they knew me, and they arranged it. Some politician probably thinks this reunion will be good for his career and wants to be front and center of the attention."

A relaxed silence fell between them as each man was lost in his own thoughts.

"Did you see a doctor about your memory loss?" J.T. inquired tentatively.

"I saw a neurologist, a man I used to be quite friendly with, I am told," Chauncey replied as he rapidly glanced up and down the street they were about to cross. "He doesn't know how or why I lost most of my memory but says I almost have a totally barren mind. They call it Tabla Rosa in new born babies, a blank slate."

"You mean that a baby has no memory at all because they were just born?" J.T. asked quizzically.

"Exactly, except I kept the ability to speak and other mental faculties that allowed me to function," Chauncey replied with a grin. "It's all pretty strange."

"It is strange," J.T. said with a gently nodding of his head. "What did they say your name is?"

"Robert Fogler," Chauncey replied absently. "Apparently I'm an obstetrician and have a family."

"That's a doctor that delivers babies, isn't it?"

"Yes it is."

"I'm having a hard time imagining you as an obstetrician," J.T. said as he eyed him. "Especially since I can only envision you swinging a sledgehammer at the farm."

"Yeah, it's a difficult concept to get your arms around, isn't it?"

They both laughed heartily as only good friends can.

When they finished laughing, a somber mood befell them.

"The priest says it'll take over a year to rebuild the damage at the church," J.T. said.

"I heard it was heavily damaged."

"The roof in the atrium, that's what the priest likes to call the lobby, was trashed," J.T. continued. "The blast totally blew it off; at least between the big laminated wood supports. The supports themselves were still intact but have to be replaced because they're structurally unsound."

"That means they'll have to tear the whole front off the church and rebuild it."

"I think that's what it means," he agreed. "The portico was ripped off the front of the building. I saw one of the terrorists lying in the doorway right underneath where it attached to the church. His bomb must have cleaved it right off at its attachment point. The whole thing ended upside down on the lawn."

"To top everything off, I heard they wanted to charge you and Sarah with illegally carrying firearms into a church," Chauncey said as he raised his eyebrows.

"They sure did," J.T. replied with a chuckle. "It was just the chief of police trying to get his name into the newspapers along with his boss, the mayor."

"What happened there?"

"He was referencing the law forbidding carrying a firearm into a place of worship without a good cause as being a class four misdemeanor in Virginia. He looked very foolish when it was pointed out that the parishioners of St. Boniface's did have a very good reason for carrying firearms since the Hallelujah Gathering scenario happened only a few months prior," J.T. stated flatly.

"He didn't look nearly as foolish as the senator who called for more restrictive gun control measures," Chauncey replied. "When a commentator pointed out that the terrorists broke over a dozen laws that were already on the books, and used bombs as well, he really didn't have an answer why more gun control laws would have made a difference."

"The fact that fully automatic firearms are already heavily regulated under the 1934 federal gun laws doesn't seem to deter the freedom haters from wanting to curtail the rights of law abiding American citizens every chance they get," J.T. stated emphatically. "You'd think the voters would get rid of morons like that."

"What was the final determination with the dead guy they found in the ditch?" Chauncey asked.

"The word I get is he was the driver," he replied. "Sarah remembers shooting twice at a man in the van but doesn't know what happened to him. They found one of her bullets in his left lung and one in his guts that nicked the abdominal aorta. Both wounds would have been fatal without immediate medical attention."

"So they figure he died trying to get away?"

"That's the theory."

"Have you heard any news from your friends whether this was an organized gang?" Chauncey asked.

"Yeah, I can't say much but this was an organized terrorist cell living in the United States; apparently for years," he replied evenly. "When the authorities searched their cars and houses they found information, mostly on computers, that will help deter a lot of attacks."

"What about the guy you shot in the church?"

"He was a heavy hitter. A real bad guy the authorities have been watching for almost a decade. They lost track of him last year and didn't know he was in the United States," J.T. replied.

Their conversation lapsed into a serene quiet while they walked side-by-side until J.T. broke the silence.

"Chauncey?"

"Yeah?"

"They found Sarah's laptop and your work computer in one of the apartments along with a few bags of garbage from my house. They'll be released to the Virginia State Police and you'll get them back after they process them as stolen property."

Chauncey was silent while his mind digested the significance of this information.

"So they were stalking us?"

"That's the way I see it. It's probably some fallout from our involvement at the Hallelujah Gathering. The police won't be able to answer any questions about where they found your computers so don't bother asking, and I can't say any more either."

An uncomfortable silence hung in the air like a toxic fog. To break the awkward silence Chauncey said the first thing that came into his mind.

"I hear the grotto was destroyed but the statue of the Blessed Virgin was untouched."

"Yeah, they're calling it a miracle."

They left the cool, dank darkness of the parking garage and stepped onto the sun-drenched sidewalk.

"It's another miracle you found out who you are."

"Yeah, it is a miracle," Chauncey agreed. "When my picture appeared in newspapers across the country, folks who saw it and knew me as Robert Fogler called my wife to tell her they found me."

"You're a hero," J.T. said solemnly. "It's only natural the media would pick up the story."

"I guess so," Chauncey said with discouragement in his voice. "I don't think I'm a hero."

"Our country needs heroes," J.T. said. "You have to live up to that role for the kids whether you want it or not."

"Thanks for keeping Sarah's name out of the newspapers," he said to change the subject.

"No problem," J.T. replied. "I gave a friend a fake name and that's what the media picked up on. She didn't need to have her real name plastered all over the world. Islamic radicals would surely declare a fatwah against her."

"I wish I could say the same thing for myself, but my story is attracting way too much media attention to not have my name, names I should say, and picture picked up by media around the world."

"You can always legally change your name now that you know who you are," J.T. offered sincerely. "But I don't think you'll have any problems. You just carried a bomb out of the church. Sarah actually stopped their plan by killing four of them."

"I'll take your point of view under consideration," he said solemnly. "But what about you? You killed the terrorist to save me. Won't they be coming after you?"

"My friend got my name wrong also," J.T. said with a smile.

Chauncey weakly returned his smile.

They stood on the curb across the street from the courthouse waiting for the light to change.

"That was pretty strange having all the electricity go out yesterday in the entire eastern part of the country wasn't it?" Chauncey asked.

"Yeah, they say it was human error and it made the computers shut down."

Chauncey looked at J.T. who refused to acknowledge his gaze. He returned his eyes to the crossing light across the street.

"So it wasn't human error," Chauncey said softly. "They're here and they're out to kill us all, aren't they?"

The silence between the two men was suffocating even amongst the din of street noise.

"Yes, they're here," was all he said.

Chauncey allowed his eyes to wander and take in his surroundings.

"What's your opinion of how Sarah's holding up?" J.T. asked to change the subject.

"As well as can be expected," Chauncey replied with despair in his voice. "The orthopedic surgeon says that since she needed a complete shoulder replacement, her career as a chiropractor is over."

"That's not going to sit well with her."

"Actually, she's accepted the news pretty well," he replied. "She's already making plans."

"That's a good sign," J.T. said solemnly. "What types of plans is she making?"

"Well, it'll depend on how much range of motion she gets back in her shoulder and that won't be known for a few months," he replied. "But if she can, she wants to train to become a defensive shooting instructor."

J.T. was silent for a moment.

"Well, she'll be a good one if she can handle it physically," he said slowly. "She did one hell of a job at the church. Only God knows how many lives she saved and how much misery she prevented."

"More importantly, she's been empowered," Chauncey explained slowly. "Now she knows she can defend herself and her loved ones unlike when your brother was murdered. I think it's a turning point in her life."

They walked on in silence, each lost in his thoughts.

Without saying a word, they stopped at the front steps of the courthouse and stood silently while staring up at the huge, ornate doors. The television vans lining the street in front of the courthouse made it obvious the media were out in full force to cover the biggest human interest story of the century.

"Are you OK?"

"Yes I am," Chauncey replied resolutely as he continued staring at the front doors of the courthouse. "You don't know what it's like not knowing who you are, what you've done, or what your future may hold. It'll be good to have a documented life again."

"You still don't have any idea what made you lose your memory?" J.T. asked without taking his eyes from the doors of the courthouse.

"I don't have a clue," Chauncey replied noncommittally.

Suddenly Chauncey turned to J.T., startling him, and said, "I'm really excited about meeting my wife and children. It sounds like I have a wonderful life."

"I'm sure you do and I'd like to stay in touch," J.T. said before quickly looking away.

"That we will definitely do," Chauncey replied with a faraway look in his eyes.

"Well, you ready?" J.T. asked as he looked at his friend.

"As ready as I'm going to be," Chauncey answered wearily. "Let's go."

Chauncey and J.T. barely had enough time for their eyes to accommodate to the dim interior of the courthouse when the media spotted them. The naked glare of television lights swung in their direction and blinded them while reporters shoved microphones into Chauncey's face. The bombardment of questions instantly turned his homecoming into a circus.

J.T. faded unnoticed into the crowd.

Chauncey answered each question with a short, courteous reply and a smile. He continued walking and refused to allow the reporters to impede his progress toward the small office where his family awaited him.

Irene Fogler, Robert's wife, had been nervously rehearsing what she would say to her husband after not seeing him for almost three years. It had been a mentally draining ordeal. Many different thoughts had run through her mind when he vanished. Had he abandoned his family because of the pressures of his job? Had he found another woman and run away with her?

Those scenarios did not make any sense and baffled her as well as the police. The stress of the unknown had driven her to the brink of a nervous breakdown. Robbery was ruled out because his wallet was found in his abandoned vehicle with cash and credit cards intact. During his absence, none of his bank accounts were touched so a romantic dalliance was determined to be unlikely.

These facts offered some solace to Irene but the uncertainty of not knowing the truth was mentally devastating.

She had asked their minister, Marvin Jones, and his wife Sonya, to accompany her to the reunion. They had been a great help to the Fogler family throughout the ordeal. Marvin was the same age as Robert and the two couples had been close friends for decades.

Chauncey courteously forced his way through the swarming mob of obnoxious reporters in the courthouse lobby. The mayor appeared out of the crowd and shook his hand briskly as the heat of camera lights beat down upon them, then personally led him toward the office where the reunion was to take place.

Irene heard the rumble from the crowd growing in volume and knew Robert was coming.

"Marvin, I feel faint," she whispered with a shaking voice while unsteadily grasping his arm.

"Here's a seat. Sit in this chair before you keel over," he said, as he led her gently to a gray steel desk. The mottled gray cloth covering the back of the chair showed signs of wearing through from being backed against the wall, but it offered her a place to recover.

He pulled the secretary's chair out and held it steady while maintaining a firm grasp of her arm. She slid onto the chair using the wall to steady herself.

"Watch yourself," Marvin warned. "There's not much room to scoot in between the desk and wall; it's pretty close."

The brass nameplate on the desk faced toward the door and informed the world this was the workstation of Mary McCutcheon.

"I'm so nervous," Irene said with a quivering voice. She was on the verge of tears.

"Calm down," Marvin said in a deep, soothing voice. "You've been married to this man for thirty-one years and have known him since you were both five years old so there's no reason to be nervous."

"I'm shaking like a leaf," she replied. "I don't want a bunch of reporters seeing me like this."

"Cross your hands and place them on the desk," Marvin instructed. "Sit up straight and keep your feet flat on the floor. Breathe deeply and evenly. You'll be fine."

Irene pursed her lips tightly together and held herself rigidly erect as her firmly clenched fingers blanched to a pale tan. She fought to keep anxiety from overwhelming her.

The unrelenting barrage of questions from the reporters was beginning to take its toll on Chauncey and showed in the strained expression on his face.

Keep your head about you.

Don't let the camera lights disorient you. Just look at the floor and keep your balance.

The clamor of the crowd was reaching a crescendo. Irene was startled when the mayor suddenly popped into the room with his hand on Chauncey's arm. With a flourish, he released his grip and gently said, "Welcome home, Robert."

The room fell silent. Even the reporters lining the path to Mary McCutcheon's desk held their breath in anticipation.

Chauncey slowly and deliberately raised his eyes from the floor and saw Irene sitting stiffly behind the intimidating steel desk. A broad smile spread across his face but his feet were unwilling to move.

A heavy veil of stillness held the room in a stony grip as seconds agonizingly clicked by while Chauncey unwaveringly stared at Irene. She could only smile weakly as tears of relief began cascading down her face leaving rivulets of saturated rouge marring the smooth lines of her cheeks.

With halting steps Chauncey forced one foot in front of the other until he was standing with the front of his thighs lightly touching the cold steel rimming the top of the desk.

Irene had readied herself for this moment but was totally taken aback when he extended his hand and said, "Hello Mary, I'm supposed to meet my wife here today. Has she arrived yet?"

The End

A thousand thanks to my proofreaders, Maria and Ronald, and my editor/cover designer/author photographer, Rose

"It's better to have a gun and not need it than to need a gun and not have it."

—CHRISTIAN SLATER

Continue the series with Book Two:
RIGHTEOUS JUSTICE

Sarah Collins must grapple with the emotional quandary of forming a relationship with a widower, Daniel Lewis, M.D., and his uncooperative teenage daughters while still uncertain about her readiness to move beyond the recent murder of her own husband and the idyllic life they shared.

When drug lord John McGuire follows Daniel Lewis's sister, Madelyn, to her historic home in western Virginia it falls to Sarah to prepare her for the inevitable showdown to save her from McGuire's savage beatings and death threats.

When McGuire's minions set up a new division of their methamphetamine distribution network strange things begin happening in the bucolic surroundings of western Virginia.

The stage is set for two parallel cases of stalking; one based on love and the other on hatred.

The fiery ending culminates on a wild Friday night shattering the serenity of a rural Virginia night. But will they survive the hatred-fueled stalkers that threaten them day and night?

Righteous Justice is the second novel of the action/thriller True Justice series. Enjoy the provoking story lines, memorable characters, and meaningful relationships that are reminiscent of the styles of James Patterson, David Baldacci, and Lee Child. Follow Sarah and Madelyn as they embark upon an unforgettable adventure in the unpredictable stream of life.

Delve deeper into your new favorite book series by visiting the author's website at: https://www.DEHeil.com/

Want even more? Sign up for my mailing list and receive a FREE copy of DELAYED JUSTICE, a novella related to the True Justice series!

One of the best things about writing is building a relationship with my readers. I love sending information to you: newsletters with details on new releases, special offers, and other bits of news relating to the True Justice series that my readers report finding very interesting.

If you sign up for the mailing list I will immediately send you a copy of Delayed Justice for your reading pleasure.

Your email listing will NEVER be sold or used for anything other than an occasional announcement pertaining to this series of novels. Naturally, you can unsubscribe at any time.

To get your FREE copy simply sign up at https://dl.bookfunnel.com/bhnevz7rhh and your book will be sent to you in the blink of an eye!

A preview from your FREE copy of
DELAYED JUSTICE
Novella of the True Justice Series

Neighbors at odds.
Predators on the hunt.
A quiet neighborhood.
A mother who just wants to defend her child.

When the urges of perverse truckers overcome their fear of discovery, and the prospect of thrills beyond their wildest dreams goads them into attacking seemingly defenseless people, they are overdue to learn a hard lesson.

Delayed Justice delivers heart pounding action from the upsetting beginning to the triumphant ending. The astonishing ending culminates in a series of mindboggling events that will change the characters' lives forever!

If you enjoy reading works by James Patterson, David Baldacci, and Lee Child, be sure to get your immediate copy of this True Justice Novella! I only need to know where you want it sent.

If you enjoyed this book...

I would truly appreciate it if you would help others to enjoy it also. Reviews of books are a vital part of helping readers find series they will love. Reviews are often what make the difference between passing over a book, or finding a series that will keep you on the edge of your seat and demanding the next installment.

Your review will mean a lot to both me and to future readers. Please write a few words and post your review on Amazon and on Goodreads.com.

Creating an account at Goodreads is very simple and you will discover a new home there with other readers who have reading interests very similar to yours. Check them out.

Thank you very much in advance for taking the time to post a review and your opinion of this book. It is greatly appreciated, and I look forward to reading your review!

ABOUT THE AUTHOR

D.E. Heil was born on a wintry day in Pittsburgh in 1956. His mother was perpetually late for important appointments, and in keeping with her tardy nature, never spent more than 20 minutes in a hospital before birthing any of her four babies.

He received an undergraduate degree in Psychology from Slippery Rock University, spent an adventurous winter in Aspen, CO as a ski bum, then attended the National University of Health Sciences in Lombard, IL where he received a BS in Human Biology and a Doctorate in Chiropractic. In a tremendous stroke of good luck, the best luck he has ever had, he met his wife, Maria, who lived nearby.

Heil has supported his wife's activism for the Second Amendment since the year 2000. Currently, she is a Member of the Board of Directors of the National Rifle Association. It is through his close association with Second Amendment issues that he has gained great insight into the world of ordinary Americans willingly accepting the responsibility of providing protection for themselves, their family, and their communities.

Because of his fellowship with typical yet remarkable Americans, the True Justice series of novels was born. In addition to writing fiction as well as non-fiction books, Dr. Heil recently obtained a Master's degree in Industrial and Organizational Psychology.

He and his wife live in Pennsylvania where they raised their four children.

CONTENTS

Made in the USA
Monee, IL
05 May 2021